M000188094

Covered With Snow

"**Best novel this year**. If Ernest Cline, Tim O'Brien, and Jack Kerouac... had a baby, it would be 'Covered With Snow'. A Beatnik-mystery dream... **as believable as it is heart-wrenching... exhilarating... the characters so honest, so deliberate, so painfully human** that I forget they're not made of flesh and blood... Hutchinson is not afraid to ask the difficult questions... [but] empathy is ever-present in this [tale] of grace and truth... A breathtaking Bildungsroman and God's lovingkindness in one..."

—M. Havens,
(Amazon review, 2021)

"**I didn't want it to end. ...like a combo of Krakauer and Alcorn...**"

—Ron W.
church leader; Atlanta, GA

"...like an elaborate sculpture or cathedral, with cornices, gargoyles, faux doorways, and steeples... **a beautifully nuanced and tailored tale...**"

—Graham Philip, author of
'A Tale of Two Vicarages'

"**Very 'Forrest Gump'**"   —Pat Holloway (Amazon review)

"**Meticulously researched**"   —KLHLA (Amazon review)

"...**excellent visual writing**... great narrative... interesting dialogue... I want to know what happens next."

—Bart Stamper
173rd Airborne Brigade, N/75Ranger, 1969-70,
blogger at SoulRanger.com, and author of the
upcoming Vietnam memoir, 'Laid in the Balance'

"**Rich, imaginative, compelling**... loaded with the details... that make it leap to life with a knowing smile... reminds me of David McCullough..."

—Ray Britt, author of ten books

"...wonderful... vivid... **gritty and thought-provoking**."

—Rob Hamel
NH Teacher of the Year nominee

Covered With Snow

a novel

Art Hutchinson

Covered With Snow
Copyright © 2021 by Art Hutchinson
All rights reserved.
Published by Carmel Head Books, Watertown, MA

This is a work of *fiction*.
While necessarily, as in all fiction, the perceptions and insights herein are
based on the real world, including the author's experience, all characters,
events, dialogues, places, institutions, names, situations, and other
elements are either imaginary or are employed fictitiously. If you *think* you
recognize yourself (or anyone else) in here, I'd urge you to sell your
Learjet, avoid both Saratoga and Nova Scotia, and go listen to some old
Carly Simon albums.
All to say: *fiction*. This book is not about you *or* me.

Neither this book nor any parts thereof may be reproduced in any form,
stored in a retrieval system, or transmitted in any form by any means
—electronic, mechanical, photocopy, audio recording, or otherwise—
without prior written permission of the publisher,
except as provided under U.S. copyright law.
That's it. Enjoy.

Paperback Edition: May, 2021
ISBN: 978-1-7358761-1-5
All scripture citations are amalgams informed by multiple translations—
but don't trust me; be a noble Acts 17:11 Berean and go look them up.

Cover design: Jason Anscomb

In memory of Ed
who saw the butterfly clearly.

Prologue:
The Face in the Deep

The Columbia Icefield, August, 2019...

Cece Paine, Professor of Glacial Geology at the University of British Columbia, is not sure, when she crunches out of her tent in unlaced, crampon-clad boots, if a spot of bright green deep in the crevasse lit by her headlamp is not a dropped hat or mitten. She hopes it is not another dead signal-free iPhone snuck up by an idiot student.

In the nineties, needful of free student labor, she downplayed the rigors of these research trips but now, with tenure, her weed-out speeches are stern. Rations are dry, tents cramped (except hers), and days long. The only rescue attempts will be for *people* who fall, and the official waiver makes no guarantees. Anything *else* lost down a crevasse will be regarded as an archaeological gift to a future century. But despite her policy, Cece is not devoid of empathy for these kids, many of whom are terrified by their first time on a glacier where spooky whale-like groans, thumps, and cracks fill the nights as the ice beneath them shifts without warning. Surrounded by snow-veiled chasms, the tiniest misstep can be unforgiving.

To forestall whining, Cece resolves to ask her students about the green object in the morning. If they can fish it out without risking a *what-were-you-thinking* mishap, she will amuse herself letting them try.

She shuts off her light, relieves herself, then stands to relish the sky: like salt tossed on moonless black velvet. Back under Vancouver's nonstop amber glow, she will miss the stars like social media "friends"—distinct, but remote. She slides her eyes to where the pinpricks of light melt into a milky sea at her feet: star glow plus a mysterious bioluminescence she hopes to study one day. She will miss the Icefield's presence and power most of all.

She ducks back into her tent and re-nestles inside her down bag. This time tomorrow both items will be draped across patio furniture and she warm and deliciously spent, spooned with her husband. She pictures tomorrow's trek down the headwall (never rote, sometimes epic) then the ten-hour drive home into sunset and night. Alistair will have chilled her favorite white, procured takeout (Chinese or Thai) and gracefully resisted Nate's pleas for extra bedtime stories.

Sunlight illumines Cece's tent walls. Camp stove roar and cheerful banter suggest a welcome shift from her team's testy exhaustion. Amiable but commanding, Hamlin Rutter's voice pierces her tent's thin fabric.

"Knock, knock, Dr. Paine. Rise and shine! Coffee! Last day!"

How can her top grad student be so resolutely cheerful? She adjusts her face to slightly less grumpy, unzips the flap, and takes the steel mug Hamlin holds out. Across the valley, peach tones inch down jagged peaks. She lowers her eyes from the hills to her mug. "I'll never get enough of this," she sighs. Transforming her words into a puff across her coffee's surface, she imagines the tiny quick ripples as her private ocean.

"Isn't it amazing, Dr. Paine? God's grace is new every morning!"

Cece hopes she doesn't look too condescending. She memorized that verse as a child. She nods her thanks, re-zips the flap, and sets down her warm brew. She puts on her least stinky socks then remembers.

"Hey guys? Guys?"

Someone kills the stove and a silence so lovely ensues that she thinks of vanilla. Reluctantly, she breaches it. "Did anyone lose something green yesterday?" She imagines glances and shrugs.

"Looks like no," Hamlin says. "Why?"

"Because I saw something in the crevasse beside my tent last night."

Booted footsteps crunch close and pause. "Holy crap!" someone yells, followed by a sound like a dozen heads of lettuce chopped all at once—a herd of cramponed boots swarming to see.

Eudora's voice trembles. "Dr. Paine? I think you need to come see this. Like now?" Eudora Dewey is flighty but full of potential, one-in-a-hundred

2

observant. Whatever it is will be unique. Cece steps out to a semicircle of student faces. They may be dismayed or delighted, but all Cece perceives is them standing still, eyes wide and locked as if she's the empress in a fool's parade, about to find out that she's naked. (She glances down just in case.)

Eudora points far down into the crevasse and hands Cece a pair of binoculars. Cece raises them to her eyes and moves them around, searching.

"Where? What am I looking for?" Suddenly, spider chills scuttle up her arms and neck to caress her scalp. A green parka sleeve is enmeshed in the ice below them. From it a grey hand protrudes as if keen to write in the air.

Cece abruptly inhales. She's slept above it all week.

Fifty years earlier: the first of December, 1969…

Snow covers the Stockbridge-Boston Turnpike.

Night falls and TVs blink on, their laugh tracks pre-empted. In one hour's labor, every ten seconds, a white-haired Washington, DC official extracts another blue-green skull-like capsule from a glass jar, cradles it briefly, then cracks it open. A cold voice decrees the three hundred sixty-six birthday verdicts, one inside each—life or death, freedom or war.

Each televised nationwide slap causes five 747s-worth of young men to cry out in shock or relief as the soldier nursery slowly fills. Except for those called and chosen, laugh tracks and sweet dreams resume. Within weeks, a lilting lullaby will freeze the night's surreal events in pop music culture: the day's snow will melt; the *date's* pall will not.

Three thousand miles west of Massachusetts (as a drafted hitchhiker might tramp the route) looms the continent's greatest snow cover outside Alaska. Canada's Columbia Icefield sprawls to the size of five Manhattans, thick as its towers are tall. Long before Babel quit building *its* version—well before nations and wars—the Ice Age left the Icefield an orphan.

The last of the first Europeans to see it worry tonight for great-grandsons but for the Icefield, both events exist in a blink—this night like any across the millennia. Snow falls softly, relentlessly, adding two stories each year. Naïve to the Icefield's secrets, next summer's tourists will throng the dripping grey tongues of this miniature Antarctica hours from the U.S. border to take snapshots, buy pre-stamped postcards, and picnic. Only a handful will venture further.

3

As his plans are buried tonight, one man among them hears far off exquisite singing—a siren song or a heavenly choir, if he believed in such things. He conceives a grand quest. He will cross the Icefield's yawning crevasses. He will ascend its toothy, confining prongs. He will master this behemoth jewel, and with it, his fate. Another man born the same hour as the first observes the night's sad spectacle and writes in his private journal:

"Watch and pray. Wait on the Lord."

One:
Octopus

The Boston Arena, March, 1965...

Otis Fletcher is used to sticky, constrained, desperate situations: man-sweat sharp with fear, arms taut, and ribs and faces entwined, high-tops scrabbling the bull's-eye mat, not sure he can hold on one more second, or wants to. Ear guards damp grunts; thrashing masks pain (blood sometimes too, if the ref fails to see). Otis knows to wait for his rival's dallying ebb, a slack that shouts: *Second feels good today. Go ahead, take me.*

Inches from the mat's edge, Coach Lester Wrangel squats crab-like, watching intently. Less than a second after Otis feels his opponent's let-up, Coach sees it, leaps up, and screams, raspy and red-faced, windmilling both arms. "Drop him! Drop him! Drop him!"

Coach's words express the team's confessional: a D.H. Lawrence poem he tortured into its current form after returning alive from Guadalcanal to teach high school English. *Full fury! No pity! Drop them like birds!* Each November, he mimeographs it, hands it around, and has the captains lead call-and-response recitations. Coach preaches that, aside from war, wrestling is *the* great equalizer of brawn and brains, a manly puzzle to solve and love. Three seasons ago, bored and a little chubby, Otis bought the vision and joined the team, shocking his parents. Running for Captain last week, he grounded his winning speech on the poem fragment, the only candidate to remind the team of Coach's gospel: You have to want to get pinned.

Today, the premise fails before a thousand people. Otis venerates those who wrestle at States, but having joined that elite a year ahead of plan—and now, having lost—his shame burns hot.

5

Octopus (real name, Theo Behm, a.k.a. The Bomb) is the latest proud product of Chandler, Massachusetts. The football-wrestling powerhouse abuts Dirkden, Otis' hometown (haven to a quarter of MIT's and Harvard's faculties). One narrow unlit road links the two, tendriling out from Chandler's refrigerator factory ("U.S.A." painted in story-high letters) past its bowling alleys and bars, through a swampy no-man's-land. Dirkden receives the link like week-old fish, plowing its pothole-strewn section last after snowstorms. Shortly after V-J Day, wielding Army discharge papers and a pay stub from Gillette, Otis' parents Charles and Ruth Fletcher elbowed their way into a treeless Dirkden tract near the road's outflow. Until Charles got promoted, their mortgaged toehold on respectability meant strict abstinence from luxuries such as fresh meat, nights out, new clothes—and from letting three-year-old Henry have a sibling too soon.

Octopus. The grim hulk is bound for Iowa full ride, but still. Feigning weakness so well that even *Coach* is deceived? With only seconds left, Otis is ahead, until *boom*. At the ref's whistle Octopus spits his mouth guard at Otis' ear and leaps up, prancing to foot-stomping roars, flexing and bellowing, neck tendons taut. Otis had rehearsed victory at this venue so often and in such detail (ref lifting his hand, Coach's crushing bear-hug, adulation at the post-season banquet) that a win here had come to feel as real as the past.

Stunned on his back, the vision plunges into a mapless void. A blizzard of post-debacle faint praise leaves him numb. *Man, you almost had him! Podium silver is awesome! That weight class is yours next year!* A year seems a long time to wait for what he can still feel as if it's part of him. He shouldn't have let his mother's worries distract him. Sure, Henry *might* join the clot of troops wading ashore at DaNang this week, but it's hardly combat and Henry is twenty-two, able to handle himself. Why did she feel the need to harp on that *today* of all days?

That spring, Otis eats ice cream (the first time in years) and puts on six slovenly pounds. Each attempt to staunch mental replay of the match fails. Finally, he decides that Octopus must have used a borderline hold that caused him to black out for a split second. Octopus had to have known—and the ref had to have seen it—but now it's too late to contest.

He let a beast loot his dream.

Two:
Brothers

August, 1966...

A year and a half later, all three Fletcher boys left home within days of each other: Henry to Vietnam for his second tour, Billy to start prep school up in New Hampshire, and Otis three hours west to the Berkshires to start Deden-Fisher College, his top choice despite it being all male. Henry had seemed different this furlough compared to last, effusive one minute, distant the next. What little he related about Vietnam dwelt on tropical fruits, exotic birds, and sunshine. Thunderstorms caused him to retreat to his room, unresponsive to knocks or calls for meals.

Their last time together, the five of them sat in the living room. Henry lingered on his watch face as if staring might slow the taxi's arrival. When Henry noticed Otis noticing, he stood and embraced him, his aftershave musky. "I'm proud of you, Otis," he whispered. "Take care of Mom, Dad, and Billy, OK?" He cradled Otis' face in both his hands, a gesture that made Otis recall him playing Hamlet in a school production with a skull borrowed from the biology lab. "Otis?" Otis met his brother's eyes. "Promise me?"

"Sure," Otis said, still thinking, *Alas poor Yorick!* "Of course, Henry. Why would I need to?" He shrugged and stepped back, regretting the pit he'd just dug for the chillingly obvious.

A taxi slid down the street. "It's here," their mother said a little too loudly, and though they'd done this already for Henry's first tour, her words this time twisted Otis' sense of being eighteen from a sunny expanse of nice options to a hangman's call: next-in-line, eligible. The time it took Henry to hoist his duffel, exchange more goodbyes, then crank down the cab's

7

window seemed an endless blur, protracted yet swift like a wrestling match. Sun glare on the cab's rear window obscured Henry's face as it roared off, but Otis could tell by the way Henry's waving hand tilted that his older brother had been looking back toward them, toward home.

The first thing to grab Otis' attention upon moving in to his freshman dorm the next day was a poster for the local Big Brother program. A forlorn child with unkempt hair peered from a cork board in the entryway. "Will you help this fatherless boy?" The picture reminded Otis of Billy in need of a bath. Figuring it would be good practice for a family someday, Otis signed up.

At Big Brother training, he studied a stapled black-and-white snapshot of Davey Green, his assigned "Little Brother." Small for age eight, his kinked hair was close-cropped, his collared shirt neat. He wore a hard-to-read, perhaps stoic, expression. Otis brainstormed lists of things he'd enjoyed Henry doing with him around that same age: hikes, crafts, movies, board games. Billy had been eight and Otis twelve when Henry left for college. Otis had tried to fill Henry's shoes and coax Billy into brotherly fun, but something was missing. They drifted apart.

Their first day together, Davey's mother nixed movies likely to spark nightmares or wrong ideas, steering the two of them instead to a Don Knotts slapstick about a haunted house. Her guidance proved brilliant. On their walk home, Otis and Davey plunged each other into laughter as they mimed scenes. Once giggles subsided, Davey spoke like an open hydrant.

"It's cool you're my big brother because I don't have a real one. My dad lives in Georgia. He went there after Vietnam. His real name's Jonas but I'm not supposed to call him that. Some kids don't know their dad so his name makes him more real, you know what I mean?"

Otis tried to look thoughtful. All that the Big Brother profile form had offered was, "father out of state; honorable discharge." Not much to go on.

"Names are important," Otis said, "but your mom is right. I'm eighteen but I still call my dad, Dad."

"But you don't have to, right? Because you're a grownup?"

"No, I don't have to. His first name is Charles."

"So if you wanted you could call him Charlie?"

Otis didn't like where this was going.

8

"I *could* but it wouldn't be respectful. Let's do this, Davey. You call your dad 'Dad' and I'll think, 'Jonas; what a nice name.' That OK with you?"

"OK," Davey said. They walked a block in silence before Davey spoke again. "Mr. Fletcher? Do they have summers in Georgia?"

"Yes," Otis said. "And I hear they're hot."

"Mom said Dad missed hot weather. Vietnam's hot and sweaty, Dad said. When he got back, he couldn't sleep; when it's nighttime here, it's daytime there. Some kids' parents fight real bad, but Mom and Dad only yelled a little, for a few weeks. He left when it got cold and snowed."

Davey's childish piecemeal impressions filled Otis with toboggan sensations. Where could he steer their conversation without further hurting this hurt child he barely knew yet? He thought of Henry, a few weeks into his second tour, and did the time zone math. The sun would be rising. Was he in his "hooch," as he called it, or out on patrol? What had Davey's dad done and seen in the war? Had the Greens always lived in the Berkshires? Were his parents still married? Had they ever been married? Why had Davey's dad really left home?

"I see," Otis said, aware that his response was lame.

"I bet my Dad will come back here next summer."

"Is summer your favorite season?"

"Duh!" Davey scrunched his face. At the movie, he'd confided his desire to try the big kids' river rope swing next July, before he turned nine.

"My favorite's winter," Otis said, shrugging and grinning so Davey wouldn't think they had to divide over it, and also to reassure him that he had no designs on his father's role.

Near the end of wrestling season, frustrated by his new coach's deafness to pleas for a less punishing diet regimen and workout schedule, Otis invented a family duty then snuck off to the White Mountains with the Deden-Fisher Outing Club. There in Huntington Ravine the club's President, Shaun Thirchton taught freshmen enough ice climbing skills to keep ambitious idiocy from killing them on a mountain before Vietnam could have a go.

In post-season wrestling competitions, Otis' secret self-coached defiance bore fruit in wins. "Whatever you did that weekend at home," his coach said, "let's plan to do it again next year."

Three:
Acceptance

Summary, 1967...

T he following June, Billy returned to summer camp in Maine. Henry wasn't due back from Vietnam until fall. Otis was working at Sucre Flambé, Dirkden's fanciest French restaurant, washing dishes, unloading delivery trucks, and keeping its walk-in fridge organized. On his day off, his parents proposed splurging for a meal there together.

"We'd love to meet your new friends," his mother said brightly.

"I think they have that day off," Otis fibbed, but accepted their offer anyway. He was not averse to fancy food, but he'd seen too many greasy scraps in the dish room to let the prospect enthrall him. Simple climbing-trip fare—crackers, GORP, canned sardines—could be just as satisfying. At his mother's behest he donned a tie. Otis wondered how his father could wear one to work every day (high and tight like his haircut) and not choke.

At the restaurant, a waiter named Frank who'd graduated a year ahead of Otis from Dirkden High pretended not to recognize him. Otis returned the favor, just as they'd done for a month working together. Frank unfolded tented napkins into their laps, handed out leather menus, and recited specials from memory. Otis craved a beer but if Frank carded him—as he was supposed to, and likely would in his case—he didn't want to deal with his father arguing on his behalf. After perusing the phonebook-fat wine list for a veritable eon, his father ordered a cheap red. Frank took the list and left.

Otis' mother leaned forward. "Tell us more about school," she said.

They'd heard all about his classes already. He'd been relieved to survive his first year with mostly B's. He filled ten minutes with trivia about coin operated laundry machines and cafeteria food, plus some of the tamer practical jokes he'd seen played. They listened eagerly.

Frank brought the wine. Otis' father swirled it, remarked on the cork's dryness, then said he was sure he'd ordered the '63. This was the '64. He asked for the wine list to compare with the label. Impassive, Frank went to retrieve it. When he returned, Otis' father read the description aloud, noted the price, and asked if it was subject to sales tax. At last, he sipped. "It's OK," he said. Frank nodded and poured three glasses. Otis imagined Frank talking to the other wait staff and wished he'd turned down his parents' offer. Apropos of customers far less troublesome than his father, he'd overheard plenty of derisive tales in the basement break room.

"So," his father asked, "what are your plans for a major?"

For years, his father had urged him toward the practical, so Otis was careful to say only that he was *thinking* of majoring in History. Appetizers arrived. "Delightful," his mother gushed. "Fantastic," his father enthused. Did their reaction relate to what he'd just shared or to the jumbo shrimp cocktails? Otis couldn't tell. Emboldened as much by Frank's alacrity refilling his wine glass as by the wine itself, Otis described the breeds of History major he'd observed. Most used the Deden-Fisher name as a springboard to law school and the top ones cannonballed into big money at white-shoe law firms. Smaller fish made honest ripples as prosecutors until a wife and kids drove them to compromise their ideals for enough pay to afford a suburb with good schools. The other coveted option was academia—pursuing tenure. Those types wore tweeds, smoked pipes, and had pasty complexions from laboring overmuch in the library's bowels.

The first group of History majors was cavalier and boorish he opined, the second naïve and hypocritical, the third stultified and stuck-up—an airless cloister. Otis felt aglow, his thoughts taking shape as he expounded them. "Why follow the crowd?" He asked. Sensitive to his mother, he noted that a less-trodden fourth path came with an occupational draft exemption. Confident that his parents followed his logic—even felt his excitement—he sat up straight and took a deep breath. "I want to teach high school and coach." They all knew which sport.

The shock of what followed would stay as enduringly seared on Otis' mind as news clips of Pacific island nuke tests. Otis was so focused on the superb indignity of Frank twisting a pepper grinder the size of a baseball bat

11

over his mushroom soup until he cued him to stop that he failed to notice the storm brewing on his father's face, or his mother's eyes darting between them. The instant Frank departed, his father set down his spoon, wiped his mouth, and lowered his voice.

"What on earth possessed you to wander down *that* dead end road? With what we're paying?" He sat back, hands in lap, and spit out the words. "If you need to go low-brow, you can transfer to UMass. We'll get the kitchen re-done. Won't we, honey?"

His mother sat stoic, eyes brimming. Abruptly, she remembered something she needed from the drugstore next door before it closed. She fled out the back. After ten awkward minutes alone with his father, Otis excused himself to the bathroom but strode through the kitchen instead. In the back parking lot, his mother stood smoking. Otis was stunned. She'd quit years ago. He tried in vain to console her, then returned to relay the news that she was no longer hungry. (He didn't mention the smoking.) His father demanded that Frank bring them doggie bags, then huffed that because they were freeing up the table early, he only had to tip five percent. Otis was mortified. Not only did he shrink from the thought of returning to work to face Frank the next day, but the career that had ignited his enthusiasm now seemed tantamount to family treason.

Alone with him later, his mother sounded more nuanced notes. Unfortunately, they changed nothing. Otis faced a choice: be honest about his career aspirations (still nascent, couldn't they see that?) and transfer to a cheaper, less respectable school or play pretend with them for three years. He waited all summer for his father to walk back his threat or else press it hard. When his father paid his tuition bill without fanfare, Otis saw that their deal would be tacit, a subject best left un-broached.

In August—Billy still off at sleep-away camp—Otis packed to return to school. They would miss each other by a day but it could have been a year. They had little in common anymore. Otis had tried the camp years before Billy and loathed it. Otis had worked every hour Sucre Flambé would give him, drenched by dish room sweat, chilled by walk-in frost, saving to buy a Mustang. Billy's letters home told of *his* hard work: on his archery, his waterskiing, and his élan, earning the tan he modeled in a posed Polaroid.

Otis was busy pairing socks when a low growl intruded on a thick pre-thunderstorm cicada hum. A black sedan filled the driveway. His mother screamed. His father thumped up from the basement. Otis clomped down to the stair landing where he, Henry, and Billy used to lie together like flannel puppies on Christmas Eve, shushing each other in imagined stealth as they watched their parents wrap presents.

Inside the screen door stood two uniformed men. His mother shook her head: they must have the wrong address. Their soft rehearsed voices shredded that hope. *Landmine... artery.* Otis' face felt suddenly hot; his ears rushed. *Quang Tin Province... our nation's deep gratitude.* His mother groaned, guttural and otherworldly then retched and stumbled to the kitchen. His father scurried to help her. As Otis crept down the stairs, white noise, rain smell, and cool rushed past him, filling the house. Lightning flashed and, out of habit waiting for thunder, Otis silently counted each step as he moved to the kitchen to join his parents.

At the sink, his father daubed at his mother's sundress. She held her hands to her head as if it might come off. "We should never have let him watch cartoons with guns," she moaned.

"It's not our fault," his father said, but his wavering voice betrayed him.

"We need to shut windows," she said and his father scurried to obey. Otis followed to help. Soon, breakfast smells filled the house, evoking routine. Otis and his father returned to the kitchen where his mother was pouring coffee from the percolator into two saucered cups adorned by silver spoons. The breadbox was open. A loaf wrapper dotted with cheery orbs lay slack and empty on the counter. Otis' mother handed him two plates, silver forks neatly tucked alongside stacks of toast. Otis held them, dumfounded. She handed his father the coffee cups. "Here, bring these out," she said. "Ask them if they take cream and sugar and if they'd like butter and jam."

The soldiers had just declined the untimely breakfast when the power cut out. Unmoving, Otis and his father stood in place as if doing so might change the men's minds not only about the food but about Henry. In the storm's dim yellow-grey, their faces looked befouled. The men reiterated their condolences, said someone would be in touch, then trod out to their government car. Despite the deluge and no umbrellas their gait stayed steady and somber.

Back in the kitchen, his mother urged Otis and his father to eat. "Toast is the best food for an upset stomach," she said, but she wasn't eating. Otis studied his piece, its rough surface like wood, a door that, with waiting, might open to normal. Nausea engulfed him. There was nothing to wait *for* anymore; normal was over. Henry was dead; he would *always* be dead.

Before his parents could see his distress, Otis dashed to the bathroom and got sick alone, quiet as ever. In the euphoria that attended flushing the toilet, wiping his sweaty brow, and rinsing with mouthwash, he wondered if sorrow might help him drop down one weight class.

Billy returned home late that night, but then the Army called about an indefinite delay returning Henry's body. With nothing to do except receive casseroles and pesky questions and rub each other raw, Billy and Otis left for their respective schools. Those first weeks, Otis avoided the back-to-school how-did-your-summer-go-mine-was-great parties and drifted through his new classes without remembering a thing. Whenever he was able to sleep he dreamt of Octopus, multiplied in jungles that lacked referees.

In October, a week after the funeral, Otis met a girl. Louisabeth Dunson had helped to plan a Cold War-themed sorority mixer at her elite women's college down in Northampton. "Coffee liqueur détente!" proclaimed banners in mock Cyrillic script. They danced, goofy and sweaty until the cloying drinks made Otis giddy and maudlin. She took his keys and made him sleep on a couch. He said he respected her forthrightness. She said she respected him for not arguing.

That winter, a string of wrestling losses caused Otis' coach to revise down high-octane hopes set by Otis' freshman season. Otis made half-true pleas about grief—and false ones about trips home—loathe to confess his cathartic ice climbing escapes that sometimes blew out his strength for days. His coach's silence made Otis think he might be on to him, but Otis cared less and less. His new outdoor pastime was exhilarating—just as intense and complex as wrestling, but without any public result to exceed or atone for.

That following February, the Tet Offensive sent a thousand Americans back to the dust in Vietnam. Their blood cried in rivers of angry news ink but no one seemed able to heal the discharge without adding to it. The blood of thirty times as many attackers ran sticky in the same torrent some noted, but the few who knew that statistic said they all deserved it. Thirty thousand was the population of Dirkden. To staunch thoughts of so much faceless carnage—his town's leafy lanes empty of all but flies and mangy dogs, flesh blurred into muck by tropical heat, bugs, and rain—Otis spent the late winter of 1968 distracting and exhausting himself in his two sports.

With far fewer bullets, the spring of 1968 felled Martin Luther King, Jr., then RFK, and—in a different way—LBJ, opening the door to vote-magnet Nixon, "the one." Jowly, tan, and elated, V-fingers up, the peace-maven swore he had a secret plan to win *and* end LBJ's war (soon, very soon, and with honor). Otis did not believe it. He was not alone.

Aside from Henry's bombshell embrace of ROTC during JFK's inaugural seven years prior, his purchase of a used 1959 Renault Dauphine was his only blatant act against parental counsel. The cars were "Parisian vanity rust-buckets," their father noted, "bound to disappear from the U.S. market." Where would Henry get spare parts then? After Henry deployed for his first tour, the black car stayed shrouded in the garage. Once a month, their father would start it and poke around under the hood. He sent away for sparkplugs, belts, and filters; he also changed the oil. A few sunny weekends each summer, he would circle it around the block a few times then wash and wax it in the shade of their front yard elm. Since Henry's death, it had not left the garage. Otis didn't dare ask if it ever would.

In August, he prepared to take the bus back to school, careful not to mention the anniversary of Henry's death lest he add to his parents' angst—high pitched already from everything else. Chicago was filling with tear gas and Prague with Russian tanks. Otis was more shocked that Ringo was quitting the Beatles. His parents let the anniversary pass. That night, his father gave him the car's keys. "Be safe. Love, Dad," proclaimed block letters on an index card, tented on Otis' pillow. Otis was so stunned that he *almost* refused them. The car seemed irreplaceably precious now, both blessing and curse. To drive it felt like taking a Faberge egg for a spin.

The most notable feature of Otis' junior year at Deden-Fisher was a satisfying rhythm with Louisabeth Dunson. Serious, and also not. The two of them took turns driving: she up, he down, each once a month, offsetting a week for sex timing. A smattering of calls and letters sufficed in between.

The following summer, the last of the decade, two proud sets of American footprints adorned the moon's dust, unruffled by wind. A half a million feet tromped Woodstock's mud, glad it was not Vietnam's. Working six days a week again washing fancy French dishes—rotating Sucre Flambé's inventory of butter, eggs, and mushrooms—Otis missed the nightly TV reports. Radio news on midnight drives home was disturbing enough, making him nostalgic for the easy-going life he'd taken for granted when Henry had been around.

Recently, the Fletcher house had felt like a minefield.

Four:
Pinned

October, 1969...

For an instant as happened most mornings, Otis thought to call Henry until he recalled his wax-like face and the dissection specimen odor, the coffin half closed to hide the jumble below his ribcage. *Funeral anniversary.* No way could he fake it through class. He stared at his ceiling. Seven months hence, upon graduation, his draft exemption would expire. Then there was Louisabeth's call last night. She was pregnant.

He liked kids. But with *her*? So soon? Married or not, her bulge would show under her graduation gown, the public shame welding their lives—and pinning him like a bug. "Drop frozen," he murmured from wistful habit, unsure anymore if Coach's mantras had *ever* had power.

His father's latest dispatch had arrived hours before Louisabeth's news. One neat capital letter occupied each graph paper square. Reading it, Otis envisioned his father shouting advice and felt again the impotent shock of Octopus grappling him into public submission. Teeming with prudent counsel, the letter filled three pages, both sides.

"The future is bright here," Charles Fletcher wrote to his middle son, ardor for his lifelong employer as conspicuous as the aftershave he slapped on daily, including weekends. "Men have shaved since the Pharaohs, and always will." But if Otis didn't care for the job he could happily arrange for him—and so live at home to save for grad school—"the other prudent avenue is the audit track down at Morrison-James." Ed Fishender (the only Army buddy his father had ever mentioned) "is among MJ's most well regarded partners," his father assured him. "MJ is highly prestigious but Ed

17

could give you a leg up there. He and his second wife made a special trip up from New York City to celebrate your third birthday with us."

MJ was a corporate accounting firm. Not as easy to grasp as shaving, but supporting a wife and baby on a teacher's salary would be tough and somehow, miraculously, no Deden-Fisher alumnus who went to work at MJ ever ended up in Vietnam. Should he roll the dice on it? His plan to teach had drawn reactions from his professors no less damning than those from his father. "High school," one had said, his beard bobbing like a drunken turtle, then, "coaching wrestling. Well then. I see." He did not see. None of them did. Most Deden-Fisher professors were blind to anything more physically demanding than strolls with their obese dimwitted golden retrievers or waxing their new Saab or Volvo, purchased on their latest academic junket to Stockholm.

The multi-underlined superlatives Otis had grown used to reaping in Dirkden's public schools were as rare in Deden-Fisher's exalted air as seagulls atop Mount Everest. Most of his professors liked him in a "competent work" kind of way, reserving their real praise for scintillatingly bright classmates who received A's but seldom waved such grades around. The reality was, none of his professors were going to kill a Saturday to write him a recommendation. Not the academic kind he would need to get into grad school or law school (and so defer the draft), not the reputational kind he would need to top supplicants from schools like Amherst, Harvard, or Yale for plumb jobs in DC or New York, and certainly not a reference to teach high school and coach. Otis had considered how to make up for being only slightly above average here. Other B students raked professors' leaves, engaged in urbane chitchat over port, or babysat their kids. Otis rejected such insincere groveling on principle. He would win on luck and merit or not win at all.

In a surprise pre-season scrimmage a few days after Louisabeth's news and his father's letter, Otis' coach unleashed a cadre of scary-strong sophomores to shake up the varsity roster. Wobbly from cutting weight and brooding about his future, Otis' heart had not been in it. Sore from the drubbing, unsure if he'd retained his spot, he skulked into the campus career office so he could tell his father he'd done so. He did not plan to tell his father he'd gone three days unshaven.

"Your father's absolutely right," the college counselor chirped. "Some of our best are down at MJ. It's a highly prestigious firm." Highly prestigious. Had his father called the counselor with that phrase in an effort to scheme his son into a job, or had the counselor called him?

Earlier that fall, the counselor had encouraged Otis to think big. Otis had expressed his wish to keep summers free to climb glacier-clad mountains. Now, using the fingers of both hands, the counselor ticked off the benefits of Otis starting his career "in the city," noting that, "the Deden-Fisher Club in Midtown discounts its dues for MJ's first-year DF alumni."

Otis feigned interest. Louisabeth was from rural Virginia. She'd go crazy in a tiny New York apartment, alone with a newborn. *If* they got married, *and* if she kept it. Still, the MJ salaries were astonishing. He could work two years then quit and climb for six months straight.

"You should do the interview for practice," the counselor advised. Before Otis could think of a plausible objection, the counselor put his name on the MJ interview schedule for three weeks hence: Halloween afternoon. His eyes raked Otis' damp sweatshirt and scruffy face. He wrinkled his nose. "You never know," he said. "We've had surprises."

The following Friday, after a brief visit with Davey, Otis drove home to Dirkden. Fire-colored leaves swirled and glowed in his wake, sparking nostalgia: his last fall break, far enough past the funeral anniversary to make the trip tolerable, maybe even mint fresh memories. The Dauphine had been making squealing noises—perhaps a loose belt—and a few rust spots had begun to bloom. His father had seemed excited about helping Otis prepare the car for winter.

At home, his father's new Lincoln sat on the lawn. The garage floor was covered in pristine drop cloths, spare parts, and neatly arranged tools. His father rushed to wave Otis in, then talked him through the supplies he'd laid out. Otis had hoped they'd be done by Saturday lunch, but on Sunday evening, his father was still finding and fixing problems.

That night, Otis couldn't sleep. He valued the sense of security that living in the same house his whole life had given him, but his memory of the other black car that had briefly occupied its driveway continued to taint what he'd once cherished about it. Unlike that day, he was starving. He made his way to the kitchen. Leaving the light off, he lifted the freezer handle, clunk clunk, felt for the cardboard ice cream container, then spooned and scraped until it was empty.

Footsteps descended toward him. The overhead fluorescent buzzed on.

"Dad!" Otis blurted, unsure whether to raise or rinse his sticky hands.

"What are you doing? Why's the light off?"

"I didn't want to wake you guys."

His father removed a tumbler from the cupboard and filled it from the tap. "I was awake." The thick-bottomed glass obscured his eyes as he drank. His father looked pale and drained, knuckles covered with Band-Aids from wrenching tight spots. Varicose veins ribbed papery calves below his bathrobe hem. When had he developed those? Otis missed their old easy chats. His father had once been open, lighthearted, eager to hear about whatever his sons were into. The last two days had instead been rigidly focused on protecting and perfecting the Dauphine.

Otis slurped the ice cream's last soupy remains. Chocolate was his father's favorite. "I'm sorry," Otis said, meaning it. "Did you want...?"

Spack. A gooey glob landed on his bare foot.

His father contrived a smile. "Don't worry. Your mom will get more." He glanced at Otis' wrist. The watch, once Henry's, was tacky and smeared. Otis wiped the glass face with his thumb, then wiped his foot too. He rinsed the silver spoon and returned it to the drawer.

"Do they not use soap at your frat house?"

Otis chose not to remind him again that he'd chosen to live in a big old *row* house owned by the college, not a Greek fraternity with initiation rites. He retrieved a handful of spoons, washed them, dried them, and put them back. "You and Mom made any plans with Billy next week?" Between Billy's prep school breaks (offset from his) and Billy's summer camp, the two of them seldom saw each other between June and Thanksgiving.

"Not really. Billy's usually got things pretty buttoned-up. It gives us all a chance to relax."

Was that a jab? Billy had set up his academic draft deferment far ahead of his upcoming Christmas Eve birthday whereas four years ago, Otis had waited and almost blown it. Otis thought to deescalate. "I can't believe he's almost eighteen, can you?"

"Around the office, I talk about Billy as 'seventeen going on thirty.'"

"Eighteen will mean more if they lower the voting and drinking ages."

His father made a noise between puffing and spitting and Otis realized he'd stepped in it. At school, the ideas were undisputed: A man old enough to die for his country should have a say in who ran it. A government that could trust a man to fire a gun in anger should also trust him with beer. But Otis had forgotten where he was. He knew what was coming. When his father got upset, his voice got cartoonish: high and fast, almost a stutter.

"Woodstock kids? St-st-stoned *children* voting for s-s-*senators*? It'd be chaos, chaos, fall-of-Rome chaos! This nation would never r-r-recover. Thankfully, it's only talk."

Otis repressed an urge to laugh. The next logical topic was the draft lottery President Nixon was putting in place and he did *not* want to go there. "So, Dad, you been busy?"

His father's face brightened; his shoulders relaxed. "Busy? Very. They've got me on a big project." He set down his glass. "I've been trying to get home for dinner a few nights a week. Twin blade technology is revolutionary, but we're still more than a year from launch."

"It was nice of Mom to cook veal parmigiana last night."

"You should tell her. This thing has been hard on her too."

"What thing, dad? The new razor?" His father stared as if Otis had disgorged a Lenny Bruce monologue laced with anathemas. Otis had meant the question honestly; now he wished he could suck back the words. Henry's death was the only "thing" anymore. Hippopotamus-like, it lurked under the surface of everything, gulping all hope into its lightless gullet.

"The Army!" His father barked, then waved as if shooing bugs. He backed into the counter corner and folded his arms. "They could have warned us. They never did it that way when I was in the service."

"What are you talking about, Dad?"

His father glanced up, annunciating each word as if firing off rounds.

"When. We. First. Saw. Him."

Him, Otis thought, as if he should have read his father's mind and genuflected. His father no longer used Henry's name—or his or Billy's either, for that matter. Pronouns didn't have old girlfriends who had to be informed when they sent a cheerful unknowing Christmas card. Pronouns didn't leave photos or weighty anniversaries: the date on Henry's death certificate, the date of his last visit, last call, last letter, of getting the news, of the wake, the funeral, tense cake-free birthdays, an appointment the dentist called to confirm. Pronouns didn't leave clothes in closets or dressers, precious scents fading. Pronouns didn't twist survivors' guts into knots searching for excuses to postpone the big final giveaway trip to the Salvation Army. Pronouns shielded from the worst stings of the hurt. Otis got that.

Yet by avoiding "the name," his father had elevated Henry to deity, impossible to ignore or exceed. No matter what Otis did, his brother's shoes were un-fillable. Yet his father's linguistic sleight-of-hand didn't make his brother's death any more bearable. It only consigned Henry to obscurity; and that made Otis mad. Pronouns might be his father's way of coping, but they weren't his, and so Otis had made Henry's name into a personal memorial crusade, wedging it into conversations as often as he could, *especially* around his parents. Was that cruel? Otis thought it crueler that Henry's name had become a kind of shameful sacred taboo.

His father continued. "I would have stopped them if I'd known. Your mother insisted she had to see him, but I was a fool. You can't un-see something like that. It was a production line in that hangar, dozens of flag-draped caskets lined up. We had to wait as they opened each one for each family. Your mother has needed sleeping pills ever since." His voice trailed off. He shook from his shoulders. His words came out half hiss, half moan. "And there were flies."

"I'm sorry, Dad. I didn't know. I miss Henry too."

At the name, his father jumped as if shot and stormed back to bed.

Unable to sleep (or imagine what he would do all day Columbus Day Monday at home after a face-off like that) Otis wrote his father a short note. ("Thanks for your help with Henry's car!") He wrote another to his mother thanking her for dinner. He told them both that he was looking forward to Thanksgiving even though he wasn't. Only after he was halfway back to school on the dark empty roads did the Dauphine's purr calm him down.

Five:
Ghosts & Goldbricks

Halloween afternoon, on his way to Davey's house, Otis kicked at piles of leaves, eager for a few hours' respite from big life decisions. In the three years they'd known each other, Davey had shot up a foot, his resplendent Afro tracking the growth of the Jackson Five's fame.

"Michael's my age," Davey liked to point out.

A cerulean sky dazzled like polished glass, temperature perfectly poised, the air windless. What would he say to Louisabeth? What would they do? He went back and forth. They had to decide soon, and three hours from now he had to regain his composure for Morrison-James.

A pair of aspen bathed the Greens' kitchen in yellow.

"I need a costume," Davey announced.

"You could go as a ghost again," his mother suggested. She looked exhausted, her second job taking its toll.

"The eyes are ripped too big," Davey complained.

Oversized empty eyes made Otis think of Jay Gatsby, the great man dead in his fictional pool. He rested a hand on Davey's shoulder. Davey would be recalling their first Halloween together three years ago. Davey still referred to it as "the inside-out Oreo fiasco." Otis wanted to restrain him from another clash with his mother. She had desired, as Otis had, to coax her son out of his natural shyness—made paralyzing by Davey's father walking out on them soon after he returned from Vietnam—but she'd been distracted, mired in her own anger and hurt.

They were not going to throw away perfectly good bedsheets she insisted, yet she would not let Davey sleep sheetless, blankets only, nor was she going to spring for a new second set. He had to make his bed properly.

23

Davey hated to cross her, but this dictum rankled. He had told Otis how much he loathed the nightly skin-close reminder of being mocked for a "cheap, loser costume," that made him "look like a Klansman." But with his voice changing and having grown to be eye-to-eye with her, what Davey viewed as a plea for fairness she viewed as revolt, a line she could not let him cross. Past her lay chaos, she had confided to Otis. It was why she'd contacted Big Brother. Otis knew his inadequacy in that role better than she did. Most Fridays were a whirlwind of improvisation.

Today, he mustered extra politeness and gently floated a question. "Mrs. Green? Would you mind if we *shopped* for a costume? It would be my pleasure—and also my treat."

Her crimped face relaxed more than Otis expected it would. "Oh, would you? This late you might find a sale." Davey looked over-the-moon relieved and excited.

Otis and Davey browsed the local Woolworths. Half the costume wrappers were open, their contents tried and found wanting, the body portions thrust together with absurdly wrong masks. Werewolf Cinderella? They cringed and laughed through a dozen pairings like it. Nothing was suitable. All were desperately white, Otis realized. Not like the cursed sheet, but like *him*: Mr. Spock, Captain Kirk, Robin, Archie, Elvis, The Banana Splits, Fred and Shaggy from a new show called Scooby Doo. They cast Caspar aside. *Friendly? Really?* The less white costumes were hardly flattering: Yogi and Boo-Boo Bear, Planet of the Apes, gypsies.

"Batman's kinda black," Otis noted.

"Maybe with his mask on. Otherwise, he's like your friends."

"Good point," Otis said without correcting him. He considered few of his DF classmates to be friends. "What do you say we make one?" At the hardware store, Otis explained his idea. Back on campus, they spray-painted a sheet black, tacked it to tree to dry, then went for cider and donuts. Otis sketched the rest on a napkin "What do you think? We can paint bones with Lightning Bug Glo-Juice." He was less sure from there but they had rubber bands, safety pins, a roll of twine.

Davey quivered with sugar-fueled eagerness. "This is gonna be badass!"

Otis finished off Davey's third chocolate-frosted. Outside, wind rose, skittering leaves. They returned to campus. The sheet was gone. They searched. Otis swore under his breath. A prank? Against a fatherless kid?

Seriously? Finally they found it, stuck on a hedge. Where the proto-costume was not coated in pine needles and leaf fragments, the tacky paint had stuck the sheet to itself. Otis worked to pry apart its stiff folds.

Davey stood, arms at his sides.

"That's alright," he said. "I can hand out candy again."

"No. We can do this, Davey. C'mon." They still had time. Otis brushed off dirt and detritus. Davey didn't move. "Davey. Trust me. This will work." Otis worked to keep his voice calm. It *had* to work. "We'll take it to your place. Your Mom will be home soon. She can help."

In the Green's tiny garage, they spread out the sheet. Davey sketched a skeleton pattern from Otis' napkin design, improving on it in ways Otis hadn't thought of. The thing looked positively creepy. Now, if they could only finish. Otis glanced at his watch. Davey met his eyes.

"Let's divide it up," Otis said. "Meet in the middle. Feet or head?"

"Feet," Davey said. He shook a hand-sized plastic container of luminous paint and daubed out two small dimples. With his pinky finger, he spread them out carefully to form precise skeleton feet. Otis opened his identical container. Nothing came out. He squeezed harder. The top burst off in a blob, filling the space for the skull, then expanding like a gnarled gourd. Otis scooped up the excess then ran to dump it on the patchy crabgrass lawn. Davey's mother pulled up.

Davey kept working, head down. "Hi, Mom. Busy. Love you."

"He's doing a great job," Otis observed.

Behind his back, glow-paint dripped from his hands.

She raised a skeptical eyebrow at the setting sun then the mess.

"He *always* does a great job."

Davey's precise artistry was amazing, but at this pace, he wouldn't finish before Christmas. Otis had zero desire for the MJ job, but if he skipped the interview, word would get back and his father would grill him. Otis returned to the garage, leaned down, and whispered. "Davey? What say we make this *really* badass?" Davey's look of eager trust broke his heart, but he was out of time and ideas. He could sell this. No one would ever forget Davey Green.

Back on campus, Otis scrubbed paint from his hands, donned the brown corduroy jacket and matching bell-bottoms his mother had re-hemmed, cinched his canvas belt, then ran to the career office. He brushed dandruff off his lapel and adjusted the tie he'd worn to Henry's funeral, relieved to learn that the previous interview was running long—fifteen minutes so far.

"Wild thing," he whispered to conjure the sense of Coach's thundering team pre-match psych sessions. The oft-repeated reminiscence slid into a pop-song hum from his pre-college summer when all things good had seemed not only possible but virtually certain. From there he recalled accounts of the Monterey Pop Festival. Transfixed by Hendrix, the crowd had doted on the guitar god's tiniest gestures and steps, his every pregnant verbal pause and amplifier distortion, his repertoire of come-hither glances perfectly synchronized with his almost magical calloused fingers until—fearlessly charging a heretofore uncaptured hill for musical history—Jimi set his guitar on fire. *On fire!* Kneeling over the transgressive blaze, he'd commanded (and deservedly received) the crowd's reverence. How could Otis go wrong following the example of someone so clearly destined for greatness? He would *own* this interview—then refuse the job offer. Once he proved to his father that he could make it without inside help, he could then go his own way.

A door opened and Otis broke off his singing mid-stanza. Wilson Ward emerged to fill the room with three-time All-American wholesomeness. The interviewer rested a hand on Wilson's broad charcoal grey shoulder "Call me any time, Wilson. Any time." The gesture evoked things Otis had overheard around Deden-Fisher: a neatly folded Wall Street Journal on a BMW wood center console, a house on the Vineyard, fresh flowers daily, landscapers, maids, and time on the links. Worlds in their grasp, DF's and MJ's in-charge higher beings *deserved* such things.

In the brown shoes he'd worn for years, Otis felt his feet shrivel like the Wicked Witch of the East under Dorothy's house. Wilson was the star center and Captain of Deden-Fisher's nationally ranked hockey team. His black dress shoes glistened as bright and sharp as his skates.

Wilson and the interviewer exchanged oaths to greet mutual friends then mouthed "Kap Sig," to knowing smiles. Otis felt furtive watching. He wondered how they knotted their matching rep ties to look so symmetrical. Their white shirts were blindingly crisp. Otis envisioned a line of little people dancing and singing about the privilege of being around them, joyfully following them down whatever twisting yellow brick roads they chose to conquer. The interviewer saw Wilson out then turned to Otis. His toothy smile seemed at once menacing and inviting.

"Fenton Carmichael," he said, extending a tanned bony hand, his clean-shaven cleft chin the epitome of Sunday Times Magazine manliness. "The third, actually. Deden '63. Call me Fent." That explained the silver cufflinks: FCIII. "And you must be?" It was rude of Fent not to know his name, Otis thought. Fent waited, then beamed. "Why of course, you must be... *next!*"

The first Deden people Otis had heard of (a U.S. Senator, always in the papers for laudable reasons, a pioneering neurosurgeon neighbor, a Dirkden High valedictorian years ahead of him) all possessed a physical verve and effortless ability to inject social ease into any situation with sparkling verbal precision. When a campus tour guide exuded those qualities, Otis put DF first on his list. Getting in had made him feel superhuman.

Yet now, being so near the quintessence of those traits in Wilson and Fent, Otis sensed he'd been gypped. Despite three years traipsing the school's campus and hallowed halls, doing his best, he still was who he was. Seven months of the same stuff would add nothing except fatherhood. And *that* thought made him sweat.

Fent beckoned Otis to a black captain's chair, the DF school crest embossed in gold. "So," he began from behind, his voice an octave lower as he closed the door. "What interests you most about our firm?" Fent came around, sat, and locked eyes with Otis, fountain pen poised like a spear.

Otis quashed an impulse to quip, "Not much." Everything about Fent smacked of the guys he'd disdained in high school. Here they were merely slicker. To break the ice, Otis related Mr. Fishender's trip to Boston with his second wife to attend Otis' third birthday party. Fent's gaze slid out the window. "The salaries sound amazing," Otis added. Fent set down his pen.

Only after Otis left the career center and loosened his tie did he note that, in their ten minutes together, Fent had never called him by name. His grades weren't the issue; they had never come up. The problem was, Otis wasn't anointed. Fent and Wilson could both smell it. The interview confirmed what Otis lacked the nerve to tell his father. Even if a firm like MJ accepted him—and now he knew for sure that it wouldn't—he would be miserable caged in a glass Manhattan tower with guys like Fent and Wilson sixty or more hours a week.

Cowed by the interview's exquisite awkwardness, Otis burned with a shame so complete that, as if on a hamster wheel, he could not move his mind off it. There was no reason to connect the interview with the farce of a blind date his cousin had once cajoled him to take with her friend. (*She doesn't get out much… but she's really sweet.*) But for years afterwards, whenever MJ came to mind, so did the interminable evening at the overpriced restaurant and the regrettably themed movie afterwards. So too in the other direction. The two humiliations tended to slosh back and forth like garbage pails in his brain, never empty or clean, back and forth, one to the other.

After the MJ farce, Otis quit the wrestling team. The move would have been unthinkable his freshman year. Three years on, it was long overdue. A second lackluster season his junior year had kept him from making captain. Then, last month, pre-season sparring had bruised not only his ego but also his body. Over the summer, two of last year's freshmen had bulked up into his weight class, their abs cut like washboards, their lat muscles like wings, eyes afire, every move snappy. They'd put in the work, sure, but they showed no respect. Why should he play dutiful workhorse just so the new thoroughbreds could stay sharp and strut? His senior season could be painful as well as depressing. In relative peace with far less hassle, he could hone his climbing. He'd never clicked with his coach anyway, and Deden-Fisher didn't offer scholarships.

He went to talk to his coach who assured him he had a place on JV. Otis said he would think about it, then asked to take a week off from practice to tend to personal matters. The coach asked him to specify what those were. When Otis refused, his coach told him to clean out his locker.

Six:
Pinnacle

O tis and Louisabeth talked round and round about wedding venues. Before driving down to visit a Northampton jeweler with her, he verified his bank balance but when he reached for his checkbook there, his arm felt like after a match or a long climb—heavy, lifeless, no spark. Before he could ask if the ring's price was the best the store could do, she had twisted it off and sidled down the gleaming case to try on one she knew was far out of his price range. After walking dark streets in drizzle not holding hands, they agreed on a resolution neither was happy with but which both felt was unavoidable.

Otis talked to guys he knew who'd been through it. He read articles on recent court cases, perused warily-worded newspaper ads, and made toll calls. Finally, he settled on a doctor in Los Angeles and booked their plane tickets. Flying out, Louisabeth was polite. Flying back, she was weepy. Hormones, the clinic people said: perfectly normal. Dropping her off at her dorm, Otis tried to confirm their next visit. Stoic, she said she would see.

With more free time, Otis looked into teaching jobs, resolved to hide those forays from his father until he had a firm offer in hand. In light of his father's wishes, typing and sending inquiry letters felt like shoplifting. Otis had never done it, but a friend had once duped him into keeping watch. Otis' imagination filled in the rest—sometimes daydreaming, sometimes in nightmares. His father was always the security guard. *Hey there son, what's that under your jacket? Oh, nothing, nothing. Only my future.* In Otis' mind they always grappled and Otis always lost.

Only a few schools wrote him back. Heavy draft call-ups had inundated schools with over-qualified male applicants while turnover among young male teachers had plummeted. Some schools voiced specialized needs. Could Otis hone up to teach calculus? No. Could he sub one day a week? No. It wouldn't exempt him—or pay him enough. How would he feel coaching swimming? Over my head he thought, irritated and dismayed. Prep schools were the worst. Which three alumni could vouch for his character? Discouraged, he continued to send out a steady stream. Persistence had always served him before.

⸻

Home for Thanksgiving, freed from having to keep to a weight class, Otis ate like he hadn't in years. Throughout the meal, he thought about ice: blue-white threads snaking down ragged cliffs, thickening, waiting. His tools were sharp. A cold front had come through. Shaun would be up for it. Laid-back in day-to-day life, Shaun had maintained his II-S draft deferment via a long series of flimsily-warranted graduate studies akin to chain-smoking. He was also a spider on walls.

Otis helped his mother clear the table, then dried the dishes beside her as she washed them.

"I don't know how they do it," she marveled, her hands immersed in soapy water, going on about the Apollo Twelve astronauts, quarantined three days already since their splashdown in the Pacific. "It will be weeks until their families can hug them again."

"Mmm," Otis murmured, still walking around Mount Washington's Huntington Ravine in his mind, mulling routes and backup partners in case Shaun refused. He had a good idea how the astronauts endured isolation but she would not want to hear it. Doing hard things in hard places to reach higher goals meant giving up pleasant things. It took dedication and focus.

Otis dried his hands. In a high enough arc for his father to hear the clinks from his recliner, he lobbed coins into the mug by the phone and dialed Shaun (in state, long-distance, but evening rates) at his run-down apartment back in Dedentown. He twisted into the basement staircase as the phone rang. Careful not to pinch the cord, he waited in the dark, picturing the college town emptied for break. If not for two years of clumsy attempts to fill Henry's chair on a holiday, he would have invited Shaun home for the

30

weekend. The trip he planned would be more satisfying for both of them. Shaun picked up. Otis cupped hand to his mouth, around the receiver.

"Hey Shaun, it's me. You up for ice?"

"What ice? Mount Bluetop's still bare. I've been staring at it all day."

"Think bigger, man." Shaun's adventure spark would ignite any second. "Like what?"

"Huntington. There has to be snow above four-thousand feet."

"Too far. My advisor needs this chapter and I need to keep my II-S."

"Pinnacle could be in shape." Otis let the proposal dangle. Pinnacle Gully was the hardest ice climb on Mount Washington and Otis had not yet mastered it. Each time he went and saw it, the sense of incompleteness irked him. He pictured calendar pages fluttering through an iceless late spring, then graduation. After that, who knew? This winter might be his last shot.

"*Pinnacle* may be in shape, but I'm not. I've been a chair-hound all fall."

Otis found it hard to imagine Shaun pudgy and timid.

"Time away will clear your head."

"Fair point."

"Then you're in?"

"If we keep to Central, I might consider it."

"Do I have a wrong number here? Central is practically an escalator."

"How about Damnation then, or Odell's?"

"You can't be *that* out of shape, Shaun. I've seen you waltz up those."

(When Shaun first taught Otis to climb, he'd told of Noel Odell, the Harvard Geology professor two generations their senior who had pioneered the route that now bore his name. Shaun had always seemed to Otis to be of the same caliber as Odell, bound for newsworthy high altitude feats.)

"OK Pinnacle then, but only if we take it easy."

Otis tried to imagine how Pinnacle and easy could occupy the same sentence, but he didn't want to offend his mentor and belayer. If Shaun sounded weary, he'd probably just woken up; he'd come around once on the hill. "Of course. Easy. Live to climb another day." Shaun had taught him to always include the refrain, the climber's motto of caution.

"When were you thinking?"

"Tomorrow." Otis dropped his voice to a whisper. "I'd go now but, you know—family." He'd told Shaun little about his family, and the only thing he knew about Shaun's family was that he'd come east to avoid being sucked into a role in the multi-generational Thirchton mining empire.

"I get it," Shaun said. "I'll crank pages tonight and be ready."

"Yesss," Otis hissed. Shaun hung up and Otis slunk back up into the kitchen. His mother's voice startled him. She, Billy, and their grandmother sat at the kitchen table, a veritable ambush.

"You sound happy," his mother said. "I heard you mention tomorrow. You remember we're taking your grandmother for an early birthday lunch."

Billy stifled a smirk and Otis thought of times he'd cuffed his little brother's ears. Their grandmother took Billy's hand. "I don't have as many birthdays left as I used to," she said. "Sit for a minute, Otis. I love having *all* my grandsons around me." She patted the chair next to her.

Otis glanced at the *other* empty chair. His mother noticed and hunched her shoulders. She'd lost twenty pounds in two years, and she'd been lean to begin with. Otis sat; his grandmother took his hand and Otis relaxed. Her doughy-soft, sun-spotted flesh and the smell of her poorly cleaned dentures evoked footy pajamas and her reading him "Goodnight Moon," before bed.

In the next room, their father's recliner thumped down. Otis tensed. His father appeared in the kitchen doorway in plaid moccasins, his reading glasses tucked in his dress shirt pocket. His pipe trailed a grey plume that smelled of cherry and leather. Billy stood.

"Hey, Pops. Fred and the guys are getting together and it's the only time they have all break. Mind if I take the small car?"

Otis thought: *you wouldn't have this problem if you went to public school.* He wasn't yet sure how—if he landed a prep school job—he would handle Billy's jabs on top of his father's.

"Fine by me," Charles Fletcher said, practiced at curbing upsetting memories of his third son. He glanced between his two remaining ones as if it had always been so. "What say you, Otis?"

The Dauphine. He would have to tread lightly. He fixed his eyes on a spot of grime where the table's metal flange ends didn't quite meet. "They can't come get you?" In silence, Billy eluded the bait. Otis sensed his mother's gaze. It meant something like: *We all know whose car it will always be, just like his wristwatch, and if you force us to spell it out you will have ruined yet another holiday.* "Alright," Otis conceded. "But I need it back in the morning."

"What for?" his mother asked.

"I've made plans to hike with a friend." There was no sense alarming them. It was partly true. He and Shaun would have to hike up to the Deden-Fisher cabin in Huntington Ravine to access the base of Pinnacle Gully.

"With Louisabeth?" His mother beamed. "What a delightful young lady. I was so sorry when she couldn't come for Thanksgiving. She's welcome here any time, Otis. Any time."

Inwardly, Otis shrank. It had been three weeks and he still hadn't told them. She was still refusing his calls.

"The trails will be there after lunch," his father injected.

Otis did the mental travel calculations. It would be a late night, but he and Shaun should have enough time. To ease his parents into the news that he would not be coming home again until Christmas break, after exams, he proposed returning his grandmother home to her Stockbridge house, an hour south of Shaun at school. Yes, he would rake her leaves and clean her gutters, he assured them. Even if they don't seem to need it, he added, an instant before they could.

As Billy slid past, he elbowed Otis hard in the ribs. "Bye," he breezed, grabbing the keys. Their parents appeared not to notice Billy revving too high in neutral and grinding the gears.

Seven:
Headlights

After his grandmother's birthday lunch, Otis drove her out the Mass Pike, silently fuming. Billy had left the tank almost empty. A pizza box in the back stank of anchovies. At a service station, an attendant came around his side with the dipstick. A fresh quart would be wise, he said. With a fiver, his grandmother paid for the gas and the oil.

"You must miss your brother," she said as they waited for change.

"Ha," Otis scoffed and she flinched. *Oh no. She'd meant Henry.* The miscue reminded him of the mortifying moment, talking while eating, that he'd accidentally spat a food fragment onto a date's sweater. "Yeah," he stammered, loathe to call more attention to his error by apologizing. "It's weird. I thought I'd be more used to it after two years."

"You never get fully used to it," she said gently, apparently unoffended.

Otis had never thought of his grandmother as a widow, only as slightly lopsided. Yet it must have been awful for her, he realized. Otis' grandfather had died of a heart attack on their fortieth anniversary. Otis recalled standing in the hallway at age seven when his mother answered the phone. "Charles? Your father is dead." Otis could see the words creasing the air, sealing the moment, each carpet fiber detail sharp.

"I remember sledding with him," Otis said, "but I'm not sure how much is from actually doing it versus what I picked up later secondhand."

"If enough stories point at the same thing, you're on the right track."

"I suppose," Otis said, recalling a paper he'd written about mass hysterias throughout history.

"Your grandfather was truly happy sledding with you," she said, as if the scene were as vivid to her in joy as his grandfather's death call had been

34

to Otis in shock. "You can scarcely imagine, Otis. He would be proud to see how well you and Billy take care of me."

Otis indulged her tea and cookies, then went out to the shed. Waiting for his eyes to adjust, smells of linseed oil and pine reminded him of his grandfather's quiet strength and how he let Otis "help" him refinish cabinets. Nine years ago, his father had marred that impression.

Henry had first voiced interest in ROTC his freshman year in college. Home for a weekend, the five of them had watched JFK's inaugural on the family's tiny black and white TV.

"He really means it," Henry said, leaning forward. "If we can help people, we should."

Their father bristled. "Your grandfather's medals are in a box in their attic somewhere, but they won't tell you the price *we* paid and the burden *we* bore." Henry had stiffened. Otis recalled it like it was yesterday. "Woodrow Wilson baked pie in the sky, but men like your grandfather had to eat that wild promise mixed with blood in the mud at the Meuse-Argonne and at Belleau Wood. He would wake screaming and crying, unable to stop. Sometimes he'd stare past us for days. Your grandmother called him in sick when that happened. It nearly killed her to lie."

By contrast, their father's war stories followed shifting chronologies that led to quickly changed subjects. Their mother Ruth had been four months pregnant with Henry when he'd enlisted, soon after Pearl. He'd been stationed in Kansas and England, performing unspecified (but apparently vital) clerical duties. If he'd had any life-altering experiences, he never spoke of them.

Two and a half years later, JFK's silent casket procession had caused Otis to reflect on his brother's eagerness to serve as an officer once he graduated that next May. Had he helped people in the short time before his death? Otis hoped so. He wished he could ask him directly.

Otis set up his grandfather's heavy wood ladder against his grandmother's house and let the memories sluice away as he hosed out her gutters. He raked her small yard, dumped the leaves in the ravine, and deflected her offer of dinner. He and Shaun would arrive late as it was. He made sure she bolted the door behind him then, as the family had always done, he beeped twice and waved out the window until he was out of sight.

<hr />

Otis was glad when Shaun said nothing about his being six hours late to pick him up. On the familiar curves up to Pinkham Notch, a bright moon peeked over Wildcat. Equally bright in Otis' mind was the narrow strip of glistening ice they would face tomorrow, wedged amidst steep rock shadows. Pinnacle. He could feel its pull. Suddenly around a bend a deer appeared, straddling the double yellow line. Otis braked hard and swerved. In the skid's split-second forever, he pictured the car upside down in the adjacent brook, frigid water swirling in, up and around them: mouth, neck, then torso, struggling frantically against jammed doors. Instead, a broom-like swish raked his side mirror, his wheels regained traction, and they were past it, unscathed.

"Nicely done," Shaun's voice was as composed as a seasoned caddy extolling a humdrum putt. Had he had his adrenal glands surgically removed? Was that how he slept slung against granite halfway up Half Dome? Otis clutched the wheel so tightly he thought he might break it, the avoided catastrophe so vivid that taking another breath seemed like submitting to drown.

On the moonlit hike to the cabin, oak leaves rustled under their feet, calming him down. Bare tree limbs striped a thin layer of snow. The path diverged and Otis thought of Robert Frost. Silently he pledged himself to tomorrow's climb. This trip would make all the difference.

<hr />

The next day at Pinnacle's base, Shaun pointed out all the route's key moves. Then he let Otis lead up. Nervous at first, Otis struck sparks with his tools, his crampons wobbling on the lichen, museum-like under thin transparent glaze of icy verglas. *Wild thing,* he thought, careful to avoid Coach's poem about dropping frozen dead. He found a tenuous rhythmic calm: swing, plant, step, step; swing, plant, step, step. He might do this he realized, fifty feet up until a sudden gust shook him. *Crap.* He'd forgotten to set protection. "No good!" he whimpered.

"Take your time," Shaun said. Otis glanced down. Shaun looked the size of a bug; and he'd stepped back from the fall line. Shaun pointed. "See that bulge to your left?"

36

How had he missed the rock nub? Otis tiptoed sideways to the perch and set a web anchor around it. He tested the rope, wrapped it around himself to rappel, then leaned back. With long friction releases, he walked backward down the steep slope to bounce level with Shaun.

"Off belay," Otis said, sitting to take up the slack.

It was the conditions, he told himself.

"Belay off," Shaun said. "Such as it was."

"I've never seen it so thin," Otis stammered. *Oh no.* Had Shaun pointed out the nubbin so he could set pro and continue up? Ashamed, Otis re-coiled rope. Shaking, he kept dropping loops.

"I'll get that," Shaun said. "Tough pitch, that one. Good try."

They slogged around to check out other gullies. Cold descended and the wind picked up, and Otis grew thankful when they agreed to make no more attempts. The Deden-Fisher cabin caretaker split logs and stoked the wood stove. Otis and Shaun stripped to T-shirts and filled the day with chess. Protection or no, he could have had it Otis thought—and tomorrow he would. Chagrined, he won only one game.

Next morning, the jet stream was scouring the summit a half mile above them. On firewood forays, its roar was so loud that it muffled conversation. "Reminds me of my close call," Shaun shouted, confident that Otis knew what he meant. Otis recalled the story with reverence.

Two years earlier, Shaun had been part of a team preparing to climb Mount McKinley, the highest peak in North America but the day he was to depart for Alaska, he tripped on a curb and broke his ankle. Shaun lost close friends when half the team perished in a prolonged arctic storm.

The ordeal had sparked hot debate within the Deden-Fisher Outing Club. In light of summit glory, some said the lost men were hero-martyrs. Yet photos of the *survivors* were gruesome: black fingers and toes like bits of rancid sausage, awaiting amputation. Club members debated apt digit-loss values for epic peaks. Everest: four. Other Himalayas: three. McKinley: two. Otis would have said one, but he didn't want to seem timid. Less than three hundred people had stood on McKinley's summit. Otis revealed his ambition to Shaun, who responded in generalities. To be invited onto *any* McKinley team, he would have to prove himself far better than yesterday.

On a shelf of tattered paperbacks, Otis found the copy of Moby Dick he'd read there before. Inside the cover was Shaun's name, from Freshman Lit. Otis had never noticed it before. On the next page, in different ink, someone had written: "White Mountains = White Whales."

Otis showed it to Shaun. "Is this you?"

But Shaun only shrugged. After a few chapters, Otis noted a scraping sound—Shaun sharpening his pocketknife on a whetstone. Shaun heated water, hung his polished steel cup on a rusty nail, and soaped his face. He shaved with quick precise strokes In the cup's sheen, he met Otis' eyes.

"You seemed more than a little preoccupied yesterday—not exactly the Otis I know. You worried about the draft lottery?"

"A little, I guess. Why?"

"Think down, fall down." Shaun rinsed his smooth nick-free cheeks.

"Of course. You taught me that."

"You remember what else?"

"No one ever plans to fall. It's always a surprise."

"Exactly." Shaun rinsed and dried his knife.

Otis protested. "But nothing happened! I *didn't* fall."

"I'm glad. You almost had it, but then you talked yourself out of it."

Otis let his muteness confess.

"You need to hear something, Otis. On one level, this weekend is easy kicks: short problems with a road and rescue nearby. Everything is forgiving at low altitude. But bad stuff can happen anywhere, and it's seldom the bad stuff you've planned for. You get preoccupied? You're just as dead down here as up on the big peaks. The guys I let on my rope? I have to *know* they'll keep a cool head when the poo flies and the team has to make choices. You may *think* it's gutsy to take a fifty-foot runout on a first pitch like that, but I'm telling you Otis: it's stupid. That much air time *never* ends well. I don't like making bad news clean-up phone calls. You hear me?"

Otis dipped his head. "OK, Gandalf." Unsmiling, Shaun acknowledged the old nickname then poured hours-old coffee from a dented pot. "Keep at it. You'll have that one by March. Champagne's on me when you do."

Otis' heart sank. He'd hoped to notch Pinnacle before *Christmas*. Hiking down and driving back, Shaun recounted a blizzard high on Rainier, then other glory tales like it—in the Alps and the Canadian Rockies, taking risks to bag higher and harder peaks. Otis hung on his every word. He ached to be Shaun. A place called the Columbia Icefield particularly intrigued him. Shaun had described it as, "a miniature Antarctica you can drive to."

Back at school, brushing his teeth in the bathroom mirror, Otis wondered: What about risks you can't choose? Risks like the deer in the road, tomorrow night's draft, or failed birth control? What glory was there in blind luck and fate? What would he do if his number came up?

Eight:
The First

T he next morning, snowflakes chafed Otis' lead-mullioned dorm room windows, drawing down steel-grey sky with them. Otis lifted his head from his typewriter keys and each inky typebar clacked back into place. Small round dents pocked his bare forearms. His hands felt numb and heavy. He shook them and felt hot pinpricks. Clumsily, he removed his headphones. Chapel bell echoes died out in the quad. The phonograph tone arm rested in its cradle. His new record album—The Band, "The Weight"—was back in its sleeve. His roommate Lucius must have tidied up while he slept—again.

Otis reached for Henry's wristwatch to see how long he had until class, but his still-gimpy fingers caused him to fumble its stainless steel heft. It skated across his scarred stained desktop and fell hard behind. He stooped to retrieve it. The second hand was frozen in place. He held it to his ear, hoping against hope. No ticking either. He muttered curses. To leave it at school over break or bring it home unrepaired wouldn't work. His mom would notice or sense his guilt (it didn't matter which instinct came first). Then she would probe and learn the truth. Grieved by his lack of confession as much as his actions, she would tell his father—because that was just how they were. Then things would really get tricky.

His father had never thought Otis should have it. *Someone* should, his mother had insisted, around the time Henry and his things had arrived in different sized boxes. Otis didn't especially want it, but Billy had been too young. (He still was, in Otis' opinion.) After a jeweler cleaned blood, dirt, and who knew what other unspeakables from its crevices, the timepiece rested in a case on his father's dresser for nearly a year. On the first anniversary of the news, right before Otis was due to head back to school, their father conceded by placing it in a box in Henry's car.

Otis put the watch on his wrist then peeled open the first Advent calendar door. A tiny angel smiled back. It comforted him that his mother had snuck the tradition into his bag three days ago. Still, he wished today wasn't *today*. He leaned to the window to see the clock tower. *Fragged.* His paper was due in an hour. Low grades increased draft risk. Last night, he had been too tired to think. He tousled his hair, rolled a fresh sheet into the typewriter, and lobbed a spray can of Right Guard into one of his snow boots. How *was* the storming of the Bastille different from last August's Chicago riots? He rifled through his notes. OK, he could bash this out. Some professors still gave Ds on assignments, but few gave them for a semester anymore. No professor wanted a man's lost draft exemption on his conscience. Emboldened, Otis typed until he ran out of time.

That evening after the library closed, Otis ambled along an eerily quiet fraternity row, load of books under one arm, pea coat collar up. He wished he could linger inside the shimmering cones snowflakes were making under the streetlights. At his campus house—probably at all of them—the televised lottery would be unfolding, relentless. Unlike last summer's spectacles (both lunar and musical) one third of tonight's news was bad *by design*. Within an hour or so, a third of the guys his age would be moping, while a third would be celebrating a clear reprieve. The others wouldn't know what to feel for months or years. And inevitably tonight, after it was all over, both consolation and congratulation would be insincere. Except for twins, each man was truly alone. Otis wished he could tiptoe past those clustered around the house television, up to his room, then look up his fate in tomorrow's paper, but no way would he get past them.

Otis had known his draft options for months but wearied of being pestered about his plans. Parents, professors, random activists. Henry's friends and former platoon-mates. Even his barber was expert at dissecting scenarios that changed daily on headlines and rumors. People debated the virtues and drawbacks of every alternative. Some were bizarre, many sad. Some men had served without fanfare, come back just fine, and gotten on with their lives—but hardly all.

Each class ahead of Otis—1967, '68, and '69—had faced the draft piecemeal on graduation. Until a man turned twenty-six, each day's walk to the mailbox was steeped in low-level dread. And as new deployments sped the flow of call-ups, that dread rose in lockstep. One year might be safe, the next not. A man might marry, start a job, buy a house, and only *then* get called up. He might serve his time loading trucks, shuffling papers, or peeling potatoes—or he might be sent to the front lines. Like ripping off a Band-Aid or plunging into a pool, the draft lottery was President Nixon's effort to condense all of that angst into one night. Whether it would dampen opposition or ignite something worse was anyone's guess.

Deden-Fisher's *ultra*-elite used high connections to enter the National Guard, but the rest of DF's healthy men avoided the draft by redirecting the cleverness that got them into the school toward failing the military physical. Which injuries were most disqualifying? Least debilitating? Debate raged. How flat did feet have to be to obtain a 4-F? What was needed to prove one was homosexual and how might one live down such a claim later? Experiments multiplied. Smoking one's way into temporary emphysema. Popping uppers to stay up for weeks and mime psychosis. Gorging oneself into "morbid" obesity like a penned veal calf. Some schemes worked to get one out. Other schemes did not. One man eschewed bathing for months and got inducted anyway. Irreversible measures were generally thought to be the most credible. Pre-med students consulted on how best to lop off a finger or toe without undue pain or risk of sepsis.

A group of Theater and Psych majors shopped the DSM for mental illnesses, then practiced them 24/7, disrupting classes by staying in character. Others stepped out of role briefly to offer teach-ins. A growing cast of the faux-deranged kept campus life amusing. The intelligence test was hard for college men to fail, it was said. Faking liver or kidney disease in urine samples had once been easy. Now an official stood with you and watched. Creepy, Otis thought. No thanks.

Administrative approaches abounded at DF and beyond. In an attempt to talk his draft board into Conscientious Objector (CO) status, a lapsed Episcopalian friend had cited a Quaker great-uncle in a grandiloquent essay on newfound pacifism. Atheists and agnostics wrote impassioned seminary applications, hoping for the 2-D exemption.

After receiving his draft notice, one man backdated paperwork to "volunteer" for the Coast Guard. Some burned draft cards in public, casting shame on those who threw theirs away with less fanfare. Did Canada or Sweden offer the best non-extradition refuge for expats? How did one go about connecting to the rumored, shady domestic underground networks?

Passionate arguments flared over labels. Were *all* draft evaders feckless cowards? Were *all* soldiers baby killers? Why didn't the military let men hire substitutes as in past wars? Wouldn't that be much fairer? (That topic proved a hot one.) It went on and on. With little warning, honest attempts at discussion could drive emotional shrapnel deep into close friendships.

The girls had their own factions, fears, and messy motives. Was it bad form to dump a guy who got called-up? Did it depend on his role—and his odds of coming back? What if he came back crippled? What kind of life would that be? Did dating a baby killer or feckless coward make you one by proxy? What did a guy's evasion say about his proclivity to lie or skip out on *you*? Was the 3-A exemption JFK had given to men with dependent children fair? Was getting pregnant to *get* a guy the 3-A a mark of noble devotion or wishful delusion? Was Nixon wrong to kill the 3-A exemption last April? Was Nixon wrong about almost everything?

On some things, it was easier to agree.

The brass-handled row house door groaned at Otis' reluctant tug. Grave faces scowled at the influx of cold. The common room was a sea of bodies, including a bevy of wool-sweatered coeds who'd extended their weekend visits for moral support. Cigarettes darted to ashtrays like nervous birds. At the room's center, a black-and-white TV flickered inside a huge carved wooden case atop which rested a half-dead plant. Otis wedged in, not quite believing this moment had come.

"I'm coming to you live from Washington, DC," whispered CBS anchor Roger Mudd in golf broadcast hush. Behind him, a man drew hand-sized plastic capsules from a large jar, one by one. Another man cracked each one open, unfurled a slip of paper inside, and called out the birthday of roughly two thousand men. A balding man in a suit two sizes too small added a corresponding white date card to a growing set of rows and columns. *Tiny headstones* Otis thought, musing as to whether the cards' proportions were deliberate. *Someone* had chosen that scary format.

"Yes!" one of his housemates barked, but quickly stifled his relief. More cards went up on the faraway wall on the screen. Stone-faced, a guy wormed out from the crowd, alone in his low number. A swarm of well-intentioned back pats caused him to flinch as if stung.

The television zoomed to the left-most column, filled before Otis arrived. Next to number two hung a card with Otis' birthday on it: April 24th. *That can't be right*, he thought. Across the full room, Lucius swiveled, caught Otis' eye, and offered a glum look. Otis' gut congealed like the first time he'd been fired. "Sorry," Lucius mouthed, grimacing in futile empathy.

Chattering nervously, most of the class of 1970 drifted from their TVs to fill the campus pub. Would the ordeal they'd just shared bind them in solidarity or would newly imposed categories of predicament, limbo, and relief tear them apart? Otis didn't go with them. He didn't care. He was tired of his classmates' bloated banter about classes aced, townie women wooed (more like used), and top grad schools applied to. Most of them seemed to Otis like insensate beasts, snared by their own prosaic feats. Having never tasted the freedom he'd tasted climbing, they could not feel the correspondingly huge loss he felt being drafted, nor the relief he *would* have felt if he'd drawn a high, safe number.

Back in their room, Lucius typed as if nothing was different because, for him—applying to seminary, almost certain to get in and obtain a draft exemption—it wasn't. Lucius Berton Hook was the son of a rural Ohio pastor, third of eight children. Freshman year, he and Otis had been paired as roommates. They had little in common, but neither did they irritate each other as much as some roommate pairs seemed to. And so for three years, inertia kept them together.

Otis found Lucius' steady routines and unflappable cheer exasperating but also comforting. Lucius never missed a class. Lucius ate three balanced meals and brushed his teeth after each. Lucius kept his desk as tidy as a tiny well-planned city with a vigilant public works department. Lucius finished his papers early and, although few were inspired (Otis often helped him) and his idea of physical adventure consisted mainly of long walks, Otis often felt slothful around him. Others with such qualities could be obnoxious, obsessed, oppressive, but Lucius' wellspring of good sense amidst things that upset most had watered in Otis a reluctant but growing admiration. Lucius might not be exciting or daring, but he was trustworthy to a fault.

Otis mentioned The Den, a half-mile off campus, downhill. One heard stories—pool hustles, ER trips, nights in jail. For three years Otis had stayed away, but after what had just happened? Studying was impossible. He had to get out, go somewhere, do something. He was also curious. He stood next to Lucius until he looked up then asked him to accompany him.

"What do you want to go there for?"

"Why not? I've got less to lose."

"You're alive."

"Dead man walking."

"The Den's a bad idea."

"I'm not stupid, Lucius. One drink, then we can leave. C'mon."

The Den's token window blinked neon, not quite in time with thumping country music. Otis stepped toward the recessed door and pulled the sticky handle. Inside, heads turned quickly then, just as quickly back. Exhilarated, Otis bee-lined for the bar. "Green death," he said.

"Ah, Haffenwrecker," the bartender said, his voice cigarette gruff. He popped the malt liquor bottle's cap, half-filled a glass, and slid them forward. Otis gulped greedily, then studied the cryptic puzzle inside the cap, wishing it offered magic reprieve. The bartender drew Lucius a Schlitz.

"Lottery?"

"Yes," Lucius said, hands in his lap as his beer's foam settled.

Otis belched and pointed a thumb at Lucius. "*He's* 2-D. Seminary."

The bartender dipped his head theatrically.

"Ah, father! Forgive me, for I run a *wicked* notorious *bah*. How 'bout I say a couple Hail Marys and you guys drink free?"

"Thank you," Lucius said, "but that won't be necessary."

"I gather your friend's *not* 2-D?"

"I'm just plain two," Otis sighed.

The bartender leaned forward conspiratorially. With his eyes, he indicated the room behind them. "Listen my friend, you're not alone. The younger guys here made me flip to the game. I served with their dads overseas but everyone knows this war is different. If they weren't more terrified of their father than of getting popped by Charlie, some of them would find a way out. Count on it. Half of 'em served, half of 'em wanted to, and half of 'em are against it."

"Wait." Otis said. "That's three halves."

"Exactly. We can't protest like you college boys then split town. We have to keep getting along. What guys have confessed to me across this bar? I could start a war in this room, right here tonight." He smiled, stood back up, and wiped the bar. "Hey, you two got names?"

They told him. With his teeth, the bartender issued an ear-splitting whistle. "Hey! Listen up!" The clack of pool balls subsided to jukebox. "My friend Otis here will be serving our country in Vietnam. And my friend Lucius here is pursuing the cloth. Let's be sure they remember us."

Hoots ensued. The bartender poured lavish tumblers of Canadian Club whiskey. Lucius tried to wave him off, but the bartender pointed down the bar to where an older man held up his glass, head slightly bowed. Otis wondered: For who? For what? But he lifted his glass anyway. "Thank you," he yelled, exuberantly enough for the whole bar to hear, eager to hide a vertiginous feeling of loneliness. The whisky brand's clever ads seemed a safe way to take the spotlight off himself. "I wonder if anyone will ever find the case they buried in the Arctic."

"If it's valuable enough," Lucius said. He had barely touched his beer.

"Your friend's smart," the bartender said. "You should listen to him." He pointed to a row of postcards angled along the mirror. "If you end up in country, don't you forget us."

Otis tossed back his whiskey, mind churning as he strained to see the Vietnam stamps. Lucius grabbed his arm and their coats, left the bartender a tip, and tugged Otis outside.

"Why'd you do that? Now they'll think we're, like... jerks."

Lucius handed Otis his coat. Otis held it, puzzled. He felt warm and hopeful, a lot better than he had an hour ago. They would talk out whatever was bugging Lucius, then go back inside.

"You once told me that it was never a good idea to drink when you had a good reason to."

"I said that?"

"You did."

"And your point?"

46

Otis stooped as if to tie his shoe but instead threw a snowball at Lucius. Lucius looked pleased. They went at it for a while, nothing icy that might draw blood but otherwise not holding back. Each took a few in the face. Finally, Otis picked up his coat, put it on, and they trudged back to campus. He stopped them at the library's rough limestone wall, recalling its sunbaked warmth his first week on campus when being at his "stretch" school had felt like Julie Andrews looked singing in an alpine field. Tonight brought the contrasting sense of being hauled into a cave by a rapacious monster.

Otis stretched his arms up and found two remembered protrusions. Gingerly he stepped up and set his weight on a thin stone lip, careful to feel for his balance. He rehearsed the familiar sequence of lateral moves.

"Spot me," he said and Lucius knew not to argue but to do what he'd done for his friend a hundred times before: step back and stretch up his arms, alert to break any backwards pinwheel fall and minimize damage. Otis climbed sideways for a dozen yards, his feet a little above Lucius' head, his trust instinctive and total. Lucius moved with him until Otis walked off onto the hill that angled up to obscure the building's first floor.

"Better?"

"Yeah. Thanks. *Now* we can go home."

The strange part was that, except for seeing a little white card with his birthday on it on TV a few hours earlier, nothing had changed.

Nine:
The Cannon

T hree days later, Otis opened a letter from his mother.

"Your father and I watched the draft lottery live and we're keeping up with everything in the Globe, the Times, *and* the Herald Traveler. We will support you *whatever* you decide."

His mother's affirming superlatives were one of her lovable quirks: her way to proclaim her devotion. As a child, they had given Otis a sense of safety beyond that intrinsic to the Fletchers' large flat grassy backyard and quiet street. (Aside from seasonal mud, infrequent bee stings, and a small patch of blackberry briars, their suburban enclave offered few ways to get into serious trouble.) Otis looked differently now at the caring safeguards she and his father had worked to sustain and the naïve faith he'd placed in her doting precepts. The more he faced adulthood's painful, protracted lessons, the more he saw that he'd grown up in a fantasy world. Beyond its invisible walls, high-stakes clock-ticking trade-offs lay everywhere.

It had taken Otis years to learn—visiting Friendly's for once-a-month family treats—that "whatever you want" did not include taking home one of the huge cardboard tubs of ice cream concealed beneath a line of stainless steel freezer lids. Nor did it mean the wide-mouthed jar of jimmies into which the waitresses in funny caps dipped what they'd scooped, nor the teetering stacks of cones, nor the whole vat of hot fudge. Instead it meant, "Pick *one* flavor within a reasonable amount of time or else we will pick one for you." Otis *wanted* to choose and please his parents. He really did. But the variety *itself* felt more enticing. Retaining near infinite options felt better than settling on any one flavor. And so, he would fight his parents on details— single or double dip, dish or cone, nuts or no, marshmallow fluff or whipped cream—and usually end up with a less appealing flavor because he had run out of time and they had picked for him. Still it was ice cream, not spinach. Once all the drama subsided, he always finished his portion.

The draft reversed the same quandary. Every option he faced constrained his freedom; every option was bad. And yet putting off choosing one of the least repugnant among them postponed his experience of any *specific* distaste. After all, what if the war suddenly ended?

His mother's ostensibly wide-open offer of support in her letter sparked an impish zeal in him which he loved but also hated—because, although giving voice to it often felt really good, it also almost always backfired. Why not a one-way ticket to Sweden and cash to settle there? Why not a secret basement suite to hide from the FBI? To test the limits of her offer with the critical laser he used to write papers and win wrestling matches might briefly relieve his unease, but it would also impugn her sincerity. If he deployed it here, her feelings would be collateral damage. He wouldn't do it. The steely-strong face she could put on hid a fragile core. Like an injured bird, she was doing her best amidst her own hurts.

Each time she spoke of her father's suicide attempt, days after the 1929 stock market crash, the story spilled out like a fresh secret—bound by oaths never to tell. Otis knew the script backward and forward, as did the whole family. "He was sad," she would say. "If only I'd been less selfish sewing my Halloween costume, I might have cheered him up."

Sepia photos showed a posh family home. French doors reflected Long Island Sound down a broad orderly lawn. Otis could scarcely imagine her anguish at age ten as ambulance personnel carried her father out, pale as a ghost, lips black from guzzling his inkwell. (Ink was very toxic back then she would note—not like now—as if someone might try it or think she was joking.) Not long after that, her family lost the big house and the life that had gone with it. Yet as much as Otis pitied his mother for those childhood hardships, it irked him that her rote emotional re-tellings did not countenance commonsense questions. Had his grandfather been patient and pure, the sole victim of those tough times? Would preventing his attempt have been as simple as her smiling more often and bringing him tea?

Otis could only guess at the truths behind her stories. *His* memories of his grandfather were of a glum divorce victim, wildly underemployed as a postal clerk, his stuffy New Haven apartment littered with ashtrays and stacks of half-finished crosswords. As Otis' interest in history and his research acumen grew, he slowly filled notebooks with clues as to how the jubilant tuxedo-clad man in the old photos had come to such a nadir. He concluded (reluctantly but definitively) that war profiteering, astoundingly poor business judgment, and shady dealings were intrinsic to the family legacy on that side back to the Civil War. It helped explain seething hostility and division among aunts, uncles, and cousins—cold fires of regret that burst out only if one or more of them drank too much at a life milestone event or a holiday gathering. Otis never shared what he found. Who was he to alter a hot mess dynamic that had been burbling for decades before he arrived? If it had led his mother to prefer a tidy, predictable, upbeat fantasy world, who was he to burst that bubble? Where was the harm in a little historical gloss for the sake of peace and sanity?

Otis supposed that his mother also wrote to him as she did lest he doubt their unity. Yet all the handwriting was hers, looping and flowing over a stationery card from one of the boxes he bought her each Christmas, dutifully taking the Green Line to the MFA because she had once said she liked French Impressionists. (Plodding the local mall, Otis could never come up with a better idea.) He thought of calling to accept her offer, but her note presumed that he'd made a decision for them to support. And he was not even close. The draft was Friendly's Ice Cream all over again, the longing and the paralysis worsened by his father staying in the shadows, delegating this first feel-good letter to come from her.

No doubt his father was busy behind the scenes. He would be churning ideas from respectable sources, pouring facts into graph paper forms, biding his time until his opinions set hard around logical rebar. Otis anticipated a letter from his father in which he quoted again from "The Three Little Pigs." In light of the draft's intricacies—Otis imagined him writing—Otis should follow the brick-solid plan *he* had come up with and not waste time attempting to construct flimsy ones of his own, founded on misinformed notions of straw or wood.

Did both his parents desire his well-being? Yes, he trusted they did. He was grateful both to them and for them. They had given him every advantage and meted out spankings, groundings, and curfews he richly deserved. But as the three of them had ventured onto the thin ice of adult dealings, it could sometimes be painfully clear (though often only to him) that what each of his parents meant was *wildly* at odds with the other. They strove to put up a united front but often it was anything but. When Otis mentioned teaching, his mother had scowled along with his father but then later urged him to follow his dreams. *Don't mind him*, she had mouthed—a protocol-shattering candor so rare and sheer that Otis had come to doubt that he'd actually seen it.

Had Henry's death created new fault-lines at home or exacerbated old ones? Were they living unique versions of such conflicts or acting out Archie Bunker clichés? (As a student of history, Otis thought it ridiculous how much people talked about a "generation gap," as if such gaps were original.) Friends—not the least Davey—had shared gloomy tales of parents separating and even divorcing, but did his parents' thirty years together (with voices rarely ever raised) obligate him to forge muddy truces for them? Did he have to pretend chalk was cheese for them so they could make it forty years? Trying exhausted him. He couldn't do it.

A few days after his mother's letter, barely half an hour into his afternoon nap, Otis woke to the dorm phone's incessant ringing. Annoyed in bare feet, he ran to answer it, ready to chew out whoever it was then leave it off the hook. *His parents*. He slumped to the floor.

Cheery, his mother began. "We found a man who can help us."

His father chimed in. "It took a little research."

Otis pictured them side-by-side, receiver between them, heads touching. Typically, they spoke to him serially. One would speak in the background while the other relayed between them. Why call together like this? And what on earth was 'men who can help us,' supposed to mean?

"Your father is being modest," his mother said. "He went through the entire Yellow Pages and made a chart. We divided it up and I made him brown-bag lunches so he could make calls from his desk instead of eating in the cafeteria. I made calls from here too—now that I'm not so busy raising you boys anymore." She paused for a painfully long moment. "We shifted dinner a whole hour later to make more calls together."

"It was an hour and a quarter, honey."

"An hour and a quarter, Charles. Of course. The point is, Otis, your father spent all weekend making photocopies from directories at the public library, then checked with the Better Business Bureau and the Chamber of Commerce. He even phoned a special clearinghouse out of state."

His father cut in. "Otis? I want you to write this down."

"Hang on," Otis said groggily.

He let the receiver swing free and went to fetch pencil and paper. His father read him a name and number then had him confirm. But what kind of person was this? A dentist? A doctor? An auto mechanic?

"This is the most reputable man taking new clients. We've moved money from savings to checking to pay his fee."

Otis' father sounded dutifully tired the way Otis imagined he would bailing him out of jail late at night. Finally, it clicked.

They'd found him a draft counselor.

His father's tone made it clear: this hack was not their first choice. He would charge them an arm and a leg to spoon-feed them warmed-over ideas Otis had gleaned already watching others deal with the draft. His parents could not protect him, but urgently needed to feel that they could. He was touched that they'd beaten the bushes to find him a fig leaf, but did he have to wear it? It was his skin on the line. The thought terrified him but inside of it lurked the familiar. Better options always showed up if he waited, alert, ready to jump hard and fast, no looking back. Whenever he'd broken his self-imposed wrestling ring rule out of fear, he'd regretted it. Trying to explain the intuitive artistry of it to someone lacking the instincts was pointless, but neither did he have to embrace his parents' illusions of safety. He crumpled the scrap of paper and lobbed it into the hallway trash can.

"Thank you for doing all that," he said.

"Will you call him today?" His mother's boldness surprised him. He respected her attempt, but he recognized the move. Fear was what led rookies to go for a pin too early in a match they might otherwise win with confident patience and a higher tolerance for pain.

"I've got class in fifteen minutes," Otis said. (A short one he could easily skip, but they didn't know that.)

"Tomorrow's fine, Otis. Call us once you've reached him, OK?"

"But Charles! What are you saying? We agreed."

"Didn't you hear him, Ruth? He said he's got class."

"Not for fifteen minutes, Charles. You need to listen."

52

Several times, Otis tried to interrupt them as they bickered. He loathed being the object. He covered the mouthpiece and mutely kept score. Takedown. Escape. Reversal. Nearfall. One more escape. Another reversal. Neither of his parents gained a decisive advantage. Then Otis realized: they were only sparring. There would be no verbal pin, no final united demand that he act. They just needed to know that they'd done all they could, united in that. All the choices remained his. In fact, he surmised, their real disagreement probably wasn't about him at all.

At last, Otis interjected to tell them he loved them.

Because he did. He really did.

Ten:
Real News

The following week, a letter arrived from Louisabeth. Otis tore it open before shutting his brass-doored campus mailbox.

"Dear Otis. I don't know how not to hurt you, but my dad says guys are tough and you won't be surprised." Cold trickled through him. Student center buzz muffled. Why bring her father into this? Wasn't she a women's libber? "As you know, I've been wrestling with my feelings. We've had fun times, but things change. I need to consider my future. You're a great guy Otis, but it's time we went our own ways. I'm sure you'll find someone sweet. Stay friends, OK?"

Stay friends. Someone sweet. *Right.* He recalled the cloying drinks the night they'd met. He should have known.

Back in his room, he tucked her letter under his typewriter, rolled in a fresh sheet of paper and racked his brain for the right words to reverse hers. No words came. He tried her dorm phone for a week but all who answered agreed: "She has a twenty page English paper due very soon."

"On what?" he asked, on the eighteenth call.

"Don Quixote," her roommate quipped and hung up.

"What would you do?" Otis asked Lucius after the twentieth futile call.

"Do you love her?"

"Yeah."

"When was the last time you told her?"

"I can't remember. What does that matter?"

(In fact, Otis recalled the last time rather vividly.)

54

"Otis, this is eating you up. You need to pursue her or else move on."

"Maybe I should go there. Find her. Talk to her."

"Your call. I'm happy to tag along for moral support."

"Her last class ends at four."

Friday at 3:59PM, Otis and Lucius idled near Louisabeth's Northampton classroom building. A dim December sun skittered low behind bare trees. Clutching a single red rose, Otis got out.

"I'll be praying," Lucius said.

"Thanks." Otis shut the door. *Whatever*, he thought.

A stream of women filed past. Those whom he recognized looked bemused and avoided eye contact. One woman glimpsed him, raised her eyebrows and turned back inside the Art History building. Otis' ears burned from cold. Ten minutes later, Louisabeth emerged, approached, and stopped. Otis strode forward, extending the frost-stiffened blossom. "I've missed you," he said.

She took the flower but didn't sniff it. He leaned forward to kiss her, but she turned; strands of loose hair stuck to his lips. "Oh, Otis. This is so sweet, but you shouldn't have come."

"I got your letter."

"This isn't a good time, Otis." She glanced around.

"I thought we were getting back to OK."

He fought the urge to disgorge accusations.

A chisel-faced man strode briskly toward them. Heads swiveled, their expressions ranging from ire to lust. The man wore a grey-blue uniform: tight black collar, black stripe up the front. Louisabeth stood on tiptoe to kiss him and the familiarity of their embrace caused Otis to recall vignettes she'd casually dribbled into conversations during the two years they'd dated, about a "next-door childhood friend, a nice boy named Connor." Play dates and grade school recesses, she'd said, notes passed in class, him carrying her books, her attending his games, them studying together, going for ice cream after school play performances, summer jobs together below the Mason-Dixon line. All of the memories she'd shared had been opaque to Otis' attempts to talk about and appreciate what she and Connor had experienced

55

dating "off and on," and then "a bit" after high school, "agreeing to split as good friends."

Connor handed Louisabeth a box of gourmet chocolates and a dozen roses, their perfect petals protected by two carefully arranged layers of clear plastic. Good friends indeed. The bottom line, Otis realized, was that Louisabeth and Connor had dated a lot more than a bit—on more than off since both of them had been in diapers.

"Connor, Otis. Otis, Connor." Louisabeth looked at the ground.

Connor held out his hand.

"Connor Trumaine. Glad to finally meet you, Otis."

The impossibility of the situation steeled Otis' resolve. He kept his hands resolutely at his sides. "Nice next-door childhood friend," he said, hoping his words sounded icy.

"Connor has been there for me when I needed to talk."

"That's not fair. I'm ninety minutes away. We agreed on phone calls."

"I left at o-four-hundred," Connor said. "Virginia Military Institute."

Otis kept his eyes fixed on Louisabeth.

"Cute. So now it's about who can drive the farthest and use military jargon. Seriously? The California trip was hard on me too."

Louisabeth's face reddened in a way Otis had only ever seen when she'd taken the megaphone at various antiwar protests she'd helped organize.

"I'll bet. But I was the one who had to go through it."

"That's rich. I found a doctor. I paid. You remember those parts?"

"You have no idea how well I remember those parts—and other parts I vowed to spare you. But it doesn't end with the mechanics any more than it began with them. I'm not sure you ever got that." She wiped a tear. Connor drew her in. "Maybe I didn't either. I'm sorry. I really am."

"I only got your letter last week! I've tried dozens of times. Your roommates keep hanging up..."

"Listen, Otis." Connor's deep voice suggested power but he kept it measured. "Louisabeth is a grown woman."

She plucked a hair from his uniform shoulder and cast it into the wind.

Otis addressed Louisabeth. "I thought you were against the war."

Connor stepped close to face him. "Let me help you, Otis" he said, so calmly that Otis supposed, for a moment, that Connor *was* going to help him. "Louisabeth isn't your choice anymore. You face a different one. A

56

simpler one. I looked up your draft number. You can obey your country's call or you can refuse it and take the consequences—like a man." Connor turned and offered Louisabeth his crooked arm; they strode off.

"Hey," Otis hollered at their backs. "Ask your drill sergeant if he'll let you watch some real news for a change!" Once he was inducted, Otis realized, someone like Connor—perhaps even Connor himself—would have the authority to run his life, down to the smallest detail. There was the rub, the thing that he could not abide.

Lucius grabbed Otis' elbow.

"Let's head home," he said and very wisely, they did.

Eleven:
Sliding

F inals week, over donuts and hot chocolate—their last day together before Otis' Christmas break—Davey told him that he and his mother would be moving before the New Year.

Otis tried to sound upbeat. "To Georgia?"

"No way. Did Mom tell you?"

"Nope. Just a good guess."

"Dad works at the Atlanta airport. Mom says you can see planes close up from his house. Flying is expensive so we'll be driving there. I have a half-sister. She just turned four."

"That's great, Davey. Really great. I bet you'll have a really great time." He let Davey pick a dozen donuts to go. "For you and your Mom."

The counter lady handed Davey the string-wrapped box. "To *share*," she said, which made them both laugh. If Davey sensed what Otis was really feeling, he didn't let on.

"Send me your new address," Otis said. He hoped his request didn't sound brittle or clingy.

For three years, he'd watched Davey grow from timid and spindly to pre-teen awkward. The occasional glimpse of manly courage, such as Davey's first river rope swing last fall, gave Otis hope. Yet it was hard not to be sentimental. Half the places around Dedentown evoked fun things they'd done together—events a father should see. Re-united with his real father, Davey would be better off. Yet having played some of a father's role with Davey and then—upon Louisabeth's news—in his mind's eye, Otis found it hard to be positive about the prospect vanishing.

Would he and Louisabeth have had a boy or a girl? It did no good to dwell on the fact that he would never know; but still, sometimes, he couldn't help wonder. In myriad recent dreams he was on the verge of finding out when something unsettling would intervene. The baby would turn out to be wrapped tightly in plastic, floating on a fast river face-down, or tumbling out the door of a speeding car. Each shift would paralyze him, mute, able only to watch the horror unfold. A month ago, the choice to abort had seemed clear but now, increasingly, he hated the nightmare-filled void it had left.

After his last exam, Otis tossed his things in the Dauphine and started home, resolved to call Big Brother. It was a long shot, but if they could assign him a new boy to mentor until graduation, he could let Pinnacle go. Until then, without the team or Davey to distract him, he should be able to tackle the gully with the kind of dedication Shaun would expect.

In a hypnotic corridor of flakes, Otis struggled to stay in dark tracks left by blurred taillights ahead. Wet clumps packed the windshield's corners, restricting his wipers. Around midnight, he fishtailed into his parents' driveway. The spotlight came on transforming the swirling white from menacing to magical. His parents appeared, framed in the storm door. His father stomped out in bathrobe and boots, but as he extended his hand Otis was already turning to open the trunk; in his peripheral vision, Otis glimpsed the gesture a moment too late.

"Your mother's been worried," his father said to his back.

Otis bent to grab his luggage.

"You guys didn't need to stay up. The Dauphine is fine in this stuff."

"We're your parents. It's our job."

Otis rolled his eyes then turned around. They caught fingers and shook as if it were the right way to do it. Otis thought to pass his father the heavier suitcase, but his snow-dappled hair, damp glasses, and bathrobe made him look old and bewildered. Otis handed him the light one instead.

"Your mom is worried sick. We need to talk as a family."

Family? He couldn't mean Billy. That would be beyond awkward. Besides, what was there to talk about? They would only drag him to the draft counselor and what could *that* charlatan do?

"Yeah, sure, Dad," Otis said.

His mother propped the door open and embraced him. Through her thin nightgown, her shoulders felt bony. Smoke smell and a hoarse voice suggested a lapse longer than her one-pack restaurant parking lot protest. "You can sleep in tomorrow but then I want to hear all about everything." She trudged upstairs, hand on the rail. At the landing, she gave a tiny wave.

His father shucked off his boots, black dress socks taut and high. He thumped Otis on the back but it felt clumsy, pre-planned. "Your mother's just tired. We're both glad you're home."

"Me too, Dad," Otis lied.

"Goodnight then. I'm on the early train tomorrow. See you at dinner."

Otis was not looking forward to the next three weeks. Did it occur to his father that he might grab a pizza tomorrow with friends? It would also be hard to pursue teaching jobs from home. Would the mall security guards mind if he brought his typewriter there and set up on a bench? He slumped on the sofa, feet on the off-limits coffee table. Like a goateed shark in a pool of crude oil, a menacing face leered from an all-black Life Magazine cover.

The day after the draft lottery, Charles Manson had been arrested for several horrific, perhaps ritual murders. With grim fascination, Otis read the feature article, "Love and Terror Cult," then a piece on "*The* Massacre," definite article, like *The* Boston Massacre had been for the American colonists until other massacres eclipsed its five dead. At My Lai, U.S. troops had outdone their forebears, shooting and burning hundreds of children and women. What sort of person would do such a thing? What excuse could they offer? Henry had said little about his time in Vietnam, but Otis was sure that his brother would never have fallen to *that* level of depravity.

Another man's face leapt to life on another page, the total opposite of Manson's. Low sun cast the man's dark beret, bushy eyebrows, and white hair in weathered relief. He had started a thing called NOLS, the National Outdoor Leadership School. "To escape any dilemma," the story began, "I would instantly, confidently ask for Paul Petzoldt." *Any* dilemma? As with his mother's letter, superlatives made Otis skeptical. He recalled a snippet of chatter he'd overheard as a clueless high school freshman. He'd been scurrying past the senior lockers, eyes downcast. "What a dilemma!" An older girl exclaimed, her eyes red and wet as friends consoled her. With Russian missiles headed to Cuba, Otis had assumed they were fretting over the apocalypse, but within weeks the crying girl had dropped out, pregnant.

Otis woke the next day to street plow rumble, clacking tire chains, and the swish of the truck spreading road salt. Once it passed, all reverted to quiet. A thin shaft of sunlight illumined the spot on his wall where seeping ice dams had left a stain two winters ago. Had his father run the snowblower already? He opened the curtains. The driveway and walk were pristine, snowbank verges crisp and straight. He blinked in the glare, grateful but also feeling guilty for not helping. He was still unpacking when milk bottle clanks made him hungry. He donned jeans, tromped downstairs, and brought the bottles in but only three spoonfuls into his bowl of Lucky Charms, his mother returned with groceries. He rushed out barefoot to help her unload.

"You don't have to go to Vietnam," she said with no warning.

"Does Dad agree?" Barefoot, Otis danced as she unlocked the trunk.

"He loves you more than you know."

Otis grabbed two bags in each hand, hurried in, and began unloading the perishables into the fridge, just as she'd taught him. "I'll finish," she said. Politely, she asked him to wipe up his wet tracks so that no one slipped.

"If he loves me, then why doesn't he say what he wants?"

"What do *you* want, Otis?"

"You know," he said. They all three agreed—and knew *that* they agreed. They all wanted him not to end up like Henry. But to say so was utterly taboo; plus, how he achieved that end was still up for grabs. Most men who served in Vietnam came back whole and honorably, without all the complications of civil disobedience.

"OK then, choose; we will support you. But don't let this slide."

"I will," Otis said, "just not yet." He hoped he did not sound too evasive or ungrateful. Her admonition was right, but hearing it felt like Friendly's; the ticking clock entrenching him into further indecision. What if he made the wrong choice? A little boy inside him wanted his parents to make the draft go away. Tell the Army they could not have their second son too, then hug him and never mention it again. He recognized the impulse as infantile and fantastic but he also hoped that somehow, they or *someone* would intervene with a new option to save him.

Twelve:
The Arena

Every Friday in January, right after his last class (and sometimes before), Otis fled campus with anyone he could coax to climb, anywhere there might be ice: the Green Mountains or the Whites, the Adirondacks or the Berkshires, steep stuff or easy, new routes or old. He could feel himself getting nimbler, stronger, more efficient and the more he climbed the more he wanted to. Why had he not done this before? There had been Davey of course, but only one day a week. He could have juggled them both. He pestered Big Brother to assign him another boy for the spring, but they kept putting him off. He also made inquiries into teaching jobs, but the month slid by with no promising replies to his many letters.

In early February, audible from across the cafeteria, Wilson Ward explained with exuberant vulgarity how his father's tailor was working up a dozen custom seasonal suits for him. To keep the suits fresh for the job Wilson had accepted with Morrison-James (reporting to Ed Fishender, the MJ partner Otis' father had once known) the Wards' full-time handyman was adding a walk-in cedar closet to the rent-controlled Midtown loft with deeded parking that Wilson's father had secured for him. In December, Wilson had drawn a high, safe draft number—well into the three hundreds. Under his leadership, the hockey team was going to the national championship again, as favorites. Otis hated simultaneously feeling violated by Wilson and envying his charmed life.

That weekend, Otis wrenched his knee in a pathetic, short, slip-and-twist mishap on Central Gully—the equivalent of tripping on an escalator. The doc said he would be out of commission until late March, well into melt. Resolved to heal it in less, Otis haunted the weight room to stay in form, leaving his crutch outside so he didn't look like a sissy. It just wasn't the same. Antsy, he checked his campus mailbox several times a day. Big Brother thanked him for his dedicated service but their policy did not allow for assignments to graduating seniors. Reading their note, Otis deflated. If three years had helped Davey, couldn't three months help another boy?

In mid-March, despite his knee still being sore, Otis funneled his frustrations into a last-ditch climbing frenzy. And it paid off. In his most brilliant lead ever, he topped-out Pinnacle Gully! The ice which had spurned him responded like never before, receiving each of his axe swings and foot-placements with what felt to Otis like joy, subsuming him into a symbiosis so focused and sublime that its ecstatic timelessness almost rivaled sex.

Just in time, too. Within days of his conquest, a heatwave hit New England. Home for spring break, Otis detailed his climb's key moves for his parents in a slide show his climbing partners had snapped for the purpose. His mother wept (in awe, Otis supposed) until his father abruptly stood, said, "I think we've seen enough," and flipped on the lights.

The next afternoon, Otis stopped by Dirkden High—his first time back there in three years. Entering the gym that had once felt like a home now felt like a break-in. A handful of pimple-faced boys sat spellbound in a semi-circle at Coach's feet. States were next week, the squad pruned to the elite. "Drop them frozen dead!" Coach hollered and the boys repeated in unison. Had he been so scrawny? So blindly trusting? Coach Lester Wrangel's bullhorn voice, thick red beard, and winding eccentric stories commanded attention the way his bear-like body had once dominated wrestling mats across New England. Attempts at interruption were fruitless, even as his heart of gold drove him to elated tears whenever one of his athletes won.

A few seniors spied Otis and hailed him. (Bob? Gary? Ralph? Otis had no idea.) Freshmen remembered their captains. The reverse was rarely true. He faked a smile and waved back. Coach turned, beamed, and told Otis to join them, then crushed him in a side-hug. With Otis under his arm, he recounted Otis' matches, move-by-move to the boys for what seemed an hour. Otis felt naked. Just as he began to wonder if it would dishonor Coach if he slipped free of his clutches, Coach released him and sent the boys off to drills. He lowered his voice and met Otis' eyes.

"I was sorry to hear about Henry."

Henry had attended many of Otis' matches. "Thanks Coach. I'm sure he's in a better place." Aside from a hole in the ground, Otis had no idea where his brother was—or if he was—but the stock line usually quenched well-meant intrusions. Nobody liked to talk about death.

"You're almost done at DF, right? History?" Coach's caring recall of hundreds of athletes' lives had always been peerless, but Otis was amazed that it applied to him, years past graduation. How had Coach learned his major? "Come by tomorrow in togs, why don't you? Show the guys your moves." Otis said he would have to check what his parents had planned. "You'd make a great coach Otis, a great teacher too, I'd bet. The pay and the prestige are low, but it's a noble profession. Rewarding. Have you considered teaching again, Otis?" (They had talked about it a few times before, but only casually.) "Young men need good role models—these days especially. There are lots of opportunities, you know."

As he had at countless after-school briefings, Coach went on like that without interruption for ten minutes, neither demanding nor expecting Otis to answer, happy to let anyone in his presence float down a cheerful river of reverie. Yet Coach never let his own monologues distract him from his work. As he spoke, he took in a thousand concurrent details—a grunt, a pause, a misplaced hand or foot, a too-high center of gravity—as dozens of boys sparred around him. He would hold up a finger to whomever he was talking to, turn to bark a concise correction, then resume mid-sentence without ever needing to ask, now where was I?

"Great kids, these," Coach said. "Your class too, sixty-six. We were really something, weren't we? You remember." Coach's beaming face filled Otis with cascades of memories neither one of them needed to specify because they'd lived them intensely together. He hoped Coach would not mention Octopus, and Coach did not let him down. The 1965 state final match might as well not have happened. Otis knew others felt the same, but being in Coach's presence always made him feel that he was his true favorite, sensitive to any scars from deep wounds like that one.

Otis told Coach of his job woes. Coach shared names to help: Principals, Athletic Directors, old friends from who-knew-where or when. "Feel free to use my name," Coach offered.

Jackpot. In the circles Otis hoped to inhabit one day, Coach Wrangel's name was pure gold, respected for transforming boys into men who won in life after the mat. Coach had influenced Otis so comprehensively—instilling a discipline and tenacity he had found nowhere else—that Otis couldn't imagine who he would have been without him. Otis could never repay him, but he could honor him by passing along his wisdom to others, creating new winning traditions.

Otis pictured his future athletes. Just as Coach did with each crop of virtual sons, he could see himself holding them in affection, calling them "my guys." Many weren't born yet. If he coached long enough, even their parents weren't born—a staggering thought. They wouldn't know that Otis' motivational pearls of wisdom were hand-me-down variants on Coach's treasures. But Otis would know and that would be enough for him to feel part of something larger than himself.

Galvanized by the vision and Coach's support, Otis turned up five solid job leads that week. By early April, he was getting interviews. Late in April, a letter arrived from a Connecticut prep school where his interviews had gone especially well. Not his dream job, but very close. "Please call at your earliest convenience," the letter said, "so we can expedite the hiring process."

Hiring! Otis called them, ecstatic.

The HR woman got right to the point. Otis' birth date suggested a low draft number. Could he please send a notarized copy of his deferment, his Conscientious Objector approval, or else his medical exemption? As soon as they had one of those on file, they would send out the formal written offer for him to sign.

Otis voiced confusion. He reminded the HR lady that teaching was a protected national occupation; teachers were the equivalent of domestic soldiers. Everyone knew the history.

"Not anymore," the HR lady said. "Didn't you hear? President Nixon changed the rule."

"What do you mean?" Since Otis could remember, few things had been more sacrosanct. In 1957, the Russians had launched Sputnik. In response— to help win the Cold War, which that shock had kicked into high gear— President Eisenhower had created military draft rules designed to "channel" young men toward "strategic" professions. Teaching was one of them.

"April twenty-third," the HR lady said. "I'm sorry you didn't know but you must understand. Parents place enormous trust in us to provide the best, most stable educational environment for their sons. They make a substantial investment and we carry the corresponding responsibility of ensuring our teachers are worthy of their investment. Can you imagine the trauma a young man would suffer if his beloved teacher was, how shall I say, snatched away in an untimely, abrupt fashion? It would disrupt the close-knit community we have worked to build here since 1750." She explained her task: scrubbing draft-liable candidates from the school's hiring short list.

"You can't do that," Otis shouted.

"Please. Civility and duty are two qualities we work the hardest to instill in our young men."

Otis argued with her from several angles; it was no use. He hung up, baffled and panicked. To not land one teaching job stung. But this development killed his entry into the entire profession. He would face the same scrutiny everywhere he'd applied—the issue as pervasive as mildewing wall-to-wall carpet after a flood. He might as well have yielded to his father's wishes years ago. And he'd been so close. But his vexation ran even deeper. He wanted what a stable full-time job enabled: a relationship with a woman that went further than pre-arranged carnal weekends. She didn't have to be rich or stunning, just kind; someone honest with whom he could be himself. Someone who wanted more or less what he did: a stable marriage, kids, happiness, home.

Was it childish gloss that the home he'd grown up in had once felt that way—much more than shelter? He warmed up his amplifier and plated the Stones album he'd bought the week after the draft. As the simple, plunking guitar line ascended toward its frantic crescendo, Otis studied the album jacket: a wedding cake atop an eclectic stack of disks: a movie film canister, a bike tire, a clock, even a pancake. On the cover's reverse, the stack had been cut and fallen in on itself, its distinctive parts intermingled perversely. Why did his thoughts of home seem like that now?

That night, on a dining hall bulletin board, a hand-lettered sheet caught his eye: one free ticket to Jim Morrison and the Doors at the Boston Arena in exchange for a ride to the midnight show. He wasn't crazy for the Doors' music or the venue—the site of his state finals defeat five years before—but if freshmen (not allowed to have cars on campus) were behind the offer, then the trip would offer a welcome distraction from guys his age.

Among Otis' fellow seniors, the December lottery had laced formerly-jovial relationships with hairline cracks. Attempts at banter often widened them into chasms, fraught to yell across. Separated into draft lottery haves and have nots, those vulnerable to the war and those freed from its clutches had less and less to say to one another, even as those in the tentative middle obsessed about which side would one day become theirs. Otis tore off a paper tab, called, and confirmed. Sure enough, freshmen—exempt from the draft three more years if they kept their grades up.

As he drove the group east Friday night, Otis refused the joint they offered. Someone thrust Led Zeppelin's new album into the eight-track. Otis smiled as his young wards wove side to side to the flamboyant stereo effects. Otis took comfort in the tunes like that with bluesy lyrics which felt more in keeping with his 1-A vulnerable first-to-the-firing-line status than did the Beatles' soporific "Let it Be" or The Jackson Five's kitschy pop "ABC, 123," that seemed to dominate all the radio stations lately like billows of cotton candy.

They arrived in Boston to a tangle of firetrucks losing a battle to save a building angry with flame. Police kept back a stream of trippy faces pouring from the Doors' first show—which had not paused—the fire more a feature of it, than a threat to it. Later, onstage at the midnight show, the fire outside finally contained, Jim Morrison interlaced drunken slurred lyrics with prohibited epithets until, well before the city's 2AM curfew, the power cut out with no warning. Jeers and boos pelted from the sudden smoky silence as hundreds of Zippos sparked to break the gloom.

For a moment, the crowd wavered between resignation and riot as a dozen cops ran onstage waving flashlights, grabbed Morrison by all four limbs, and dragged him off, howling like a banshee. Otis imagined the clean-cut Wilson Ward, bound in place of the wriggling singer, and let a poem his mother used to recite to him twist the scene into a new fanciful form.

James, James, Morrison, Morrison,
highly prestigious indeed.
I don't care for your New York job;
I would much rather be free.

Dying for open space, Otis wormed his way through a scrum of stumbling bodies as tight as any wrestling match. Outside, he felt for his wallet. It was gone, as were the freshmen. He waited by Henry's car. After an hour, he considered leaving, but what if he got stopped with no license?

Around 4AM, the freshmen finally returned. Otis was freezing. The freshman looked flush.

"We found this underground place that took our IDs," said the one who most resembled Otis. He handed Otis back his wallet. "Hey, I noticed your draft card. Bummer, man."

Seething with rage, Otis drove them home. One of them threw up on the way. Otis spent the morning cleaning and airing the car. Never again, he vowed. That afternoon, with housemates he trusted not to be jerks, he watched Apollo Thirteen on TV. One beer per launch event was the standing agreement: ignition, liftoff, stage one, escape tower ejection and on it went, a six-pack inside of twelve minutes, the beer buzz trailing behind like the rocket's contrail. When live shots of the hurtling lunar module turned grainy and wobbly and the network cut to artists' renditions, the whole thing felt to Otis like the concert—horribly wrong in ways he couldn't pinpoint.

Only two days later, when Apollo Thirteen ran into trouble did Otis' foreboding coalesce. Houston, we have a problem. Understatement of the century. Otis hoped for the best for the stranded crew, but he was also glad it wasn't him dying slowly in dark and cold, far from help.

After the men didn't die, he and Lucius went to see the M.A.S.H. movie. Others laughed, but Otis whispered to Lucius that a mobile Army surgical hospital seemed grim, the humor tasteless. Lucius countered that the doctors and nurses were doing their best in trying circumstances. Otis broke off what might have become a spat to go and get popcorn. In Otis' isolation—team-less, iceless, jobless, and girlfriend-less—he was reluctant to do anything that might alienate the one friend he had with a refreshing perspective. Otis' respect for his roommate was grudging but growing. Lucius took seriously the same news items he did (the Manson murders, the My Lai Massacre, Nixon's recent speech on Cambodia) but never lost his cool. Lucius would express sorrow or anger, but he never circled an endless whirlpool of angst as many did.

Thirteen:
The Wire

The first Monday in May, Otis learned who had gotten his prep school job from an overheard lunch conversation. Jealous, he seethed at the news. Bob Pachis' doughy physique matched his clingy manner. Deaf in one ear, Bob's right elbow was fused from a childhood fall; handshakes were awkward. Bob sat in the front row of every class, infamous for posing tortuous questions, oblivious to eye-rolls behind him. As a freshman, he'd pestered Otis for eccentric social advice at all hours, but a year later, when Otis was trying to catch up in a class they had together, Bob had acted as if he was doing Otis a favor to give Otis' term paper outline a perfunctory skim. Bob might get by teaching history, but why would a school make him their assistant *wrestling* coach? Even in kickball, Bob always sat out and kept score. This must be what it felt like to be held back a grade, Otis thought. When the military released him two years from now, Bob would be well entrenched in the job that *should* have been his. How could Otis compete then?

Otis finished his lunch and walked back to his room, mind churning with the unfairness. The quad was busier than usual. He plowed through the crowd, eyes ahead, dying for his nap. In his room, he shut his windows, pulled the shades, and lay down, rehearsing a rant he would share with Lucius over dinner. Within minutes of Otis falling asleep, Lucius burst in and dropped his books. Mutely, he fumbled with his transistor radio.

"Don't you have class?" Otis was startled; Lucius was never impulsive.

Lucius slumped into a chair. "They're all cancelled."

He tuned in the college station.

"...this just off the wire, from local station WKSU in northern Ohio..."

Otis couldn't believe what they were hearing. He knew about the Kent State University ROTC building arson, but ten students shot? Four of them dead? Two of them *women*? The ROTC news had felt like an assault on Henry but it was only a building, and Otis could empathize better with the protests than he had before. Yet this sounded like war. Even-keeled Lucius also looked stunned. Suddenly, Otis remembered. "Oh crap! Your sister."

Lucius looked up. "I already tried. Her dorm phone is fast-busy. My dad wanted to drive up and get her, but the whole town is locked down. No one is allowed in or out."

Otis stood, silent. He wished he could fill the role for Lucius that Lucius had so often played for him: ballast, confidante, wingman. But what to say? After Henry's death, he'd been startled at how many people's attempts at consolation achieved precisely the opposite. Lucius closed his eyes and leaned forward, hands tented beneath his nose. His silent intensity in prayer made Otis recall their freshman fall when, getting used to each other's routines, Otis had asked him about it.

"Aren't you just talking to yourself?"

Lucius had paused before responding.

"God promises to hear those who trust Him."

"How can you trust what you can't see?"

"You trust gravity, don't you?"

"That's different."

"You said you trusted your coach."

"That's different too."

"Is it? You trust well-corroborated firsthand accounts of historical people and events."

"Of course. I'm planning to major in History." (Otis had been far from sure, but expressing the false resolve as if it were certain had helped to cement it in fact.)

"Well, have you considered that the Bible is a reliable collection of historical documents? Did you know it was penned by eyewitnesses during the lifetime of hundreds of other eyewitnesses, each with varying motivations and perspectives, who *could* have contradicted the eyewitnesses' written accounts but never did for the rest of their lives?"

"No, but I'm pretty sure the professors here would say you're nuts."

(Otis recoiled to recall how zealously immature they'd *both* been: two intellectual carnivores, used to the top of his local academic food chain, fresh off long successful high school quests to get into DF or a top school like it. Each had been conditioned to empty a full clip of cerebral ammunition into *any* target in-range without hesitation. Both had since grown more selective.)

"Have you thought about how consistent the Bible's message is across forty human authors and wildly different linguistic and cultural contexts over fifteen centuries? Have you reflected on how that diversity serves as a crosscheck on error and validates the Bible's repeated, unavoidable claims to supernatural origin? Have you looked into how the superlatively unmatched profusion of extant manuscript copies authenticates the Bible's clear message and its specific words?"

"Not really. Why should I, Lucius? What's your point?"

"My point is that you couldn't corrupt the Bible if you tried—and many have. It depicts God as the unique, omnipotent, omniscient, omnipresent supernatural being who created and controls everything both seen and unseen in every instant of time, from the largest galaxy down to the smallest sub-atomic particle—the sole author of history, past, present, and future."

Lucius' claims had struck Otis as absurd. How had he gotten in here? Otis had clapped his hands in mock adulation. "Good for you Lucius, but now tell me: did God make me do *that*?"

But Lucius had only smiled and said, "In time I hope you see." Then, to Otis' astonishment, Lucius had *continued* spouting. "The Bible says God defines truth, beauty, love, and goodness. It shows Him entering into history in the form of a baby named Jesus, living a real physical human life yet as the perfect, sinless image of God, dying on a cross, then rising from the dead to prove that He is, in fact, whether we like it or not, the sole and forever creator-king of the universe. No other book is remotely like the Bible. It's God's love letter to His people and simultaneously, His unilateral judgment on His enemies."

"OK, you win," Otis had jibed. "I'm late for practice. I prefer fights that aren't rigged."

A year later, Lucius had put his words into action, consoling Otis about Henry late into many teary nights. Otis still cherished his roommate's singular investment in his comfort that year. But ever since the milestone

Bible lecture from Lucius their freshman year, Otis had made sure to avoid topics and situations that might trigger another soliloquy like it.

The dorm phone rang. Lucius blinked. They scurried to it. Otis nodded and Lucius answered.

"Yes, Mrs. Fletcher." Otis detected his mother's voice rhythms but could not make out her words. "Yes, we're awaiting news also. Thank you for your kind thoughts, Mrs. Fletcher. Yes, he's right here, Mrs. Fletcher." On weekdays she often called around this time: hours until Otis' father got home but too early to start dinner. Sometimes Otis would sit and let her talk, receiver hanging loose next to his head while he did his homework. Lucius handed Otis the phone.

"A letter came for you today," she began. "I was going to speak with your father and call you later, but then I heard the awful news. Is anything like that going on there?"

"No, Mom. Guys are hanging out in the quad playing Frisbee. It's a beautiful day." He didn't mention the joints and hasty placards.

"How many guys?"

"I don't know. A bunch. Thirty? Forty?"

"Promise me you'll stay indoors if a mob forms?"

"I'll stay inside if a mob forms, Mom. You said I got a letter?"

"Yes. From Selective Service."

"Go ahead," Otis said, "open it." He leaned heavily against the wall. "Draft," he mouthed to Lucius. His only curiosity was how long he would have between graduation and induction.

She read aloud right away, with no sound of tearing paper. "It says, 'You are hereby ordered for induction into the Armed Forces of the United States and to report at...' It gives an address in Kendall Square, Cambridge. June eighth, at eight in the morning." She sounded agitated.

Great. After receiving his diploma, he would have less than forty-eight hours of freedom.

"OK. Thanks, Mom. You can hang onto it. I don't need to see it."

"Don't you think you should call the draft counselor again?"

Otis recalled the smarmy mustachioed lawyer—Theodore, or George, or Dwight-David—a name that escaped him, wholly at odds with the man's

72

drab office, droopy shoulders, whiny voice, and stained light-blue polyester jacket. Otis wondered what had kept his legal practice afloat between a correspondence-school legal degree in the mid-fifties and the recent mushroom-like inception of draft counseling as a lucrative thing. As Otis had expected, the Fletchers learned little more from their two-hour meeting than what he'd already gleaned from friends. His father had written the man another check then his parents had bickered all the way home.

"What can he do, Mom? My number came up. I passed the pre-induction physical. We don't exactly have a close friend in Congress, and I'm not going to chop off a finger or toe."

"You don't need to be flip, Otis. He seemed well informed. He might have fresh ideas."

"I have his number."

"Promise you'll call him?"

"I'll think about it."

"Well, speaking of such, we got a lovely Christmas card last year from your father's cousin Beatrice and her husband Andy. Up in Thunder Bay?"

"OK."

"In Canada?"

"I got an A in eighth grade geography."

"Be nice," Lucius mouthed.

"Your father doesn't care for their politics, but I'm sure they would love to see you."

"Mom? I have to go."

"Hug, kiss," she said. Otis hung up.

"It was nice of her to call," Lucius said. "They obviously care for you."

"I just wish she wouldn't worry so much."

"Give her some credit, Otis. Have you considered how hard it must be for her to worry so *little* about you right now? She's probably holding back."

"Yeah maybe, but it's oppressive. They never did this with Henry."

"Um, Otis? Have you noticed how much has changed since he enlisted? On top of grieving for him, your parents are struggling through all of this along with the rest of us."

"I suppose." Otis wasn't going to volunteer as Henry had, but he wondered what his parents would do if he did. He started cleaning his desk:

tossing candy wrappers, receipts, crumpled first drafts, re-capping ballpoint pens—anything to avoid talking about Kent State or induction.

"Look," Lucius said after a while. "With classes cancelled, nothing is due tomorrow. We can hike the Stillwater Trail and be back by dinner. Clear our heads. What do you say?"

"What about your sister? Won't your parents be trying to reach you?"

Lucius laced his boots. "There's nothing I can do that I haven't done."

"I don't get you," Otis said, thinking but not saying: She's your sister, your flesh and blood. She might be hurt or dead; why would you not wait to find out she's OK?

They walked in silence, trees gauzy pale green, just coming out, sunny where summer's onset would soon bring shade. But the further they went, the more Otis' thoughts churned in surprising, disturbing directions.

Who was he to judge Lucius for not waiting for a phone call? Who was he to chastise Lucius about his care for his own flesh and blood? He'd failed in the same realm, and failed big. He'd caved to expediency and let fear talk him out of the biggest, boldest, scariest move he could have made— embracing fatherhood. He'd scarcely even tried to persuade Louisabeth to carry the baby to term because he'd been just as ambivalent as she—about them, about it, about being tied down. No amount of regret or wishing could reverse what he'd accepted, even encouraged.

Fourteen:
Faces

Otis shivered, hung over. Drizzle drenched his cap and gown. Commencement pomp could not end soon enough. But if Monday never came, it would be *too* soon. Was jungle rain warmer? He pictured guys who'd sat in these folding chairs the past few years who'd lost limbs, minds, and lives to take nameless hills only to give them back. Some he knew only by sight or voice, but he'd shared classes, bathrooms, and meals with others whom he could still picture carefree.

Drizzle slowed to mist and then stopped. In the bleachers, his father's umbrella stayed up. Two-toned and golf-sized, he twirled it conspicuously. Otis glared a smile, mortified. The family all waved. His father put the umbrella away. Did they have any idea?

Otis hated the term evasion. The prospect of physical danger wasn't what bothered him. He'd taken hard climbing falls and blown tendons on wrestling mats. What irked him was the thought of submitting to orders: all kinds of orders—pompous, pointless, deadly. He preferred to think of things to run toward: pure, cold, high places with built-in rewards. Besides, if he let himself be sucked into the system, his mother would have to relive the whole Henry ordeal.

Six years ago, Henry had made the rounds at his active duty send-off picnic: a graduation party and Memorial Day celebration rolled into one. Neighbors brought extra grills and hot dogs. Friends spilled over the Fletchers' lawn, paper plates heaped and drinks cradled, sunburn galore. At last, under a high bright moon, a hardy few slumped in lawn chairs, telling tales as the dew came. Henry had been fit and relaxed Otis recalled, almost aglow, his orders stateside, mundane, but proud to serve just the same.

75

Twenty thousand advisors were plenty for LBJ to handle a skirmish as small as Vietnam. Ten months later, Henry got orders to join them.

His father would mask his reaction to Otis' Monday induction better than his mother would, but whether he was secretly relieved (if Otis evaded) or secretly miserable (if Otis submitted) his father would also be angry. Aside from yielding to the draft counselor visit, Otis had not sought his father's counsel. In his father's eyes, that made him responsible for his mother's worry. Since there seemed no way to win that battle, sparing *both* of them more drama and pain seemed like sufficient reason to keep his embryonic plans private.

On the dais, the college president recounted the grizzled speaker's imposing resume of heroic deeds and selfless service. The school paper had opined that the retired General would rouse few, enrage many, and change nothing, hinting ominously that, "even amidst these bucolic lavender hills, a Berkeley-like outbreak of violence is possible." Wilson Ward—and capable seniors like him—had been advised to listen for protest rumors and quash them as they saw fit, no questions asked. Should they fail in their duty, diplomas *might* be held up on technicalities; job offers from alumni firms *might* mysteriously evaporate. In light of such existential incentives, the appointed young men had been zealous to please their elders. Other colleges and universities had cancelled their 1970 commencement ceremonies. Short of *nuclear* war, Deden-Fisher would not.

The former General stood to a crosscurrent of boos and cheers, then waited until patrician instincts performed their expected function. The microphone caught his medals jangling. In a gravelly voice, he disarmed his audience in a way few on either side expected.

"Twenty-six years ago this very day," he intoned, "we fought true evil. I fought true evil. Newsreels barely hint at the horror. What we did was vital. To dally too long is to act, as Neville Chamberlain sadly discovered." Several clapped. "Yet, even knowing what we now know—of death camps and marches and squads—I cannot tell you what to do now, in *this* troubled time. That choice is *your* generation's special burden."

The row of white-haired men behind him blanched. No speaker had been better vetted.

"Some things don't make it into official records," he said. The old men glanced at each other. "I signed up after Pearl then got cold feet. I went AWOL from training for thirty-six hours. On Omaha Beach, I lost my breakfast and froze. Deeper inside France, a sniper got my best buddy. When the sniper surrendered, I shot him point blank. War is ugly. Evil has many faces." As if holding a gun, he pointed a finger at his own. "Young men? Don't flatter yourself. Take a long look in the mirror. You might not *think* you'd behave like I did. You might say, 'I'm no Nazi or Nero or Nixon,' but each one of us is *capable* of the worst this planet has seen." He paused and grinned. "I added the Nixon part to wake a few of you up."

A few chuckled nervously.

"What kind of graduation speech is this, you ask? What does this have to do with me? Young men, I will tell you. God made us in his image." He swept his arm over the sea of faces and Otis felt simultaneously filthy and hopeful. "Even now, He restrains us from being as bad as we could be. Once I got past my cold feet, I did what was asked of me. Not always well, but I stayed out of trouble. Now look around you. Here we are, free. Take just a moment to think about that."

Clutches of students whistled and hoisted clandestine beer bottles.

"But mark this. History need not have turned out this way. The freedom you enjoy here today was hardly a foregone conclusion. Close friends of mine fought and died to protect it. Others will try to take it from you in less evident ways." He paused again. "I'm not a prophet, or the son of a prophet, but some of you will be among them. It has always been thus. Elite, well-trained minds like yours have the power to propagate great good or terrible evil. The distinction can be hard to see on the front end. Your duty is to reason well and give thanks to God that you can. Don't you dare forget history or settle for slogans, especially your own. I'm humbled to bear witness here on behalf of those who did not make it back. Names with no special meaning to you, but faces." He paused. "Faces." He cleared his throat. Bird chirps seemed suddenly loud. People shuffled programs. He'd seen too much carnage to choke, but his next words came so softly and slowly that the hush they draped over the crowd seemed like an encroaching eclipse. "Faces I will not forget."

He wet his lips as if to say more, paused, then stepped down. The white-haired men checked their watches, eyes wide, eyebrows raised. This had never happened before. It was ludicrously, embarrassingly, unprecedentedly far ahead of the official schedule. But an ovation built slowly until all were shamed into standing and clapping with them. Otis glanced over at his father who was shaking with full-body sobs like nothing Otis had ever seen.

⌖

Receiving his degree, Otis knew he should reflect, proud and happy, but all he could think of was Monday. Like the moment he waited for in each match—and knew for sure only once he felt it—the commencement speech had crystalized everything he'd been mulling the last six months. It felt like contemplating a first move above a belay anchor, familiar in theory but never in the particulars. Would this route "go?" Maybe or maybe not but bold move time had come. Where was his next place of safety? He had no clue. Two days from now (or two years) he might peel off the route he planned with a truncated shriek, lacking so much as a head-shaking onlooker to clean up the mess. But that could happen regardless. Answering to himself beat the alternative.

After the recessional, half-friends swarmed half-dead grass paths, intersecting obliquely, recalling the shallow congenialities of collocated life. Sincere-in-the-moment goodbyes mixed with wishful, distracted thoughts about new friends, commitments, and etiquettes elsewhere.

Lucius slipped an arm over Otis' shoulder and handed him a wrapped gift—a book small enough not to overburden a military rucksack. "Write me when you decide to read this."

"Sly dog." Otis pivoted to a firm handshake. "Don't hold your breath."

"I'll be praying for you."

Otis avoided eye contact. "You and what, a seminary class you haven't met? You're wasting your time with me, but where I'm headed? I won't say no." Otis hated himself for the head-fake. If he told anyone, it would be Lucius. He was tempted to drop a broad hint, but he didn't want Lucius to feel guilty later for failing to talk him out of it. And fail he would.

Shaun found Otis and greeted him with a boyish grin, long curls unkempt like he'd rolled out of bed minutes before—which he probably had. He wore a T-shirt peppered with carabiner pinch holes near the waist

78

from countless rock-climbing belays. Shaun asked, "What am I going to do without a partner next winter?"

"Get out of shape," Otis grinned to conceal the fact that he meant it and that he was jealous. Shaun's draft board had bestowed a reprieve: four months to finish his graduate thesis.

"You'll show 'em what tough is," Shaun said and Otis beamed. Shaun had been the sole witness to his Pinnacle triumph, sweeter for his having also witnessed his whimpering failures. The fact that Otis was about to apply that toughness to a different set of problems from those going through Shaun's mind didn't bother him at all.

Immediately after his freshman year, Otis' parents had made a reservation for this day at the best place in town. The idiosyncratic vote of confidence had warmed him but then, two months later, Henry had been blown to bits. Otis tried to reconstruct the sunny world in which such long-term planning for celebration had seemed an irrefutable tenet of how things worked.

An elderly waiter ushered the family to a table sparkling with enough cutlery to arm a small militia. Otis' father ordered a fancy wine. The waiter filled every glass. Otis pushed his away without touching it. His father looked askance; his grandmother stifled a giggle. "Moderation in all things," she said, and took a big gulp of hers. "*Including* moderation." A jellied beef tongue course arrived; she split Otis' portion with Billy while Otis swallowed bile. From her purse, she fished out a bottle of aspirin. "Take these and drink water," she whispered. She handed him a fat envelope. "Your grandfather said cash made things easier overseas."

Otis stuffed the enveloped in his jacket pocket and swallowed the aspirin. He didn't mind if his parents noticed his hangover or his grandmother giving him money, but not telling her his plan bothered him more than hiding the same fact from them or Lucius or Shaun.

After the meal, to everyone's surprise, Billy stood, clinked his glass with a knife and cleared his throat. "Otis, with both of us away at school, we maybe don't know each other as well as we used to. And OK, so I haven't always been as nice to you as I probably should be."

Everyone chuckled, but Otis sat rapt. His bratty brother had put actual thought into this. Billy quickly caught Otis' eye then continued.

"Now that you're going away, I realize I might actually miss you... a little." He grinned. "Seriously though, I wanted to say how proud I am of you, Brother. Take care of yourself over there." He raised his glass and winked. "And also, thanks for the car."

Otis realized he would miss even this awkwardness. His mother leaned close and spoke. "What if Billy's lottery draw next month is like yours?"

In his mind, Otis finished her thought: *Then the worry might kill you.* She had barely come to grips with the idea of a *second* son in Vietnam. A third would flummox her completely. For now, his words might have the reverse effect as their plain meaning, but he had to say them anyway because he alone knew they were true. "Don't worry, Mom. Everything will be fine."

For him it would, anyway. What Billy might choose later was anyone's guess. Back home, Otis shoved Lucius' gift in his sock drawer and packed up the things he would carry.

Fifteen:
Well Done

Charles Fletcher's knuckles gripped white on the wheel, his shoulders tensed tight toward his ears. "Cambridge!" he blurted. "That's three times around the block! Where are the police? If they don't move these double parkers, he'll be tardy. The Army does not brook excuses."

In the backseat Otis grit his teeth. What was he, a postal parcel? The last two days, through graduation festivities, his parents had told and re-told the story of him being born a week late: "If he'd come on time," his father had chimed, "or *eight* days late, he would have had a *safe* draft number."

From the front seat, Otis' mother tried to calm his father. "You've done all you can, hon; let's just say our goodbyes here." Did she recall that those had been the funeral director's exact words at Henry's wake?

Muttering, his father checked all three mirrors and stopped the car, then fumbled under the dash for the hazards; but his foot slipped off the clutch, lurching the car into a stall. Inches from the bumper, a man toting a duffel bag banged on the hood, snarled curses, and flipped them the bird.

"Ignore him," his father commanded. Trembling, he daubed at a trickle of blood from his forehead that ran toward his nose. When their attempts at goodbyes interrupted each other, Otis reached over the seat and shook his father's hand. Outside, through the open window, he kissed his mother.

"Write us as soon as you can," she yelled as they pulled away.

Otis tightened his pack straps and donned his '67 Red Sox World Series cap and sunglasses. He waited until they were out of sight, then joined the line in the stone building's shade behind the jerk his father had almost hit. Otis tapped him on the shoulder. The jerk glanced without recognition.

"Those were my parents," Otis said.

The jerk sneered without turning. "Yeah. What about it?"

"You want to apologize?"

"Not really. Your old man should learn how to drive."

Otis' vision narrowed; his senses crisped; time seemed to slow. He stepped out and faced the man. Knowing he'd never see him again filled him with wild, righteous elation. "Apologize!"

"Stuff it."

Otis punched him hard—once—surprised at how deep his fist sank in the unprepared gut. The man dropped and folded: fetal, retching, screeching curses. Faces peered. "Next time, show some respect." Otis ambled back up the lengthening line as if to rejoin it.

Tony, a high school wrestling teammate flashed surprise. "Otis?" They'd been co-captains. "Otis!" Otis ignored him and picked up the pace, careful neither to turn nor to run. He passed the line's end and kept going. Behind, a stern voice quenched the buzz of nervous conversation.

"Well done on winning the lottery, boys. We've been looking forward to meeting y'all."

At the building's corner, Otis pivoted and strode briskly away. Before he'd gone three blocks, a cruiser roared by, blue light flashing and siren wailing, back toward the induction center. Otis willed himself on toward sailboats, Mem Drive, and a chance at a saving ride. A dark green VW bug pulled alongside, its top down; a familiar voice thundered.

"Otis?" Otis looked over. "Well, I'll be! It is you! You need a lift?"

"Coach Wrangel!" Otis was dumbstruck. "Um, yeah sure," he said and got in. On countless winter nights, Coach had saved him a long hungry slog home after late practice. In the tiny car Otis felt fourteen again, several weight classes below his college competition trim.

Coach slapped him on the knee. "What a coincidence! An old teammate of yours sat in that same seat only minutes ago. Tony Burck's parents refused to drive him to induction. Told him he should burn his draft card and go to Canada. Can you imagine?"

"Wow," Otis said. "Heavy. I haven't seen Tony in a while."

Like five minutes, he thought.

Coach's face mottled as during matches, searching for words fervent enough to praise one of the many young men he jealously treated as sons. "A guy like Tony? Makes me proud. To stand up to bald-faced cowardice in his own home? You coach a young man and you get to know him at his best and worst, at practice and in the ring. You get a good idea who he's going to be as a man. But the parents? Ones like that get me steamed. Driving Tony was the least I could do."

Coach kept on talking: service, valor, duty. The withering fire at Guadalcanal. How could Otis tell him? Compared to deceiving a man he revered, hiding from the government seemed nothing. He pondered the irony. He had crossed not only the ripe-smelling Charles, but also a personal Rubicon. Draft inductees would be inside the building. Names would be called and absences noted. Warrants would soon be issued. For a few miles Coach was his safety, yet if not for the fateful rule change in April that put him back in line for Vietnam he wouldn't be here. The teacher/coach dream wasn't just dormant; the profession was closed to him, tomb sealed-up, dead. Whether public or private, no school would hire a felon.

But he had a shorter-term problem. Coach seemed to be driving and talking on autopilot. Otis had to make sure he did not drive him home out of habit. At the Mass Pike tollbooth, Coach took a ticket from the attendant, then thrust the small car into a torrent of outbound traffic. Over the slipstream's roar and madly threshing small engine, Coach yelled to Otis.

"So, what has you strolling around Cambridge on a Monday morning?"

"I'm headed to California," Otis yelled, his gut churning at his chump response, designed to lead Coach astray. Coach was a people person, trusting, not big on maps. He would follow Otis' blatant non-sequitur without asking or even wondering why he'd traveled east to go west.

"A lot's happening out there these days, I hear. You have a job?"

"Not exactly," Otis said, frantic to change the subject.

"What will you be doing then?"

"I don't know." Whenever Coach sparred with him, Otis always ended up pinned, Coach's weight on him as the team circled to hear the lesson.

Coach glanced over, silent in the way he was with wrestlers full of vain boasts, but without follow-through discipline. Never him. Until now. Despite hot June sun, Otis felt cold. Coach let him out at the Route 128 cloverleaf. His well wishes reminded Otis of a time when he'd believed Coach's words inerrant, his expectations sure to come true.

Within minutes, a slim mustached man with dark shoulder-length hair picked him up. Two guitar cases filled the back seat. "Otis," the man echoed. "Like in the Berkshires or Redding's Dock of the Bay." Otis smiled. Otis Redding had died shortly after Henry. He'd replayed his brother's forty-five single of the doleful ballad until his copy became irredeemably scratchy. "Then there's my man Otis *Blackwell*—just as big but he likes to stay in the shadows." The man spoke as if he knew him. "Folks know lots his stuff without knowing they do." To illustrate, he sang several Elvis Presley clips with a dulcet ease that left Otis amazed. The man bridged seamlessly into an unfamiliar fresh-sounding tune about heartbreak.

At Stockbridge, Otis felt bad bypassing his grandmother, but to drop in on her would raise hard questions. He quickly thumbed another ride. Late that night, several rides later, he reached northern Indiana. He hiked over dunes; Lake Michigan opened before him, vast and shimmering. A setting sliver of moon hovered above Chicago's glow. Not bad. He'd made almost a thousand miles his first day. The draft seemed much further. Two more days and he could be in California. He would figure those details later. He burrowed into the warm sand, soothed by the rhythm of low lapping waves.

Seagull squawks woke him. Otis waded a bit; then, against a river of families lugging picnic baskets and plastic pails, he waded back toward the main road. The scene recalled family trips to Singing Beach on Boston's North Shore. Henry would take Otis to the water's edge where they'd stand side by side, each wave sucking their feet down in pleasantly deeper, until their mother saw and yelled. "Pull out your brother this minute!" Their father would beckon his confirmation and Henry would twist Otis up out of the ooze and carry him to a warm towel. Otis always ran back to the water. Only once had he doubted that his brother would extract him in time.

Rides came easy across Illinois' green fields, then Iowa, Three Dog Night's "Mama Told Me Not to Come" on every radio. Halfway across Nebraska, the land dried and browned. Hidden by willows, beside a wide river, Otis spread out his sleeping bag, found the Big Dipper, and traced its handle to the North Star. Freedom.

Whatever he might face next, he was glad he had come.

Sixteen:
Down Heavy

The next morning at a truck stop near his impromptu campsite, Otis loosened his belt and let his fork slide into an ocean of artificial syrup, conceding the 'Super Colossal Pancake Special.'

From several booths away came faint sobbing.

Tears rolled from a young waitress' reddened blue eyes, wetting her girlish cheeks and her white uniform blouse. Her simple braid seemed more congruent with laughter. Across from her, with his back to Otis, a man with neatly cut light brown hair held her hands across the empty table, speaking too softly for Otis to hear. Otis wondered if she would compose herself before her break ended. The man squeezed her hands and she rallied with the radiant sort of smile people use who've looked on one another naked and fully expect to do so again. Her revived expression led Otis to guess that the man was smiling back in the same way.

"I know it's the same country," she said, "but can't we...?" Loud talk from adjacent tables interfered, "...write you... phone calls?... Christmas?" The man stood and raised her up. They embraced a long time then left the diner arm in arm, her head tipped to his shoulder. Otis never saw his face, only a quick faint distorted reflection as they walked past the plate glass.

Otis' older waitress topped-off his coffee. Eager to keep her from thinking he'd been eavesdropping on her co-worker, Otis asked, "Why is this place called Grand Island?"

A man at the next booth spoke up.

"Big island in the riv*ah*. Isn't that right, Rhonda?"

Otis startled. The man had a thick Boston accent. In his mid-fifties or past it, the man's face was oddly uneven: lined and tan all over, but ravaged down the left side. A dearth of grey hair hinted at dye or a wig. The past hour, whenever Otis had looked over, the man had glanced quickly away. A short-sleeved plaid shirt emphasized heft that might once have been strength: solid, broad-shouldered, but paunchy. With his cigarette hand, he drew a line in the air. "Platte runs along the interstate almost to Denv*ah*. You crossed it to get he*ah*. Nice on coast-to-coast runs." Despite Otis associating such accents with blue-collar towns like Chandler, the man's voice had a friendly quality to it. He sucked his cigarette butt to a brief angry red, ground it out, then studied Otis. "College boy? Headed to California?"

Otis' waitress—apparently named Rhonda—looked up and frowned. "Oh Jack, not that stuff again. You leave this nice young man alone." She piled more soiled plates onto one of her arms.

Otis arched his eyebrows. "I graduated three days ago. How did you...?"

The man coughed a smoky laugh. "Let me guess," he continued, theatrically touching his meal check to his forehead. "You're trying to find yourself. San Francisco?"

"I was thinking about it." Otis folded his arms, envisioning the city as a jumping off spot for Yosemite's sheer granite walls. He tried not to think about his sad secret trip out to LA last fall.

"Ha! Call me 'Carnac." The man snickered. "Rhonda, you owe me a quarter. Johnny Carson's got nothing on *this* trucker-man!"

"I didn't bet you, Jack. And you take it outta my tip? I'll salt your coffee." She stared lasers over her reading glasses. He laughed nervously. "Don't think I won't. Now you let him be."

"Don't mind him," she said, careful not to spill Otis' syrupy plate. "Too much time alone."

Otis paid and went to the restroom. Jack entered and stood one urinal over; he rested a hand on the white tile above him. "Coffee never stays with you long, does it?" Otis grunted and stared at the grout ahead. "You've got a big appetite. I've never seen anyone get that far on the Super Colossal." Otis let his eyes blur. Jack spit, flushed, and zipped. Otis heard Jack wash his hands then grab the endless towel. "You like Italian food? Of course you do. Who doesn't? There's this place in San Fran, corner of Pacific and Morrell. The waiters are from the old country and they all know the wine list by heart. If you're headed to California, I'd be happy to take you and show you. Your choice. I'll wait outside."

Across the heat-shimmering lot, among a cluster of semi-trucks, there Jack was, his arm high as a flagpole, waving from the wrist like an eager student. "Otis! Over here!" Otis ambled toward him and felt sweat blossom under his pack straps. "Sorry I didn't wait," Jack said, "but the cab can get pretty steamy on a day like this; and my old unit takes its sweet time." He pointed to an air conditioner condenser above the cab's rear window. Its drips mixed with those from a larger one on the trailer behind it to form an oily rivulet that ran between Jack's feet. Jack sang: "Cal-i-for-nia here I come, right back where I started from. You ready for San Fran?"

"I'm not sure yet." Otis assessed the near-silent highway and thought of the Rockies. What was the rush for California? He could find plenty to do in Colorado for weeks.

"We can stop wherever you want. Beats a lonely wait in this heat."

Otis thrust his pack up into the cab, leapt up behind it, then shoved it behind the seat. Jack got in his side and slipped the truck into gear, out of the parking lot.

"You look strong. Did you play sports?"

"Wrestling," Otis said. "It's not play."

At the turn onto the highway, Jack swirled the wheel wide. Between their seats was a picnic-sized cooler but Otis felt queasy, ready to burst, unable to bear thoughts of food. An eight-track tape hung in the slot. Vanity Fare. Jack poked it in. Last spring at school, everyone had mocked the inane, bouncy lyrics about a lonely hitchhiker. Otis couldn't believe he'd met someone who had actually paid for such garbage.

Jack glanced over, expectant. "Groovy! Isn't that what young people say?" Otis tried not to roll his eyes but when the song ended, Jack removed the tape. "So," Jack said. Tell me about wrestling. I bet you were good."

Otis related basic outlines of a few matches but Jack's enthusiastic response led him into more and more detail. "You pinned him that fast? I'll bet *he* was surprised! I wish I'd been there to see you. That sounds so exciting. I'll bet all your girlfriends loved watching you."

"I guess," Otis said. Each of his three high school girlfriends had been too involved in her own activities to attend his matches. After months of cajoling, Louisabeth had driven up to see one. When Otis asked her her impressions, she'd tightened her face like a cat biting a dill pickle.

"My wife used to ride with me," Jack offered. "But she's been sick a long time."

Otis closed his eyes, willing down pancake taste.

"I'm feeling a little sick too," he confessed.

When he re-opened his eyes, Jack held an open cold bottle of Coke toward him as if it were a microphone. "Bubbles help. Drink." Otis took it and sipped. Jack offered him a cigarette but Otis waved him off. "Of course," Jack said. "What was I thinking? You need to maintain that healthy young body of yours."

Jack turned up the AC and smoked in silence. Every minute or so, he glanced over at Otis. Otis finished his Coke and felt better, less queasy, no longer peeved about Jack reading him so accurately at the diner. He had a free, cool, comfy ride all the way to California. Jack was alright. Otis held out the empty Coke bottle. "What should I do with this?"

"Out here? Who cares? Pitch it."

Otis felt a pang of guilt to recall a TV PSA, a small girl chiding her parents: "every litter bit hurts!" But he didn't have energy to argue. He rolled down his window and watched the bottle explode on the shoulder, thrilled and aghast to be so cavalier. "Back at the diner," he yawned, "how did you guess I was going to California? Why did you think that was funny?"

"Not funny. Sad. The last few years, young people have been flooding out there like its Eden. Fifteen, fourteen, some young as twelve; tired of mom and dad, church and school—and who can blame them? Too many parents see beautiful, natural things as shameful. So the kids see pictures in the news magazines and think, 'Wow! Why can't *I* have flowers in *my* hair?' But if they're not prepared, the world can deal harsh lessons. So innocent. They need someone to listen and guide without judging them. I show them *real* love and affection, but also prepare them to fend off the creeps. Sometimes, sadly, I have to pick up the pieces after someone gets hurt.

"Take the Altamont concert last December. No cops. A quarter of a million kids riled up after the draft lottery. The Rolling Stones play 'Sympathy for the Devil,' and some Hells Angels stab a black kid to death. Stones keep on playing like nothing's wrong, then swoop off in a helicopter and back to England. A young man from Ohio told me about it. Kevin. What a sweet boy." Jack paused and sighed. "Fit and trim like you. At the concert, he cut his foot on a broken bottle. The next morning he was thumbing outside Stockton at the start of my run east. Freezing, poor thing, not even a blanket. Wanted his mama. He laid down up there back to Columbus." He gestured to a single bunk behind the seats. "You seem more mature than that, older, more... experienced?"

"Sounds like Hendrix," Otis slurred, feeling a pancake nap coming on.

"I have some Jimi tapes if you like that kind of music. Feel free to take off your seatbelt and get them up there behind." He gestured. "Lie down if you like—if it's more comfortable for you. There's nothing up there that I'd be embarrassed for you to see, Otis."

"That's alright." Otis grabbed a greasy tattered map and traced blue and red interstate veins from Nebraska. He tried to do mental math but his brain was sluggish. Getting to San Francisco meant stopping to sleep. Jack was alright, but not worth the complication. What direction should he go? The South had been out from day one. The ending to last year's film, "Easy Rider" had taken place there: young life unworthy of life, the grisly climactic scene cruelly discordant with the freewheeling Steppenwolf soundtrack Otis loved to croon.

It looked like the highway would fork an hour ahead. Otis would have Jack let him out there. He would get fresh air then decide his next step. The coffee and Coke pressed at his bladder. He wouldn't make it. He asked Jack to stop at a small-town turnoff; Jack did not slow.

"Oh, you don't want *that*. The public restrooms there are awful, horrid, no ambience. You're a big boy. I know somewhere much better. You hold it. You'll see."

"Sure," Otis said, but it came out like a sigh, his eyelids drooping. They passed another turn-off. Otis looked over at Jack, but his vision lagged his head movements. "Where are we?" His lips felt weighted.

"You need to trust me," Jack said.

Jack roared past a truck stop. Otis mumbled. "What are you...?"

"Hold it. I promise. It's nice. I like my friends to have nice things."

Jack pulled over in the most desolate place Otis had ever seen. Aside from I-80's two strips of shimmering asphalt, nothing broke a flat waste that stretched to the horizon in every direction. A tuft of dry grass looked enough for a ten minute nap. Jack would understand. Otis slid down and out of the cab, then leaned on the idling truck to steady himself as he peed.

He closed his eyes. In the oven-like heat, his head felt like a watermelon. He re-opened his eyes to zip up.

"There," Jack said. "That must feel better."

Otis turned. Everything swirled. He grabbed for the cab door.

Nearby, unmoving, Jack crouched, his hand on the truck's front tire as if examining it. "It's important to relieve pressure on hot days," he said but there was no hissing, no gauge, no pump or tools. *He must have been there the whole time*, Otis thought. *But what did that mean?* "Don't you just love the solitude of this place?" Jack stood and stepped toward Otis. "Here. You look faint. It's nice and cool in the cab. Let me help you."

Jack had angled his rig so they were hidden from any sporadic cars whizzing by. He'd heard only two since they'd arrived. Jack gripped Otis' forearm with surprising strength. The Coke. He hadn't seen Jack open it. Fear shot through him. Drop him! Otis could feel the moves he should make, but his arms were impossibly heavy. To stagger around the truck to flag down help would take speed and balance he didn't have. Jack pulled him close. Coffee and cigarette breath made Otis gag, and gave him an idea—how he'd made weight—not fun but simple, routine. He thrust two fingers deep into his mouth, to the back of his throat. Gagging, he let his breakfast flow. Jack leapt back, doused by a torrent of half-digested pancake, Coke, and coffee puke.

Cursing, Jack reached around behind him. A gun glinted silver: tiny, but real. Strength surged on instinct and Otis took two quick low steps straight at Jack's knees, his shoulders like missiles. Pop, pop went two aging tendons. Falling, Jack fired. The shot zinged off. The gun flew from his hand. On his belly, Jack wriggled after it with startling energy. Otis leapt on him and yanked his arm back like a chicken wing. The motion thrust Jack's face into the dirt.

"Enough!" Otis roared crackling with rage and fear unlike any he'd ever known. The thought of killing Jack felt right, even exciting. He knew it was wrong. He yanked back Jack's trigger finger instead. Jack shrieked, more from surprise than from pain. Otis had suffered far worse injuries wrestling and barely felt them. If Jack had another weapon, the break would slow him down. Otis stood and backed away, watching him.

Jack whimpered and rolled over, his face dusty and bloody. He clutched his hurt hand. "Brute. Why'd you do that? I wasn't going to hurt you."

"Liar." Otis picked up the gun, aimed it at one of the truck's tires and fired. The tire hissed, deflating. He emptied the magazine into several other tires until the truck listed. He retrieved his pack, shut off the engine and both AC units, and locked up the truck's cab. He set two uncapped Cokes out for Jack, then made a show of pocketing Jack's keys.

"Please don't take those! My cargo will spoil. I'll lose my job."

"You should have thought of that before." Trying to look less rattled than he felt, Otis stuffed the empty gun into his backpack then staggered backwards up the highway, careful to keep Jack in sight. Jack spewed a string of obscenities at him, but made no move to follow.

Seventeen:
States of Grace

<hr>

Adrenaline offset whatever it was Jack had slipped him. Except for scraped knuckles, the fight had been bloodless but beside the road, barely out of Jack's sight, he felt trapped in a stranger's nightmare, nameless, filthy, disembodied. He rinsed from his canteen; desert dryness cooled his skin. He'd never experienced—or even thought to dread—anything like this: the stuff of movies his parents frowned on. Jack's tactics were practiced: smooth pick-up lines and rationales, drugged Cokes, a gun, a remote spot. Not his first time; likely not his last. Should he report it? They were near the state line, but which side? Nebraska or Colorado? Or had he slept all the way west to Wyoming? The scenery offered no clues. He pictured filling out police forms. To what end? He was on the lam, a non-person, unable to stick around to testify. They might well detain *him* on a vagrancy charge—or something worse. No. He'd done his part, slowed Jack down; hopefully Jack would think twice with someone else.

Nervously, he extended his thumb. A station wagon pulled over: an Omaha family headed to Yellowstone. Otis envisioned Old Faithful, hot springs, and languid bison. The mother offered green grapes; Otis nibbled, grateful to taste the crisp cool. The family sang songs: "King of the Road," "If I had a Hammer," "Rise and Shine." Reluctant at first, Otis hummed, then murmured, then added his tenor to the family chorus, enjoying it so much that he almost stayed with them west past Cheyenne. When he realized his error, he thanked them, and walked back ten minutes to the northbound interstate. There was nowhere to toss Jack's gun and keys so he kept them.

After a while a newish white pickup pulled over, its driver alone. He leaned across the seat toward the open passenger-side window. He had coppery features and wiry-short grey hair. Cautiously, Otis approached. "Hop in!" the man said. "I'm headed to Dayton."

Otis froze. Jack had bragged of "helping" a boy hitching home to Ohio. "I passed there already. I'm headed north now."

"Dayton, *Wyoming*," the man's tone was matter-of-fact and cheerful, not like Jack's fawning slime. Otis scanned for weapons and suspicious soft drinks but saw nothing. The man's left arm ended in a gnarled stub just below his elbow. A one-armed assault seemed unlikely. Otis got in. The man accelerated, took his hand off the wheel and extended it sideways.

"I'm Mike Running Bear," he said. His grip was among the firmest Otis had ever felt. With guidance only from Mike's knees, and going ninety, the car slid across the double yellow line. Mike kept his gaze and his grasp on Otis, expression unchanged, waiting as a huge truck loomed rapidly toward them, leaning on its horn.

"Otis," Otis bleated. Mike held on. "Otis Fletcher!" he squawked. Mike released his hand, returned his eyes to the road, and calmly guided the car back into the proper lane at the last possible moment. The truck zoomed past, its horn still blaring.

"It's nice to meet you, Otis Fletcher." Mike looked utterly calm.

Over a couple of hours, in a casual way that also seemed caring—light-years removed from Jack's flattering, thinly veiled agenda—Mike drew from Otis more than he'd planned to reveal. "So, Mike," Otis asked, after spilling half his life story, "what is it you do in Dayton?"

"We run a ranch."

"We?"

"With my business partner. Mark and I grew up an hour apart, but only met in the Air Force: Pacific islands, then the China-Burma-India theater. I got shot down three times." Mike held up his stump. "Mark? Only twice." He grinned. "We're a little competitive. Stanford; class of '49. GI Bill. Mark returned to help his dad. I stayed for B-school plus a JD. When Mark's dad passed, he asked me in. Shocked my parents when I told them what I'd done. How can you trust a white man? They didn't get it. We'd been under fire together, escaped from a POW camp together. M&M, they call us now. Brothers. My parents are coming around."

The falling sun silhouetted a string of mountains to their left. "Listen," Mike said. "You're not likely to catch another ride out here tonight and Mark cooks a mean steak—fresh and rare. Most of the ranch hands are up on the mountain with the herd so we've got spare beds."

Otis flinched at the word bed, but his mouth also watered; he hadn't eaten since breakfast, and he'd lost most of that. Mike seemed to be all that Jack wasn't. Humble yet smart, fearless, highly degreed. Stanford was half a step *above* Deden-Fisher. Plus, they had a business and presumably a reputation and ties to the community (such as it was in this empty land). "If it's not too much trouble," Otis said, curious about how men from such different backgrounds got along so well. Moments later, Mike turned onto a one-lane road. He slowed only slightly to rumble across cattle grates. After a half dozen, he turned in at a metal archway, 'H3 Ranch' welded rusty on top.

"H-cubed?" Otis asked, thinking of Hubert H. Humphrey. "Like the '68 Democrat nominee?"

Mike's laugh burst like a firecracker. "After the Chicago convention I sent the DNC a cease-and-desist. Never heard back, but if you can't have fun as a lawyer, why bother? The ranch is named for Mark's father, Henry H. Hopkins. Henry the Third you might say, though I'm a better fit for the part, don't you think?" Mike held up his arm stump. "To shrink mine arm up like a withered shrub... to shape my legs of an unequal size; to disproportion me in every part."

Otis grinned, delighted that someone out here knew Shakespeare. "I had a brother Henry," he offered. The car slowed. Many people heard what they wanted (present tense *have* a brother instead of *had* one) and breezed on as if all were well, Henry still alive. Others heard rightly and breezed on so as to avoid discomfort. Mike did neither thing. Mike did not breeze.

Mike's solemn eyes testified that he'd seen more than his share of death. "I'm sorry," he said simply and somehow Otis knew he really meant it. They drew near a sprawling ranch house, large barn, and cluster of outbuildings. "That's Mark there," Mike said. Mike's business partner stood tending a grill spewing smoke. Tall and silver-haired, with a weather-beaten face, his introductory grip and gaze—long and sincere like Mike's—seemed to read Otis' soul.

Through a long relaxed meal around a rough-hewn log table, Otis relished listening to Mark, Mike and their respective wives talk. He'd never

94

tasted steak or red wine so good. Even the potatoes were sweet and fresh, unlike any he'd known. After dinner, Mark talked Otis through his collection of Western art, his rare books, and his antique and 'working' guns. Otis wanted to ask how big the ranch was and how they could refer to a Republican president as a "Pinko," but he was grateful to his hosts, happy to have a large, clean, safe bedroom and bath to himself.

⸻

Before first light, Otis slipped from the guest wing into silence so deep that, until a horse snuffed and swallows flitted from the barn, close then away, his ears made up rushing sounds. He ambled stealthily toward the main road, his boots crunching on gravel, feeling exposed.

A shout came from behind. "Hey there!" Otis spun, shocked to see Mark holding what looked like a rifle. He ducked. It was a manure rake. Sheepish, he shuffled back. "We can't let you go empty," Mark said. A wad of tobacco distended his cheek. He went to fetch coffee. Standing together, they watched the sun rise. Mark asked, "You still headed north?"

"Montana," Otis offered; he hoped that was enough.

"Keep going and you could be in Canada by this afternoon."

Was that a test or an invitation?

"I wasn't necessarily... I mean... I hadn't settled on a..."

Mark held up his free palm. "Son, I wasn't born yesterday. A man's got to fight for what's right, but Vietnam?" He spat at a dung beetle which had been busy rolling a piece of manure. Engulfed in brown jiggly restraining goo, the beetle struggled as Mark continued.

"I hate the Commies' lies more than Nixon says he does, but that war went bad long ago. Let Saigon elect leaders with backbones to fight their own war if they care. The French were stupid to back them, but we don't have to be. The draft signals weakness. Hanoi sees that. Ho may be dead, but he taught the North well. Unless we've got their resolve to endure ten times the blood we have and take decades of pain, they'll just wait us out; wait for us to decide that *this* win isn't worth it, and that withdrawal is honorable and wise. What do you think? Are we that patient?"

Was it a trick question? Otis shook his head. "Probably not."

"Exactly. Sad thing is, that *should* be common sense. Now, don't get me wrong. You won't catch me burning the American flag. This is a great

95

country. Not as great as before FDR hired busloads of bureaucrats to put sand in the gears, but still basically sound as long as we've got the Bible and the Constitution. I've never heard anyone propose any better. You can live out your choices here, climb to the stars if you like. You may fail—in fact you'd better; that's how you learn—but you can't whine that you didn't have a chance to see what you're made of. Canada is nice on the surface, but going there isn't a decision to take lightly, son. In the time we're living, it's not a choice you can rescind if you change your mind."

"Thank you, sir. I appreciate you sharing your wisdom." Otis was sincere and respectful the way he might be on safari, facing an exotic carnivorous beast. He braced for Mark to press him about his destination, but Mark only slurped his coffee. As they watched, the beetle extricated itself from Mark's tobacco spit glob and scurried off, rolling the manure chunk as its trophy.

Mark flung away his mug's dregs. "Well OK, then. Let's get you some grub and get you on your way north." In the kitchen, deftly with his one hand, Mike tended three sizzling pans. "I'd take you myself," Mark said, "but I'm flying the Cessna to check on a couple of our Colorado herds."

"I'm inking that deal up at Fort Belknap," Mike said.

"You have time to give him your take on the battle?"

"Of course."

Otis was puzzled. *The* battle? Fort Belknap?"

"Just trust him," Mark said and both he and Mike laughed.

Eighteen:
Russian Dolls

O tis was glad that Mike's errand freed his last U.S. ride from the chance of another Jack ambush. They sped past a Montana welcome sign.

"I hope this isn't out of your way," Otis said.

"It's not. I planned this trip weeks ago. Lord willing, I'll be home tonight."

"Lucky for me."

"No such thing."

"Come again?"

"Chance is an illusion."

"How do you figure?"

If the universe operated on randomness, you couldn't rely on anything. We exercise our free will within the bounds we're given, but human beings don't have access to all the parameters God does. You may think something is luck—good or bad—but God ordained it already from *outside* of space and time. He made space and time itself. His order is perfect and His providence is meticulous, impossible to foil or avoid. Neither you nor I planned our meeting yesterday, but that doesn't mean it wasn't planned."

Otis tried to process Mike's assertions. He vaguely recalled Einstein's relativity theories from high school physics—time as a dimension of space, or something like that—but not enough to confront Mike's full-force intellect. He thought about the draft lottery, a roll of the dice if there ever was one. If he'd been born just hours later, he'd have been safe. Mike pulled in at the site of Custer's Last Stand and parked in the near-empty lot. This must be the battle Mark mentioned.

"This is one of the most ironic places I know of," Mike said. A flagpole halyard struck erratic notes in the morning breeze.

"What do you mean?" Otis said, again feeling stupid at not quite getting Mike's confident statements, and also uncomfortable coming to a place like this with an Indian.

Mike looked at Otis over his sunglasses. "Use your noggin, man. You majored in History, and at a decent school too." He ambled away toward the U.S. soldiers' cemetery—lone hand behind his back, monk-like, as if clasping the missing one—then Mike stooped to examine a lichened headstone. What did Mike mean about this place being ironic? To holler guesses seemed gauche.

A man in a khaki uniform approached, a bugle in one hand, a triangle-folded flag in the other. Mike was still some distance away. The man's badge read, 'H. Smith.'

"Would you help me raise the colors?"

"Me?" Otis looked around, then pointed at his own chest.

"The ghosts aren't much help."

"Yeah. Wow. This is so..." Otis almost said 'cool.' He took a deep breath. *Courteous, kind, obedient, cheerful, thrifty.* It had been years. He would fake brave, clean, and reverent.

Mike moseyed over. "Hey, Howard."

"Morning, Mike. Friend of yours?"

"We're getting there."

Ranger Howard handed Mike the flag.

Mike leaned toward Otis.

"Relax. You told me you were in the Scouts. It'll come back."

Ranger Howard inspected each end of his bugle then puckered as if practicing kisses. "Most days I manage on my own, but the boys deserve the best, don't you think?"

"Don't forget the other boys," Mike said.

Otis detected no malice between them.

"You know I don't," Howard said.

"That's why I can say it." Mike smiled warmly.

Otis secured the flag's eyelets and tugged the cord. Mike let the fabric run through his hand. Howard played reveille. Otis' throat tightened and his thoughts flooded: stoic faces, rifle shots, bugle taps, a folded flag. He imagined many who'd never seen this place—their loved ones' final rest. A six-year-old who lost a father here would turn one hundred this year.

Otis secured the cord to the cleat. High above, the flag luffed like sheets on a clothesline. The sound made Otis think of bright summer days at Shurwood, his grandparents' place up in Maine.

Otis bought postcards at the gift shop. While Mike drove, he filled them out: to his parents, his grandmother, Lucius, Shaun, Billy. "I'm out west. Can't say more. Hope all's well!"

"So," Mike said. "How are the ironies simmering?"

"It was a Pyrrhic victory. You won the battle but lost the war. Sorry."

"Don't apologize for facts. That one's truer than you know. Continue."

"Don't start wars you can't win? Don't let pride cloud your judgment? Know when to quit and when to double-down?"

"Term paper truisms. What else? What's *ironic* about that place?"

Otis' face fell. He thought he'd done well to recall those tidbits. What had he overlooked? Mike let silence build until Otis thought he'd moved on and forgotten. "Borders," he said at last.

"But there weren't any back then."

Mike clicked his tongue, scrunched his cheeks, and held up a finger.

"There were? Seriously? I never learned that."

"Sadly, I'm not surprised. Indian nations had plenty of borders, one to another—different from how we think about them, but very real—not things to mess with. Stanford doesn't teach it much either."

"So what do you mean?" Saying it for the third time, Otis felt like a dunce. He stared at the rolling empty grass hillocks—terrain he assumed made borders indefensibly pointless.

"That piece of U.S. federal property where we just raised the American flag? The Little Bighorn National Monument? It sits smack in the middle of *our* Apsáalooke sovereign nation. The Americans are *still* surrounded."

Mike raised a playful eyebrow and for an instant, Otis wondered why he'd never thought to escape the draft on an Indian reservation. There was probably a catch, otherwise someone at Deden-Fisher would have tried it. And it would probably be unwise to ask a thrice-shot-down combat vet for such a favor. He gave Mike a puzzled, helpless look. "What did you call it? Absolute nation?" (Years later, Otis would recall their chat with fondness when clever ads for Swedish vodka began blanketing billboards and magazines: Absolut this, Absolut that.)

"Sounds like it, but no. Apsáalooke means children of the large-beaked bird. We're Crow."

"If that's all you meant, then what's the big deal about borders?"

"The U.S. sovereign land sits inside the Crow sovereign land that sits inside the sovereign state of Montana, which many here view as trapped inside a sovereign nation less federally coordinated—as it was constituted to be—than it is centralized and overweening, tumbling toward tyranny."

"Like Russian dolls," Otis blurted, proud of his analogy, though not ready to insist on it.

"Exactly!" Mike thumped the wheel with Socratic satisfaction. "Like Lesotho, or Vatican City, or the Republic of San Marino. Monaco is a close variant on the same idea."

With Mark and Mike, Otis had been elated at the challenge of employing a vocabulary and thinking at a pace he'd taken for granted at Deden-Fisher. But the last eighteen hours had also brought back a humbling latent fear he'd learned to live with for four years around smarter, better read people capable of snubbing him with little effort if they cared to—and plenty had. Otis struggled to call to mind a world map.

"San Marino's in Central America, right?"

"Italy. East of Florence. Near the coast. That's a hard one. Point is, such places are sovereign only in a technical sense. Their power is perfunctory and ceremonial. They exist at the mercy of a greater power around them. Embassies work on the same norm. A host country lets a foreign one have a building or a compound inside their territory, but if they decide to invade it's no contest. POW camps are *supposed* to operate on similar principles with certain protections, but I can tell you that's not always true. They march in whenever they please." Mike held up his stump arm. "At the highest level, Geneva Convention or no, nations are drops in God's bucket. That understanding is where true freedom lies, regardless of physical borders. Your peace of mind depends on how you look at this, Otis."

Otis wondered what any of Mark's philosophizing might mean for what he faced today and couldn't think of anything. Canada and the U.S. were cordially separate. He could barely recall his father's Ontario cousin. What if he went underground inside the U.S. instead? Continued out to Seattle where housing was cheap? Got a cash job on a salmon boat or a logging crew? On his days off, he could bag the nearby volcanic peaks: Rainer, Baker, Saint Helens.

After a while, Mike asked, "My meeting is up near the border, but if you like, I could let you out up ahead where the road forks. What do you think?" He pointed to an escarpment dotted with buildings and smokestacks, then flicked on the radio and twirled the dial to a DJ speaking over a drumroll. *Good morning, Billings! Here's a new, hot tune on K-Bear, your hits station. Many won't like it, but you need to hear it. Here's Edwin Starr, with "War: What is it Good For?"*

Mike turned up the music. A drumroll seemed to strafe the car, before giving way to a guttural call-and-response: aghast angry pleadings to a wailing chorus. Otis had never heard anything like it. Parsing the words, he recalled his ashen-faced father, writing a check to the undertaker, his mother slumped in an ugly chair in the softly lit room with the casket, torturing a soggy tissue. As the song faded, its lyrics refused to.

Mike found the Billings post office. Otis went inside to mail his postcards. Adamant posters papered one wall. *Have you registered? These colors don't run. I want you.* As he waited in line, Coach's pep talks vied with Uncle Sam's wagging, flattering finger. *Run toward your fear boys. Make a bold move and see it through!* He rehearsed statistics on his top ten big Canadian peaks: heights, summit rates, and mortality figures—none worse than Vietnam. Calgary offered central access to all of them. With his grandmother's bankroll, he could rent a room. He would find a job and work until the snow up high slacked off, then he would buy new gear and climb for the rest of summer, two months at least.

Otis returned to the car. Mike started the engine.

"What's it going to be?"

"North."

"You sure?"

"As sure as I'm going to be."

"OK. I'll take you to a sleepy little crossing I know. A guy like you will get a kick out of the name."

Hours later, Mike pulled over in what seemed the middle of nowhere, the road ahead the same as the road behind. Except for a white rabbit dashing for cover, it was as desolate as Jack's spot. Mike gestured. "Saskatchewan is up the road about a mile."

Otis wished he could linger. He thought of asking Mike if he could work with them on the ranch but decided that would be awkward. He recalled a radio anthem about wanting more time. Why not pitch his tent here, decide tomorrow? No. He'd chosen already. What Neil Armstrong had *meant* to say: one small step for *a* man. "I don't know how to thank you."

"Then don't. Own your choice. Now get out and get going." Mike grinned and Otis obeyed. "See you later," Mike said without explanation. Abruptly he turned the car and sped back south. The hum of his tires took a long time to fade. Otis unclipped his cloth-shrouded canteen and unscrewed the cap, glad that this wasn't a truck route. He walked north a while, the road so empty he could have napped on the double yellow, but instead he dawdled to either side.

Nineteen:
Mirrors

head, amidst a sea of waving grass, two modest whitewashed structures hugged the road: one closer, one further away. If not for different flags, Otis could imagine one building real and one not, a giant mirror between them. Tingling, he approached the first. A century ago, he'd have been shot for this. Oh no! Jack's gun. Buried deep in his pack he'd forgotten it. No way could he dispose of it here in the open between the buildings. Smiling, he approached the second building. After a few friendly questions he was in Canada—over and done. Why had he worried?

The rest of that day cars and trucks slowed but only gawked. What if no one picked him up? At dusk, bone tired, he set up his orange tent in a field. Would it give him away amidst the short green wheat stalks? After dark, he buried Jack's gun and his keys. All that night, thunderheads flashed and rumbled, but when dawn came, he was still dry. He thumbed his first Canadian ride: a pig farmer's truck bed, partly-cleaned of manure. That afternoon, he walked more; he ran out of water. He wished he could ask Mike: How should I "own my choice" now?

Finally at a tiny town, he bought a bus ticket. Waiting, he studied a poster of a bucking horse and cowboy amidst fireworks: "The Stampede." In Calgary, well after dark, he disembarked in pouring rain. Bedraggled, he wandered. For this, he could have gone to Seattle. Home seemed remote. At last, a YMCA sign jutted over the puddled sidewalk.

Mercifully, they still had beds. "Mark well the rules," a clerk droned, doling back change for one night. He pointed to a sign dense with fine print at the head of a dimly lit hallway. "Down this corridor on your left. Lights out in twenty minutes. You'll find plenty of company."

"What do you mean?"

"You'll see." Two words leaked disdain and pity.

Worn lines crisscrossed aging hardwood. Amid a warren of improvised shelves, high ceilings that had once echoed sneaker squeaks now echoed coughs and snores. Dejected eyes tracked him like those of beaten dogs. Most of the men looked his age and wore bandanas, beards, or both. Extension cords snaked to salvaged lamps used to illuminate tattered paperbacks and crosswords.

Otis found a rust-pocked empty bed, shrugged off his pack, then changed quickly out of his wet things which he spread out as best he could. With his pocketknife, he carved apple and salami, feeling smug to have smuggled them. The attendant hollered and threw a master switch to a chorus of groans. In the musty gloom that followed, Otis finished eating by feel then lay down. He recalled Mark's words: *not a choice you can rescind if you change your mind.* Already he wished that he could. That afternoon, his bus had rushed by red poppy fields and he'd recalled the traditional November poem: "If ye break faith with us who die, we shall not sleep, though poppies grow in Flanders fields." The poppies also made him think of Judy Garland—Dorothy the late queen of Oz dead too young, scarcely a year. *There's no place like home*, Otis thought. *There's no place like home.* He closed his eyes and wished he could wake somewhere else.

After a fitful night, Otis re-packed his damp things and left. He tried to banish self-pity. Once he found a job and a place he would feel better. He bought a newspaper, circled ads, and found a pay phone. Traffic noise made it hard to hear but he didn't have to hear much. Every employer not closed for the weekend interrupted him. *American?* "Yes." *The position is filled.* He used all his spare change. No store would break U.S. bills. The banks were closed. He bought gum to get coins, surprised at the mix of U.S. and Canadian pennies: Lincoln and the Queen. No one seemed to notice the faces and care that they were different. He called about apartments and got the same response as with the jobs. How would Monday be any different? He needed time to think, and a new plan. There must be a park beyond downtown where he could camp and reassess—anything but the morose Y again. He faced west, began walking, and worked up a mood-raising sweat.

The Rockies' tops poked out from clouds, their tops dazzling white. As their steep flanks disrobed, he thrilled to recall Shaun reading from a dog-eared area guidebook: "Early one August evening, in 1898, British adventurer-scientist J. Norman Collie clawed his way to the rocky crest of one of the Columbia Icefield's guardian ridges and glimpsed a heretofore hidden leviathan. 'A new world was spread at our feet,' he wrote in his journal, 'a vast ice-field probably never before seen by human eyes, surrounded by unknown, unnamed and unclimbed peaks.'"

Some of those peaks had recorded only a handful of ascents since that time. Unlike ho-hum New Hampshire, the Icefield's far side still sheltered virgin routes on which *some* intrepid soul would one day put his name. Why not him? His grandmother's gift would set him up with gear; and closer to the ice he was bound to find someone competent to clip in with.

He took a bus to Banff and found a climbing store. "I need your best nylon rope," he declared to a salesman inside. To have packed his old rope in his induction rucksack would have tipped off his parents, and after several falls, it was due for replacement anyway. The rep stared at Otis as if he'd asked for Cheez Whiz at a top Michelin restaurant.

"You ever see a big ship moored with *nylon* rope?"

Otis tried to picture it. His family seldom ventured in to downtown Boston from their home in the suburbs. He shrugged. "I don't know. I've never really thought about it."

"Well, you haven't seen it, and that's for good reason. Nylon stretches. If a fat nylon rope were to snap, it would be like an Anaconda on speed. The rope would have its way with you." Without warning, the rep thrust his hands forward and clapped an inch from Otis' nose. Otis leapt back. "Folks have lost limbs or been killed by nylon ropes. You with me?"

Otis frowned. What was this guy trying to prove?

"Now, imagine yourself on the Titanic. The crew takes a coffee break and lets a fat nylon rope trail in the water. Nylon is heavy; unlike hemp, it sinks. So, the rope those deck hands *should* have coiled neatly drags in the water. Give it a minute and voila! It snags the propeller, ruins the engine, stops the ship dead. Would you want to be stranded near Labrador, waiting for an iceberg to sink you because someone was lazy and chose the wrong rope? No, of course you wouldn't."

Otis chafed at the inept attempt at a cautionary folktale. "Are you saying I should go back to hemp for *technical climbing*? What kind of place is this? I've used nylon for years. In fact, one of our Outing Club alumni who summited Nanda Devi said..."

"Whoa, whoa, whoa. Hold your horses, Sir Edmund."

The rep held a hand toward Otis' face, not as close as before, but close enough that Otis envisioned a quick move that would put him on the floor. "Did you hear me say *not* to use nylon? You need to listen. And trust me."

With every fiber of his being, Otis wanted to leave the store and never return, but this was the last place to get gear, and the Icefield was a hundred miles north. With the lousy hitching he'd experienced in Canada, he might already be pushing darkness. Wordlessly, the rep slipped into a back room and returned with a short length of colorful, intricately woven rope.

"You want this. Kernmantle, German, means core and sheath." He removed a buck knife from a leather waist holster and sliced the strand at an angle as swiftly as if he were dispatching a goat. You see this outer sheath here?" Otis touched it. "It's there to protect what's inside but this isn't a bris. Don't ever cut it. You got me?" Otis nodded. "This kind's dynamic."

"Dynamic?"

Otis was transfixed by a toothy ridge outside the window.

"In a leader fall, it stretches and bounces the perfect amount. Not like piano wire, but not like a rubber band either—the best trade-off between ripping you in half and letting you crater. It's been on the market only six years. We're the first store in Canada to carry it. It's perfect for the mixed rock and ice terrain you'll find around here. Come and take a look."

The rep ushered Otis into a back room where climbing gear Otis had seen only in magazines hung on all four plywood walls. He walked around slowly, eyeing and fondling. This place was amazing and this guy knew his stuff. "I'll take a length," Otis said.

"There's just one thing," the rep said. "This rope is almost *too* good. Some guys imagine it's magic and try routes they shouldn't. Get in over their heads in those crevasses." He waved north—toward the Icefield. "But gear won't save you. Sober judgment will. We won't sell this to just anyone who waltzes in here." His eyes probed Otis, assessing.

106

"Live to climb another day," Otis said then told mostly true stories from Huntington Ravine which seemed to assuage the rep's conscience because he let Otis pick out a bright green coil, plus other gear and supplies. Otis staggered out of the store, his pack clanking. He paused to marvel at Lake Louise's iconic turquoise, then ambled north, his thumb out.

Traffic was sparse, but an icy escarpment kept him enthralled. When the ridge fell into shadow Otis stopped to don a sweater and finish his salami. Should he camp here or turn back? This tourist road would empty at night.

Headlights peeked over a rise. The Mercedes braked hard on the gravel beside him, a swirl of dust in its headlights.

"Grizzlies! Behind you!" A braceleted arm stabbed out the window.

Before he could swivel, a burly driver bellowed. "Get in, son! Now!"

Otis sensed dark hulking shapes. He threw his pack then his body prone into the car, which sped off. He wriggled up, pulled the door shut, and looked back. A clutch of brown bears had converged where he'd stood.

The woman whistled. "A mother with cubs? You were lucky. When we hike, we wear bells and sing songs so they hear us coming."

The couple was older, dressed too nicely for hiking. Sherry, perfume, and cigar smell suggested dinner out. They carried the conversation: hiking, grandkids, the park's history. The man found Otis in the mirror.

"If they're in a bad mood and you're not good with a shotgun, you just have to pray that the first impact knocks you out and it's over-with quickly."

Otis was glad he had not tried to camp. The couple was headed home to Jasper, the only town for two hundred kilometers. As the man swung the car through rising switchbacks, Otis shared his plans. Before his ears had popped, the campground sign sprang into view and the man pulled over.

"Be careful up there," the woman said. "Glaciers are unforgiving."

"Especially that one," the man added.

Otis stepped out. *That one.* He'd apprenticed three years with the best and now he had the latest gear. He'd made the big leagues at last.

"Thanks for the lift," he said over his shoulder.

Twenty:
Tents

G iddy to finally smell glacier, Otis stuck to the forest road's gravel crown so as not to trip in the dark. Faraway roars like hornless car wrecks told of falling ice blocks. Languid crickets and goosebumps jacked-up the caution. This place was ice climber mecca, *the* place to solicit rope partners. Only that fact (and bears) restrained him from tenting free in the woods. As he drew closer to the campground, disembodied voices grew louder while fire shadows jiggled on tree trunks like jousting ghosts. At a picnic table, inside a cordon of Harleys, large men clutched long-necked bottles and longhaired women. Cigarettes flared between too-hasty laughs.

Otis strolled past and crooned his favorite Steppenwolf song about wild highway adventure, climbing high, and not wanting to die. Most of the bikers nodded in knowing agreement. Otis smiled without slowing. He approached an official-looking cabin, hopeful that the 'No Vacancy' sign was incorrect. Inside a screen door, a mustached man sat reading. The insignia on his drab green sweater also looked official.

"I had a little grizzly encounter," Otis said. "Can I come in?"

The ranger sighed, poked a marker into his fat bird book (the Western version of one Otis' mother kept on the kitchen windowsill back home), but then he kept on reading. Otis glanced behind him. The woods were utterly black, his night vision gone. Did the ranger not see the urgency here? It had been foolish to eat by the roadside, but he'd been starving. What if the Mercedes hadn't stopped? Picturing what lesser luck might have wrought he dashed up the rough wood stairs, yanked the screen door, and stumbled in. The door's spring twanged in complaint, slapped his backpack, then whapped the doorframe behind him, loud as a gunshot.

The ranger winced, closed and set down his book, and then stood.

"The browns do prefer Americans," he said.

He ambled to a table topped with hard transparent plastic, maps and brochures spread out to view underneath. Otis set down his clanking pendulous pack and joined him. The ranger studied a campground diagram. Otis shifted from foot to foot. "My tent's small," he said. He reached for his wallet but thought of Mountie ethics and slipped it back. Canadian Park rangers probably disdained bribes as well.

At last, the ranger fingered a spot.

"We don't usually allow this, but this late it's the best we can do. I don't think this fellow will mind. He's American *and* quiet."

Otis thanked him, eased the door closed, then found the numbered site. Dusky campfire embers pulsed in a light breeze. Otis cupped his hand over his flashlight. The car bore Nebraska tags, a sixty-four Pontiac Tempest, sky blue, like the tent beside it. The trunk lid was scratched. Otis erected his tent, but in the small space he couldn't help crossing guylines. In the hard soil, several tent pegs required repeated blows with a rock. How selfless were Nebraskans that they didn't mind such a noisy intrusion? He thought about opening a can of corned beef hash but seeing the trunk lid and fearing more bears, he instead stifled his hunger.

Inside his tent, Otis nestled into his sleeping bag and lit his brother's watch face. Midnight. Not bad. Rather amazing, in fact. Six nights ago, he'd been under government orders. Now he was master of his fate, able to stroll to the bases of dozens of epic climbs.

Crawling up from sleep, Otis thought to throw a pillow at Lucius for typing so early, hitting each margin bell but then he saw the orange glow of his tent walls and remembered. Elated to not be in his dorm room, he squirmed to his tent door and poked out his head. Sun shafts sliced campfire haze that smelled of bacon. At the site's picnic table, a man about his age lowered his hands from a typewriter. He wore a bright green down parka. His smooth cheeks were peppered with blood-pipped bits of tissue. Why would anyone bother to shave while camping? Otis' beard scruff was on its eighth day already. Unlike the contrasting faces, the man's parka was startling, identical to the one Otis had stuffed in its nylon sack to use as a pillow.

"It was kind of you to be so quiet last night." The man's voice was composed, his accent hard to place: blandly Midwestern, but proper and clipped ('kind' like 'pint'). His face was as relaxed and open as if Otis were an old friend who'd just slept on his couch.

"The caretaker thought you wouldn't mind."

"I do not. I am sorry if I woke you with this." He pointed to the ancient-looking typewriter. Beside it a gilt-edged tome rested, splayed flat; ribbon markers poked out from between pages.

"No, no. I hope I didn't wake *you* so late. I'm happy to move and pay my half for last night."

"You are welcome to stay. I have already paid through tomorrow."

Otis was relieved, and ravenous. Niceties could wait. He shrank back into his tent, gobbled corned beef hash, then mixed powdered Tang with the rest. The night's worst chill was past, but to break the ice with this guy he donned his bright green parka and re-emerged, spoon upright in his fatty-sweet breakfast mess. Sure enough, their same-color parkas sparked lighthearted chat.

The man's name was Ulrich; born in Berlin. That explained the accent, and his odd syntax, though not what seemed a mild and forthcoming nature. The few German immigrants Otis knew tended to conceal their heritage as long as they could. Ulrich was driving to a job in Alaska, he said—from his home in Grand Island, Nebraska.

Otis paused chewing and spoke with his mouth full. "Grand Island?"

"Yes. I grew from thirteen years there."

Seeing the license plate, Otis had assumed its driver was from one of Nebraska's population centers—Omaha or Lincoln. Grand Island was the last place on earth he wanted to recall. Four days had barely dulled his dismay at the close call with Jack that began there.

"I might have passed by it on the interstate. Is it by a wide river?"

"Yes," Ulrich said. "That is the Platte."

"Aren't the summers beastly hot there?"

"Yes," Ulrich said. "Last week was that way. But heat or cold I do not mind. Summer and winter each have a purpose."

"C'mon. Even kids have favorite seasons."

Ulrich smiled and shrugged and Otis chose not to press it. Ulrich was headed north to survey an oil pipeline route—a job he'd secured with his new engineering degree from the University of Nebraska at Lincoln. Otis guessed the gig gave him an indefinite occupational draft deferment, but he didn't probe. Draft status was typically a divisive topic.

Otis sketched his own circumstances: also fresh from college, traveling to "find himself." (Jack had brandished the phrase as a jab; it felt good to steal it back.) Otis didn't bother to name or offer details about Dirkden or Deden-Fisher. No Midwesterner was likely to know either one.

On a clunky two-burner stove, Ulrich made coffee and pancakes which he shared with Otis, honey instead of syrup for topping. Then, as if plucking an orchid, Ulrich removed a worn photo from his wallet and held it by a corner. His face seemed aglow, his eyes lingering on it so long that Otis began to wonder if he should excuse himself. At last Ulrich spoke. "This is Calia. We are engaged to be married." He held it for Otis to take.

Otis pinched the opposite corner cautiously and examined it. Married? The girl looked barely fourteen: freckles on babyish cheeks and a sandy-blonde bob. He turned it over. 'Love, XOXO, Calia Doe,' read the girlish script. Each 'o' enclosed a tiny smile. With a matured face, Calia's double-barreled name and girl-next-door looks made him think of the Beverly Hillbillies' Elly May, spunky but sweet. Ulrich was lucky. And he had a good job lined up too.

Otis feigned indifference. "She's pretty. Have you set a date?" He held the photo out to give back, but before Ulrich could grasp it, a gust swept it out of his hand. "Oh no, I'm sorry!"

Otis gyrated to retrieve it from the dirt, but Ulrich beat him to it. From his knees below, Ulrich answered in a jaunty tone. "Next summer we marry. At Christmas, we visit." He stood back up, returned the photo to his wallet, then patted his typewriter. "It is good. For years from school, I write. She writes much too. Phoning is costly."

"You *type* to your fiancée?"

"Calia is dyslexic. She writes. I type. To help I typed her school papers."

Otis set his own wallet on the table top, and clasped his hands over it as he half-listened to Ulrich's adoring accounts of Calia's godly poetic and musical talents. Should he use his photo of Louisabeth as a prop to warn him about long-distance relationships? He had considered sending it back to her or throwing it away (briefly, he'd considered burning it) but none of those options felt right; and though it was only a formal head shot, leaving it at home would have complicated matters if his parents found it by accident. Determined to hide their breakup's cause, Otis had hidden the fact as well— eight months so far. "She's a great catch," his parents opined (even on the way to induction!) baffled as to why Louisabeth did not attend Otis' graduation, or he hers. He wished he could dull his recall of her curvaceous ivory skin, her sharp mind, and his wildly oscillating emotions since last fall. He'd been excited to imagine himself a married father, but petrified once he weighed what it meant for those two big life changes (plus graduation and the draft!) to all coincide. LA was not the kind of last date he'd envisioned.

The dreary retro muse made Otis yearn to see the glacier, touch it, gauge its persona. Could Ulrich be the partner he needed to climb it? Was it this easy? Nebraska was an odd place to find a legit climber, but Ulrich's parka and tent were modern. Why not take a shot and ask?

"Are you a climber?"

"Sometimes yes, I climb. I learned with top-ropes."

"Where? I thought Nebraska was flat."

If Ulrich thought him rude, his face didn't show it.

"In the northwest, with the Boy Scouts."

"The northwest. Awesome! Where? Rainier? Baker? Saint Helens?"

"The Nebraska National Forest."

"The Nebraska National Forest," Otis repeated, deflating.

Was Ulrich serious?

"The buttes there are good for learning. Later, we went to Colorado."

"I see," Otis said, not wanting to ask how many fourteen-thousand footers Ulrich had bagged there. Otis had only one to his credit so far, Pike's Peak, and that in a car, when he was ten.

"Also I went to Wyoming. NOLS—The National Outdoor Leadership School. Do you know it?"

"Of course!" Otis exclaimed. "So you have climbing gear?"

This was auspicious.

"Yes. I have some things." Ulrich indicated his claw-marked car trunk as matter-of-factly as if pointing out the difference between spruce, fir, and pine. His serene energy reminded Otis of his worthy wrestling opponents— not Tigger bouncy but not Eeyore dull. To ask for an equipment inventory was premature. If they roped up, Otis would have a chance to inspect any shared gear. NOLS was a good sign. Hemp rope would be a bad one. It was time to take a chance.

"It would be cool to get up on the Icefield."

"I have heard that it is difficult. I have thought to try a day trip instead." Ulrich pointed to a tidy adjacent campsite. "At two thirty, these men left to climb Mount Athabasca."

"Silverhorn?" Ulrich nodded. Otis was jealous. The route was a classic; departing two hours before sunup meant they were serious. Otis asked the obvious: "Why didn't you join them?"

"The Lord's Day is a gift."

Otis twisted his lips at the non-sequitur, bracing for a pushy pitch or more explanation; none came. Was the remark a put-off? Today it was moot, far too late to start a climb anyway. Snow would be softening, rocks and ice blocks loosening. Anyone on open slopes would be in for knee-deep slogging, while those beneath would be like bowling pins in an alley.

"What about tomorrow?"

"Perhaps. July first I must be in Alaska."

"Almost three weeks! That's plenty of time. A friend of mine who climbed here talked me through the guidebook and maps." Based on Shaun's reports, Otis knew the Icefield's contours as intimately as his own face in the mirror. The best peaks took days of hard effort to reach.

"The ranger can tell us good trips."

Ulrich's quick shift to 'us' made Otis wary. Was he a poseur? Had the Athabasca pair turned *him* down? Otis was loath to let some small-time local official talk them into a girly lunch hike, but for now Ulrich was his best bet—plus, he had a car. Staying in his good graces would save him the half-hour trudge down to the glacier's grey tongue. Until a better offer came along, Otis would go with what fate had served up.

While Ulrich finished his letter, Otis strode back past the ranger station and the silent bottle-strewn biker camp. He paused at a tree break. Across the valley, silhouetted against the sky, two ant-like figures inched along a wind-carved snow cornice that cast a soaring rock face in shadow. Otis vibrated with expectancy. With luck, he would soon be in a scene like it. Clouds obscured the climbers and Otis walked back to the campsite.

Ulrich had put away his typewriter and Bible and washed the dishes. Otis' wallet lay on the table. He had not meant to leave it. Ulrich pointed.

"That is yours?" Two pine needles Otis had been fiddling with remained crisscrossed on its leather, unmoved. Ulrich's honesty bode well.

They made the short drive to the main glacier's dirt parking lot. A family picnicked from a camper van tailgate—bread, apples, cheese, sausage, beer. Ulrich engaged them in German. "They are from Berlin," he said, beaming. He handed Otis a pair of binoculars. "You go ahead."

Otis scrambled over a mound of sharp scree, happy to be alone again. He knelt to touch the ice. Embedded grit made it look friendly to street shoes, not slick like it would be up high. He scanned for routes through the jumbled river of ice-blocks that spilled down the steep headwall a mile away. The binoculars made it seem like a scale model he could rearrange with his fingers. He scanned to each side. To hug the side cliffs would be suicide, yet a tangled maze of fissures that crosshatched the glacier's center could tie them up for days. The sound of a far-off cascade trickled through the crisp air but after minutes trying, he did not locate its source. He lowered the binoculars and took in the glacial bowl's vast circumference. The scale made Huntington Ravine seem quaint. But Shaun had climbed harder things with cruder gear—tools acquired in the Alps, bartered from the car trunks of climbers who had improvised them in metal shops and forged them in backyard kilns. If Shaun could succeed here, then he could too.

His eye caught soundless acceleration: an ice block the size of a tractor-trailer, already well down a cliff. Moments later, delayed by distance, came the thunder of its separation. The block hit an outcrop and exploded. Refrigerator-sized fragments bounded down a steep dirty snow fan. Several figures in the path of the huge chunks dumped packs and scattered. Otis' gut surged as if on a swing's arc. Would he see them die? A second delayed boom mixed with echoes of the first. Several chair-sized pieces chased one of the madly sprinting figures. Otis zoomed in, curious but sick for what he might see. The blocks sent up an ice-crystal rainbow, obscuring the figure. The cloud dissipated to reveal the figure erect, cap in hand. Otis resolved to set them up with better odds. They would start early and move fast to get through that danger zone before sunup.

Ulrich emerged over the scree mound. "Did you hear thunder?"

Otis shrugged. "Mountain weather, I'd think." The sky was clear.

"OK," Ulrich said. He pointed back at the lot where they'd met the Germans. "They used to buy bread at the same bakery my mother did."

"Who?"

"The Schaeffers. Before the wall. It was two blocks away."

"That's nice," Otis said, surprised by how fast Ulrich got cozy with strangers. Otis handed him the binoculars. "Here. I shouldn't be so selfish."

As Ulrich scanned, Otis unfolded a map, watchful for the moment when caution impinged on excitement. "Hmm," Ulrich said. "This looks hard. I would not want to slow you down."

There it was. "You won't. Look at these." With scrupulous patience, Otis led him through their route options, back and forth between map and binoculars, careful not to mention decades of calamities on this glacier that he'd read about in detail in climbing magazines.

"I do not know."

"We'll take it slow. You'll enjoy it. We can turn back if it doesn't feel right." Otis wished he were this good with women.

After more cajoling, Ulrich said OK.

Later, at the campsite, they sorted gear. Ulrich suggested they take his stove. There was no way. A good stove was essential to melt snow for water. (Eating snow could cause hypothermia.) But Ulrich's clunker was an Army surplus beast, heavier than the rope. It would slow them down and hold them back. Now that Ulrich was on board, Otis could afford to be pushier. He held out the spider-light model he'd picked up in Banff. "Feel this."

Ulrich rotated the stove, assessing design and detail. "It *is* very light."

"Better, watch this: this baby *cooks.*"

Otis took the stove back from Ulrich and attached a fuel canister. He twisted a valve then touched a match to the burner. A hiss attended the 'whoomp' of blue flame he expected, but fuel like spit also oozed from the hastily threaded canister top. Too late, Otis lunged to shut off the gas. A ball of flame singed his fingers, arm hair, and eyebrows. Ulrich tossed a blanket onto the inferno but it knocked the blaze against Otis' tent. In seconds, flame consumed its orange nylon. Otis smothered the mess with another blanket, glad to find the rest of his gear largely unharmed.

Ulrich apologized for his imprecise throw, then helped Otis move his things to his intact light blue tent. Otis volunteered to carry the tent the next day—along with Ulrich's behemoth stove. It would do. It would have to.

Twenty-One:
Chasms

They got a late start, after four, twilight distinct by the time Ulrich parked in the muddy, near-empty lot, exactly where they'd parked yesterday. It made for a longer walk to the start of their hike, but Otis bit his tongue. He had figured a week to snag a half-competent belayer. To find a self-effacing NOLS vet within hours of arriving was the best luck he'd had in months.

Otis stashed his wallet in the glove box then stepped out of the way to let Ulrich do the same. Ulrich slid something from his wallet into his parka pocket and shut the glove box. He locked the car, then beckoned to Otis to show him where he had slipped the key inside the front fender. The gesture seemed pointless but Otis took it as positive. Ulrich seemed to trust him.

They cinched waist straps and hiked in silence, the glacial headwall pristine and pink-purple before them. Sunlight kissed its top, then moved down until long-striding shadows formed before them and shortened. Sweating at the access road terminus—on the verge of real blue ice at last—they sat to strap on crampons and smear their faces with zinc oxide. The preparations felt to Otis like a wrestling match, sober and serious, except that, out here, no corrupt nearsighted ref could steal his reward.

There was no need to rope-up here on the lower glacier where it was easy to hop narrow shallow crevasses or quickly skirt them, but Ulrich insisted and Otis yielded. Fifty yards' distance between them curbed small talk, and using the rope saved him having to carry it. Thoughts of the icy tableland above thrilled him. They would run out of food before exhausting its potential. Years ago, it had struck him that the euphoria he felt while climbing was similar that which some people sought in the drug scene, yet what was the point without a tangible feat to point to and say, "I did that"?

Too many people were far too easily sated with imitation accomplishments: chemical crutches or tourist parking lot snapshots. Yesterday, waiting, swarm after swarm of children had squealed the same obvious things. *Look mom, ice in summer!* As if they were the next Ernest Shackleton. Their mothers in Jackie headscarves and gingham dresses were no better. *Be careful*, they said, then, *let's go, hon, this looks dangerous.* Very few fathers pushed back. *Alright kids, back in; let's go*, most of them said, so accustomed to self-gelding that they'd forgotten they'd ever had any boyish sense of adventure. It reminded Otis of the "This Car Climbed Mount Washington" bumper stickers back home. As if *their* gas pedal were extra special, worth a blue ribbon.

Danger imposed on peoples' complacent cowardice. Once someone grasped that you lead-climbed, *above* an anchor, on routes where falls were inevitable, they got irritated. Otis despised their anxious questions: "What about weather? What if your gear breaks? Don't you value your life?" Failure mindsets were moth-like, gnawing away at resolve until *nothing* felt safe.

Otis had found a refreshing antidote to such malaise in Climbing Quarterly. When the DF Outing Club received its copy, Otis was always first to consume it. A recent story had detailed Austrian climber Reinhold Messner's first ascent of the Eiger's forbidding north face. Europe's most audacious route had been deemed "impossible and foolhardy," until four days of radical suffering while dangling made Messner a revered legend. As a reminder not to accept others' limitations, Otis had taped Messner's long-haired, strong-faced picture on his dorm room door beside one of Paul Petzoldt—older, but, he thought, just as determined. (Lucius neither objected nor posted any pictures of his own.)

This month, Messner was in Pakistan with his little brother Günther to push a bold virgin line up Nanga Parbat. Otis looked forward to hearing how *that* trip went. The Himalaya: he had to go, dedicate himself. One could live on almost nothing there, he'd heard—pennies a day for rice, tea, and yak cheese—free from the clutch of duties that pecked at potential. To summit a peak that breached the "Death Zone" was to enter a priesthood nearly as elite as the astronaut corps.

Until then, his practice ground was here. The guidebook described the rarely-climbed peaks on the Icefield's far side in British Columbia as, "advisable only for veteran parties equipped for self-rescue," but it didn't elaborate on what that meant. Surely their combined experience came close enough. Later, he would share specifics with Ulrich, but before they got to the treacherous headwall—where untold tons of ice decanted, erratic and abrupt, like cubes caught in a narrow-lipped pitcher—he had to test Ulrich like Shaun had tested him. On modest slopes, Otis had them rehearse self-arrest (slide, turn, and dig in your axe point at chest level) and tying Prusik knots to re-ascend the rope if that failed. To Otis' relief, Ulrich proved deft with both skills.

The air warmed; the gradient steepened. Ulrich tiptoed around crevasses Otis easily leapt. Otis steamed. They had to get through the tricky headwall section to safer ice up top before midday sun turned crevasse snow bridges into uncrossable mush. To be stuck, forced to wait overnight for refreeze would invite calamity as ice blocks and rocks melted free and rained down.

Around ten they came to their first real snow bridge: no way around to either side. Still in shade, it looked sturdy, shoulder-width and about as thick, spanning a gap of five yards. Ulrich asked Otis to set a belay. It was gratuitous, but Otis obliged with a quick boot-axe loop. With delicate, metronomic care, Ulrich inched across, then set an identical anchor on his side of the chasm to belay Otis. Otis tracked across, careful to keep to Ulrich's faint footprints. A cold gust wafted up. He looked down. From directly above, the pit seemed much darker and deeper than it had just a few feet away on safe ground. The ice made a sudden rumbling popping noise. Otis took small rapid breaths. He should freeze and weigh his options, but a peskier part of him shrieked as if scalded: *get off this bridge right this instant!*

He took two lunging strides and was taking a third when his outstretched leg punched through the snow bridge like a pencil into soft-serve ice cream. Only his protruding pack and awkwardly buckled back leg kept him from sliding straight through. Below, head-sized chunks he'd kicked loose shrank away, flickering as they spun down into the gloom. Ulrich was only a body-length away, but if his belay was as casual as Otis' had been, the slightest move could be disastrous for them both. Worse,

Otis' plunge had weakened the bridge. The whole thing could crumble. What should he do? His mind was muddle.

"I have you," Ulrich said. "Extend your axe. There you go. Easy."

Otis slithered to Ulrich's feet, ebullient but embarrassed. He despised what fear sensations did to his poise, but each time he pushed through them he got better, and better at hiding them. How had Ulrich kept his cool? Quaking, Otis stood and profusely thanked him.

Proceeding upslope, they skirted crevasses of every size and shape until a house-sized serac blocked their path. The massive collapse had been recent. Near it, fresh boulder-sized fragments gleamed like enormous sapphires: sharp and pale blue. Steep ice at last!

Otis led up the side of the huge block, ankles flexing to give his crampon points traction. His arms burned with the effort of hacking steps for Ulrich to follow. He pushed ten yards or so past the crest, then dug a belay snow seat, and wedged his feet downslope. Firmly ensconced, he yanked the rope to signal Ulrich it was safe to start. Belays without sight lines or voice contact weren't ideal, but in such terrain they were unavoidable. Ulrich should be able to walk up in the evenly spaced toehold divots in far less time than it had taken Otis to carve them.

Slack confirmed that Ulrich was climbing—slowly. Otis' fear grew with his irritation. At this pace, making the Icefield plateau today seemed less and less likely, a dangerous night here far more so. At last, Ulrich emerged into sight. Still well away, he plopped atop a serac. Otis waited as Ulrich unsteadily opened his canteen and took tentative sips. Otis fished a chocolate bar from his pocket, took a big bite, and waited. Then he waited some more. As in a minefield, it was instinctive (but stupid) to draw near a partner in such terrain. Earlier, lower down, where eroded ice features lay in plain sight, it had been fine to stand side by side, but up here, and for the rest of their trip, thin snow veils would often hide chasms. Without time to react, a short rope gap was a death pact. If one climber fell, the other went with him. Without a third party to help from above, it was almost impossible to re-ascend the near-vertical walls inside most crevasses.

Ulrich looked limp, not budging. From where he perched, the crevasses below him would look like sharks' gills. That should motivate him. They didn't. Otis yelled. "What's going on?"

Trembling, Ulrich removed his goggles and undid his waist strap.

"What are you doing? Buckle back up and let's go!"

"I am feeling poorly. I need to rest a moment."

If Ulrich merely slumped over, Otis could likely hold him, but if he tumbled over the serac's sharp edge, Otis could not stop their fall. The snow in which he sat was too mushy. Otis shed his pack, unclipped from the rope, and post-holed down ten steps down to Ulrich, each stride within his own body shadow. Hoping to convey the gravity of their situation, he squatted beside Ulrich, lifted his own goggles, and waited for Ulrich to meet his eyes.

"Listen. I'm beat too, but we can't stay here. Do you hear me?"

Ulrich nodded weakly, mouth slack, breath fast and thin. "Why don't you try standing?" Otis held out a hand. Ulrich took it and tried, but lost his balance. Feet entangled, they slid together to the serac's edge. "Don't move!" Otis shouted, mind racing. Ulrich only moaned.

The taste of blood and chocolate reminded Otis of a junior high biology project. To show how capillary networks delivered oxygen and energy to muscles, he'd traced a transparent overlay in the World Book Encyclopedia: a leering anatomic cutaway. What if Ulrich had merely neglected to eat and his blood sugar was low? Gingerly, Otis reached for another half-melted chocolate bar, opened it, then pulled back Ulrich's lips. He rubbed the melted mess around Ulrich's gums.

Within seconds, Ulrich opened his eyes.

"Thank you," he said. "I feel much better."

"That's it? You're fine?" Otis stood and threw the candy bar at him, as disgusted by the intimacy of what he'd been forced to do as by Ulrich's sudden blithe flip back to normal.

"I am sorry I endangered us." Ulrich sounded meek and sincere, but mountains didn't care about that; such inattentiveness didn't bode well.

Why had Otis assumed a Nebraskan could handle himself in the mountains? Ulrich might be a NOLS grad, but if he was this out of shape—lacking even the sense to eat—then incidents like this would recur. Worthwhile routes were off the table. He needed a new partner. Yet explaining a turnaround would be ugly, their return to the campground awkward, and it would take days to audition another partner with different quirks—if he could find one. Plus, on any existing team Otis would be the outsider, a follower, even less free. No, despite Ulrich's distinct weaknesses, he'd shown himself capable in other ways, guileless and straightforward.

Besides, Otis no longer owned a tent. Going on with Ulrich was his best worst option. He trudged back up the slope, set a more solid snow picket belay, then let Ulrich finish his candy bar and climb up to him.

Soon after that, as if cresting the lip of an ultra-slow-motion waterfall, they left the headwall's disarray. Far-off, greyish peaks poked from a vast snowy upland. Behind those, rows of hazier peaks recessed to the horizon. Shaun had warned him that smooth snow here didn't mean safety. Hidden crevasses could lurk anywhere; this close to the headwall they would be everywhere. Only closer to the Icefield's center could they relax. Otis paused. He was drained, tempted to stop. How bad could it be to tent here if they were careful? He was about to propose it when Ulrich began to sing. *My eyes have seen the glory of the coming of the Lord. He is trampling out the vintage where the grapes of wrath are stored.*

How could one chocolate bar make him so suddenly vibrant?

Despite himself, Otis joined the refrain—*glory, glory, Hallelujah!*—and started plodding. His head pounded from altitude and dehydration. Scale—hard to judge in the void—made him dizzy. After a dozen rounds of the hymn, Otis said enough and they walked on in silence, the swish of their clothing the only mark of their progress in the midday glare. As soon as Otis estimated they were within range of a Mount Columbia day trip, he shucked off his pack. He would wait a little longer to plant the seed for that trip. They probed a perimeter and spread a tarp. Ulrich prayed and they shared lunch: dried fruit, crackers, sardines. The weather was fine. The tent could wait. From his jacket pockets, Ulrich took postcards, a pencil stub, and a small spiral notebook. "I write for a bit."

"Suit yourself." Otis pulled his hat over his eyes and leaned against his pack. Any postcards he bought later would be souvenirs. There was no one he wanted to tip off to his Canadian whereabouts.

"Otis. Otis? Otis!" Ulrich held out a tin mug. "Here is soup." Through Otis' fogged goggles, smeared zinc oxide made Ulrich's face appear ghostly. His own reflection in Ulrich's bug-eyed goggles looked wraithlike too.

Otis sat up and took the mug. Shadows had shifted to transform the blanket-like landscape; years could have passed. "What time is it?" Groggy, he almost asked where they were. He did not want to admit it, but leading had been far more taxing than he'd expected. Nearby on the tarp, the map was spread flat, its corners held down by food cans.

"Almost seven. I slept a bit too." Ulrich sounded excited. He brought the map over. He must have slipped it from Otis' pack. If he'd discovered a solid multi-day route on his own, Otis was ready to smile and say, *great idea; when do we leave, Partner?* But he was also wary of flaky ideas. Maps were not gospel. Nuances emerged only after study alongside the guidebook. Bleary, Otis gulped his soup and yelped in pain, the roof of his mouth sunburned from open mouth breathing in reflected snow glare.

"I'm sorry," Ulrich said. "Mine is burned too." He scooped snow and offered it. Otis nibbled, brooding on the day's mishaps and moods. The next week might be as much of a rollercoaster as today, but it would be worth it if they managed a rarely-climbed—even a virgin—route. From his pocket, Ulrich pulled a hand-sized metal contraption that looked like a woman's compact crossed with a compass. He gestured at a bulge in the glacier's surface. "That is Snow Dome. It is unique. It shares its meltwater to three oceans: Pacific, Arctic, *and* Atlantic."

Otis knew this trivia already, but Ulrich's comment made him envision thousands of melting rivulets forming then combining to form streams and rivers and make their way east to Boston Harbor.

"It's a mound of snow," he said. "There's a lot of that here."

"I would like that we climb it," Ulrich said in a reverent tone.

"Climb? It's a walk-up. Any Jack or Jill could..." Otis stood but feeling faint, he lurched and knocked over his soup. He kicked at the stained snow. "Look, we don't have forever up here." He pointed in the opposite direction at Mount Columbia, its steep gullies and ridges more evident now in evening shadow. "*Those* are *real* climbs." Shaun had spoken of the mixed rock and ice there as providing some of his most important practice for the Himalaya.

"I did not know you felt strongly. Why do we not try both?"

Otis didn't like words like 'try,' but he could see he'd been outflanked. The weather was fine and an extra acclimatization day couldn't hurt. Reconnaissance from Snow Dome's high vantage might prove useful. "OK," he said, "half a day, but that's it."

After dinner, Ulrich proposed a self-timed picture. Otis was not in the mood, but figured he could pepper Ulrich's camaraderie shots into his post-climb slide show. The smattering of wives, girlfriends, nieces, and daughters who attended DF Outing Club alumni gatherings would appreciate the human angle. Ulrich seemed like the type who'd be faithful to send copies.

Ulrich cocked the self-timer and scurried back. In the evening calm, the mechanism sounded like a swarm of locusts. Otis counted, trying to smile. Ulrich held "cheese" like a deflating tire. Right before the shutter snapped, he slung his arm around Otis' shoulder and tipped his head fondly toward him. Otis startled but did not suggest a second take. He would use his own camera for the real *wow* climbing shots.

Twenty-Two:
A Broad Place

The next morning's layer-cake sunrise billowed like an atomic scare film. As Otis watched, orange and red gave way to gentler flesh-tones that tinted the snow. Its cheerful pink reminded him of the Cat in the Hat coming back to clean runaway bathtub cake rings. He warmed his camera and captured the scene, amazed to think he might be the only witness to this grandeur.

Rustling inside the tent broke the stillness. Ulrich emerged and beamed. "Oh my! Lovely. Like cotton candy. We will have plenty to eat!" How childish, Otis thought. How would he take a week of this? Ulrich slipped on his boots and stepped to the edge of their camp to pee. Otis looked away. Ulrich spoke over his shoulder. "The water cycle. Do you know of it, Otis?"

Otis couldn't tell if Ulrich perceived—maybe even intended—the irony. "Of course I know it. They *inundated* us with it at the Earth Day teach-ins. Clouds drop rain which collects in rivers which run to oceans which evaporate to make clouds." Ulrich zipped and turned, his face neutral, oblivious to Otis' attempt at humor. Initially, two months ago, the teach-ins had intrigued him. His feelings changed upon learning that the celebration (oddly set on a Wednesday) had been orchestrated to coincide with Vladimir Lenin's one-hundredth birthday. Days later, Nixon invaded Cambodia, adding to Otis' (and many people's) vexation.

Then, days after *that*, Ohio National Guardsmen caused blood to run down storm drains at Kent State University. The news photos of that event had made the water cycle seem almost obscene.

"Don't forget snow," Ulrich said, but Otis was still picturing bayonets, tear gas, and bodies on sidewalks, kids his age sprinting and stumbling,

124

wailing in disbelief. "Thousands of years of snow formed this glacier. The Bible speaks of snow and glaciers. Do you know of Job, Otis?"

"Of course. Poster boy for arbitrary suffering."

Meanwhile, he was thinking: *four dead.*

Otis knew plenty about suffering for big goals. Seasoned with enough self-discipline toward a purpose, suffering made you stronger. It helped you go harder, faster, longer, and higher. You learned and improved and edged past guys unwilling to suffer as much. Whether or not you reached the bold end you had in mind, the hurt accomplished worthwhile things inside you.

At Deden-Fisher, he had taken a religion course to fulfill a requirement. From what he recalled, Job's suffering had been largely pointless. His life had sucked, and he'd been unable (or unwilling) to fix it: a cosmic punching bag who sat around feeling sorry for himself—a rung lower on the contempt scale than D.H. Lawrence's frozen poetic bird. And if there were ever an illustration of why freedom from groupthink was vital, Job's friends had provided it. Those confidence-killers had been *less than* useless.

The professor for Otis' course—an ordained but churchless Christian minister—had spent years in Asia as an acolyte of Tao, Chi, and Zen. His perennially over-subscribed class, *Primitive Faith in Contemporary Society*, featured archery and martial arts practice alongside selected Old Testament readings (like Job) which he described as *laughably violent, hegemonic relics*. He said that Otis' generation carried a special responsibility to, "restore balance to an irascible society gone utterly putrid." The term paper offered a choice: report on daily solo nature walks or attend an all-night "vision-quest" in a local cow pasture (clothing optional; peyote encouraged) and write a lyric poem about the experience. Otis spent two hours typing invented reflections about walks he never took. His 'A' still made him chuckle.

But Ulrich seemed bent on making a point, and he needed his belayer to like him, and so Otis pretended to listen as Ulrich continued, unruffled.

"God asks Job: 'Hast thou entered the storehouses of snow?'"

Otis flung his arms wide. "Yea verily, we hath entered!"

"Oh, yes. That is good, Otis. Now, think like Job. Perhaps he saw flurries in ancient Iraq or snowy peaks far away, but he did not know a place like this, or Antarctica, or Greenland."

"Every civilization has its myths. What's your point?"

Ulrich's eyes widened.

"Oh Otis, it is not a myth. Look around! Job never saw *this*, but God told him to expect it. Job trusted God and wrote what God wanted him to write. The water cycle is wondrous. According to physics, the earth's water should evaporate off into space. How is it replenished? Some think it's by tiny pieces of comets being added to our upper atmosphere."

"UFO snowballs?"

Ulrich chuckled—a first. "I do not know. Maybe we will someday. But is it not wonderful that God gave us science to learn about His creation?"

Otis considered asking him how a good God could allow Vietnam, but why should he lend him ammo? Ulrich's beliefs seemed immune to debate. Could his fixation on Snow Dome spring from a maverick analogy between the three-way watershed and the holy Trinity? As long as it didn't distract him from climbing, Otis would let him believe what he wanted.

While they'd been talking, the flaming red sunrise had given way to a low but un-menacing overcast. Ulrich retreated into the tent. Red sky warnings were for sailors. Up here, four-hundred miles from the coast, a sunless day meant hard snow, easy walking, and a break for their sunburned palates. Otis would keep a close eye on conditions as they went along.

Ulrich reemerged, cradling his Bible as if it were a butterfly. Did he not give up? He slid a ribbon marker up through a clump of pages, flopping them side-to-side like parting waters.

"Look here. King David writes about water cycles and glaciers in Psalm thirty-three. Listen." Ulrich pulled back his shoulders as if to sing.

"'God gathers the waters of the sea together as a heap: He lays up the depth in storehouses.' Job and David wrote centuries apart, in different countries and languages and yet because these are God's words, they harmonize perfectly. Two-thirds of fresh water is locked in glaciers, Otis. God gives and preserves what we need for life!"

"I guess," Otis said, unsure what Ulrich thought he might have proved. "If it works for you."

Ulrich's response came so softly that Otis envisioned the butterfly that had been his Bible lifting gently from his lips, gliding into flight. "What kind of snowstorm would affect only one person?" Otis remained impassive, tired of verbal games. After a few minutes of silent reading, Ulrich put his Bible away. They ate and talked gear as if the previous conversation had not happened. Their outing would be short, they agreed and so they pared to essentials—food, water, the map—and set out after a leisurely lunch.

Atop Snow Dome, Ulrich took another self-timed buddy shot then stuffed his canteen with snow. Out of respect, Otis waited to pee until they turned off the gentle summit. Ahead, Mount Columbia gave the illusion of rising from the Icefield like an escalator but Otis knew better. Its crevasse-riven glacier was scarier than anything they'd faced—and also further from rescue. It would be wise to scout routes. Why had he not brought the binoculars? If they slogged back to the tent to fetch them now, Ulrich might call it a day. Squinting, Otis could still see the tent; the cloud cover was steady. He resolved to glance back now and then to keep the tent in sight as they advanced for a better look at Mount Columbia. He would turn them around before dinnertime, a little longer than they'd agreed, but it was important; Ulrich would go along.

Hard snow rendered their earlier footprints hard to see. In a scoured icy portion of the route they'd taken up Snow Dome, they disappeared altogether and Otis took the opportunity to veer them toward Mount Columbia. If Ulrich noticed, he made no protest. He stopped when Otis stopped and moved when he moved, following Otis' lead, the rope never sagging or tugging. Today, that was nice. Tomorrow, it would be essential. "That baby's ours if we want it enough!" Otis thrust his axe up and ahead, conscious of imitating the world's tallest statue (in Stalingrad) that he'd read about in the Guinness Book of World Records.

Unable to read Ulrich's reaction to the gesture behind goggles fifty yards away, Otis upped the pace. Ulrich kept up without complaint. As they got closer, climbing route details sharpened and Otis grew excited. Soon he would have all the details he needed for planning. Sweat fogged his goggles. He stopped to pull them off. Freed from the tunnel vision of leather side flaps, the effect was disorienting. The light had dimmed and flattened, blending horizon and sky into an edgeless grey that absorbed the far-off peaks. Snowflakes speckled the air around them. As Otis watched, a wall of dark cloud swallowed Mount Columbia.

He turned slowly, full circle, distressed to have lost his bead on the tent. If the rope were not there for perspective, Ulrich could be ten feet tall—or two inches. Otis motioned him closer and took up slack as he came. Ulrich stopped a snowball's lob away. A rumble made them both cock their ears. "Airplane," Otis said, hoping it was, fearing it wasn't. "Oh by the way, have you seen the tent?" He wished his orange one hadn't burned. Light blue blended in. In any conditions, an overnight bivouac on this open plateau would be unpleasant.

"I have not," Ulrich said. "We should retrace our steps."

What steps? Otis could barely see the pinholes his crampons had left in the icy surface around him. He gestured toward where—in his mind's eye—he felt the tent had to be: a half-hour stroll across gently rolling terrain.

"Over there. It will be quick." He wished he fully believed it.

"I do not think that is wise."

Fat snowflakes came between them. In his peripheral vision, Otis thought he saw flickers; dehydration mirages, he hoped. "Did you bring that compass thing you were using yesterday to sight directions?"

"The Brunton?"

"Yeah that, whatever. You know what I mean."

"It is in the tent."

Otis remembered. He had insisted that Ulrich leave it. The dark wall moved rapidly toward them. Lightning flashes were obvious now, thunder like metal trashcans tossed down stairs. The air smelled zippy. Otis' face felt enmeshed in cobwebs. The ice seemed to hum. His wrist burned; Henry's watch became suddenly hot. "Crap! Saint Elmo's fire! Get down!"

Otis dove flat and ripped off the watch as a flash-roar ripped his senses. He slung his metal-topped ice axe away. A burst of thick snow obscured sound. Was Ulrich OK? Had he thrown his axe away too? More lightning crashed close. Standing could kill him, or crawling, or staying put. Otis pictured doe-faced Dorothy Gale, kicking at her family's storm shelter door in the Wizard of Oz. *Let me in!* The door hadn't budged; the tornado had swept her away. As thoughts of shelter filled his mind, so did Rolling Stones lyrics: a woman assaulted, her shriek shockingly authentic. Time crept and Otis wondered: what had Henry seen, heard, and felt at the end?

At last the storm tapered to steady snow and distant rumbles. They both stood; neither could spot the tent. At a break in the clouds, they lined up canteens with a rocky landmark that Ulrich recalled. Now at least they could aim—*if* he was right.

Unwilling to venture far without axes, they crawled through the fresh snow, feeling for them, each one's weight spread in case the surface hid a crevasse. When that turned up nothing, they dragged the rope sideways to cover more area, trying to snag the axes with it. The method turned up Otis' axe, but after several fruitless hours, Ulrich's remained missing.

"I have a light." Ulrich offered.

Otis was surprised; they'd both agreed not to bring them.

"Then you should go ahead."

If Ulrich fell, Otis might save him. In the reverse case, if Otis fell? Ulrich wouldn't be able to do it. Self-arrest with only hands in this fluff would be a joke. Ulrich needed to exercise caution, but Otis needed perfect precision—for both of their sakes.

Ulrich turned. As he walked away, Otis payed-out rope and prepared to follow precisely in each of Ulrich's footprints.

Twenty-Three: Darkness

Within a few steps, Ulrich vanished into a dense whirl of flakes. Such snow would be sublime anywhere else, Otis thought as he waited for the rope to uncoil. Once it did, he tracked behind, each step increasing his awareness that Henry's watch was now lost forever.

After a while, his saliva grew thick, and his thoughts fixed on glasses, cups, and mugs—water, milk, orange juice, beer. He wished they'd brought the stove to melt snow. Gradually, darkness descended. That meant they'd been out over eight hours. Their chances of stumbling over the tent now were as good as a monkey typing Hamlet, but beneath several inches of new surface fluff, the surface was far too hard to dig a cave. Moving would keep them warm through the short early summer night. Ahead, veiled by sheets of snow, it seemed like Ulrich had flipped on his light.

The rope jerked taut. Otis fell to his knees, ice axe clutched to his shoulder, pick out, ready to fall to his face and self-arrest. Minutes passed. The rope's tension eased. Otis stood, wary for more. "Ulrich!" he yelled. Blood thumped in his ears, backbeat to the wind's drone. He tipped his head to listen. Bulbous flakes wet his face. If Ulrich had not pushed for Snow Dome, they'd be back at the tent, warm, fed, and unhitched. But until Ulrich replied, it was foolish to move.

Otis mused as he waited. Mount Columbia was still possible. Let this fresh snow slough off the steeps, then lend Ulrich his spare axe. Maybe the day after tomorrow. He wiggled his tingling clenched fingers. His nose ran a ticklish salty plume. He twisted to wipe it on his sleeve, but the attempt dislodged Henry's knit cap which slid out of reach. His ears chilled, painful then numb. Heat loss through the head was a serious thing, but to relax his self-arrest pose to retrieve it could make their outing a cautionary tale. Snow transformed the hat into a mound, too far downslope. Otis hoped Ulrich had not strayed them back near the steep headwall they had struggled up.

Ulrich's silence worried him. What if he'd passed out again? Did he expect him to get him out of *every* jam? Why had he roped up to a virtual stranger? The thought made him nostalgic for safety and family.

When he, Henry, and Billy were kids, their father would spread a gym mat across the back of their station wagon. On long car trips, the three of them would lie on it and look up through the windows. Each found fun in calling out what he saw: cloud, tree, airplane, tollbooth, street light, green highway sign, red stop sign. Nothing they noted had to connect because one of their parents was always driving. Eventually, after campgrounds, motels, restaurants, and making their parents nuts singing a hundred bottles of beer on the wall for the hundredth time, the regal elm in their front yard would always come back into view.

"Ulrich!" Otis yelled. "I'm freezing. What's the hold-up?"

No response. Otis lowered his ice axe, resolved to fix a belay and go search. Just then the rope leapt up, rigid as cable.

Before he knew what was happening, Otis was off his feet on his back, accelerating as if hitched to wild horses. His ice axe flew from his hand. Attached to his wrist by a lanyard, it caught hard and wrung out his shoulder with a flash of blinding pain. Fearing it could eviscerate him or slice the rope, he tried to reel it back in but his wrenched arm disobeyed, gimpy. Frantic, he dug in his heels—the only thing he could think of. One foot caught and his ankle felt like an exploding star, the center of everything. His body cartwheeled over his stuck crampons and slammed him face-first; his head downhill, leading the slide. His mouth and nose packed with snow, but the motion brought his axe under his torso. On instinct, he thrust its tip down and in with his good arm and pulled his weight over its shaft. Like clock-hands to six, his momentum slung his feet around past his head, downhill where they should be. He wrestled as his axe point skittered and grabbed on the ice beneath him until at last, he slowed to a stop.

The snow rushing with him did not; instead, it piled on to encase him. Face down he fought to spit, clear his mouth, and breathe; it felt as if sock balls were jammed down his throat. He held back a vomit gag reflex. The rope gouged his hips. Ulrich might be hanging free. He was Ulrich's lifeline but he could be inches from a crevasse lip himself. Holding them both felt like holding a weighted one-handed chin-up. He dared not raise his head lest his balance shift and his axe tip pop loose. Gently, he swiveled his head to the side as if swimming. Nothing. His face was still beneath the snow's surface. His chest heaved, lungs begging.

About to black out, a scene from fourth grade came so vividly to mind that he felt transported, aloof, a spectator. Principal Goode sprinted across the school playground, ripping off his tie, kicking off his shoes. He leaped a chain-link fence, strode into the murky off-limits pond, and dolphin-dove, over and over. Adults joined to help, bedraggled and confounded. Other adults kept kids back and tried to console them. Fire engines came. Someone asked, *how long?* Adults shook their heads at all the answers. Finally, Principal Goode staggered out through broken cattails, Fred the class bully draped in his arms, bleach-faced and snarled in weeds. At the wake, Otis hid his relief with tears.

Fred, the class bully, looked much smaller dead.

Unable to resist any longer, Otis arched up from the snow and gulped cold air. Wild pleasure coursed through him; he yelped panting sobs.

Too fast for shock, his axe point popped free of the ice.

Otis plunged, flailing in darkness.

Part II

Twenty-Four:
Abyss

Otis floated in pre-memories of comfort, his mother cradling his head above kitchen sink suds, cooing melody snippets. She swaddled him in a warm towel that smelled of clothesline-fresh breeze. Was he dead? As in a summer afternoon hammock nap, the question didn't seem urgent. An aura of wrongness eclipsed that sense of wellbeing. His mouth was blood-salt, dust dry. Each breath brought sharp stabs. Shapes he knew not to trust filled the blackness around him. As he swam back up into consciousness, more of him ached. At erratic intervals, the dark around him yielded to a thin swath of pinprick stars. *That must be up.*

The idea amused him. *Up. The stars are... up, and they're pretty.*

A sterner, wiser part of him broke in to chastise.

Stop it. I'm serious. That isn't funny.

Windless snowflakes caressed his eyelashes. He wanted to brush them away but both arms were pinned. He must be on a ledge inside a crevasse. How wide? How strong? Crevasse. Ice. Snow. He no longer shivered. That wasn't good. Something he ought to remember seemed just out of reach. Reach. Hand. Arm. Pinned. Lying motionless was what *a losing opponent* did. Otis tried one arm, his shoulder on fire, but was relieved to hear his axe clatter, still strapped to his wrist. Without it, he might stay entombed. He wiggled his toes in his boots and thought he felt them. One ankle was bad, but it didn't feel broken.

A thought roared in train-like, commanding alertness.

The rope was slack. *Ulrich.*

He scrabbled for the knot at his waist. His mittens impeded feeling. He slipped them off to stash them in his pockets, but they scuttled away.

134

Seconds later, they flopped softly below. He had no spares or even spare socks. Bare hands meant faster frostbite. To trade digits for glory here (far below the height of peaks he was capable of) was shameful. How soon was dawn? He tugged on the loose rope and quickly found its end. In the dark, it was hard to tell how it had severed. It would be unusual for a new rope to fray without the defect being obvious. Had his crampons nicked it? Had his ice axe? He couldn't remember.

Suddenly, horror seemed to distill from below and around him. Was he still awake? The dark crevasse seemed to take on substance and bind him, inside and out. Like a sentient tapeworm, it found his brain and whispered, *blood for blood*. The thought felt icy, devoid of all hope.

"No!" Otis shouted. He felt silly replying to an illusion. He yearned for a real human voice—a cry of anger or anguish, *something*. "Ulrich!" Only dark thoughts cackled back.

Once, on Otis' ride home from elementary school, too far from the schoolyard monitor or the crossing guard for either to see or hear, a cordon of fourth-grade bullies had ambushed him with a stick into his bike spokes. *Goodness*, Fred Sheowin their leader had taunted as he stood above him, heedless of Otis' oozing road rash. *What's this? No big brother to save you?* He'd shrugged and mimed Otis' grimace. Otis had kept his eyes down and stifled his pain. (Otis' collarbone had been broken, but neither Fred nor Otis knew that yet.) He'd worked to forget the others bullies' names but he'd been unable to forget their faces. One of them extracted library books from the bag Otis' mother had double-stitched for him. *You think you're so smaht.* He read the titles in a fake-British accent, then flung each into a patch of poison ivy. Another ripped pages from Otis' assignment notebook, some of which blew into the nearby swampy pond in which Fred would later drown. *Now that don't look so smaht, does it? Geek!* They chanted. *Geek! Geek!* They all kicked him, then walked off slowly, laughing together.

The five minutes Otis had lain there alone had seemed like five days.

In the inky crevasse, Otis yelled until he was hoarse, feeling each cry as if the bullies' rib kicks were fresh. "Help!" *Help, help, help*, teased the fading echoes. Another time, as a boy, a strange fever had hospitalized him for weeks. Open-eyed night terrors had plagued him. Why was a tube strapped to his hand? Who was laughing at the TV's blue-grey flicker? Why did his parents not come? At first, the night nurses had been soothing, but when he woke the ward with screams every night they got brusque. "Get hold of yourself," they barked, shaking him. One time, one slapped him. "Wake up! Think of the people around you." If only he could have.

A faint glow textured the darkness below and around him. In sports he'd taken 'bell-ringer' hits; they always sparkled and danced. This light stayed still. Had it been there before? Slowly he twisted so as to peer over the edge. The light was diffuse. If he were Ulrich and conscious, he would flip his light on and off or wave it to signal. The light stayed still. But what else could it be? Otis gathered breath. "Hey!!"

Again, only echoes came back: *Hey, hey, hey.*

Only days ago, solitude had felt freeing. No draft, school, or hovering parents. Extend a thumb; go where you liked. Solitude here evoked horror. *Ulrich was probably dead.* The realization felt like the one time he'd been held for detention in the Vice Principal's office—accused, convicted, and already serving a sentence—the lair of the dreaded Mr. Van Thaile.

Fred Sheowin, owned the detention bench there, his initials carved deep despite a multi-year battle with knife confiscation and the janitor's efforts at sanding and lacquer. Mr. Van Thaile had leaned close to their faces, his eyes rat-like, bulging and darting, his haircut stiff as a wire brush. *Don't blame me for your mischief,* he barked. *You brought this on yourselves. My job is simple: punishment. Eye for eye, tooth for tooth. If you don't like it here, clean up your act.* While Otis had choked back fright puke, Fred had remained dead-faced, his conscience seared long ago.

Like that day, Otis felt trapped. The storm had erased their tracks. As far as he knew, no one knew where they were or would miss them for weeks. And if someone happened to be up here (and they'd seen no one) why would they bother looking into *this* crevasse among hundreds of dimples like it on the city-sized glacial plain? If he got out of the crevasse—and in his state he didn't know if he could—how would he pick his way through the steep headwall labyrinth the two of them had barely made it through yesterday, fresh and together with an intact rope?

Otis would have no belay, no second chance if he made a misstep. The likelihood that he would die struck him as unfair.

The grim prospect made him recall the day after his hospital stay when he was still too weak for school. While he'd been away, a robin had nested above the Fletchers' back door and the newly hatched chicks were making a

136

cheerful time of it, echoing his feelings of reprieve. Otis had slept through their insistent chirping—better than he had in weeks—but when his mother brought his breakfast tray, she told him that the neighbor's outdoor cat had screeched half the night. They'd lain awake, concerned for his health. What if Otis didn't get enough sleep to recover properly? Otis told her he had slept just fine, but that news never reached his father.

As was his morning custom, his father gathered egg shells, coffee grounds, banana peels, and toast crusts to take outside to the compost. Otis heard him return inside, sounding animated and disgusted. The mother robin was on the back porch; he was late for work. Otis watched out his bedroom window as his father (wearing rubber gloves) carried the cat-torn dead mother robin's body to the compost pile, and tossed it on. Then his father returned. The peeping grew louder.

Otis had not been sure how they would raise the tiny chicks, but his father was good at fixing things; Otis assumed he would figure it out. Instead, his father carried the still-peeping nest to the compost pile. Raising a rusty shovel to shoulder height, he chopped and churned at the steaming black soil until all Otis could see were traces of blue shells. Trembling with horror, Otis recalled the blue hospital gown he'd worn the day before in which he'd lain alone and helpless. His father returned inside to wash up. From upstairs, Otis heard him talking excitedly about how the extra nitrogen would make better fertilizer to grow redder, fatter tomatoes. Otis still hated tomatoes.

He set his jaw to quell the painful swarm of memories, but crunching growls from deep within the ice caused the nightmare vignettes to repeat. He thought of the English class in which he'd memorized the poem which Coach's mantra had mangled. To get the class's attention, the teacher noted that D.H. Lawrence had been banned in England. *Wild things don't feel sorry for themselves*, Otis had summarized, when called on, *and so we shouldn't either*.

The idea had seemed beyond question and won him dozens of matches. Now in the crevasse's clutches, it felt harsh and inhuman. Why *shouldn't* he feel sorry for himself? No one could see.

Besides, what did he have to go back to?

Twenty-Five:
Relentless

ranslucent sapphire framed a bright strip of sky. The crevasse's lips looked higher than Otis' attic dormer back home—about four stories, he guessed—but the prospect of having sun on his face again steeled his resolve.

With singular care, he drew up onto his good foot and steadied himself against the ice wall. The ice above him was not as steep as Pinnacle, but it was steep enough, no chance of self-arrest if he fell again. He must have rolled and bounced to get here. Yesterday, cutting steps up to get out would have taken half an hour—strenuous, but not heroic. But today? In his condition? Half a *day*, *if* he could even cut one, *and* if his bad leg would take his weight. And if it didn't? If he couldn't? He refused to think about it. There had to be a better, safer way.

He studied the crevasse, bulbous like a funhouse mirror. The other wall, across the gap, was too far to touch—or hit if he fell. Ice ledges sometimes angled toward a crevasse's top, but his seemed a dead end, the only flat surface around. All else was sheer or overhanging. The only way out was up. He *had* to get out. He *would* get out. He wished for a belay, abashed to be so chicken. He'd snuck pitons into his pack in hopes of reaching Mount Columbia's rock but they were ill-suited here. Under pressure, they would melt out of any ice crack into which he jammed them. And even if one held briefly, clipping in to it by such a short length of rope was liable to *cause* him to fall. Like stuck dental floss, it would jerk him back as he moved up.

He re-examined the rope's end but it told him nothing he'd not learned by feel. Whatever had cut it had been near his end—his flailing ice axe, most likely. He untied the rope from his hips and recalled the salesman. *Some think a rope is magic.* He wished he could charm it to lengthen and tie to sky hooks. Six feet was a glorified dog leash, dead weight. He fished the pitons from his pack, strung them on the short length of rope then tied its ends together. He flung the bundle out over the chasm where it writhed on an air current before disappearing. The metallic echo of it hitting hard ice took longer than he would have expected. Any mistake here would likely be his last. As such, Shaun's wisdom was crucial: fear is self-fulfilling; think down and eventually you *will* fall down. He would clear his mind and think upward thoughts.

He took a deep breath, turned, and faced the ice. He chipped steps at knee, waist, chest, and shoulder height, then flipped out his Swiss Army knife corkscrew and balled it claw-like in his fist. With his good arm, he swung his axe high, pleased by a solid thunk. He tugged to set it, reassured by a snug feel. Slowly he relaxed and let the axe sling take his weight and set the axe tip firmly in its divot above. He raised his good foot, kicked into the first step he'd cut, and pushed up. *Nice and easy. Steady. Relentless. Pace like for an all-day elimination tournament. Do only what needs to be done to advance; stay in the moment. Don't trust the highs or the lows.*

He moved his corkscrew hand up, re-swung and set his axe, then raised and placed his weight on his bad foot. Fighting jets of agony, he puffed through pursed lips and readjusted his balance. The familiar movements guided his alertness to the stakes into total concentration. Painstakingly he repeated the sequence, never pausing long enough to relax and hope. His arms felt like wood. His legs jiggled. Drenched in sweat, he didn't dare pause to remove layers. In a far corner of his mind, he registered the sun moving down the crevasse walls, surprised when it blazed into his eyes. The lip was right there! He swung his axe past it, pulled hard, and lunged up.

Warmth. Skyline. Safety. Impossible. He'd written himself off. He wriggled away, bathed in relief. After a while, he rose to his knees. Squinting through glare, he took in his surroundings. Mount Columbia taunted, unchanged. On the crevasse's far uphill side, a groove showed where he and Ulrich had slid. Behind it, a maze of meandering boot prints muted by more snowfall showed how much they'd wandered. Where was the tent? He scanned the homogenous white until his eyes burned. A faint shadow suggested its half-collapsed outlines.

He had to reach it before dark.

He shouted repeatedly into the crevasse. Silence. If Ulrich were alive, he would have to climb farther than Otis had (probably a lot further; aside from the diffuse light below, Otis had seen no sign of him) and all without an ice axe. Impossible. It was over. He'd done all he could.

To spread his weight across any concealed crevasses, Otis slid slug-like, rising to his knees only to get his bearings. Hours later, he reached the tent. Snow-bowed walls cramped the interior like jostling pigs. He cleared some away and crawled in. Ulrich's clothes and Bible were wrapped in a plastic bag. His sleeping bag was neat and flat, a few stray hairs at its head.

Otis stretched out on his own bag, careful not to touch Ulrich's. If their fates were reversed and he was the one late returning, he would appreciate room to lie down and his things just as he left them. *Ulrich was fine, only late.* The notion had a pastel-vague plausible quality to it, as if he'd entered a rabbit-hole land with magical rules. With his rational mind, he knew Ulrich had to be dead, but before he could unlace his boots or think which version was true, exhaustion greyed his delusions into dreamless sleep.

More snow came that night, then two days of fog and hard rain, pinning him down. (Soaked, he would freeze in the time it took to find the remaining rotting snow bridges.) He envisioned his tent as an ocean raft, surrounded by sharks; he huddled in his bag. He did not light the stove. He'd burned one shelter already. A mishap here had much higher stakes: poisonous fumes in the tight space or else exposure. He ate snow then set out the cook pot for rain. In the tent ceiling's glow, over uncounted hours, his eyes made up patterns. He nibbled dry food, and peed in a cup he poured out the door. The wind seemed to cloak mumbles just shy of music, almost alive. The disorienting effect made him recall other times he'd been cold and scared.

Trees bare and mud coming unfrozen, he'd pedaled his banana-seat bike home from school, hands and ears red. He skipped the snack his mother had left out—and the Superman rerun he never missed—then all was blank until his bedroom ceiling swam into focus. His arm vibrated. Acrid smell tweaked his nose. He glimpsed the fan motor that had gathered dust on his father's workbench. Otis had brought it to his room to fix as a surprise. A screwdriver clattered from his fist. Footsteps clomped up the stairs. Henry rushed in, his face troubled in a way Otis would not see again until the end of his brother's last combat furlough.

"Otis! Never try something like that again, you hear? You ask me first."

"OK." Otis fought tears. Henry slipped an arm under his shoulders. His rough white work shirt smelled of fryer oil. He laid Otis on the bed and opened a window to vent the ozone smell. He replaced the motor and screwdriver, fixed the blown fuse, then slid the dresser to hide the singed plug socket. As his big brother bustled, Otis felt safe, sure that Henry would keep the secret. And he *had* kept it—to the grave. Only Otis could ever tell, and he had no reason to.

As sleet lashed the tent, Otis' mind wandered to another winter afternoon a few years later. Otis and Billy had hunched in their snow fort by the street, pilfered candle and matches between them. Their snowballs sat ready, each hard and perfect, baseball size, stacked in a pyramid. Some cars they hit only slowed or honked. Then one car fishtailed back. Otis snuffed the candle and peeked out. Red glow and exhaust filled the fort. The rhythmic wet squeak of a window being rolled down revealed a tattooed forearm; fingers pointed as if its owner wore X-ray glasses.

"How old are you, punk?"

"Eleven," Otis mumbled, frantic to run, but the house was too far and he should protect Billy.

"You wanna live to be eight?"

Otis stifled a giggle. The man had misheard his age. Another car pulled behind and the first roared away in a plume of slush.

"Otis, you knucklehead hooligan, come out of there!" Sheepish, Otis stood, then Billy. Henry pointed at Billy but stared at Otis. "Seriously, Otis? He's seven. Look at him. He's your little brother—our little brother. He needs a Kleenex. Where are his mittens?"

Otis recalled being angry at Billy for unclipping them, yet Henry being right had made Otis feel like he weighed two tons. He crawled back into the fort and found them, stiff with red candle wax. He cracked off the worst of it, glad the mittens were the same color. In the driveway, he re-clipped them to Billy's sleeves, said he was sorry, and mostly meant it.

Henry drew them together, snatched off their hoods, and tousled their hair. His leather jacket smelled earthy. Otis craved his brother's hipness, his wisdom, his caring. Despite sports, jobs, girlfriends, and homework, Henry

141

always asked Otis how his day was and listened through winding tales of recess and hallway intrigues. When their parents went out and they got Billy to bed, the two of them would watch Dragnet and Hawaii Five-O, wary for returning headlights. Inside the house that winter afternoon, pot roast smell had enveloped them in a delectable haze as Otis and Billy sat to take off wet things. Henry brought a fresh loaf of bread to the kitchen.

Pot roast and fresh bread. Why had he let himself recall that? He was down to a half sleeve of damp biscuits. His sleeping bag was drenched from drips from the tent's walls. He wished the wind's murmurs would resolve into Henry's voice. A ghost might terrify him, but after he got used to it *Henry's* ghost would be alright. *He* would know how to get him home safely.

The third day, skies cleared. The things Otis could carry, he packed. Injured, it wasn't much. There would be no triumphant DF Outing Club slide show and his camera was heavy and old. He left it and Ulrich's things in the tent. More snow would soon subsume it, but leaving Ulrich a refuge helped assuage his guilt. He almost abandoned Ulrich's Bible, but changed his mind. To do so felt wrong. Plus, it smelled like Henry's jacket. Otis also took Ulrich's three pre-stamped finished postcards. He owed Ulrich's family that much.

Beneath a bright midnight moon, Otis began the trek down. Each step was an ordeal. Rain had unveiled dozens of crevasses they'd not seen on their way up. Zig-zagging around them added painful steps. His second night out, dreams became hard to distinguish from hallucinations. He envisioned gravity and cold as demons, flipping a coin for the chore of killing him. Freeze first then fall? Or fall first then freeze? Either way, the patient glacier would get its runaway meal.

Twenty-Six:
Younger Sun

August, 2019...

Cece let Eudora's binoculars dangle then stepped away from the crevasse edge. She felt five again, wishful for any adult to make sense of what she'd just seen. The grey hand in the green parka sleeve looked perfect, as if reaching out, begging. It wasn't of course, but the impression lingered and without a sat phone or cell reception, the next moves were hers. She took a deep breath, held it, and turned. A solemn half circle of students stood respectfully back. To make her words sound relaxed, she exhaled through them so slowly that it felt like she was back on Xanax.

"Hamlin?" Eye contact, pause, loyal serious nod. "I need you to set an anchor and a Z-pulley rescue rig—just like we practiced. Grab whomever you need to help you and triple check it. This set-up has to be bomber. The rest of you? Melt snow for water and pack the tents and the gear. We need to get down and report this."

Eudora wiped snot and tears and plopped onto the ice. No one else had seen the hand magnified, but a mutual pity party would do no one any good.

"Pull yourself together," Cece said. "And put on your toque."

"I'm not cold."

"I don't care."

Meekly, Eudora obeyed. "What do you think happened?"

"We don't know yet."

Cece retreated to her tent to give herself a pep talk. She couldn't evade this. She had to go down in the gloom close to the thing. Once Hamlin readied the set-up, she mutely clipped in, went through the belay command sequence, then leaned back into her rappel, taking care not to pierce the grey exposed hand with her crampons. (If it had thawed, she thought, the result would be like cleaning dog mess off shoes.) Once into position, she used her ice axe and Swiss Army knife to chip gently near where the hand suggested a face might be. Once it came into sight, the team lowered her jugs of hot water which she used to clarify her view into the solid ice.

The face was a man's, his complexion blotchy but intact. Zinc oxide was smeared against a younger sun, his beard scruff and mild acne like some of her students. His closed eyes reminded her of how, only inches away, an airplane seatmate might pretend to sleep to forestall small talk.

His clothes were a mix of nylon and wool. Nylon meant post-war. Fleece had arrived in the mid-eighties, her high school years, to mostly replace wool. The man had either shopped thrift stores or died before then. That left a span of about forty years. How strange to think: a kid the age of her students, yet perhaps as old as her folks—past retirement age. She took photos then zipped her phone in her pocket and hollered for her team to haul her up. The process seemed to take eons, causing her panic she hadn't expected. A glacier was one thing; an open tomb quite another. *And she'd camped above him all week!*

Back on the surface, Joe—a less-than-gifted freshman—bugged her to share her pictures. Instead, Cece related a sanitized gist. Miffed, Joe told a Popsicle joke. No one laughed.

"Shut up!" Eudora screeched. "Just shut up! You have no idea what you're talking about." The group stood stone-faced. Cece's gut churned. Now what? Someone handed Eudora a tissue. Willing her best command voice in hopes it would forestall further strife, Cece explained how they would leave together for the hike down in exactly one hour.

Hamlin spoke up. "Would you mind if I prayed for us?"

She should have guessed.

"Go ahead," Cece said. What was the harm if a brief foray into myth kept the kids from freaking out long enough for her to get them to safety?

Hamlin's prayer made Cece recall her old departmental assistant doing the same thing to zero objections. The weekly meeting had been going nowhere anyway—everyone reeling from what the TV was showing: Manhattan's skyline spewing slow smoke, soiling a crystalline azure sky, but better than the hellish close-ups of plummeting bodies. Half these kids had

144

been in diapers that Tuesday morning. Was she really that old? For a moment after Hamlin's "Amen," the tidy narcotic ease of Cece's mid-continent upbringing threatened to reassert itself, but she could not afford that distraction here. She had to stay 'on' until she got these kids home. She returned *her* toque to her head and let her sense of control slink back to its established place.

———

At the base lodge, Cece shared photos and GPS coordinates with a young ranger who studied a computer monitor, then shook his head. The Parks Canada database listed no unresolved local cases within that timeframe. Cece took down his contact information and promised to upload her crevasse photos to a cloud folder in case he might recognize anything. "You can if you want," the ranger said. In the glacier's measured flow, they both knew it would be decades until the body reached the heavily trodden tourist areas where someone might care.

Twenty-Seven:
Hidden Things

June, 1970...

Near the southern end of his duty area in Western Alberta, just as he'd done since the "Dirty Thirties," when fine blowing dust had coated, colored, and flavored every square inch of life and no one had heard of metrification, Doug Moiry McKeon, Assistant Senior Warden for Jasper National Park, turned right off the Icefields Parkway and trundled down the mud-gravel road to his favorite spot early on summer mornings: facing the glacier. Several new climbing parties had parked and departed in the wee hours. Drunks were elsewhere, sleeping it off. By sunset, most climbers were too spent for any serious shenanigans. They told tales and nursed blisters over schnapps-laced cocoa but that was about it. Anything more rambunctious was the evening shift's problem. *This* hour was his.

Doug shut off the engine and reveled in a quiet marred only by the faint hint of rushing water that wafted in on a zephyr. Between him and the ice, the surface of Sunwapta Lake was glassy at this hour, tinged with what the tourist brochures insisted was turquoise-emerald, but which was, in fact, grey-blue-green, reflecting the stunning elevation of rock and ice behind it, and the sky above it in exquisite likeness.

Within an hour, a half-kilometer behind where he sat, wrinkled tourists in expensive cardigans would swarm the hillside lodge, gorge on rich foods, and wait for chipper tour directors to herd them onto idling busses. Last year, bug-like diesel tractors had joined the sightseeing menu to carry those whose late-life vacation excursions barely dented their retirement kitties

146

onto the lower glacier to snap trophy photos. Sacrilege, Doug felt. But he had no say in the rules.

Toward the end of his shift, in the afternoon, Doug would return here to talk with descended climbers. Cracked lips, raccoon tans and jolly exhaustion made them easy to spot. Their vehicles used to be distinctive too: rusty late models held together with coat hangers and strapping tape. With more flying in, rental cars confused things, though gear in the back seat was still a 'tell,' as were daubs of zinc oxide on trunk lids and door handles. The best clues though were the smells. No climber's vehicle ever exuded aftershave, dirty diapers, or perfume. Sweat or beer: always a climber. (Sometimes now, albeit rarely: marijuana.) Peanut butter or moldy cheese? Ambiguous. Claw-scratched paint or shredded soft-tops were usually tourists. Most climbers read the warning signs better and put smelly food items away.

Long ago, as a rookie grateful for *any* job, Doug used to examine the visitors' log first thing, name by name, party by party, climbers or trekkers— in twos or more if they had any sense. Then he would crosscheck sign-outs against license plates. It was years before his diligence bore fruit.

Shortly after the war, rescuers found an Ottawa pair shivering—and twelve hours overdue—midway up a route they had no business attempting, one bleeding from double compound tibia fractures and his partner severely concussed. The second case a few years later had been simpler. A Calgary accountant had come to shoot amateur photos and wandered under an overhang. His final skyward photo won posthumous awards. The third memorable case, ten years ago, had ended at a Jasper bar. Three Frenchmen had been shocked to learn that efforts to rescue them were underway. Chagrined, they paid their fine in cash and poured Doug a glass of wine. Politely refusing, Doug sealed the revenue in an official envelope, watched each man initial the flap, then wrote them a Parks Canada receipt. (Later, he stapled the receipt's carbon copy to his report.)

More recently, the log entries had grown haphazard. (Since when, Doug couldn't say, but it seemed to correspond with the increasing length of men's hair.) A false-alarm confrontation like the one with the Frenchmen was now unthinkable, but so were time-sensitive search-and-rescues like with the Ottawa pair. If two went up, two should return. Lacking the log, Doug now relied on instinct and Sam the cook to make those links. Sam's frenetic work preparing fresh elk and smoked trout for well-heeled guests from Toronto, Vancouver, New York, and LA did not dim his near-photographic recall of everyone who passed near his kitchen.

Doug rolled down his window. With a pensive satisfaction made bittersweet by numbered days, he inhaled the glacier-scrubbed air. Though healthy, age rules made this his last season. He poured coffee from the thermos his wife had filled before dawn, then unfolded the Edmonton Journal's sports section, relishing the aromas that filled each day with a sense of possibility the way spiral notebooks had once initiated each autumn. After Sam had had time to examine his copy (but before his prep cooks returned to fix lunch) Doug would mosey up to the lodge for a refill, deliberate with Sam over box scores, then ask about any climbers he might have missed.

A muffled sneeze nearby caused Doug to slosh coffee all over his paper. He cursed his rookie mistake. Always scan the scene. Was he losing his edge? He slipped out and left the door ajar. Another sneeze. There. Fogged windows. He crept toward the sky blue Pontiac Tempest. Last Monday the hood had been warm. Six days was a long outing, but two big storms had socked things in. Body odor was no surprise. The bear-scratched trunk lid was.

Something moved in the back seat. Confronting couples was always awkward. Morning was an odd time, but hardly unprecedented. Doug rapped on the driver's side window. "Would you please show yourselves?"

"Just a sec," came a raspy male voice, then a convulsive cough.

A young man stepped out barefoot. He stumbled and swore, breathing in short puffs, all his weight on one leg.

"I'm sorry," said Doug, "but camping here is not permitted."

Doug usually addressed anyone old enough to drive as 'sir' or 'ma'am'. Here it felt wrong. He'd seen many climbers in extremes of pain, exhaustion, and dishevelment. This battered beast was off that scale: black eye, broken nose, hair matted with blood, sunburn-scabbed face, eyebrows singed off. Bits of food clung to a week-old scruff that failed to hide two broken teeth. His hands were swollen and scratched. One finger was oddly bent.

"I'm sorry," the man said with a smoker's rasp. "I got in real late last night." He coughed, winced, and clutched his ribs. "We were; I mean I *was* over on the BC side. What day is it?"

"Sunday, June twenty-first. Father's Day, the Summer Solstice."

"Thanks," the man mumbled. "I suppose I should call him."

The man blinked often, his eyes badly bloodshot. His narrow squint made snow-blindness a more likely cause than lying, but Doug wasn't yet certain. Without any telltale odors of illegality, he would start at the other end and work up. He pointed at the man's swollen ankle. "Medical attention might be wise before driving manual."

"I'll be OK," the man said. "Took a little tumble, that's all. No big deal." He turned away.

If other people were around to witness a situation like this, Doug would deploy his command voice and ask for ID about now, but this guy seemed more of a danger to himself than to others. Engage and disarm seldom failed. "My name's Doug," The man turned back around.

"Listen man, last night was late. I was too tired to drive. I'm not bothering anyone. I'll be out of your hair in a few."

The man's defensiveness was troubling. Doug regrouped.

"How about coffee?" The man bobbed his head in such a way that Doug thought he was about to faint. "Why don't you sit down? I'll be right back." Doug moved toward his cruiser, his ears alert for jangling keys. Sometimes, poachers he stopped would take their chances and zoom away, a half-closed trunk lid chopping half-heartedly at a trophy bighorn or an elk carcass sliding around a bloody pickup bed whenever its driver cornered hard. With only one road for fifty miles in each direction, north or south, the morons eventually either regained their wits, crashed, or ran out of gas. This guy didn't seem the type to spray gravel and flee like that.

Doug was happy when his assessment proved correct. Returning, he set the homemade cookies he'd been saving for lunch on the man's car roof. The man's eyes darted to them like bait. "Help yourself," Doug said and the man wolfed down a handful. Doug filled the screw-top lid cup from his thermos and held it out. The man took it in both hands; small ripples agitated the coffee's surface.

"I've never been to Nebraska," Doug offered. The man looked confused so Doug clarified. "Your car?"

"Oh, right. It's nice and flat. Not like this."

The man-beast tilted his head toward the glacier and sipped.

Most climbers were socially awkward, plus, this one had just woken up. Still, his behavior was shifty, not fully explained by a concussion. And his injuries were pretty bad. Mirroring the man's movements, Doug tipped his head at the glacier, hoping to relax him enough to get a name.

"So, besides this beauty, what brings you here?"

"I just finished college."

Doug had heard sillier answers. An American his age probably meant Vietnam. Not his concern. If they'd cared, the border guys could have stopped him. He would try a simpler tack.

"Looks like you had a rough outing. Were you up there alone?"

Twenty-Eight:
Don't Blink

Otis muttered. "Up there alone." He was glad that the ranger—whose name he'd already forgotten—was not the one he'd met his first night, but did they trade notes? He took another swig of coffee, hopeful it might fetch a brilliant retort free of contradictions.

"Yes," the ranger said. "Were you up on the Icefield by yourself or were there other people there with you?"

Otis pursed his lips. He was still coming to grips with the surprise of making it down alive. He studied the mud at his feet, his eyes like hot sand, not *fully* snow-blind, but a dark room sure would be nice.

"I, um. Yeah. Alone. Up there." The ranger raised an eyebrow. "Alone for the last bit, I mean, in those storms. My partner went down before that. Home, I mean. I didn't know him so well. We met last week."

He came close to adding, *at the campground.*

The ranger spoke slowly. "I need you to do something for me. I need to see a driver's license or a passport—something official."

Otis froze. "What's this about?"

"It's policy for cars here five days or more."

Otis had memorized the guidebook. It said nothing about such a rule. Still, refusing an order from a uniformed officer in a foreign country might be pushing his luck. He plunked into the seat, opened the glove box, and removed a sheaf of papers. The top item was a letter from Ulrich's fiancée. Under it, a 1963 document certified Ulrich as a naturalized American citizen. Under that was a letter from the U.S. Selective Service Administration. Otis scanned it and gasped. Ulrich didn't need an occupational draft deferment;

he had been safe all along. Otis fished for Ulrich's wallet, found his draft card, and confirmed. Ulrich's number was three-hundred and fifty-one.

Otis reeled with a sudden idea unlike *anything* he'd dared to dream. Was this the lucky break he'd hoped for since last December—his chance to cast off his draft burden once and for all?

The park ranger cleared his throat. "Is there a problem?"

"No," Otis said. "I'll be right with you."

The two wallets lay side by side in the glove box. Visually, Otis weighed their leathers, shiny from wear, conformed to the bodies they'd clutched. What he was thinking felt miles past crazy, yet Calgary had shown that he couldn't make it in Canada. And if he returned to the U.S. he'd have to hide, always on the move, vulnerable to Vietnam, jail for not going, or both. He'd never intended Ulrich harm. He hadn't known his draft number. The fall had been an accident. Days ago, he would have dismissed the idea that was forming as chancy and wrong but then why should he refuse a gift dropped in his lap? Ulrich was dead. Whatever Otis did, *Ulrich* couldn't be hurt anymore. Yet by using Ulrich's name, *Otis* could live free, much better off.

A thousand doubts flooded his mind. It would never work. He would trip up; get arrested. He picked up his own wallet and slid out his Massachusetts license. He would manage somehow, no worse off than before. Just as he was about to stand to hand it over, his mind filled with news clips he'd watched of blood-spattered arms bouncing limply off stretchers being hustled to hovering Med Evac choppers.

Behind the car, the ranger spoke again.

"Some licenses have pictures now."

Don't be a dope, Otis thought. Nearly all his classmates had hoaxed their way out of the draft. Even ROTC-minded Henry would think of the war differently now. Besides, the ranger had seen the car's Nebraska plates. To offer his Massachusetts license would raise questions that might leave him worse off once the ranger saw Ulrich's registration. *Neither* state's license included a photo. Otis swapped wallets. Slowly he stood and held out Ulrich's driver's license and draft card. As if illuminated by lightning, a life's worth of possibility swept his mind clean. *Freedom.* The ranger made notes on a clipboard. What might he ask? He had one chance to get this right. Would he have to sign Ulrich's name?

"I grew in college," he offered.

Fright-sweat cooled his palms. *He couldn't go back.*

"That's a healthy thing for a young man." The ranger handed him back Ulrich's draft card and license. "Don't forget to renew this next spring."

Had it been that easy? As Otis slipped the cards back into Ulrich's wallet, he half expected them to burn him, or leap away yelling 'fraud!' He looked through the wallet's slots. Where was Ulrich's photo of Calia? Was that what he'd slid into his parka pocket when they set off?

"It looks like you're a reader?"

Otis was startled.

"Oh yeah, sure. College, y'know. History major. English minor."

The ranger pointed through the windshield. "I mean that one. It's nice to see a young man with a Bible handy. It looks like it's seen some use."

To make room to sleep, Otis had wedged Ulrich's Bible on the dashboard. Its ribbons drooped from its gilt-edged pages; a gold cross embossed its cover. A wave of guilt struck him as stifling as his claustrophobia at the Doors concert when, for a moment, he'd feared that all sanity might have vanished *outside* the venue as well as inside it. Otis stammered. "Oh, yeah, that."

"Those were more common when I was young. What's your life verse?"

Otis hesitated. "All of them, I guess." *That was lame.* He couldn't let something like this smoke him out. He had to go back on offense. He recalled his grandfather saying grace. "To be honest? Right now I'm thinking about, 'Give us this day our daily bread.'"

The ranger chuckled. "I'll bet. You must be starving. The lodge starts breakfast at eight. It's too fancy for my taste—or our budget—but to each his own." (Doug enjoyed the gourmet plates which Sam slipped him free, but he also hated wasting the lunches his wife prepared him.)

"Thanks for the tip. I'll find some grub on the road."

"It'll be a while. Where you headed?"

"Alaska." His heart swelled at the thought. He was free! He could change his destination the instant he left the parking lot; no one would care.

"Jasper's an hour north. Beyond there make sure you have tools. The road gets rougher the further you go; after Dawson Creek you're committed. Take extra fuel too—the big Jerry cans, not those dinky squat things—and also water. There are plenty of ponds and streams for the radiator, but look sharp. The bears drink at them too. They'll smell you a long way off."

Was that a comment on his hygiene?

"I'll look into it," Otis said. His ankle throbbed.

"You should get yourself looked-at." The ranger handed Otis a business card: Dr. Ephrem Hoyt Shields, MD, Jasper, Alberta. "My son-in-law; goes by 'Eph'. Stop by first thing Monday. Most afternoons he does rounds on the reserves. He'll work things out if you're short."

Since they'd begun talking, several cars had arrived. The ranger walked off to engage them. Otis plopped into the driver's seat, his heart thumping. He ran a hand through his tangled hair. From behind the seat, he grabbed his Red Sox cap. The ranger came back. Otis whipped it off and sat on it, hoping the ranger's view had been obscured by the windows' reflection.

"One more thing, Ulrich. For my report." Otis stiffened. "Where was your partner from?"

"Boston," Otis said, his tongue brassy-tasting all of a sudden.

The ranger chuckled with boyish glee. "I expect he gave you this already but, how about them Bruins? Four-game sweep. Incredible, eh?" The aging ranger stretched out both arms and leaned so far forward that Otis felt sure he would fall on his face.

Otis tried not to laugh. Guys at his on-campus house had gotten annoyed when Kent State interrupted the Stanley Cup playoffs. Bobby's Orr's winning overtime dive—his body horizontal to the ice, stick extended—had become an instant icon. Wilson Ward and his noxious teammates had endlessly pantomimed Orr's move, culminating in hoots when they each repeated it, diploma in hand, at graduation. Virtual gods on the ice, they were little boys everywhere else.

"I don't follow hockey," Otis said, hoping the heresy sounded blasé.

"Oh, you don't know what you're missing! Johnny's our local boy."

"Who's Johnny?" Otis reveled in his specious deadpan delivery. From interviews with, and fawning profiles of the Edmonton-born Bruins team Captain in the Boston papers, every New Englander felt they knew Johnny Busiek as intimately as did his family.

"You *must* be from Nebraska."

The ranger walked away, shaking his head.

Otis worried. Had he seen through his story? His grandmother used to "can" by lowering metal lids and glass jars with forceps into boiling water. "But they're not cans!" he used to protest, awed nonetheless by rows of tomatoes, peaches, cucumbers, and beans in his grandparents' basement, sealed in glass to eat many years later. The tale he'd told the ranger was also sealed—but he had to keep its contents hidden.

The Icefield glared in his mirror, too bright to look at as he drove away. The week's events looped nonstop in his mind: storm, dark, fall, then climb out, more storms, then pick his way down through the icefall—two nights and three days. Now, after all that, he'd stumbled on a way out of the war, a fact that seemed too good to be true. It reminded him of a story.

A condemned man stands noosed on a bridge, hyper-alert to his watch. A plank is released and he drops, but the rope breaks and he escapes. Within sight of home the false reverie ends. His neck snaps; he swings dead. It made Otis wonder: Was a safe draft card death's last false tease? Even as all around him seemed normal, could he in fact still be up on the glacier half frozen, dreaming this, dying? What did you do with a notion like that?

He'd been certain he would find a way to skirt the draft, but he'd dallied (Coach's cardinal sin). He should have groveled for recommendations to grad school. In hindsight, even amputating a pinky finger seemed attractive. His injuries testified to the fall's force. His ice axe *could* have sliced an artery. He needed to see a doctor. There was no sense compounding the tragedy. He was no longer evading, only trading places with someone who no longer needed a safe draft card. *How* he came by it wasn't important.

His inability to recall details bugged him, but whether his axe had cut the rope, nicked it, or it had frayed didn't matter. He'd never *set out* to cut it. He was no murderous monster: no Manson or Lieutenant Calley, destroying a village. He'd shouted and listened and waited. No reasonable person could have expected him to do more. He could report it from a pay phone.

He nudged Ulrich's car onto the highway—the Icefields Parkway— back tires on the gravel, no traffic to push him. He could go anywhere he wasn't known. Anywhere except home. Was that such a bad trade-off? For now, the choice was simpler: north to new or south to old? Out of habit, he put on his blinker. North offered bigger mountains.

Twenty-Nine:
Legacy

August, 2019...

Cece backed the geology department van out of its space in the Icefield lot and turned south on the Icefields Parkway. In Banff, she would turn toward the sunset, Vancouver, and home. Some of her students slept or pretended to, earbuds in, hoodies up, lost in unshared music. Others thumbed madly at smartphones like lovers rejoined, frantic to resurrect social media status or set new game records.

The ice man's face ruled Cece's thoughts.

In her hour in the crevasse, gingerly chipping, melting, and taking photos, he'd taken on a vague familiarity, like a nameless handsome stranger at a fine restaurant, a few tables away over Alistair's shoulder. Then, months later, in the checkout line at Whole Foods, there he would be, distant anonymity replaced by close quick wordless eye-contact courtesy (*set-down-the-belt-divider-for-you?*), a whiff of remembered cologne, and the sense that they must have met—even spoken a while—at some cocktail party or other. And so, in those situations, Cece always stayed quiet unless such a one brightened and said, "Cece!"

Which almost never happened.

No, her sense of acquaintance was bogus, ephemeral; bound to fade with a good night's sleep at sea level, reunited with her husband, responsible for no one except their son. Still, she wondered: who *was* the young man? What kind of misfortune had left him trapped in the ice? And why could the ranger find no record of a matching mishap?

Cece parked the department van outside her condo and tiptoed inside. On the granite counter, a Post-It note read: *Welcome back, hon! Thai & Sauv Blanc in fridge. Xo.* Alistair was the most thoughtful, patient man in the universe. Cece opened the stainless steel door, peeled back the takeaway lid, and dry-heaved. The cold meat reminded her of the frozen man's face.

She filled a wine glass and crept upstairs.

In the nightlight's glow, Nate's steady breaths calmed her. The last year had been sweet for the three of them. She wished she could press pause on Nate's first-grade innocence, then fast-forward through the awkward years. The man in the ice had looked barely a man himself. How often had his mother stared at her son's empty bed, dusted his knick-knacks, and put off taking down his adolescent posters lest they reveal how much his room's wall paint had faded?

Downstairs she grabbed pretzels, refilled her wine glass, and slipped outside. The warm patio stones felt pleasant on her feet, sore and crinkled from time in heavy boots. She stretched out on the lounger, went through her pictures again, and felt herself gripped by an instinct she'd learned to distrust—a nasty trick her brain played when she was tired.

At two conferences—one in New Zealand, shortly after defending her doctoral dissertation, and another a decade later, keynoting in Norway—Cece had been positive that a woman across a hotel lobby was Ellen, her childhood best friend. The actual woman (the same exacting Swiss colleague both times) had spun from Cece's excited attempt at a hug, furious at her spilling her drink. Both times, Cece stumbled away mortified, apologies wriggling out of her like maggots, unable to shake a sense that the real Ellen had shape-shifted and betrayed her. She paid the hefty hotel dry cleaning bills and sent boot-licking e-mails to patch the rift each time, but a befuddling low-level fear made its home in her mind. When might she again be thrust into that upside-down, backward universe? She wondered if the sense would ever leave her.

Her inability to link faces, voices, and names was the source of her unique problem, and it was pathological. The identifying features of those she met occupied distinctly separate (and leaky) buckets in her brain. She accommodated her unusual handicap by sticking to data and waiting until data's secrets spoke clearly.

The summer she was thirteen, her family moved and Cece found an upside to her limitation. In the Midwest, her father had missed Spumoni ice cream, a regional favorite (vanilla, pistachio, and cherry together in one chunk-filled box). Their first night in their new place, near where her father had grown up, he bought two boxes but—it being summer—both boxes melted. Once they refroze, Cece held a bread knife over the stove's flame, then sliced cross-sections from each re-hardened block. She then documented the complex samples with a Polaroid camera. Colors and flavors flowed but did not fully mingle. Some inclusions sank; others floated. On a basement rec room easel blackboard, Cece gave her first lecture, serving each sweet example to her sibling-students only after she had fully described how it had come to be the way it was.

Cece's unconventional interests and abilities amused a small circle of female acquaintances not scared, bored, or offended by them. She could picture abstract problem spaces quickly, and intuit rafts of complex ways they might change. For a time, she'd thought her skillset common. When she learned it was rare—and potentially lucrative—she considered physics, theoretical math, aeronautical engineering, high finance, and even detective work. Finally, she fell in love with the tranquil pace and tactile beauty of glacial geology. Like melted ice cream, huge masses of ice and rock flowed and warped, expanded and shrank—very slowly. Temperature, pressure, chemistry, and microscopic inclusions (pollen, dust, algae) varied in telltale ways on different rhythms, but all of them slowly as well. Few people had the patience for it. Cece found it endlessly fascinating.

Only in grad school did Cece accept that her gift came at the expense of social skills women were expected to deploy with fluent grace. One night, when Cece was out cold after double all-nighters, her housemates borrowed putty from the Theater department and gently fastened pointy ears over her real ones. On her door's mini whiteboard, they taped Polaroids of her wearing them asleep and replaced "DO NOT DISTURB" with "Ms. Spock." When the nickname stuck Cece made it her own, but the reality which inspired it remained privately painful.

One especially promising man was dumbstruck when—on their third date—Cece forgot his name. It was on the tip of her tongue she protested, her thesis defense just months away. She had a lot on her mind. She asked him to give her three guesses. Shocked to discover that she wasn't joking, he cut the night short—politely, but still. Such a strange innate handicap seemed unfair. People were kinder to those missing something obvious, especially if they had done something noble and selfless to end up that way.

Still, logic made science fun, and there was no danger the universe would run out of obscure questions to answer and problems to solve. Once a year, in hope that students would remember her class, she made a fool of herself by reprising the Spock props. If some took up the baton of discovery, the world would be a better place. Nate's future depended on it— his progeny's too, though when the time came, she was loath to push for grandchildren and overfill the planet.

Cece took a long gulp of wine and dismissed her sense of unease at the crevasse images. The cure for brain blips was data. She pulled up the "Accidents in North American Mountaineering" app on her phone and re-read the Icefield entry. "The Columbia Glacier is a violently broken icefall, extremely treacherous to navigate, even under ideal conditions. Crevasse mishaps are a virtual certainty." She had copied the blunt sentence verbatim on her trip disclaimer. Except for one kid's picky lawyer parent (who sent her a long e-mail, receipt requested) she knew of no one it had stopped. Her glacier trips always had waiting lists.

She knew the Icefield's habits as well as she knew her husband's. She'd checked the site's database before, but in case something had been added recently, she checked it again. Several fatal accidents had occurred from 1945 to 1985, the period she'd surmised by the man's clothing. She would run her computer model to confirm, but none of them appeared to have taken place upstream in the ice from where this year's team had camped.

She drained her wine and closed her eyes. She hated loose ends. Think, Cece. Think. UBC pays you to solve complex, multi-dimensional puzzles no one cares about with utterly inadequate data and pass on those cognitive tricks to future generations. She re-awakened her phone and studied her jpegs. The man had been lying at an odd angle, most of him embedded too deep in the ice for her to chip for more clues and still get her team home that night. Did his family know he'd gone up there? When had they given up? Who had mourned him? The man's ring hand was hidden. Had he left a girlfriend or wife, perhaps even kids?

On one image she thought she saw something. The rope around the man's hips twisted deep and away into the ice. She fiddled with brightness and contrast, then zoomed in until she found the rope's barely visible end. Near it lay what looked like a separate, much shorter piece of the same rope. She'd been around glaciers for a quarter century. Such a length was useless and who would have cut it? Around it were rust stains. *Pitons?* Less than useless. And what the heck? It was tied up neatly in a bow. Discarded climbing detritus—dumped precisely here, next to the body. Something weird had happened. Her face flushed with a sudden intuitive theory.

Someone else had been there when this man died.

Thirty:
Jasper

June, 1970...

After a week in pure air, Otis was hungry for civilized odors. At the "Slow Jasper" sign, an olfactory barrage filled the car: bacon, coffee, pancakes. He cranked down the window and leaned out, dog-like, his face wet. In the hour or so since he'd left the Icefield parking lot, a chill drizzle had descended—a sign of more snow up high.

At a small white-trimmed brick building, he slowed to read a placard: "Sunday Pancake Breakfast: FREE!" A mossy sign near it read, "Pastor Eric Connett Dupin." A midget steeple reminded Otis of the inflatable chest-high Bozo-the-Clown punch-down toy Billy had thrilled to receive one Christmas. To see how tough it was, Otis had popped it with a pin. When Billy refused to go along with his freak accident story, Otis had popped *him* with a quick shove.

A line of ragged men in sweatshirts darkened by rain and grime snaked toward the church's side door. Other men in narrow ties and short-sleeved shirts rushed boxes of food from a rusty car, past them, inside. Otis hobbled to the back of the line. Beards and sun-battered faces made most of the men appear three times his age (and double theirs). Wishing for his Red Sox cap, he shielded his face against the drizzle. *Nebraska.* He was from *Nebraska.*

Inside, in flowered aprons, short-haired women tended rows of steam tables. Years of Job-like patience serving moral suasion with hot food had failed to stem a tide of stinky, tipsy, obdurate souls who, the last few years especially, had overrun their small, once-tidy community. Practiced smiles hid private urges to reclaim Sunday mornings for romance novels, mugs of

161

tea, and phone calls to grandchildren in Vancouver and Toronto whom they feared were forgetting them.

"Not much of a Father's Day," said the man ahead of Otis.

"I guess," Otis said. "I'd forgotten until someone woke me."

"I hate when they clear the benches. Bad night?"

"Bad week."

"Mmm," the man said in a kind-sounding way. He indicated the door ahead. "This thing's a life-saver. My kids used to cook me pancakes."

"What happened?"

"She took them."

"I'm sorry. We used to make pancakes for my dad."

"Why did you stop?"

"We got older." Otis had been only an infant when Henry started what became tradition. He couldn't forget how it ended. Billy had been tending the bacon, but left it to take a call from his girlfriend. The pan erupted in flames. Otis ran in, smothered the fire, and threw the mess out the back door, but the neighbor's dog found it, seared its tongue, and got sick. His parents got the vet bill *and* a lawsuit to put up a fence. Father's Day. This year the thought felt doubly heavy. Today *would* have been his first—the baby a week old—except now, forever, it wasn't.

The line inched forward. On his first helping, Otis recalled Ulrich's campground pancakes and the self-timed photo Ulrich had snapped with him on the glacier. On his third plate, he recalled the Super Colossal Pancake Special at the Grand Island diner and the blue-eyed waitress, crying goodbyes. *No way.* Could it be the same girl? Had he glimpsed Ulrich from behind with her a week before he met him?

With nowhere better to go, Otis attended the service, jerking awake at the final 'Amen'. He would have sold his soul to keep sleeping. Across the sanctuary, he spied just-in-time Mercedes couple. His last thumbed ride; his rescuers. Explaining his injuries would be an I-told-you-so chore and also risk exposing his new identity. He scurried out before they saw him.

At a nearby motel, he paid extra to check in early. In his room, a cadaverous mix embraced him: mildew, smoke, stale sweat. He pulled the moth-ravaged orange-brown curtains closed, hung the Do Not Disturb sign, and ran a hot bath. Only when the water chilled and seeped down to leave a dark ring did he wake. He should call his father. *Later.* He dried and crawled into bed.

⚬⚬⚬⚬⚬⚬⚬

Crisp steps clacked on concrete. Dress shoes. A shadow moved past a gap in the curtains. "Mr. Sterbender?" A breathy stage whisper, female, familiar. A few soft taps at the door. Otis breathed through his mouth. The bedsprings would squeak if he moved. "Mr. Sterbender? It's Mrs. Wood. From the church? I didn't want to disturb you, but the ladies put together a bit of food for you: apples, sandwiches, chocolate, some pop. For your trip? I hope you like deviled ham. I put it on ice out here so it keeps. I'll be going now." She paused. "You would be most welcome next week at church if you're still in town then. God bless you, Mr. Sterbender."

Otis waited for Mrs. Wood's steps to fade. In such a small town, she and Mercedes couple, and Ranger Doug and his son-in-law Dr. Shields, plus the motel proprietor probably all knew one another. He was surrounded. Naked, he limped to fetch the food, glad like a hungry beast would be after beating a baited snare.

Thirty-One:
Smiling Tiger

⊙tis ate, dressed, then opened the curtains. Low sunlight lit the walls. He lugged Ulrich's things in from the car, eager to learn enough to perform the Ulrich illusion under closer scrutiny than he'd endured so far. Curious, he opened a box labeled, "Humble." Inside, an exultant tiger dominated an envelope from The Humble Oil and Refining Company. Otis extracted a single sheet of matching letterhead dated February 7th, 1970.

The paper was bright and soft like old bleached sheets.

"Dear Mr. Sterbender: Per our recent phone conversation, we expect to deploy new pipeline route survey crews the first week of July. It is my earnest expectation and hope that we may include you in this history-making infrastructure project, vital to our nation's future."

Mr. William C. Washington, (Humble's Director of Artcic Operations) had signed with the kind of splotchy aggressive scrawl peculiar to confident men used to moving mountains with fountain pens. The salary he offered Ulrich was higher than Otis would have guessed—in the stratospheric range of the transcendent beings at Morrison-James, but outdoors. Otis had never dared hope that such a confluence of adventure and money existed.

Another letter, posted ten days later, was also from Mr. Washington. "We're delighted to receive your acceptance, Ulrich. Upon your arrival in Anchorage, please contact Miss Brenda Collins for your field assignment. Meantime, as you complete your studies, I hope the enclosed items help you feel part of our Humble Oil team!"

Otis set the letters aside and fished further through the same box but found no evidence of a face-to-face interview. Could he pose his way into Ulrich's job? The thought hadn't occurred to him until just now, but why

164

not? Even if Ulrich *had* traveled to Alaska—or a recruiter down to Nebraska—he and Ulrich looked similar enough. In such a big company, Ulrich was likely just a name on the payroll. Who would challenge him based on months-old memories? Besides, if he left the job empty, Humble might make inquiries to find him. How hard could surveying be? He'd once helped his uncle fence his Maine goat farm. He simply had to be a good company man like his father: not make waves, not draw attention, show up on time.

Near the bottom of the box, a goofily grinning Humble tiger dominated a jigsaw puzzle titled "Great Moments in American History," and a board game: "Northwest Passage!" On its cover, an elongated oil tanker, the S.S. Manhattan, stood red and erect, thrusting through slabs of Arctic sea ice. Behind the caricature, between a Canadian and an American flag, another Humble tiger beamed. Otis laughed. The tiger wore earmuffs. A map in the game box showed the tanker's maiden voyage, from a Philadelphia shipyard to Alaska's North Slope via the Canadian Arctic and back last August. Otis had heard nothing of it, its fanfare eclipsed by Apollo 11 victory festivities and also by Woodstock. From a history class, he recalled the Franklin expedition disaster a century prior. Two British Navy ships had vanished somewhere in Canada's Arctic Archipelago. Only sixty years later did a man fleeing creditors make the marine transit successfully—a feat not repeated again until the Second World War. Why was Humble pouring money into a pipeline on land if the Manhattan's trip had been as viable as the farcical tiger implied? But what did he care if they paid him?

Otis closed the corporate box, eager for subtler clues to Ulrich's life. Otis had once played a silent bit part in a junior high production of My Fair Lady. He'd known better than to audition for Henry Higgins who—like all the other lead actors—possessed an effervescent self-assurance in real life as well as on stage. Otis was glad that unlike those roles, he could take his time, prepare for each audience he faced, and improvise galore.

Inside a box labeled "Nebraska," tucked inside the oldest of Ulrich's journals was a 1961 "Boys' Life" cover. On joining the Boy Scouts, Otis had received a subscription too. He'd thrown all his copies away. One of the articles featured on the cover was an Eisenhower retrospective.

The cover picture was equally retrograde.

In a gym devoid of females, a boy in white canvas wash-and-wear shoes grasped free-hanging rings. "TEAM," read his pristine-white T-shirt—as did all the rest, including a sculpted Phys-Ed instructor who clapped keep-at-it approval. Henry had made Eagle Scout, but Otis had endured Scouts for the camping trips. Only when threatened with expulsion had he ticked off a few merit badges. How far had Ulrich gone with it? Why had he saved *this* cover that positively *dripped* structure and optimism? Otis searched for more clues.

Ulrich had kept journals for years. One dated the same month as the Boys Life cover helped explain why he'd kept it. "Boys here are weak, they cannot do high bar or rings! I won a speed rope-climbing contest. Rufus got scared up high. The other boys tease him about his husky size pants. Mr. Brutus yelled too, but Rufus did not let go. I climbed up to help him down. At recess, the monkey bar boys asked me to teach leg-grapple tricks."

Interesting. Otis' attempts at elementary school monkey bar battles had helped spark his interest in wrestling. He skipped backward several pages.

"Gymnasium not like Berlin. Only throw, catch, and hit. American 'football' has almost no kicks! In flag football, some tackle instead. Aunt Greta took me to dentist for a chipped tooth and doctor to stitch my lip. She read Isaiah 26:3 and said not to be upset when they call me 'Kraut.'"

Otis winced at the glimpse into the hazing Ulrich had endured. He skipped further back to an entry first written in German, then later rewritten in English. "School bus first day very hot. To sit I tried but the seat a boy blocked. He then punched me. (Devlen and I are friends now. Prayers answered!) Cottonwood fluff came in windows and stuck in girls' hair. Devlen has a dark tan. Many boys tease him. He chews tobacco."

Otis wondered how Ulrich had made peace—*even friends*—with both bullies and victims. Terrified to tattle and stir up the ire of the roving pack *he* had faced daily at school, Otis had offered his parents a terse fib about "a silly fall off my bike." He'd hit a bump and lost control beside a poison ivy patch, he said, but his silence bothered him as the same band of bullies moved on to harm other targets.

Otis flipped to the first entry, also translated by Ulrich's hand. "My bedroom at Aunt Greta and Uncle Walter's house is at third floor. Windows on all sides see far. It smells of paint, cedar, and old books. Big and soft is my bed. Brass is the frame. On two walls, English books fill tall wood shelves. I want to read them all and go to college!"

Otis imagined the Grand Island house with horizon-wide pastoral views. He wanted to read more, but instead he set the journals aside. He needed to cram for the Humble job if he was to start Ulrich's job July first, ten days away. He browsed a box of textbooks: Physics, Chemistry, Calculus, Advanced Geometry, Sedimentary Geology, Infrastructure Project Management. The diagrams in Fundamentals of Hydrology seemed straightforward enough. Otis had dug backyard holes and watched water seep in. How difficult could this subject be?

With the ice from Mrs. Wood's food, he numbed his aching ankle and lay back to read the Principles of Civil Engineering textbook.

Before finishing the first paragraph, he was asleep.

Thirty-Two:
Summit Postcards

A lone on McKinley's summit, Otis dropped his gaze from the sunset to his frozen feet. *Small price to pay.* He could bivouac until sunrise. He jolted awake, his motel mattress wet from ice melt.

A nearby train shook the room. Clack-clack, clack-clack, clack-clack. He sat up, ran his hand through his hair, and plucked the doctor's card from the nightstand where the clock radio indicated six forty-five. *Monday first thing.* He wished he didn't need help, but every part of him hurt.

He threw on clothes and drove to the address: a rough-shingled house with a wrap-around porch. Mist rose from wet grass. A wood sign listed a dentist and "Dr. Ephrem Hoyt Shields, MD," in white neatly carved letters.

The front door swung open as Otis approached.

"Ulrich?" A trim, blond bearded man extended a hand. "Eph Shields."

Eye-corner creases completed an impression of autumn alders on faraway cliffs. Otis drew back and displayed his bruised twisted fingers; Dr. Shields winced. "Oh dear. Well, then. We'll see about that." He ushered Otis in to an examining room and indicated a chair but Otis leaned against a stainless steel table and waited until Dr. Shields sat on a rotating stool.

Otis read upside down from Dr. Shields' clipboard:

Ulrich Sterbender, June 22, 1970, 7:00AM.

"Doug said you were in a scrape up on the Icefield?"

"I suppose." Otis tried to cross his arms, but it hurt too much.

"It's treacherous up there. 'Live to climb another day,' is my motto."

Uh oh. A climber meant more ways to get this wrong. He wondered what else Dr. Shields' park ranger father-in-law had told him. "Everything happened so fast," Otis began. "My partner was ahead of me when he fell. I

168

got dragged, but then self-arrested. It feels like I went fifteen rounds with Ali." He flared his lips to reveal two broken teeth.

"Were you and your partner fighting?"

Otis recalled his morning spat with Ulrich and the weird Bible thing about snow. "Only little climber squabbles," he said. "You know." A sudden strong urge to cry surprised him; he swallowed it with a nervous laugh.

"I'm afraid I *don't* know. Tell me. Is he hurt? Is he OK?"

"No. I mean, yes. We got separated. When I got down, he was gone."

"Doug said he's from Boston. Have you spoken with him?"

"Not recently."

"I see." Dr. Shields wrote on his clipboard, then stood and reached for Otis' blistered face. Otis flinched. "Quite a scorch you have there. Glacier sun is unforgiving. What else can you tell me that might help me treat you?"

Otis worked to slow his hammering heart before Dr. Shields used his stethoscope on it. This was the crux.

"After I fell I blacked out. I thought I might be dead."

"It seems you were wrong. You probably suffered a concussion. Between that and your eyes, and what I'll prescribe you for pain, you should avoid bright lights, and not drive for a week."

"I got here OK," Otis protested, thinking how he'd woven slowly down the empty highway, squinting and blinking, trying not to cross the double yellow too far or too often.

"Doctor's orders. We have a spare room. My father-in-law does too."

Great. They were all in on it, just like he'd feared.

"Thanks, but I paid ahead at the motel."

"Well, tomorrow then. But first, let's see what we're dealing with." He handed Otis a johnny and stepped out. Otis stripped; he was still struggling to wrap himself in the thin blue gown when Dr. Shields knocked and popped back in. "Just for my records, what was your partner's name?"

"Otis," Otis said. "Otis Fletcher. Nice guy. I already miss him."

Dr. Shields patched Otis up, then passed him over to his dental associate. Otis declined both of their offers to dinner. He felt bad about that, and about giving them a false address in Alaska to send their generously discounted bills but—doctors' orders or no—he had to leave. Not only did Ulrich's job start soon—a hard two thousand mile drive away—but such a tightly-knit hamlet would surely compare notes and burn

169

his only draft haven: Ulrich's name. Then what redeeming purpose would Ulrich's death serve?

Back in his motel room—two teeth capped, ankle braced, and one arm in a sling—Otis went through Ulrich's suitcase, its contents neatly folded and clean. He tried Ulrich's polished brown shoes (too small) then a brown tweed jacket that smelled of mothballs, its elbows patched with navy blue iron-ons. He stretched out both arms to check the fit in the mirror. Perfect: sleeves to the wrist bone at the base of his thumbs. Suddenly, Ulrich's serene face flashed in his mind. He jumped back and shrugged off the jacket, creeped out by whatever that was. He would drop the suitcase in the church bin on his way out of town.

At nine o'clock Anchorage time, he dialed Mr. Washington's secretary.

"You sound different, Mr. Sterbender," she said with cordial curtness.

"I had dental work," Otis mumbled, as if Novocain altered accents.

"We hope you feel better soon, Mr. Sterbender. We expect you next week for training, then out in the field. Bring boots and bug spray. There's no sense getting an apartment. On days off you'll be our guest at the Fairbanks company bunkhouse. I've heard it's cozy. Have a safe trip."

Otis bought what she recommended, plus food, tools, a cooler, ice, and a cheap watch. Losing Henry's watch grieved him more than losing Ulrich. He recognized the thought as ugly but there it was. He'd known Henry longer, and there was nothing he could do about either one. Seeing his arm sling, a service station attendant helped him fill two metal Jerry cans with "petrol," and another with water, then wedged them all behind his car seats.

Later that day Otis called home with belated Father's Day wishes but he was working late again, his mother said. Before Otis could ask her to pass on his love, she said she would. Now came the hard part. Her nose for deception limited him to truth. He thought of how Pentagon spokesmen droned, stiff on the news. "I'm currently stationed in a remote location out west. We will be moving out soon but I'm not at liberty to disclose more." His activities were physically taxing, he said, but he was sleeping and eating well, getting good medical care.

"Is your work classified?"

"You could say that."

"Are they sending you to Vietnam?"

"No, Mom. Definitely not. That's out of the question."

"Oh!" she exclaimed, "I'm so..." She breathed fast puffy sighs. "I'm so relieved. That's simply... wonderful. Your father will be happy as well."

Otis was sure he'd done the right thing, but only if he kept to the discipline he'd begun on the Cambridge sidewalk could he maintain her peace. Still, an honest hint might help. "I'll be living in a tent in a cold climate," he said. "Don't wait by the mailbox. I may be some time."

After hanging up, he examined Ulrich's unsent postcards. All had "Columbia Icefield" in bold type over a glacial panorama with a grand red-roofed hotel in the foreground. Three were complete; one was blank. With Canadian postage affixed already, he had to decide before reaching Alaska. He wanted to send Davey the fourth one, but for now it had to remain a souvenir. Late in the spring, Davey had written to Otis at school. Atlanta was nice. His baby half-sister was cute, but sometimes a pest. His dad was teaching him how to play baseball. They'd hiked up Stone Mountain together. Otis wanted to tell him how happy he was for him, but Davey had not shared his new address. Otis had tried to locate him, but the directory assistance operator had said she was sorry. Of the twelve hundred Greens in the Atlanta phone book, all three *Jonas* Greens were unlisted.

Otis scanned Ulrich's three completed postcards for his name, relieved but miffed not to find it. Was *Frau Sophie Sterbender* in East Berlin Ulrich's mother? Probably. On the card to Calia, Ulrich had written that he loved her, and wished he was with her, but they must be patient—apart for now. The third card was addressed to, "Greta Schrank, c/o The Farmview Rest Home, Grand Island, Nebraska." The script was huge: "Dear Aunt Greta. These mountains are very big and snowy. Uncle Walter would have been amazed to see them. Love, Ulrich. (P.S., Have a nurse help you remember.)"

Ulrich had written "Waren hier!" (We are here!) on each with an arrow toward the Icefield. Eerie, but hardly a map and 'we' could mean anyone. Did he dare send them? They merely confirmed what Dr. Shields and Ranger Doug thought they knew: that Ulrich was alive. The glacier was vast. Ulrich's uncle was dead, his parents locked behind the Iron Curtain, and Aunt Greta lived behind a mental veil just as impervious. Sending the cards would put them off. The Jasper postmark would clinch it. Ulrich was en route to Alaska as planned. Calia would surely need more—likely soon—but he would think of something.

He dropped Ulrich's three cards into a red Canada post box slot then returned to the motel. Before shutting off the light, he packed the car, set the clock radio alarm, and dug out his just-in-case stash of Bennies, leftover from exams. He couldn't let Dr. Shields' well-meaning fears run his life. He set the small plastic baggie beside his car keys. He could do this. He *would* do this. He was a wild thing. A good job, mountains, and freedom awaited.

Thirty-Three:
Waiting for Word

Grand Island, Nebraska, earlier that same day...

Calia Doe Leuchter had lived two lives. She liked her Nebraska one better. If she kept her mouth shut and her smile sweet, most people smiled sweetly back and let her pass as a native. Only her childhood friend Philis Troy knew of her nostalgia every April for seats at major league baseball games. Only Philis knew that, in dirt parking lots or driving long empty roads, Calia got wistful for culture—dashing up from the subway on her way home, downtown from prep school, to visit a world-class museum or two. Only Philis knew that her blackmailing seared-conscience thief of a mother had taken her to Italy for a whole summer or how horseback riding, tennis, and golf lessons had once been her routine. Only Philis knew that one of her mother's man friends had staged sham Sunday Times Magazine fashion shoots with scantily-clad models not much older than Calia right outside her bead-curtain bedroom "door" in their SoHo Manhattan loft.

Philis knew how to listen and when to keep secrets.

As Calia toted plates of generic food to diner patrons—semi-retired locals, a steady stream of truckers, or the occasional sunburned hitchhiker: men fighting loneliness with coffee refills—she tried not to dwell on memories of tasty take-out, cooked in immigrant restaurants on every block. In the minds of most folks here—unless someone they knew had fought for freedom there—the nations from which such people hailed were colored blobs on a globe. Often, as she delivered a plate, she mused on the shapes of eggs, pancakes, or meatloaf: Pakistan, Bangladesh, or India? Belgium or The Belgian Congo? Portugal, Brazil, or Mozambique? Few who ate the bland fare knew the geographic (much less the colonial) histories of the places that filled her mental games, but most were solid, trustworthy people. Only a few times, when she'd let herself talk too much, had a patron noted her faint Brooklyn accent. Such unmaskings made her blush with nostalgia.

The two wildly different places lived inside of her, their co-existence as improbable as her conception. Her first memories were of Dodgers' games with her father a year before the team (and the two of them) decamped west in the early fall of 1957. Last month, she'd passed two milestones she expected would keep her here. She'd turned eighteen and gotten engaged. A little too engaged. She'd felt godly sorrow at stepping past bounds, and confessed that in prayer (with Ulrich away, another prenuptial lapse was unlikely) yet she still battled longings for what they'd tasted too soon—and for his first card or letter from his trip north.

Ulrich had been the first to suggest that Calia might be dyslexic. (She could read only ten minutes without a headache.) Whether she was or not, she was grateful for his support, typing her papers. Though she hadn't taken a class since graduating high school, she continued to build up her sizable deck of vocabulary flash cards and the Bible her teacher Miss Hansen had given her back in Manhattan had gotten dog-eared. She reserved the rest of her reading stamina for Ulrich's letters. Her teachers had encouraged her toward college, but they had other plans. Kids were a blessing (neither of them enjoyed being an orphan) and jobs like his on the Alaska pipeline would support a passel of them. She also felt she would be a good mother because she knew a catalog of things never to say, do, or be in that role.

Calia had moved to Grand Island twice. The first time she'd been whisked here by her father. (Stealing her from her Brooklyn kindergarten rest hour to hop a train west with a suitcase full of embezzled cash had perhaps been his greatest departure from prudence.) The second time she'd moved here, just shy of her thirteenth birthday, her mother had handed her off outside a notary public's office. After the Troys signed the paperwork, Philis had joked that Calia's mother had released her back to Nebraska like a jigged non-native trout. No, Calia had retorted, her mother had returned her like an ugly Macy's Christmas sweater. Later, she regretted being so harsh.

"Heart of the country, heart of the state," customers liked to quip about Grand Island to spark chitchat on the rare days when the weather was too mild for comment. It was hardly heaven, but poised (some said) between two temporal versions—bucolic collegiate Lincoln two hours east and the striking Rockies six hours west. Yet it was home, and bound be more so.

Life here was spacious, soothing, and static. No late-night shouts, whistles, or breaking glass; no sirens, car horns, or jackhammers. The traffic was eerily thin, the land obstinately horizontal. Only on a south wind did the faint whine of interstate tires compete with the clatter and groan of long trains. Sonic booms sometimes rattled windows. (That had taken some getting used to.) But sunrises often felt like refreshing breaths, sunsets like contented sighs. The daytime sky between them often felt like floating atop a pristine pool, while nights here could be eerily dark, vast, and vivid. If she looked up, Calia often felt that without effort, she could float up into the stars (some nights it felt like billions) and never be lonely again.

She glanced at the calendar beside the cash register. It had been six years, seven months and seven days since she and Philis had found her father after school as if napping on the carpet—except that his face was blue. Philis had run next door to tell her mom who was already crying about President Kennedy. Best the doctors could tell, the two men had died the same hour, though the violence to her father had all been internal: "a sudden, massive coronary," she'd overheard the ambulance people say.

Where were you when you heard?

Inwardly, Calia still laugh/cried each time someone forced her to recall: enduring fifth period English, and *her* first period. She found it hard to imagine another day as relentlessly, comically awful but if one came, she trusted her heavenly Father would stay with her through it as He had before. Until then, she was thankful He'd given her some of her earthly father's alacrity because such a demeanor made waitress tips enough to live on.

Even at age five, back in Brooklyn, Calia had sensed that her parents were enemies. When her father was home, her mother had taunted him mercilessly—on top of her serial adultery, heavy drinking, and manic depression. Calia had admired her father to the moon, yet the same intellect that enabled him to craft actuarial tables without a slide rule and retain decades-old baseball box scores in his head also drove him to overthink commonsense things.

If he'd hired a half-decent lawyer (he certainly had the money) and faced her mother in court, custody would have been less of a long shot than for most men, but in the Lord's providence, he had not done that. Instead, he'd hidden Calia from her mother then from foster care—her last-ditch, scorched-earth threat. Calia admired him for those unflinching efforts on her behalf, but his death from the stress of shielding her had left her angry *and* unprotected.

Philis' parents, Mr. and Mrs. Troy had done their best to keep Calia in Grand Island after he died, but without legal standing they could only stall. In effect, her mother had legally kidnapped her back to New York at age eleven, still mourning. Only after her mother methodically stole the trust fund her father had set up for Calia from *his* embezzlement from his former employer did her mother lose interest in her only child.

Calia blamed her mother for her father's death, but it no longer surprised her that no one else saw it. Once her mother had found them, she'd blackmailed him, using custody (plus his crimes) as cudgels. His heart had literally broken. Yes, he'd been big (massively so near the end) but also jolly and she thought, healthy. She'd watched her mother pull off far more intricate schemes then bat her eyelashes and walk away, playing the victim. It was obvious she'd planned the hands-free method to take him out. Calia's teacher Miss Hansen had been the only one to talk to Calia about forgiving the unforgiveable and at last—understanding how much *she'd* been forgiven by God in Christ—Calia had done so. The joy-soaked change had been so abrupt and total that she'd felt lighter than air that day in Miss Hansen's Manhattan church.

Calia had harbored hope and prayed for her mother, but only two postcards came between the last time she saw her and the day a short obit arrived with no note. Its cagey wording ("a sudden illness") made Calia suspect an OD. It described "a memorial gathering of friends" to spread her ashes in the Pacific. After her mother's latest beau Steve caught a big break with a San Francisco band that later headlined at Woodstock, he had lured her into drugs.

The idea of her mother in hell made her sad, but there was nothing she could do anymore; plus, one couldn't be sure. Before becoming a Christian, she would have wished Steve in hell too, his forehead tattooed in warning but now she wrote reminders on the kitchen calendar to pray for him and asked her roommate Ethel to hold her accountable by praying with her.

Such full-life tumult would never happen in her home, Calia vowed. She and Ulrich would marry, move into the big house, and fill it with kids. Then Grand Island would *truly* be home. In the meantime, she checked her mailbox twice a day, eager to hear how his climbing trip went.

Thirty-Four:
No Day Like It

Otis set out north, thrilled to be moving again. A town called Grand Cache reminded him of Grand Island, then of Ulrich's homily about storehouses. It wearied him to think he could never share *his* cache of secrets—not even someday with a wife. After only a few hours, midday glare got to his eyes. Seeking a break, he turned down a gravel track. Tall dry weeds whacked the car. He parked by a turbid torrent strewn with bleached tree trunks, their roots entwined. Nearby, logging trucks thundered across a rusted truss bridge. Occasionally, two of them would bellow jake brakes at one another and rev their engines, playing chicken for the wood-planked single lane—face-offs that reminded Otis of wrestling match moments when all grips came loose.

He unfolded a map and traced the river's blue line to its source among the Rockies' highest glaciers. Only a tenth of those who tried for Mount Robson's summit reached it. Mindful that its meltwater might bring him luck, Otis stripped to his skivvies and perched on smooth stones until the river's cold numbed his battered legs.

After he dried off, he went through more of Ulrich's boxes. An unmailed letter to Calia detailed Ulrich's drive from Nebraska to Canada. The picnic table letter! "I just met Otis: a Boston man who climbs. I sense he is here because of draft trouble. His number is two. Let's pray for him."

What? Otis re-read it. Pious Ulrich had snooped his wallet?! What if Otis had mentioned the draft after all? *Man, I drew a short straw last December. How did it go for you? Oh, I did OK.: three-fifty-one.* Otis would have been too jealous to see straight; they would never have roped up. Then why had Ulrich gone along? Had he been sure Otis did not know *his* number?

Sending the letter unfinished seemed stupid. Calia would wonder why it was incomplete *and* she'd have Otis' name and draft number to gnaw on. Sending her a confession to accompany it would ease his conscience, but even if he did it anonymously, playing the bad news messenger would put him at risk and nullify his draft card. Plus, he'd have to scrap Ulrich's original; that didn't feel right. What was the rush? Nothing could change the past. He slid the letter into a box of typing paper. Let her be happy a little longer. Once he got to Alaska, he would alter identifying details, and the date, add a short coda in Ulrich's style, and send it off.

Further down in the box, a receipt confirmed an Anchorage PO Box Ulrich had set up. Otis would remind her of it. Later, he could cancel it and let return-to-sender notifications paint the picture. No one had to tell her outright that Ulrich was dead. She could simply infer that he'd lost interest. Engagements sometimes didn't work. That was life. She would get over it.

Otis wrapped Ulrich's typewriter in his sleeping bag to cushion it for the long bumpy drive. With his Swiss Army knife, he sliced a crevice under a backseat cushion and slid in his driver's license and Dirkden library card. He moved his cash to Ulrich's wallet then, on a flat rock that poked up from the stream, he lit a small fire and burned his own wallet—with his draft card and Louisabeth photo inside then sloshed the ashes off into the rushing water.

Late the next evening, the verdant Yukon stretched empty, sun dipping but failing to set. A caribou herd swarmed the horizon like a blanket of ants. A dust plume chased the car. Rabbits darted, none yet crushed by his wheels.

Soon, at the U.S. border, he would face a test trickier and more consequential than his quick jousts with Canada's best. The gravel washboard road made his injuries throb. Earlier, he'd split a pain pill in half to take the edge off, but it made him too sleepy to drive and when he'd stopped to nap, hordes of mosquitoes found ways into the car and swelled one eye half shut with bites. He'd taken an upper to get himself going again, but when he stopped to refuel from a Jerry can with a funnel, he could have sworn a grizzly crouched behind a bush snorting in German and brandishing an ice axe. Terrified, Otis had sped off, the tank half-full, his hands and clothes smelly with splashed gasoline; the fumes added to a constant low-level headache.

With no sharp demarcation to alert him to his most recent pills wearing off, his ruminations drifted into gossamer incoherence. *Ulrich must have died quickly. Nothing else he could have done. He'd been forced to think of himself, save himself. Save who? He had to keep the names distinct: Ulrich, Otis. But if they were them, then who was thinking? He should call his family. Whose family? He mustn't let on where he was. Where who was? Him. Who's him? The body. What body? Where was he? Whose body? What had he done?*

He envisioned blood seeping from Ulrich's corpse. A grey finger beckoned. He shook his head to rid himself of the specter. Eager for company, he spun the radio dial. Static. Chocolate would help. He groped at the snack bag on the passenger seat. Its contents had melted and oozed. He licked his fingers and returned his hand to the wheel. He could clean up near people, a truck stop. He cranked down the window for fresh air. When he grew sleepy again, he slapped himself in the face. Sunburn! The pain more than revived his attention.

You killed him. The thought formed like steam, ephemeral but distinct, accusative like in the crevasse. *Don't try to deny it*—Mr. Van Thaile's line with him on the detention bench. *Come on Fletcher, come clean.* Otis objected. *I didn't mean to!* His bad breath seemed close and real. *We hear that a lot, Fletcher. Why, I'll bet you're pure as the driven snow!* The voice burst with derision. *Ya' think?* Like a skipping record, the phrase repeated. *Ya' think? Ya' think?*

Otis startled, tires thumping in rhythm. Again he protested. *I was about to pass out. The rope was cutting me in half. I couldn't have held on one more second.*

OK, so why not stomp an SOS in the snow? Use a shiny cup to signal? Ask the ranger to send a rescue team up?

Otis was about to respond with objections when he thought of Coach's advice. An opponent setting the tempo was never good. Going on offense was vital. *I risked my life,* Otis insisted, still inside his mind. *I revived him the day before. In a way, I earned his name.*

Nothing came back. Mr. Van Thaile's voice was gone. Instead, doubt hacked at his bravado. The body would eventually emerge like a freezer-burned veal chop. How long might that take? He'd heard of century-old bodies melting from glaciers in Europe, but was this glacier faster? What if say, ten years from now—once he'd set up a life: wife and kids, job and dog, a modest Cape house with a lawn—the phone rang with bad news. His life would come crashing down.

No. He was scaring himself. Ulrich had brought his camera on their Snow Dome excursion, but a picture without names was *not* worth a thousand words. What about Ulrich's pocket spiral notebook and pencil? Otis didn't recall finding them in the tent. What if Ulrich had written his name? *Oh God*, Otis thought and abruptly his Philosophy 101 professor popped into his mind to take over from Vice Principal Van Thaile.

Come now. Really? You think you're the first student to bring "god" into my classroom? Don Saager, PhD, had mimed air quotes: small letter 'g' god. Bushy grey eyebrows matched his wild hair, a brown tweed jacket over a maroon turtleneck that day. He'd run a gnarled finger down the class roster. *Fletcher, is it? Freshman?* He'd leveled a withering stare. *The boy whose wrestling prowess hoodwinked Admissions into lowering their standards?* He'd grunted and mimed a bicep flex and the class had erupted in laughter. Otis had thought he would move on to another subject or victim, but pacing like a caged tiger Professor Saager had redoubled his rant.

"Lest we be too hard on Mr. Fletcher here, let us ponder for a moment the value of physical dominance in the fertile young male. If Mr. Fletcher were allowed to kill his opponents instead of merely pinning them would he enjoy an evolutionary advantage?" Puzzled expressions had spread around the room. "Yes," someone yelled. "Excellent. Presuming he was good with the ladies, we would expect many well-muscled children. His genes would be better off. You see, death is the way of the world. Natural in every species. Let the fittest survive. Prevent overpopulation. Make room for the new! Evolution is vital to progress. Would anyone care to dispute me?"

No one had. The memory made Otis cringe.

Professor Saager's persona assailed Otis again, forceful and buttery.

So you killed Ulrich. So what? Fate handed you what you wanted on a silver platter. No Vietnam. That reminds me of a first-century locust-eating freak we cover in my False World Religions seminar.

In Otis' mind, Professor Saager paused to wink.

But be that as it may Mr. Fletcher, that body you're worried about is very well hidden. Trust me; I know of these things. Relax, live your life, enjoy your freedom!

It did make some sense, Otis thought and with that realization, relief washed over him. Time passed. Suddenly, his head snapped up, the car skidding through sand. He yanked the wheel and braked hard and the car's back end slid around, leaving the car stalled, its suspension rocking by a steep embankment. Below, a swamp littered with stumps reflected the late Arctic light. Trailing dust caught the car. Nearby, a raven flock relinquished a moose carcass, cawing in ravenous protest as they ascended.

Otis restarted the car. It rumbled louder. The muffler. Underneath, he strapped it back into place with a wire coat hanger. A few hours later, at a sign for "Destruction Bay," he took another upper. He disliked the paranoid hallucinations it produced, but it wouldn't be fair to his parents if something worse happened because he fell asleep at the wheel again.

Thirty-Five:
Cutting Away

Otis reached the Alaska border in thickening rain. A stern-faced guard in a long slicker and wide-brimmed hat waved Otis aside, then had him get out to open the Tempest's trunk. He said nothing about the bear claw marks. While Otis stood aside, another guard helped the first unload the car's contents. Otis moved to save Ulrich's typewriter from the mud but they barked at him to step back. Be cool, he thought. They could search the car all they liked. A few miles back, he'd moved his Otis license and Dirkden library card to his underwear. *Ulrich's* license, draft card, and job offer would argue for him here. Humble was vital to Alaska's future. The guards asked him long strings of linked questions.

Where did you cross *into* Canada? Why there? What time of day was it? What color was the border guard's hair? What have you done since? Where have you gone? Who have you met with? Otis was glad he'd rehearsed a plausible story. After an hour, the guards let him repack and go.

In Anchorage, he found a motel and slept all day and all the next night, unsure where he was when he woke until he read it on a bar of soap. He ironed a shirt, found a bank, and got in line—an easy errand compared to the border. So then why was he so nervous? He imagined himself and Ulrich as two sides of a coin, his luck bound to run out with more tosses.

Ahead of him, cigarette smoke ascended the arm of an older man in a red checked wool shirt. The man *two* ahead looked like a younger Mike Running Bear: black hair river-like below his shoulders. Facing them behind bronze bars, a freckled teller's face danced with energy. Another teller next to her looked mousy: demure fine short hair framed by thick glasses.

The smoker turned and coughed, ashy and loud. "Hold my place, will you?" He walked to a waist-high ashtray and pressed his cigarette into its fine white sand. Otis wondered whose job it was to clean and smooth it each night. The freckled teller beckoned to the raven-haired man who stepped forward and said something to her. She laughed, tossed her head back, and blushed. The smoker sidled over to Otis and muttered. "You see that? Can you believe it?"

"See what? Believe what?"

The smoker ticked off points on his stained fingers. "We give 'em land, defend it from the Japs, work our tails off to get statehood. And what do they do? Demand pipeline jobs or else handouts." He wheezed, red-faced then nearly blue. Otis was about to shout for help when the man recovered enough to finish his thought. "Now they want our ladies too. Disgusting."

"I see," Otis said. He shifted from foot to foot, silent, wary of making a fuss even as he wished that the man had been carried out on a stretcher with an oxygen mask over his face. Finally, the man turned away. Two weeks ago, Otis had despaired of returning to U.S. soil but now, back on it, home felt even further away. Alaska's frontier culture had sounded like it might be an easier place to hide than communal, by-the-book Canada but how long could he endure norms like this—so foreign to those he had known?

The owlish teller beckoned to the smoker who left Otis without saying goodbye. Otis moved ahead, velvet ropes to each side. In a nearby pink granite column, he caught his faint reflection. Contrary to his unease moments before, the stone's solidity gave him a sense that—far beyond any immediate worries—things would somehow be alright. The bank vault and typing sounds drew his attention and the sense of the world having something like a keel expanded, the bigot inconsequential. The war would end someday, with one side or both exhausted. The expansive sense lingered and grew—beyond Alaska, the earth, and the now-conquered moon—as if the cosmos had revealed its ballast. Civilizations would rise and fall as they had since the Pharaohs; people yet to be born would continue to flow like a great steady beautiful river. As the vision passed, Otis retained a sense like after a stop at a vast scenic vista to stretch his legs.

Bubbly as if she sensed it too, the owlish teller beckoned. "Good morning, sir! This month we are offering a free toaster to new customers who open an account with us with fifty dollars or more."

"Where I'm going I won't need one."

"For $100, you get steak knives. They're super nice."

"And you get a bonus?" The teller admitted she did. "Let's go for that then. Graduation, and his grandmother's gift seemed years ago.

"We'll need two pieces of identification."

Otis handed her Ulrich's license and draft card and quashed an impulse to try a German accent to make it all more believable.

"Thank you, Mr. Sterbender." The teller studied Ulrich's draft card. "My cousin drew 362 but he had already enlisted. You can do that, you know." Otis waited. "Now, if you'll put your John Hancock on this card, I'll match up your signatures and we'll have you on your way."

Otis pointed out his sling and splinted right hand.

"I'm afraid it may be a little wobbly."

"Oh, I am terribly sorry, Mr. Sterbender. The best you can do is fine."

Otis made a messy indistinct lefty scrawl that the teller accepted.

Later, steak knives under his good arm, Otis registered Ulrich with the Anchorage draft board. A man who looked like he'd fought in World War One and endured a stroke took his paperwork. "Thank you, Mr. Sterbender," he said. "I wish all young men were..." He struggled for a word, then looked at Otis admiringly. "Do inform us if you move." Otis knew he should feel like scum, but he didn't. He was official. And they would never call him.

At the post office, Otis retrieved a letter postmarked Grand Island and addressed to Ulrich in neat rounded script. Calia; had to be. What harm was there in indulging his curiosity? Ulrich had looked through *his* wallet without permission. Back at his motel, Otis used one of his new steak knives to slit the pink envelope. He removed Calia's letter and smoothed its pages.

Thirty-Six:
Like a Brother

⁘

Her unhurried handwriting flowed over three sheets.

"Dearest Ulrich: How I long for you to kiss me again with your mouth, for your love is better than wine! Because of the scent of your good ointments, your name is like ointment poured forth, therefore the virgins love you." Otis snorted, bemused. She'd filled the entire first page with racy poetic allusions. Her photo had given no hint of this side of her. The next page stunned him: "Oh that you were like a brother to me, who nursed at my mother's breasts! I would bring you to the house of my mother. I would give you spiced wine from the juice of my pomegranates!"

Brother? Mother? Was Calia Ulrich's sister?

The thought made Otis want to wash his hands, but if they were involved in incest, why be so elliptical about it in a private letter? Why talk in terms of exotic fruits? He had an idea. Once a month, he and his college housemates would procrastinate over a whisky or two by reading Playboy letters aloud and debating which ones were made-up. Calia's letter had a similar fictional spirit that piqued his curiosity to read on.

"I'm sure you'll not let S.O.S. tempt you to miss the great prize."

S.O.S.? Was she in trouble? And what "great prize" did she mean? Had Ulrich held an Irish Sweepstakes ticket or a Publishers' Clearinghouse entry?

"I should be more patient, Ulrich, trust God more, look to Him to renew my strength and not let myself grow weary as we run our separate paths. I know He has set us to run apart for now but I still miss you! You once said that no matter how far apart we are, we see the same moon and stars each night and the same sun each day. It was a wonder to me when you pointed that out—one of those things I'd never thought much about. And it's a comfort to me now. Each day I pray for you climbing mountains.

"That reminds me of the night we walked along the river that first time just us two. (Not the times with church.) I can't believe it's been a year! I told you how confusing it was coming here with Daddy as a girl, changing our names but how amazed I was seeing the Milky Way without city lights. That *serious* face of yours actually laughed. It had been like that for you too you said, coming from Berlin. And I was surprised because we're so different. You said you gave Uncle Walter and Aunt Greta an astronomy lesson from Genesis fifteen. When I came, I asked Daddy, "Who will pick up the spilled salt?" I don't recall saying it, but if he said so then it must be true. The stars remind me of your faith that God made us curious to discover His creation. When you help engineer things like the pipeline, I love that you want to do it well for God's glory."

This sounded more like the engaged couple he'd expected. The sibling thing had to be some secret code. But which big city had she come from? And why? Was her father still around? In what sense were she and Ulrich "running?" Did he do track? Did she? That would be odd. Otis knew of only one girl who ran after grade school. Then there was all the God stuff.

Within moments of meeting Ulrich, Otis knew he was religious. No surprise, Calia was too. Otis had no problem with that. Forced to accommodate Lucius, he'd come to see the benefits of a steady, scrupulously honest roommate. To read the private correspondence between two such otherwise intelligent people though highlighted something he'd long chafed at. Why waste a mind on impractical things? Why devote time, energy, and money to unprovable ephemera?

Some said all religions were mostly the same, but Otis had studied enough to know *that* wasn't true. It therefore came down to logic. Each religion made a few hard claims and so the number of those opposing absolutes meant that most of them *had* to be wrong. Draining that swamp with no assurance of finding a true one seemed pointless: all cattails and mud. Otis was willing to concede that some higher power might have set the universe in motion but if so, it had been on vacation for a long time, or preferred to stay subtle, or else it had quietly died. His last year in high school, Time Magazine's cover had asked, "Is God Dead?" Most at Deden-Fisher (and in Dirkden) seemed surprised that Time's editors would even bother to ask the question. How could an invisible he, she, or it be alive in anything other than peoples' imaginations?

Like a rogue wave, Henry's death had driven his parents back into a church habit, but only briefly; the sixties' outgoing tide had been unyielding. Within a year the Fletchers were sleeping late most Sundays, carving up a fat New York Times over brunch. That same tide made people like Ulrich and Calia objects of pity: boats high and dry, tilted on keels. Otis wanted to argue with her. What kind of god allowed Vietnam? And if "he" had *let* Vietnam happen, then how could "he" claim to be good? What was "he" good *for*, exactly? Believe whatever you like, Otis had concluded, just don't hurt people. Live and let live. And in that spirit, reading Calia's letter was proving a useful exercise in toleration—akin to the restraint he applied in certain museums, concerts, or restaurants where one ran across things not to one's taste but where it was rude to turn up one's nose too conspicuously.

Her letter continued. "How grand the stars must be up in the mountains! I want to hear all about your trip. Write soon, OK? Until we meet again amidst the great multitude no one can count (like the stars!) I remain your dear sister, and future bride, Calia Doe."

There was that family thing again. "Sister." Was she a nun? Ullrich's *adopted* sister? That would be weird, but less icky. Wasn't Doe the generic name assigned to anonymous orphans? Wanting to solve the puzzle, Otis slipped into free association. Doe. Deer. John Doe. John Deere. Tractors. Mud. Music. Stars. *Of course.* The "great multitude" was Woodstock!

He was a little vague on pomegranates, but if Ulrich and Calia were health food zealots *and* Jesus-freaks, the letter made sense. Otis pictured them throwing off Midwest shackles, grooving amidst a sea of hippies in muddy tie-dyed shirts to Joan Baez, Canned Heat, and CCR—though maybe not to Jimi or Janis. Yes, it was all fitting together. Calia would be easier to handle than he'd first feared. All he needed for her to think was that Ulrich was alive and that there was no need for her to come to Alaska. And for that, the PO box was perfect.

Otis kept the letter and re-read it often. Steadily, though he couldn't say why, its poetry began to seem exquisite. Much later, like a far-off, fair-weather cloud, he would entertain the idea that the woman who had written it might not be so strange after all.

Otis went through more of Ulrich's notebooks. Each entry included a date and time of day—as early as 4AM, seldom later than seven. Precise block writing in several fine-tipped ballpoint colors filled every page. Straight lines divided entries into boxes like classified ads. The older notebooks were spiral-bound. Were these assignments? Nothing indicated that—no grades or comments. Yet if all this was private, why be so meticulous? And if he'd not been able to afford clothes without patches, why shift to leather-bound notebooks with ribbon markers?

Bible quotes dominated the notebooks' pages, each referenced by chapter and verse. Adjacent were paraphrases, cross-references, and analyses, along with bullet-point self-admonitions. *Fear God. Pray. Love neighbors.* Occasionally, a faint line would connect a circled verse to another elsewhere on the page. All the effort amazed him. Academically, he'd never been this organized.

Red ink was for Jesus, but many such quotes were startlingly blunt. *Woe to you!* Really? Book names amused him. Habakkuk? A kids' western story Indian chief. Nahum? A geezer clearing phlegm. Malachi? Like spaghetti, Otis guessed: an Italian prelate. He skimmed arcane terms like eschatology, soteriology, and doxology. Justification and sanctification seemed alike.

Here and there, Ulrich had noted things beyond Bible study: weather conditions (*rainy, 49F*), conversations (*edifying coffee w/ DB*), or hard-to-fathom tidbits like: *sunlight; curvature; water; rest.* If Ulrich had kept a traditional diary Otis would be all over it, but it seemed that he hadn't.

Thirty-Seven:
The Fifth

Fearful of being unmasked in Ulrich's job, Otis pored over his textbooks and college course notebooks, cramming more diligently than he'd done for any final exam. He scrawled crib notes which he tucked into clear plastic bags for quick reference.

At Humble's orientation, briefers told survey recruits how much was riding on their work in the short Arctic summer. Vast tracts of bush from Alaska's barren North Slope down to its Gulf had to be mapped in detail—slopes and river crossings assessed, soils examined, flora and fauna carefully studied. The crude oil reserves at Prudhoe Bay were vast and needed to flow. Engineers needed data to draw up plans; lawyers needed it to fight like wolves. Humble and its partners had spent billions and expected to spend (and make) billions more, but environmental groups bound to oppose them had fired off lawsuit salvos, including one aimed at the state's former Governor, U.S. Interior Secretary, Walter Hickel. The tension in the room was palpable. Pipe sections large enough to crouch in and duck-walk along had arrived from Japanese steel mills, piled up at ports, and begun to rust. The Alaska pipeline had to be built faster than anyone thought possible.

"This is war," one briefer quipped.

Teams could expect swollen icy rivers and all types of weather from blinding snow to baking heat. Swamps had to be waded, trees cut, and cliffs scaled. (Otis looked forward to getting paid to do that.) Bears also lurked: black, brown, and scariest, polar. Crews should post sentries with stopping-power weapons. Mosquito netting and bug repellant were mandatory. Every ten days—*if possible*—crews would get thirty-six hours of R&R in crude cramped company quarters.

On the Fourth of July, he drove a few hours to the crew pick-up point: a muddy scar scraped from the tundra. He arrived late. Blake, the crew-cut crew boss checked Ulrich's name off a list; he looked peeved. Otis crammed his duffel into the hard-seated van but held Ulrich's typewriter on his lap. "Suit yourself," Blake said. The van pulled away. Otis asked to go back. He thought he'd left food in his car. He wouldn't see it again for at least a month; between heat and bears, he wanted to double check. "Tough luck," Blake said. They had to get to their first work site.

Blake was a three-tour Army vet. His wife and infant son had remained home in Oklahoma; Blake—like everyone—had come north for the money. Otis listened to one-up stories: bar brawls, farm woes, construction mishaps, epic firefights in Korea and Vietnam. Otis' injuries were evident, but he refused to say how he'd gotten them. Mountaineering seemed like a poor fit with this crowd.

At their first camp, Otis hiked a nearby ridge for photos. Blake chewed him out for venturing beyond the shotgun-protected perimeter and said it was his last warning. To ingratiate himself, Otis did tasks others shunned: fetching gear and pounding stakes. He held theodolite receivers while real surveyors aimed scopes at him. When mosquitoes didn't obscure the sun, cold rain did. Days averaged sixteen hours. Everyone got trench foot in constant muck. Still, Otis felt, it was better than being shot at or wearing a choking tie in a glass cage every day.

Everyone on the team carried a Brunton compass like Ulrich's. Otis' tent-mate Pat was the team's second hire, his New York accent strange here. Each night, Pat rested his head on a stack of classics, softened by recent paperbacks such as "In Cold Blood," and "Slaughterhouse Five." Paired together on the crew's first day, Pat asked Otis to take Brunton readings.

"Can I use yours? I lost mine." He asked Pat for a quick tutorial. ("Yours is a bit different." He didn't mention that he'd abandoned Ulrich's Brunton and tent on his Icefield retreat.) He thought he was getting the hang of it until he made an error that led the whole crew off course. It was three in the morning before they got it corrected. Pat took the blame. In their tent, Otis expressed his gratitude. "How can I make it up to you?"

"Oh, you don't have to," Pat smiled. Otis detected no sarcasm. Pat would surely cash in the favor chit later, ballooned by interest. Otis wondered how he would be asked to pay.

Blake let the team sleep until eight. Pat awoke to eyes swollen almost shut, his mosquito net sliced. Everyone on the team had a reason. Otis' net was intact. Otis wanted to press the issue but Pat let it go. Otis helped Pat through the day then helped him repair his net. Unable to see well that evening, Pat asked Otis to read Dostoyevsky. As Otis dramatized Detective Porfiry's pursuit of Raskolnikov's murderous secret amidst Saint Petersburg's onion domes, he couldn't help but think of his half-snow-blind talk with the Icefield park ranger.

At the end of their first ten-day stint, another company van picked them up. The air inside it reeked in more ways than Otis cared to identify. Blake swiveled to face him.

"You've been a quiet one."

"I'm tired."

"You don't know tired until you've done back-to-back night patrols north of the DMZ."

"Mmm," Otis said, his face stark. "I guess some might say that."

Blake raised one eyebrow to call out the snub. Otis said nothing. At last Blake bit. "So, I've been meaning to ask. How'd you get so busted-up?"

Otis replied in a monotone.

"Situation went bad in a foreign country. I was lucky to get out alive."

Blake's eyes widened and softened. "Cambodia?"

Heads turned and ears cocked.

"I'm not at liberty to say."

"Laos?" Blake looked expectant, excited.

Otis held a steely stare until every head in the van nodded in reverence. Blake's face flushed with respect.

"I knew it! I could always spot the intel guys."

The van dropped them in Fairbanks mid-evening. Blake invited the crew out for pitchers. Pat demurred, retreating to the company barracks hundreds of men rotated through—eight to each unfinished room—waiting in line for cold "showers" that spit from bare pipes. Otis bought one round of beer for the crew at the Flame Room then followed them to other bars: Hideaway, Nevada, Gold Rush and others he lost track of, thrilled to pass his toughest

Ulrich audition and bypass fights which swarmed around them. About two in the morning, the sun neither setting nor rising, Blake offhandedly proposed they hire prostitutes.

"You're joking," Otis exclaimed.

A half-circle of smirks said he wasn't. They assured him they knew the best spots. Young and clean, next-door types, blondes, brunettes, redheads, whatever you like. One quoted a memorized menu. A bargain with the money they made, another noted to nodding agreement.

"What's the big deal?" Blake scoffed. "You're single. You were in country. This can't be your first time. Who are you afraid of, the clap or your mother?"

"Pat's made him a prude," one man half-slurred, half-drawled.

"Or a homo," Blake wisecracked, leading the laughter.

"Let's go," someone else said.

"Meet back here for shots in an hour," Blake said, and they scattered.

Otis persisted in shock. It was one thing to know hyenas existed and another to be caught up in a cackling pack of them. Why did women selling themselves bug him so much? Who was he to judge? It *seemed* wrong, yet to voice vague objections felt pointless, even dangerous. Maybe it was Blake's blasé remark: *Meet back here for shots.* He thought of the men's girlfriends and wives back home. Some had to know or at least surmise. How could they overlook such a thing?

Outside the Humble barracks, a bug swarm flitted around a lightbulb—pointless in constant daylight. Others twitched, dying below. Otis tugged at the water-stained plywood door; wood-on-wood screech cut the stillness. "Top bunks are safer," Pat had said, "and drier once the bars close." Otis slouched inside, took the last bunk he could find, and hoped for the best.

The next morning, Otis showered, found a phone booth, and got in line.

"Otis! Where are you? What's happened?" His mother's voice echoed, distorted and tinny as if through an under-road culvert.

"I'm fine, Mom." Otis' voice echoed back, delayed. "Busy, that's all."

The delay made his head hurt and threw them both off so that they spoke over each other. "Otis, you have to listen." "Did you not get my postcard?" The line hummed. Neither spoke. "You go." "No. You. Go."

"FBI men came by last week, Otis. They said you didn't appear for induction. Did we drop you off at the right place?" He'd known this would come. He hated that they were involved.

"Yes, Mom, you did."

He was sure they wouldn't *knowingly* let the FBI listen in, but what if their phone had been bugged without their permission? If the FBI traced the call and she thought she'd led them to him, she would be crushed. He rested two fingers on the chrome hang-up lever. No. He had been careful. They had no way to connect the names. Alaska was huge, and he was mobile. With his free hand, he picked at bites and sunburn scabs.

"Otis? Are you still there? Tell me what happened."

"It's complicated, Mom. You shouldn't worry. I'm fine."

"Fine? They said you could go to jail."

"What did they say exactly?"

"They were pleasant. They said if they spoke with you, they could work something out. They left a card." She read him a name and number. He had no pen or paper. "Will you call them?"

"I don't think that's a good idea, Mom."

The operator asked for fifty cents.

"Why don't you call back collect, honey? I'll wait."

"That's OK Mom." He dropped in two more quarters. Collect would be easier to trace.

"Tom Metcalfe came by the house."

Metcalfe was his father's boss, a hard-nosed stickler who served on Dirkden's draft board. Otis closed his eyes and pinched the bridge of his nose. "What did he want?"

"We told him you hadn't called."

"Did you show him the postcard?"

"No. He didn't ask." Her impish tone made Otis imagine her smiling.

A sudden thought sprouted. "Why don't you call that draft counselor, Mom? I'll bet he's advised other parents in these situations."

"What situation are you in, Otis? Where can we write you?"

"The less you know the better, Mom. I'm sorry." The realization that he couldn't go home hit him with new force. His parents would have set up and filled the aboveground pool to let it warm in the sun. She would be frying up garden zucchini slices the size of 45-speed single records.

A man outside hollered. "Look at the antlers on that sucker!"

Otis covered the mouthpiece.

"You're up with Andy and Beatrice in Ontario, aren't you?"

"No, Mom. I'm not." As Otis watched, a moose strode down the street.

"That's alright Otis. This can be our little secret; like spies."

"I'm OK Mom, that's all. Trust me."

"You have to trust *me*. I lost one son. I will not lose two. I need to know you're safe."

He said, "I'm sorry you have to deal with this, Mom," but really he meant for everything. How often had he failed to thank her for listening to his frustrations and sympathizing with his fears? For preparing him canned fruit for an after school snack, dolloped with cottage cheese and dimpled with raisins? For darning his socks, hemming his pants, and sewing him a book bag? For excusing his routinely late Mother's Day cards and lame gifts?

"Mom? I'll let you know more when I can. Now, tell me. How's Billy?"

"You didn't hear about the second draft lottery?"

"No, Mom. I haven't been near TVs or newspapers."

"Billy got assigned number two, same as you. The Christmas babies got three-sixty-one."

"What? You're joking. Two? The same number as me?" Billy had been born Christmas Eve, minutes before midnight. Schoolmates had teased him that, because he wasn't one of the three wise men or a shepherd, he must be a donkey. Billy had taken that stoically, but never well.

"I wish I were, Otis. Penn is a great school and Billy has time, but it cuts down his options."

"I should call him."

"Oh yes, Otis. He'd love that. You should." She burst into a sob. "It's so... arbitrary! If each of you had been born a few hours later, everything would be different. Your father still watches Walter Cronkite, but I can't. I take a bath with a good mind-flusher book."

"None of this is your fault, Mom."

"Henry was three when Dad returned from fighting Hitler. It made a big impression on him. Dad was a hero to him. It's why Henry enlisted."

Otis had heard this fanciful theory often enough to know that he couldn't reason her out of it. Their father had *discouraged* Henry from military service. Henry had signed up for ROTC based on JFK's 1961 assertion that the country would "pay *any* price." No one would buy a sandwich without knowing the price—at least roughly—but many men had bought the catchy line. A new thought rose in his mind. Had his father enlisted on the same kind of youthful impulse after Pearl Harbor? Had his grandfather enlisted the same way in 1917 when it came to light that the Kaiser was seeking an alliance with Mexico? Was Otis the first one to break the family mold?

A large man rapped on the phone booth's glass. Otis held up two fingers—two minutes, man, peace—but the man's outraged glare suggested that he'd taken a different meaning from the gesture. Otis flipped his hand around and shrugged.

"Mom? I have to go soon. People are waiting. What else is new there?"

"Billy's been a dear, driving your grandmother to her appointments."

"Appointments? What appointments? Is Grandma staying with you?"

"She's in your room. The hospitals here are better than in Berkshire County. We thought it might be stress but the doctor ruled that out. He said the tests are routine for this."

"Routine for what?"

The next man in line pounded on the glass door.

"Public phone, buddy! Get with it! C'mon!"

"And why doesn't she take Henry's room? It's a lot bigger than mine."

Before his mother could answer, the operator broke in, demanding more money. Otis fumbled for coins. The waiting man saw his moment and shoved at the door.

"The doctor says it could be cancer." The man reached inside and hit the hang-up lever.

"I love you, Mom," Otis yelled at the dead line.

Thirty-Eight:
All Our Options

Otis rented a Fairbanks PO Box in Ulrich's name and arranged for Ulrich's Anchorage one to forward to it. He did not set up one for himself. To go by two names in such a small town would invite scrutiny and besides, he was already in touch with his parents by phone. They didn't need letters. Calia did. If he didn't write to her as Ulrich, worry would lead her to contact Humble; then they would track "Ulrich" down for her. The jig would be up.

After mailing Ulrich's postcards, plus a redrafted version of Ulrich's campground letter, continuing with more replies to Calia seemed less of a big deal. Nonetheless, his first try from scratch took several drafts. He avoided overt mention of Calia's racy "S.O.S" letter and stuck to job trivia. His assignments were long and remote, he warned her. He *might* get a chance to write on his R&R furlough, but then again it might be three weeks. Despite the caveats, Calia wrote to Ulrich often and sent regular care packages. Cookies and brownies were sometimes stale by the time Otis picked them up, but he relished them anyway, as did the crew. On each brief break in Fairbanks, Otis would peruse all Calia's letters in one sitting. Then, out in the field, he would draft a single summary response and mail it whenever the crew returned.

Otis' nightly obsessive typing bemused his crewmates. How should Ulrich's writing sound? What should he talk about? It was not a scripted role, like Hamlet or Romeo, but he tossed draft after draft into the campfire, anxious lest anything give him away. He recalibrated each letter based on Calia's reaction to his most recent one, reassured by the fact that Ulrich could—even should—change. Her letters smelled floral, a nice contrast with

197

the tarry tang of the Ole Time Woodsman's bug dope the crew slathered on. Rereading her letters, replies would blossom in Otis' mind, each thought inviting the next until, inattentive, he would slide too far into his own style—or mention things Ulrich would not know or be likely to say—and have to start again.

Nevertheless, to his delight, the rhythm of correspondence proved more pleasant than the communications battlefield he'd tried to navigate with Louisabeth. In one note, curious what Calia might see in it, he enclosed a snapshot of Mount McKinley with a herd of moose in the foreground. She passed the test: "it's gorgeous!" she wrote, "and the moose are cute too."

The problem he faced was anniversaries. He'd already begun crafting his replies in ways that might get her to reveal (even roughly) the date of their meeting and her birthday, but what other special days might she expect Ulrich to commemorate? Had he stepped on any such calendar land-mines already? She seemed the type to overlook much, but eventually she would have to lose patience. When that finally happened, Otis planned to apologize, but not too fervently. He would let Ulrich's ardor seem to cool, giving Calia more and more reasons to get fed up. Let her be the one to call things off. Then no one would care what had happened to Ulrich.

Otis would be free to use his name as long as he needed it. Thinking about the utilitarian end game felt mildly distasteful, but at this point it was unavoidable and besides, inducing a gradual break-up was a sort of kindness. War widows often pined for a final letter. He was giving Calia far more than that. She could move on with her life unburdened. She never had to even *know* she was a widow. A girl like her? She would quickly bounce back.

In August (understandably, after two months apart) Calia expressed wanting to see Ulrich or to at least hear his voice. To outflank her, Otis began a letter saying that they should perhaps wait to marry, but before he could finish it, Ulrich's typewriter ribbon broke. On his day off, Otis combed Fairbanks for a replacement. When he found it, he bought several extras and finished the letter. His message was hard, but he managed a supportive tone he felt. Her reply came attached to a massive box of the best cookies he'd ever tasted. She not only forgave Ulrich his doubts but reiterated how much she respected and loved him. Unable to eat the cookies after reading that, Otis gave them to his hyena-pack survey crew who finished them within an hour.

In Calia's next note, her tone changed. She *pleaded* for him to call, "soon it's urgent. Monday after next?" She would wait by the phone, evening her time. Otis had not shared Ulrich's schedule, but his crew in fact had that day off. At the time she'd specified, Otis paused outside the Fairbanks phone booth near the barracks, fumbling with coins in his pocket. The booth was empty. He stepped forward, paused, and stepped back. To imitate Ulrich's voice would be the height of insanity. He turned and went for a walk, feeling every second of her waiting as if she were walking right beside him, her breath making wordless clouds alongside his in the early fall air.

Around Labor Day, Calia wrote to say she was pregnant.

Otis read her letter twice in the Fairbanks post office. He wanted to scream: *This* child is not mine! The thought didn't budge. *Ulrich is dead and a father.* No one else knew that pair of facts. Otis could never *not* know them. A phrase he'd once heard came to mind. *You break it, you own it.* He had to move, think, get fresh air. He dashed outside and broke into a run, his legs loose, then burning, low afternoon sun in his eyes. He ignored stares and pain and kept on, the purge deep but not deep enough.

Pregnant. And due in March. He did the math. June. Right before Ulrich left—an extra special farewell. Given their faith, he'd assumed they were virgins. At least they were human. Wobbly, he paused in gravel wastelands near an impassable river. Over the sound of rushing water as his breathing slowed, he listened for bears or hunters who might mistake him for one. The yellow rustle of Aspen and birch leaves returned him to calm. He unfolded Calia's letter again.

She hoped the baby would have Ulrich's eyes. She was glad they were forgiven. For what? They were engaged. The second page of Calia's note was tear-stained. Her words seemed to howl:

"Please come home, my love! I need you. I'm excited but also scared."

A year ago, Louisabeth had been angry. Though Otis' lapse disqualified him from a deciding say in how *she* resolved *her* predicament—her future, her body, her parents' ire, she'd said, over and over—she'd insisted that real men fix things. What did that mean? They'd talked in circles. Finally, he'd agreed. They'd fixed things alright. So why wasn't Calia angry? He thought of Davey's mom, tired-eyed and working two jobs. A diner waitress with no college must struggle to support herself even now, alone. Since he was the only one who knew about the glacier accident, it seemed unfair to let Calia go blithely ahead with a pregnancy that would dog her for decades.

Otis stuffed her letter in his back pocket and began a slow jog back toward town. The steady blood-thump in his ears recalled Poe's Telltale Heart, a man murdered, hidden, but not forgotten, or starving transgressive vestals, shut in forever to appease Rome's ancient gods. His place in this drama was odd, yet it came with a responsibility. Only he could see her pending hardship. Only he could help fix her mess. To let it blindside her would be unmanly.

He took special care to write in terms of "we" and "us."

"Since we're not married, we should look at all our options. I did some research for us. Colorado loosened things three years ago, then Kansas last year. Either is a day trip." (Otis knew most about California, where a recent court case had slowed a tide of girls crossing to Tijuana, but Ulrich would be less familiar with it, and no way could Calia afford to fly there.) "We'll need a special circumstance for the form," he wrote. Recalling how he'd misread Calia's first letter, he noted how, "obviously, neither rape nor incest apply, but if you look upset, the right kind of doctor will be sympathetic. It's your body of course; I'll support whatever you choose. But in consideration of our being apart, and our uncertain future together, I think this is best."

He hoped that last bit—alluding to a future he knew and she did not—didn't sound too heavy-handed. He debated sending money. Not yet, but he would if she asked. He owed her that much.

Turning away from the blue mailbox, Otis pictured his letter inside and felt suddenly shaky. A moment before—able to withdraw it and leave her free of his furtive influence—he had been fully resolved, his case cogent and correct. Now though, unable to change his mind, seasick doubts wracked him and he wondered again what his child with Louisabeth would have been like—not just the gender, but learning to walk then to talk, his or her first day of school, then first date, learning to drive, getting married, bringing grandchildren to visit. Was he offering Calia the gift of hard-won wisdom or pushing her to repeat his folly so he could feel better about Ulrich's death? Was his letter noble or wanton? He went back and forth, seeing both sides.

Thirty-Nine:
Peace of the City

Grand Island, Nebraska, that same day...

When Ulrich left in June to drive north, Calia bought a small plastic alarm clock, set it to Anchorage time, and placed it on her nightstand next to an identical one she'd purchased at age fourteen for her first job. With a black magic marker, she wrote "ME" on one and "HIM" on the other, in letters big enough for her to tell them apart at night by each face's faint luminescence. Each morning, she prayed for Ulrich to sleep well and wake refreshed a few hours behind her.

One day, before she knew she was pregnant, Calia had dashed out of the shower to grab the ringing phone but slipped and missed. Lying in a puddle, her towel askew, she reminded herself not to get angry too fast or for the wrong reasons. Later, when she no longer dashed like that lest she hurt the baby, she reminded herself not to get upset when people had the wrong number, or tried to sell her things, or when a call turned out to be for one of her roommates.

In time, Ulrich *would* call. She was sure of it.

Last year, when Philis Troy's family moved away, Calia had moved in with another church friend a few years older. Sarah Toft went by her middle name Ethel. Despite her sober, bookish personality, it made Calia think of 'I Love Lucy'. Ethel had the inspiring habit of taping Bible verses to the refrigerator, or the bathroom mirror, or inside Calia's car which—like everyone else in Grand Island—she left unlocked. (Most left their house doors unlocked too.)

More recently, Calia and Ethel had taken pity on a woman from Ethel's office by letting her sleep on their sofa. Thea F. Dashwood was in her mid-thirties. She joked that her middle initial stood for 'F-bomb.' Months earlier, her husband had walked in on her in bed with his best friend. He filed for divorce, locked her out, and closed their bank account. Thea chipped in for rent as she could, and sometimes helped clean, but mostly she kept to herself, watching TV and reading glamor magazines. When Ethel left town in August for a few days, Thea broke that pattern. Calia was mixing cookie dough when Thea strode into the kitchen and hopped onto the counter.

"Mmm! Chocolate chip! These for me?"

With two fingers, Thea swiped up a dough gob.

"They're for Ulrich, but here." Calia handed her the teaspoon she'd been using to carve even-sized dollops onto a cookie sheet, then grabbed a clean spoon and continued.

Thea licked her fingers, set down the spoon, then slid her fingers again around the mixing bowl's inside rim. "Typical," she said. "Guy knocks you up on his way out of town. Now here you are, barefoot and brainwashed."

"Ulrich is different." Calia spooned out more cookies.

"You mean all those phone calls?"

Thea fingered up a chunk of dough the size of a golf ball.

"He's earning and saving money so we can have our own house when we're married."

"Listen," Thea said. "You and Ethel have been nice to me so I should be honest with you. Last spring I was in a jam like yours. I saw this doctor in Kansas." From her pocket, Thea extracted a business card and slid it across the counter, making a track through the flour. "It wasn't cheap or fun, but I was in and out of there in a few hours. No worse than pulling a tooth."

"That's awfully kind of you," Calia said, "but my teeth are fine and I like my doctor here."

Thea offered a smug, impatient look. "Honey, this ain't about teeth. The handwriting's on the wall with this guy. He's done with you. You need to think and look out for yourself. No doc here will do what you need."

"My doctor says all I need is to eat well and be patient."

"Sweetheart. Listen. This early? No one has to know. Last year I took a friend to Colorado. I'd do the same for you. We can grab a drink or three on our way, or back—both if we want. Forget together! My treat; what say?"

Shaking with sudden understanding, Calia finished baking in silence.

By mid-September, Calia had not yet received the call she'd hoped for.

At home one day with a bad head cold *and* morning sickness, she brewed tea with honey and returned to bed with one box of Kleenex, one box of Melba Toast, and three boxes of Ulrich's letters arrayed within easy reach. She began with the 1966-67 school year, his first at college in Lincoln. They'd written one another off and on: birthdays and church news, mostly. Their friendship, though casual (bridled by a four-year age gap plus shyness: his, mostly) had been sincere on her part—and also on his, she learned later. Re-reading a steadier flow of letters Ulrich had sent her the following year, Calia cringe-laughed to relive their earnest meanders into misunderstandings and their flailing attempts to soothe one another's hurt feelings.

In January, 1969, he'd enclosed a Life Magazine cover: a picture taken from Apollo Eight. The rising earth reminded him of her eyes, he wrote. "My schatz, I love you," he concluded. "P.S., schatz means 'treasure'."

Calia had leapt. He'd used the L-word! At last! Almost seventeen, she'd been eager for her life's next chapter—not unhappy, just *ready*. She knew what school friends would do with a twenty-one-year-old boyfriend (and how they'd let everyone know). *That* was not her thinking. Yet who could she confide in and trust to tell her if reciprocating his love was out of line?

Philis had been a high school senior. She was only a year older, but had been a believer far longer. Calia had asked her to read all of Ulrich's letters and pray. Go slow Philis advised several afternoons later as snow slashed the Troys' house while they did their homework together. The doorbell rang. Calia and Philis looked at each other, then outside, down the driveway. *Ulrich's car!* At the front door, covered with snow, Ulrich handed Calia half a dozen carnations and three almond Hershey bars. Calia blushed, melting, speechless. In good weather, the round-trip from Lincoln could take half a day. In that day's blizzard, it was a sunrise-to-sunset act of devotion.

Calia lay back to nap and recalled other times together. Him picking her up after work just to drive her home. Sunset walks holding hands. Riverside picnics on muggy days. His Uncle Walter teaching her German. His Aunt Greta teaching her dozens of ways to cook potatoes. Her cutting his hair on their lawn (but not the other way around; she had her pride, and he knew his limits.) Her talking-out papers too fast for him to keep up typing. The way his Bible spilled over his knee in a study group. After recounting these things, Calia wondered: was she being impatient—even picky and selfish—to expect him to call her instead of sticking to letters as they'd agreed?

Later, she spread his letters over the kitchen table—so many that they overlapped. She was blessed to have these reminders. Some men never wrote letters, she'd heard. She wanted to hear his voice, but abstaining from calls meant they could eventually have more children and give more to missions. When he got a permanent phone number, she would gift him a quick surprise call. She'd already looked up rates and set the money aside.

Years earlier, Calia had begun inventing ditties to help her recall Ulrich's letters at a glance. When she'd shared her method for reading and remembering, he had worked to be more poetic. It touched her that a man with an engineering mind would go to that trouble. She stood back now to take in all his letters and felt his years-old words coalesce into comforting symphonies. His recent letters lacked those rhythms. She hated the unkind thought, but a few seemed discordant. Ulrich had less time to compose them she reasoned, but even still, something seemed off.

She put on a Miles Davis record—the cadences sometimes complex, but always purposeful, harmonic. Soft trumpets reminded her of her father's love, care, and protection, and of his skill at seeing both pattern and detail. She was getting better at that too. Twice a year, vast droves of migratory birds descended onto the Platte, north in spring, south every fall. When things got slow at work, she would watch through the diner's plate-glass windows. She had learned to identify most species and to tell the males and females apart.

Calia let her eyes wander over the stacks of letters. Like all typewriters, Ulrich's had unique quirks and flaws: the thin parts of the 'g' and the 'a,' and the '8,' for example. Aunt Greta and Uncle Walter had brought it with them from Germany despite having to sell other possessions fast and cheap to finance their pre-war escape. Ulrich enjoyed the challenge of maintaining and repairing it. Like a familiar signature, Calia could glance at the typeface and know it was his.

Ulrich had addressed many of his earlier letters by hand and written, "my schatz" over the envelope flap. That had stopped in June. Had he hurt his hand? She walked slowly around the table, examining the pile, giving thanks for his faithfulness, silently praying. On her seventh circuit, she thought she saw a distinction. She separated the letters into two piles. In his pre-Alaska letters, Bible verses and paraphrases flowed around and through his other reflections, each one informing the other. The Alaska letters *included* Bible verses but far fewer, and almost none from the Apostle Paul's letters or the Old Testament. Worse, some seemed out of context, an error Ulrich would *never* make. What was wrong? Could he have lost faith? The thought sent her spinning. He had never mentioned a church in Alaska. He'd been busy with work, but still.

No. She knew him better than that. If Ulrich had veered away, he would veer back. She had been shown patience and been forgiven much. She would forgive and be patient. She fetched her Bible, sat at the table, and continued from where she'd left off that morning. "Behold, the LORD hath put a lying spirit in the mouth of these thy prophets." By mistake, she bumped the table and a stack of Alaska letters cascaded to the floor. None of Ulrich's older letters budged.

A week later, when Calia received Otis' next letter, she would feel as if dropped through thin ice into dark water with nothing to grab. Ulrich could not have changed *that* much, could he?

Forty:
Humbled

In October, Humble froze the pipeline project and let Otis go. Winter was the offered excuse, legal tie-ups the actual cause. He had plenty of company. Anyone tracking the news had seen it coming. Still, it stung. He applied for a head office job with Humble but didn't hear back.

It had felt good buying rounds for the crew—sometimes a whole bar—dozens of smiling people chanting his name. He missed that rush. And taxes had consumed much more of his paycheck than he'd expected. Knowing what he knew now, playing monopoly with real money had been a bad idea.

He moved to a motel. (Humble had fenced its Fairbanks barracks; Dobermans now patrolled its grounds.) Drunks came and went from the motel's rooms at all hours. Groans and shouts pierced the thin walls. The fumes from heating canned food over Sterno canisters gave Otis headaches. He called apartment listings exhaustively, but on learning he had no job, all demurred. His dejection grew with the lengthening night.

Should he stay in Alaska? Returning to Canada would free him to be Otis again, but Calgary had shown an animus toward young American men that was probably no different in other big cities—Montreal, Toronto, Edmonton, or Vancouver—while Jasper had shown the converse. A small town would quickly unmask him. Another job anywhere on Ulrich's credentials was also dubious. Careful letters to a fiancée were one thing. Faking engineering expertise in real time had been something else. If Pat had not covered for his bumbling at Humble, Blake would have canned him within days.

Otis applied for entry-level newsroom posts at Anchorage's big newspapers, the Times and the Daily News, as well as substitute-teaching slots at local schools. The *gist* he shared was true: his college major and GPA, accurate dates and his job history. Nevertheless, a frustrating pattern repeated. Despite call-backs and interviews, lauding him for his writing samples, employers' interest dissolved when they tried to verify details. Otis was tempted to reveal real names and phone numbers—at Deden-Fisher and back in Dirkden—but then he would have to use *his* real name and social security number. And that would start a clock ticking: six months at most until the FBI found him. Why couldn't people just trust him?

One night on Otis' motel room TV, a young lady reporter interviewed a local professor of economics who predicted that Humble's cascade of pink-slips, when added to the annual surplus of idealistic summer holdovers, would make jobs *very* scarce. Tell me about it, Otis thought. The station's stodgy anchor countered the reporter's spot as if stooping to pat a toy dog. *Every* spring since "the war," the picture brightened, he said. Easy for him to say, Otis thought. *His* war ended a quarter century ago. *He* was nearing retirement. *He* had an expensive haircut.

Coach would say to keep positive, recount his strengths, and get his head in the game. He was in Alaska, McKinley so close he could sense its pull through thick clouds. On rare clear days, the iconic peak seemed to hover *above* the horizon, a majestic white gumdrop like Mount Olympus, the place of gods. To think that he was breathing the air that had swept over its summit just hours before gave Otis the kind of ethereal goosebumps he'd felt upon hearing Purple Haze for the first time. Shaun belittled McKinley as a non-technical yawn—a month-long "snow slog." Easy for him to say. He'd stood on its rite-of-passage summit. *Shaun* was experienced. If a crappy job was what it took to stay in Alaska, cozy up to a team with a climbing permit, and knock off McKinley next June, then so be it. No excuses. Otis would kiss *that* piece of sky.

But what if he ran out of cash before then? No. He couldn't give in to fear. The right moment would come. It always did. Otis finished his can of beans—half-burned, half-cold—and slid his attention to the sitcom laugh tracks that soothed him to sleep each night.

Despite such hardships, he kept Ulrich's official life tidy. He renewed a safe deposit box at a Grand Island bank, cancelled the Fairbanks PO Box and reverted Ulrich to his Anchorage PO. He authorized the Farmview Rest Home to move Ulrich's Aunt Greta to a locked ward, "in the event it should become necessary for her well-being": their boilerplate not his he reasoned signing the form. Plus, being contentious might raise suspicions.

Weeks passed. His cash dwindled faster than he'd planned. Snow fell every few days. When owners and apartment managers tried to hang up on him, he now bartered. He would clean, cook, or walk dogs. He would do repairs, paint, or cut trees. He would clear snow, run errands, even babysit—anything for a roof, heat, toilet, and bed. He looked at two unfinished basements with chemical toilets. (At one, he offered to shovel coal.) But both wanted a check to clear before he moved in or else cash he didn't have.

On the brink of vagrancy, someone finally had mercy and listened.

Forty-One:
Changes of Clothes

~~~~~~~~~~

Sidwell Reuily was new to Alaska. That fact surprised many. Except for a few broad-striped cashmere sweaters he'd worn on a handful of Phoenix winter mornings—golfing or, far less often, to Mass (and which made him look even more mountainous than he was), Sid's desert wardrobe had stayed behind with his wife and two daughters. Despite a chill over his coming here, they would take him back: this venture was banking their palmy backyard-pool lifestyle.

Around Anchorage, where physical bulk was humdrum and formal dress conspicuous, Sid layered untucked XXXL lumberjack shirts in generic checkerboard patterns. Under them, to hold up his pants, he would have preferred suspenders (to accommodate his nearing-forty paunch, and because he knew too many unpleasant things that could be done with a leather belt) but his back holster had to attach to *something*. The shirts were common as moose (confusing eyewitness reports) and as easy to shed as snakeskins, fast and clean to burn when splattered.

Sid came across as breezy, yet simmered at people who hesitated at green lights or stole glances at him in the corner bar booth where he sipped 7-Ups. A barber who had once butchered his haircut also got his silent ire. Sid's hair had been thinning on top since ninth grade. At six foot five very few noticed but the old taunts still hurt. From every angle, his head appeared distinctly square. Thin, tusk-like sideburns ran low along his jawbone. Day and night, he wore aviator sunglasses so that no one could tell if he was looking at them, past them, or through them.

Sid's most distinctive tool of misdirection though was his mouth. Even when not speaking, his lips, cheeks, and tongue darted like a wall of silvery

209

herring. The mesmeric display bought him time to assess motives. Phone calls were harder, but Sid's jocularity led otherwise savvy people to second-guess their second guesses and give him the benefit of the doubt. Predators sensing deception might lurch at some of his synthetic cues, even catch a few, but no one ever caught them all. Instead, when Sid spoke, those he faced tended to empathize with him against their self-interest. People *wanted* to like and trust Sid and for that weakness, he despised them.

Sid's misanthropy differed little from thousands drawn to Alaska for over a century: miners, missionaries, trappers, and traders, plus a timeless pan-civilizational cadre of those who served them for a price: bootleggers, arms dealers, pimps, and their half-enslaved entourages. But if that century gap were removed, Sid would have found his closest amity with those whom the Civil War had ejected to tame the west: inured to death, risk, and mercy, gratified only by conquest.

The idea for this particular northern conquest had come in a haze of hand-rolled cigar smoke in a private back room at a Phoenix restaurant after rare steaks and several bottles of Cutty-Sark. The surprise Prudhoe Bay flare that illumined the North Slope's slinking dawn in 1968 quickly ignited an ambitious plan to slice the forty-ninth state north to south with an oil pipeline, but it also ignited less visible blazes of opportunity. Others would remedy Alaska's limited supply and pricey selection of wilted produce, the cigar-puffing group reasoned, but why should the state's burgeoning, soon-to-be-wealthy population not have access to the quality and quantity of *extra*-legal goods and services the group offered in the lower forty-eight? When back-of-napkin figures showed that aggressive market penetration could bring vast returns, all eyes turned to Sid.

"North to the future," they'd toasted, wowed by the potential profits. Left unsaid was that their lives would be safer with Sid far away.

For Sid, the move offered freedom from those a decade older, eager to leech off his ingenuity and discipline but unwilling to buy overcoat liners and gloves to fly up and nose into his setup. Oil was years from flowing south, but just two years into the venture, dope was flowing steadily north. Sid's job was to keep the southward torrent of money clean and out of view.

A sonorous voice answered Otis' call. A man named Sid had a room to sublet. Otis pictured a well-sated bear lumbering off to hibernation. To save time, Otis confessed to being jobless and short on cash. He was about to launch into his barter spiel when to his astonishment, Sid described the place in cheerful detail: roomy, modern, and quiet. Moose routinely strolled through the suburban subdivision's spacious yards. Sid said he was unfussy, away much of the time. The rent seemed too good to be true.

"Why's it so cheap?" Otis asked, wiser now to Jack-the-trucker traps.

"Well," Sid said with a sigh, and Otis pictured him lolling his head to the side. "I'm in a bind with business travel. Last month, I advertised free rent for a house-sitter. *Huge* mistake! Only crazies responded: addicts, hookers, hippies, gamblers. Character matters, my mother used to say. Now I have to spend a month on the West Coast. Maybe Miami too. I'm behind the eight-ball, as she would say. The place is safe and tidy, of course. The landlord lives right downstairs."

"Why can't *he* watch the house?"

"I don't mean to speak ill Ulrich, but do you watch Mr. Rogers?"

"I used to." Otis imagined Sid singing reassuringly, changing into a cardigan sweater, removing his shoes, playing with puppets.

"Well, the landlord has funny notions of what it means to be a good neighbor. One day, he's got his hearing aids out, totally oblivious, and the next he's nosing around in things that are *none* of his business. I need someone responsible, disciplined, and discrete. Those qualities seem rare these days. Do you know what I mean?"

Otis agreed; he knew very well; he valued those qualities too.

"That's fantastic, Ulrich. I'm getting a good feeling about this. What about you? What do you think?"

"Uh, great. Yeah. Fantastic."

Otis could afford exactly one more night at the motel.

"OK. But I have to ask you a favor." *Oh no*, Otis thought. "I send and receive a significant number of business packages. Between you and me, Ulrich? Quite frankly? It's become a point of friction with the landlord. I hate to impose. It sounds like you will be busy searching for a suitable position in your line of work, your own profession, but do you think you could bring them inside in a timely manner? Sign for the important ones?" Otis said it was no problem.

"Marvelous, Ulrich." Sid chuckled, and Otis did too, though he didn't know why. "Now, a few packages might need to be re-bundled. That's a big ask, I know. In your shoes, I might be thinking, 'Is this guy running a warehouse?'" He chuckled again. "But if you could do that for me, and take them to the post office, that would be a huge burden off me. I'll leave you detailed instructions and money for postage. And truthfully? For tax purposes, I'd rather you not pay rent until January. It would only confuse my accountant. What do you think?"

Otis dissolved in relief.

"Sure. Of course." He visited post offices all the time, he said, and with Sid gone so much, another Jack-the-trucker scenario seemed unlikely.

Otis packed his few things, counted his motel change, and drove to the address. Snow dusted a row of interlaced spruce that hid the house from the road. The stately cordon made Otis think of the Nutcracker ballet's life-sized silent toys. He snaked past them up the long drive and shut off the engine. A chainsaw's mechanical whine sang nearby, up and down, busy.

Sid emerged from behind a shed. Except for his blood-spattered goggles, he could be Paul Bunyan: warm smile, huge beard, thick hands, layered wool shirts, and leather work gloves. He set down the sputtering chainsaw, pulled up his goggles, and removed his right glove. His handshake was startlingly gentle. "Word to the wise, Ulrich? If you hunt, don't let a carcass freeze! Listen, I've got to finish—get this thing arranged in the basement chest freezers." He put his glove back on, picked up the running chainsaw, and used it to gesture. "You go on up and make yourself at home. I'll join you shortly."

As Otis moved his things upstairs and unpacked, the chainsaw noise continued intermittently. A new-smelling maroon rug filled the center of his room which, like the rest of the house, was spacious and clean, just as Sid had promised. He could get used to this.

Sid clomped up the back stairs and took a long shower. He then showed Otis where to put inbound packages: not in Sid's bedroom, the door of which was shut, but in a kitchen cabinet amidst canisters of sugar and flour and at least a dozen burlap bags of what smelled like ground coffee. Otis was free to use those or any other staples.

Having begun the day thinking he'd end it homeless, Otis could not have been more relieved.

Throughout that fall, Otis called home from different phone booths. It irritated his father that he varied the days and times and so often missed him, but links to his old life made Otis nervous. The FBI could trace calls. Inside the booths' frosted panes, headlights refracted in mesmerizing patterns. Northern Lights too. He fancied being encased in a diamond. Freezing was supposedly pleasant. Ulrich could not have suffered too much.

He set up an Otis PO box near Elmendorf Air Force Base (across town from Ulrich's) and gave his parents the number. If they checked where it was, they could imagine him working on base and doubt what they'd heard from officials. Ten days after telling them, he picked up a box of mail from them there. He scanned the street, carried it a quarter mile to his car, and drove home by a roundabout route.

In his room, he set aside the letters his mother had steamed and resealed—from the Army, the FBI, and Selective Service. Letters from his parents and his grandmother warmed him more than he expected. Billy's short note made him laugh. In their minds Otis realized, he had never faced danger at all. Near the bottom of the box was an August letter from Davey, forwarded from Deden-Fisher.

Atlanta was "super-hot," Davey reported, deploying the phrase Otis had used the day they met. His Little League coach had put him in center field. Not quite shortstop, Otis thought, but better than bench. Davey shared his address. Otis' heart sang. He wrote Davey back, illustrating Alaska with wildlife stories he'd heard. He'd been in an accident over the summer he added, but he was fine now. That was enough—the truth if not the *whole* truth. After all, he'd told Davey never to lie.

In late October, his mother reported vivid fall colors. Indian summer was still yielding garden tomatoes. Otis did not mention that where he was snow wasn't melting. His grandmother had "a pre-cancerous thing in her liver," his mother reported. "Probably treatable," she said. Otis tried his grandmother directly, eager to hear her say it was nothing, ready to level with her about what (and how) he was doing and seek her advice, but her phone always rang without her picking up.

He checked Ulrich's box every day but for weeks, Calia sent nothing.

Forty-Two:
Smokestack

A lone on Halloween night, Otis reminisced about Davey's return to trick-or-treating a year ago, dosed with cathartic confidence as little kids fled from his glowing skeleton costume. Had he reused it? Bought or made a new one? More importantly, had he made friends to go with? Otis wrote him another note to find out.

Around ten, a car backed up the drive. Moments later, the doorbell rang. With Sid's porch light off, no one had bothered all evening. The bell rang again. Cautiously, Otis went to look. Three figures in plastic masks stood on the stoop: LBJ (with glasses), Nixon, and Billy Graham. Otis cracked the door. "Trick or treat," they said in unison and despite himself Otis chuckled. Their adult stature and deep voices made their masks more realistic even as their grungy down jackets patched with duct tape made their get-ups ludicrous. As Otis dropped a Hershey bar into each pillowcase bag, he noted that they were all empty.

Nixon growled. "Can I use your bathroom?" Otis laughed; it was a good imitation.

"Sorry, it's not my house."

"He's not lying," Graham said, his voice rising and warbling with evangelical passion.

"He really must go," LBJ drawled.

Otis smiled. "OK guys, but stomp the snow off your boots."

Graham stayed in the foyer. Upstairs, Nixon dashed to the bathroom. LBJ lingered in the kitchen. With his mask still on, he opened cabinets and drawers. "You have any Alka-Seltzer?"

"No." Otis scurried to close what he'd opened.

From the bathroom came a metallic clack—the medicine chest being opened—then a heavy porcelain scraping sound: the toilet tank lid. Otis moved toward the door but LBJ blocked him, smelling of cheap cologne. Without flushing Nixon emerged and addressed Otis.

"Are you the carpenter who handles the caskets?"

"What caskets? What are you talking about?"

"Do you work at the airport?"

"No. Who are you? What's this about?"

Nixon nodded to LBJ and they both strode out. Otis set the deadbolt, heart pounding. At the wheel of a dark sedan outside facing the street, a fourth masked man started the engine as the three others hopped in. The car sped down the drive and away.

What did they mean asking if he was "the carpenter who handles the caskets"? What had they been after? Whoever they were, no good could come from telling Sid, yet this must relate to him. Otis examined Sid's bedroom door for the tricks he'd once used to catch Billy snooping—paper scraps, hair strands, slivers of cellophane tape, or a light talcum powder dusting inside to show any tracks. Satisfied, Otis entered. It didn't take long to search the room. Sid's closet and dresser held barely enough for a weekend. An unlocked desk held only a stapler, pencils, and a legal pad. Abruptly, the apartment felt cavernous, the suburban silence creepy. Something was wrong, but what was it? What choice had he had? What choice *did* he have? He still had no job, nor any good prospects. However strange he might feel about the place, about Sid, or about the men who'd come by, Sid's deal remained his best option.

To make the space feel homier, Otis thought to rearrange his room. He rolled back the maroon area rug, but the hardwood beneath it was ugly: patchy and dark, even tacky in spots. Sid must have brought a hunting trophy indoors to skin it before fully draining the carcass. He'd probably bought the rug to hide the stain. Otis rolled the rug back into place and left his room as it was.

By mid-November, with no pressing reason not to, Otis typically slept until noon. He knew he had to do better. On January first, Sid might end his free rent. He bought an alarm and shaved, resolved to take the best job he could

215

find by Thanksgiving. He retrieved the newspaper from the stoop and skipped past the Vietnam obits to the classifieds. The airport needed baggage handlers: gritty work but outdoors, and he could live on the pay, well above minimum wage, the best he'd seen in a while. He just hoped the job didn't involve handling caskets.

The woman who answered his call droned through a rote script. "Did you finish grade school? Does anything prevent you from heavy lifting? Have you ever been convicted of a felony?" She said to come in the next day. "A tie would be out of place," she advised.

Otis donned a clean pair of jeans and three hooded sweatshirts. The hassled-looking fiftyish secretary he'd spoken with ushered him through a door thick with grey glossy paint, its wire-reinforced window stenciled: "Assistant Director, Airport Operations."

Hanging fluorescent lights nagged the air like bug zappers. Behind a metal desk, a large man held a grimy beige phone hard to his ear. His pocked, red-veined nose looked like an overripe strawberry. Stray long hairs spanned his scalp, which he kneaded periodically with the free hand that held his lit cigarette. *As if his brain had a smokestack*, Otis mused, tilting his head to read a plastic nameplate hidden amidst towers of manila folders: Roy Camfert. He motioned Otis to a metal chair, the vinyl seat of which had been repaired with several different kinds of tape.

"Yep," Roy said. "Yep. Of course they did. Oh yeah!" He covered the receiver, and rolled his eyes at Otis, but said nothing directly to him. Finally, he erupted at whomever he was talking to. "Ya' gotta be kiddin' me!" From a row of steel-framed windows above a painted cinderblock wall, the scream of jet engines rose to a level that made Otis want to cover his ears, run from the room, and never return. The folder stacks quivered. Roy shouted. "No way can they do that!" For several minutes he kept on shouting (and, apparently, listening) before the plane rumbled away. "OK, Frank. Thanks a bundle. I'll let you go."

Mr. Roy Camfert waved at the nameplate, his voice stuck at high volume. "Don't you confuse Camfert with comfort!" His laugh made his ample gut jiggle; he leaned for an overfull ashtray. "Someone told me that once." Otis smiled politely. "OK son," he continued. "We put out the ad because three of my employees just quit to head south."

"This time of year that seems understandable."

"Don't interrupt me! This happens every fall and I'm sick and tired of it. Young people nowadays don't value loyalty. They say they want to 'find themselves.' Buncha bull, if you ask me. Look in the mirror. There! You've found yourself!" Mr. Camfert looked expectant—so Otis laughed nervously. "You wouldn't be here if you were like those pansies though, would you?"

Otis shook his head. "No sir, I would not. I want this job." The words tasted like sawdust.

"Good. Then let's get to it. I'm busy. If you work for me, we need some things straight." He looked Otis over in a way that reminded him of being alone with the pediatrician the first time, after he started puberty. "Obviously you're not a woman, and you don't *seem* like a faggot, but if you are—or if you're a hippie, a commie, or a draft dodger—then there's the door." Theatrically, he pointed. "Walk out it now or run out it when I fire your sorry lying behind. Is that clear?"

Otis stared, stunned. Back home—outside of Chandler's dingy bars or Dedentown's Den—it was rare to hear such jejune labels past junior high. Yet Mr. Camfert exuded smug idiocy below that of even an obnoxious third grader seeking culprits for silent farts. To avoid being unmasked as a draft dodger under the scrutiny of someone keen to sniff out that specific offense felt like an impossible task—unlike the quick interactions he'd weathered so far and more like the time he'd blithely dared the college chess champion Mayer Croft to a public game. How to answer? Otis would rather feed swine, but he needed the cash. Then it hit him. Mr. Camfert was a parody of himself—a blustering, strutting Hakka dancer at a checkers match. Otis needed very little game here, and thinking of Roy by his diminutive first name would remind him of how far he outmatched his soon-to-be boss.

"Yes sir," Otis said. "Clear, sir. Thank you, sir." Meanwhile, he thought *Roy, toy, boy, coy.* At least here he could quit without being court-martialed.

Roy relaxed the way a wounded bull might partway through a fight in Spain. "So, tell me," he said, his eyes suddenly wary. "What makes you think you can handle this job?"

Otis cast his eyes down. "Well, Mr. Camfert, sir, I'm glad you asked." He described how he loved working hard in the cold, then related a fanciful,

217

college-free biography. When Otis said that his brother had been KIA in Vietnam, Roy leaned back and waved him to stop.

"OK. That's fine. We're done here. You start at four Thanksgiving Day. Second shift."

Otis wanted to ask if he could start sooner, but Roy stood, grimaced, and put a hand to the small of his ample back. "Nadine!" he bellowed. "Get me aspirin and get this young man his paperwork." He turned back to Otis. "What did you say your name was?"

"Ulrich," Otis said. "I look forward to working with you sir."

"*For* me," Roy corrected him. "*For* me. You'll be out there." He gestured at the wall behind which another jet was revving to a piercing scream. "And I'll be in here!" Yelling seemed not to strain him—his natural pitch. "Keep that straight and we'll do fine! Isn't that right, Nadine?"

"That's right, Mr. Camfert," Nadine said glumly. Roy flashed a pompous cursory smile that made Otis wonder how much of this Ulrich would have tolerated.

Forty-Three:
Grounded

Otis punched in around sunset Thanksgiving Day, glad for nothing about his new job except being outdoors. Mid-evening between planes, he recalled where he'd been a year ago: phoning Shaun to plot an ice climbing escape. Devotion had turned that failure into a triumph that still gave him chills, but now on the dark tarmac, he was just cold. Would all adulthood be like this? Grinding work that used two percent of his brain? Why did planes taxi so slowly?

Near midnight, he pressed mitten-clad hands to his ears as his shift's last jet slid in to refuel. The DC-8 charter was among dozens that paused in Anchorage en route between Vietnam and the West Coast. This one was bound for Seattle. As soon as the pilot shut down the engines, Otis scrambled to chock the warm tires.

A co-worker unlatched the cargo door. Above them, oval windows framed a row of olive-drab collars. Most men slept. A few gazed at the bleak tarmac as if it were Eden. One soldier waved. Otis waved back. A heavy canvas mailbag caught him in the chest, knocking him to the ground. The man who'd thrown it hollered.

"You want love from soldiers?" He pointed to the stairs rolled to the plane's door. "Then put on lipstick and hike right on up there."

Everyone laughed. Besides being broke, the only thing that kept Otis from quitting was not wanting to let them conclude he couldn't hack it.

As they finished unloading transfer cargo, Otis recalled his cursory training. Double-check and secure everything. He ducked into the plane's belly and bumped a pallet. Behind it, in the dim light of the hold, a row of flag-draped caskets thumped against one another like muffled dominoes.

Behind them, Otis thought he spied a hooded figure. Mortified—and wildly thankful that no caskets had fallen—Otis scurried out of the plane. As he prepared to seal the hatch behind him, one of his coworkers emerged, sweatshirt hood up, screwdriver in hand, zipping up a bulky jacket. "Sorry," he said. "I forgot something. You can close it now."

The next day, he helped service a charter bound for Vietnam. Distinctive paint scuffs marked it as the same DC-8 he'd worked the day before. How far had it flown since he'd last touched it? The West Coast at least, likely the East Coast as well. The thought made him homesick for his family's Thanksgiving leftovers: turkey and mashed potatoes and stuffing and gravy. More men waved than eastbound. Otis curtly acknowledged a few without stopping work. In their shoes, westbound to battle, his mind would be doing ninety in frantic circles. He should have been in their shoes. His heart raced with guilt. Was keeping the secrets he had to keep like what cancer patients felt lugging a tumor around? He couldn't point to one man, but the draft slot he'd fled had rolled down to *someone* fighting in his place.

No, he thought. Stop it. Why was he making such a big deal of this? The Army was no worse off than if *he* had died. His simple, sensible post-mortem swap with Ulrich netted things out.

The plane taxied away. Otis' crew went inside to warm up. He'd just poured coffee when a metallic din shattered the quiet, followed by a floor-shaking boom. Screams emanated from the passenger waiting area upstairs; then came the sound of sirens. The crew dashed back outside where a pillar of fire pulsed against a wall of black smoke. Red lights raced across the tarmac toward it like tracer bullets. From nearly a mile away, Otis could feel the heat on his face.

Roy told Otis' shift that until a crash investigation could be completed, they were all on unpaid leave. He did not like it either. He told each to write down what he could recall. Someone from the government would arrange personal debriefings within a week or two. Otis filled pages with his best stab at what he'd witnessed, hopeful it would bring him catharsis, but all it did was to reinforce his horror. That night he could not sleep.

The next day's newspapers splashed banner headlines: *40 Dead! 100 escaped!* The plane's landing gear had locked, keeping it earthbound. To an alarming degree, the news photos resembled Led Zeppelin's first album cover; a guy on Otis' floor at school had blasted it to vent his rage the day of Nixon's inauguration. Now, those same dark lyrics gave Otis a sense of dazed confusion he could scarcely believe. The Army was sending another plane to ferry the least injured survivors on to Vietnam for more of the same.

That next night he lay awake again, unable to dismiss a disturbing possibility. He'd removed the plane's tire chocks—the last person to touch what was now a tangle of burnt metal and flesh. *Ulrich, now this.* Otis had harbored no ill intent in either case. He'd tried to do the right things. Yet both situations had spun out of control with startling speed. It seemed unreal. To distract himself, he grabbed a paperback he'd found tossed aside in the terminal after the tumult.

Jonathan Livingston Seagull invited him to high, happy thoughts. The crash kept bringing them down. Page after page slid past his eyes without his recalling a thing on them. Finally, grey dawn light came up and he slept. He wished he hadn't. He dreamed himself on the burning plane, his seatbelt locked. He woke with a shout, convinced he smelled smoke. He raced through the apartment, then outside. Nothing. Upstairs again, he shuffled to the bathroom. His face in the vanity reminded him of LBJ, haggard and dour, mired deep in the messes he'd made. A terrible insight replaced the phantom smoke scent. Actual people had felt what he'd merely dreamed. Was it his fault? Was whatever he touched cursed?

Seeking anything better than the dense choking smoke he'd imagined, he opened a 1969 Ulrich notebook he'd only skimmed before, curious as to what Ulrich had thought about the draft. He flipped to December, but Ulrich's entry for the first of that month was unremarkable. Otis turned to the next day. It looked like Ulrich had also slept poorly that night.

"Monday, December 2nd, 1969, 3:18AM. Thankful for deliverance from the draft; prayed for the men selected; thought of Samuel's warning about earthly kings who, 'will take your sons, and appoint them for himself, for his chariots... and to craft his instruments of war.'"

Otis had written papers about ancient military drafts. The fact that they were common did not make them right. He skimmed forward page by page but the only other draft citations involved mentions of praying for people he identified only by initials. He switched to the 1970 notebook and flipped to February, around the time Ulrich would have received and accepted Humble Oil's offer. One entry jumped off the page.

"Sunday, February 15th, 1970, 5:17AM. 'You meant evil against me, but God meant it for good so that many people would be kept alive.'"

You meant evil against me. Ulrich's use of the second person felt like a rifle aimed at Otis' chest, but that made no sense. He hadn't met him until June. Who *had* Ulrich meant? And who were the people being kept alive?

Otis flipped to the next page.

"Monday, February 16th, 1970, 4:44AM. Whom shall I send? Who will go for us? Here am I! Send me!" Otis skimmed down a column of quotes from Isaiah to where Ulrich had concluded the day's entry with a short, triply-underlined sentence: "I *AM* being sent."

Sent where? By whom? The assertive tidbit was unlike anything else Otis had read. Obviously Ulrich didn't mean Vietnam, nor could he mean Humble. They had *invited* him. Could 'sent' refer to a missionary group? Alaska seemed an unlikely destination. Was someone else expecting to hear from Ulrich? Had he missed vital papers? Otis flipped ahead:

"Tuesday, February 17th, 1970, 6:10AM, Slept late; fasting to know the Lord's will. 'Present your bodies a living sacrifice. Teach us to number our days.' I was bought at a price by Christ's death. I need to deny myself. Lord, help me submit my earthly tent to your glory!"

Tent? Body? Sacrifice? It all seemed uncanny, but did it mean anything? Brains were good at finding patterns, but also good at inventing them: animal shapes in clouds or shared impressions with staying power like New Hampshire's iconic Old Man of the Mountain rock face. His time alone in Ulrich's tent had seemed endless, voices and music filling the wind. Was he doing that here? Was what he was seeing like back-masks in pop songs? *Number nine; number nine.* That stuff led to the asylum. To tame the wild theories, Otis resolved to verify the Bible verses Ulrich cited. Until work cleared his return, he had ample time.

Forty-Four:
A Land I Will Show You

Ulrich's Bible had heft. Solid and earthy-smelling, it flopped on the bed as if poured. Otis feared to rip the near-translucent pages which made reedy sounds as he cautiously turned them. Faint stains at the page edges seemed to say, "I was here." *Years of Ulrich's fingers*. Uneasy, Otis wiped his palms on the sheets then looked up "tent" in the Bible's index. Overwhelmed by the number of references in the Old Testament, he sampled from a much smaller list in the New. One verse gave him pause.

"If our earthly tent is dissolved, we have one from God, a house not made with hands, eternal in the heavens."

He pictured Ulrich unzipping the tent flap to see his last sunrise. Red sky in the morning. Sailors take warning. If Ulrich had had inklings of doom that day, why had he not spoken up? *Stop. This is nuts.* The storm was a surprise, the bad luck over quickly for Ulrich at least. Pushing the thought away, he looked up more tent verses and then returned to the notebook.

"Wednesday, February 18th, 1970, 5:38AM. Snow heavy. No classes. Still fasting, waiting on the Lord. Verses for today: 'The lot is cast into the lap; but every decision is from the LORD.' 'Let a bear robbed of her whelps meet a man, rather than a fool in his folly.' 'Our friend sleeps; but I go that I may wake him.' 'My brother would not have died.'"

Otis guessed that, like much that flowed from Ulrich's mouth, his pen, or his typewriter, these too were Bible excerpts, but why this odd conglomeration? And why right *then*, around the time he'd accepted the Humble job? Otis' first impression of Ulrich had been one of unimaginative earnestness—big state school, big company job, his aim to return to central Nebraska and, with his sweetheart, raise kids as bland as that landscape. Yet in Ulrich's notebooks, Otis was starting to see an immigrant's vigor. His sermonette on God orchestrating the weather had been rife with presuppositions he didn't agree with, yet he could respect that he had firm thought-out convictions. His journal entries were similarly avid, crackling with intellect. He linked ideas in ways that forced Otis to think. Ulrich's viewpoints could be brilliant or batty, but they were hardly dull.

The lot is cast. Like the die is cast; like rolling dice. Mike Running Bear had denied chance. Had he been right? *My brother would not have died.* It was as if, before they met, Ulrich had known Otis' deepest pain. He tried to stem an image cascade triggered by Ulrich's words, but the effort was like a doctor thumping his knee with one of those little brown mallets. *Shined shoes in damp grass, his mother's and Billy's clammy hands clutching his tighter with each rifle volley: Fire! Fire! Fire! Soldiers folding the flag, robot-like, then kneeling to hand it over.* The scene played in his mind like an old Hitchcock film—the dismay only accentuated by repetition. At home, his father had placed the blue-and-white triangle on the mantle in a special plastic case beside Henry's formal picture, now faded. *Enough!* Otis grabbed another notebook.

"June 11th, 1970, 5:10AM. Leaving Grand Island and Calia for now. Sad, but she is in God's hands. This journey is right. 'Behold, I show you a mystery; we shall not all sleep, but we shall all be changed and the dead shall be raised incorruptible.'"

Had he seen this entry before?

No. He was certain he'd never opened this notebook.

"June 12th, 1970, 4:30AM. Last night, a man at the Little Bighorn battlefield struck the colors at the soldiers' cemetery and played taps on a bugle. I helped him fold the flag."

Otis re-checked the date. *This was crazy.* There were dozens of routes from Grand Island to the Icefield yet half a day after he, Mike and Howard the ranger had stood at the Little Bighorn battlefield flagpole, Ulrich had handled the same piece of hallowed fabric. His spine tingled with a sudden wild thought. *If Ulrich had met Howard, had Ulrich and Mike also met?* After dropping Otis off at the Canadian border, Mike would have attended his nearby meeting at Fort Belknap, then sped back south. Otis flipped ahead in Ulrich's journal but found no mention of Mike, Mark, or a ranch. Still, the likelihood that the two men had passed on the highway left him spellbound and shoved Mike's assertions back to the fore. Either everything was under

God's control or nothing was. Either everything was random or nothing was. Either every human life was imbued with vital meaning and purpose or none of them were. There was no splitting the difference.

Mike's claims still seemed way too black and white, but until he could slam-dunk *refute* them, he couldn't dismiss a guy with three Purple Hearts *and* three Stanford degrees.

Otis' philosophy professor would have retorted that if nothing is random then we must all be automaton puppets, lacking free will, but clearly Mike had not thought that. He'd spoken and acted as if *every* choice mattered. He and Mark had been more than hospitable, concerned for his future despite it being highly unlikely they would ever see him again. They'd impressed on him the gravity of the choices before him and voiced strong opinions, yet they'd listened and let him make up his own mind. And both men were over thirty!

Otis' sense of their wisdom reminded him of the Pleiades constellation. Looking off to one side, the seven sisters seemed distinct, but gaze at them head-on and they blurred. Timeframes changed perspectives too, Mike had said. Victories became defeats and vice versa yet such vast realities were hard to grasp inside of any specific battle. Otis knew this viscerally. If an opponent had him in a cross-face cradle with seconds to go in a match, he would dwell inside each intense second, forgetting the team, the score, and even what day it was.

He wished Mike were here, or Lucius, or Coach. Coach's silent disappointment still bugged him, but—despite his doubt in the crevasse—it hardly annulled his gospel of winning. Rather, it underlined its importance. Wait for the right moment, then go big, act boldly, never look back. Bluffing the Icefield ranger had come on instinct. Sure, the fallout from that had been tricky; corresponding with Calia might not have been the best idea. But anything worth doing came with trying moments—bad patches, Coach called them. The prospect of quick relief by giving up might sparkle as if not an abyss of shame but then when you grasped its shiny sucker bait and *actually lost*, it would mock as it widened to consume you. He had to persist in the course he had chosen; redouble his faith; apply Coach's wisdom more fully. In time, his next move would make itself known. It always did.

Otis set the Bible and notebooks aside, shut off the light, and nestled under his comforter. In that time between waking and sleeping, he imagined his bedsheets as pages and felt enthralled by moonlight sparkling absurdly bright through a window he'd never seen. He slid out of the book to examine frost patterns on its panes, so beautiful that to avert his gaze seemed unthinkable. The moonlight felt warm and pure on his face, erasing concern that the room was not his. Then, as if beckoning, the light shaft redirected his attention to a thin form on the bed—a boy—who slid to his knees on the floor, hands clasped before him, lips moving, soundless.

'Love not sleep,' Otis thought as he watched the boy pray, face to his mattress. *Ulrich had written that.* The same sense suggested he open his eyes. But they *are* open, he thought, the scene more vivid than being awake.

Unaware of interim movement, he stood over the boy whose hands—blue-white like the moon—were shaking so violently that Otis thought they might shatter or that the boy might topple. But the boy kept them clasped, resolute. Strange, Otis thought. Why did *he* feel so warm? Then the boy stood before him, his face serene, Ulrich as man and boy, timeless. Otis felt no terror or shame, only gladness to see him.

Then, for a split second—barely long enough for Otis to recognize himself—Ulrich's face became his own, as in a mirror. Before he could think what was happening, the vision zoomed back and he was looking down at *his own* body, twisted and trapped in deep darkness, a speck in an ice block so massive, ancient, and menacing that he felt it had desired to swallow him up since long before he was born.

His dream view changed again and he was looking up to where he'd been and from there, far above, a faint voice cried, *Otis!* A pinprick of light zoomed down at him—headlamp size in his eyes, then like a train to full sun strength and more, blinding, far brighter than midday June on the glacier.

Then, as happens with dreams that end in more sleep, droplets of detail soaked in like rain on soft soil to water a place deep inside him. Later, upon waking, Otis would recall only a sense of having witnessed something horrific, lovely, and intensely true.

Forty-Five:
Hooked

On Monday, Otis called his boss. "Check back in a couple of days," Roy snapped, touchy on top of his usual crabby. Otis asked if "a couple" meant two, but Roy hung up.

From Ulrich's PO box, Otis retrieved a short letter from Calia and read it by the dim light in Ulrich's car.

"Please come home for Christmas, Ulrich. I miss you. Ethel has been a dear, but people I thought were friends are avoiding me. Some customers have been generous, but tips are way down. The landlord wants extra rent on deposit in case you don't return and I can't work. We don't need a big ceremony, darling. I'll understand if you have to go back to Alaska."

Her earnest words felt like eating glass shards. She had gently detoured around his scheming August request that they wait to marry. After all, *she* didn't know she was asking the impossible.

Otis' Otis PO box yielded a letter from his father. Unusual. And not on graph paper either.

"Son, I'm writing because it's important you know a few things. I trust you will weigh them as a man, ready to live with the consequences of your choices. First, the FBI came by my office to ask after you. I hope that will not happen again. I gather you pulled a stunt last June. If that's true, I am saddened you could not be honest with us but frankly, I'm not as sure anymore who to believe. I cannot endorse your actions, yet I can appreciate your perspective better. At least I try. Second, the FBI came by the house to press your mother—alone, on a weekday. That upset her greatly, and it angered me. I hope you get the picture. Lastly, your grandmother is doing poorly. This will likely be her last Christmas."

227

Otis was torn. His father seemed warmer and more straightforward, but was he? The scene he described at work would have hurt his pride, yet his mentioning it hinted at the old manipulation. It hurt to hear that he might not believe him, but why should he? Otis hadn't exactly leveled with them. He hated to think of his mother upset or his grandmother dying, but he could barely afford food. Cross-country short-notice holiday airfare was out of the question.

If he asked, his parents would buy him a ticket, but then they would tussle over the timing (why not two weeks?) and ask other questions he wasn't ready to answer. To be consistent, and to steer them away from the FBI's viewpoint, he would have to come up with a plausible military job and mix the tale with the truth of a crappy civilian one that offered little time off.

They would insist on having Midge (the perky Dirkden travel agent they'd used since forever) send him the ticket special delivery. Otis imagined a chat in which he coaxed Midge to write the ticket in *Ulrich's* name. Crazy. No way. Yet one in his real name would expose him. The FBI spot-checked passenger manifests. He might make the round-trip without incident then get a visit from them months later. He would be done, caught, inducted.

He hadn't been thrilled about going home, but as the impossibility of the trip sank in, he felt like he'd dropped his keys down a storm drain. He tried to cheer himself up. *Likely her last Christmas* might mean his grandmother had a year. She might still be fine next July or August. He hoped so. Mount McKinley still loomed for next June.

Otis wandered downtown past window displays strewn with cotton balls. Foam snowmen leered amidst fake trees decorated with colored lights and shiny balls. "Advent!" declared a sign atop a stack of plastic-wrapped calendars. December first. The acute distress of last year's lottery had caused every cherished childhood memory of anticipation to wither and blow away. Instead of twenty-five tiny paper doors opened in patient family wonder on each of twenty-five mornings (to sheep and frankincense, angels and myrrh) men whose childhood wonder had petrified long ago had rushed to split open three hundred and sixty-six hard plastic canisters in one great hurried public obscenity. On most TVs, in black and white, the canisters appeared to be skull-grey. In fact they were blue-green—like the eggs of gigantic vipers—cracked to make one huge undercooked national omelet to feed the voracious war. Nearly one million men had been judged in one hour—some birthdays blessed, others cursed; countless others still in limbo even now.

Why had his birthday been found wanting? Why had *anyone's*? As arctic nights lengthened, his perverse luck had grown a why-bother numbness that mocked last summer's can-do bath of round-the-clock light. He forgot small things often, recalled big ones only with effort, and became quickly irritated by trivialities. Reading Ulrich's journals alieved his malaise temporarily, but whenever he put them aside, Sid's empty place seemed even creepier. It wasn't as if Ulrich were some cheesy poltergeist, knocking and moaning and placing cold spots. (It being Alaska, those were routine around the house.) Rather, the house could feel like a bell jar being watched. Why should he stay? Why not move to LA, Miami, or Hawaii? He remembered why. He was broke. The best he could do to dull a sense of despair was to sleep.

Otis felt no loyalty to his airport job, but as he waited for a call to return, it remained his best option. Job ads barely covered a page in the newspaper now and he wasn't about to wash dishes again. Wistful for weekend waffles with his brothers—enthralled on the sofa to Popeye, Gumby, and Boomtown—Otis ate dry corn flakes alone, tuned to the only Anchorage station with decent reception, soothed by Mother Moose, a quintessentially Alaskan kids' show. He tried baking bread with Sid's staples but it emerged rock-like, and once he ran out of butter (and then mayonnaise) it was nearly inedible. He tried Roy daily but kept getting busy signals.

A few weeks before Christmas, Sid returned, tan and jaunty. Otis could expect more business parcels soon; then he should wait for instructions. The next day, Sid left without mentioning the January rent. Sure enough, most of the day after that, Otis was up and down the stairs signing for packages until they filled the cupboard. Days passed with no word from Roy or Sid until finally, fed up early one morning, he drove to the airport.

"Is he in?" Otis asked Nadine, who looked careworn.

"Perfect timing!" Roy bellowed from out of sight. Chair hinges protested. Roy burst from his office, waving a sheaf of papers. "The investigators need to see you *right now*. If they clear you, you're on first shift. We have five eastbound planes to turn before noon: two DC-8s and three

707s. Bedlam! Happens every year. The mommas call the politicians who lean on the Army for home-leave rotations."

Otis was not dressed to work. It was below zero outside. His stomach growled. He thanked Roy and bowed slightly. He asked Nadine about his check. She said she'd mailed it. Otis verified Sid's address. "You'll get it soon. The mail's slow this time of year." Roy returned to his office. Nadine studied an accordion-like pile of perforated paper, striped with green lines. "It was only nine hours, I'm afraid. I know you stayed to help after the crash, but the punch clock stops when the airport shuts down." She lowered her voice. "I'm sorry you had to start with that."

"Me too," Otis said softly. "It's hard to forget."

"I've seen thirty years' worth. Two last October The crews come for donuts and you get to know them. The big crash down Cook Inlet seems like yesterday." She looked suddenly paler. "You remember the faces."

Otis spied a box of donuts atop Roy's filing cabinet. Roy's back was turned, engrossed in a call. Otis snuck into his office, grabbed three, and set one on Nadine's desk on a paper napkin. "To cheer you up."

"Oh, I really shouldn't."

Otis split it in half. "There."

Nadine took it, held it, giggled, then nibbled.

Just then, an investigator emerged and beckoned.

Nadine reached out and wiped powdered sugar off Otis' face the way his mother used to. "Just tell them the truth," she said. "You'll do fine."

The interview was over in twenty minutes. Otis was fully cleared, the accident not his fault. He wished someone could acquit him as easily from last summer's mishap but the fact that no one even knew made that impossible. He asked guys on the crew to take pity on him and swap duties so that—wearing only one sweatshirt—he could work inside. "Not today," came the nicest response. In the men's room, Otis stuffed his clothes with wadded paper towels for insulation as best he could. The crew cleared the clot of big planes, but then someone on second shift called in sick. Otis grabbed the open slot. An hour before midnight, two more charters from Vietnam were delayed for repairs. Soldiers shuffled inside and spilled across the waiting area, playing cards, reading, and smoking. Some lay unmoving on the worn carpet, a mix of eyes open and closed.

An officer asked Roy to unload the men's bags from the stranded planes and he agreed. He'd fought island-to-island in the Pacific. He knew how it was. He asked for volunteers for the third shift task.

Otis was chilled, Roy's donuts a distant memory, but he shot up a hand. Twenty four punched-in hours would resuscitate his finances. The crew didn't need to deliver bags to specific soldiers Roy said, but when a guy who'd worked hotel jobs rushed to do just that and received tips, all the other guys hustled too. (As a result, the crew served the sleeping men last.)

As he worked, Otis took in the sea of faces, anything but uniform, even as their routines were alike. Soldiers fumbled for shaving kits and fresh clothes, their minds on tomorrow. The waiting girlfriend or wife would be improved—or at worst unchanged—ready to bestow the same doting adoration on her fighting man as that which he'd given her gazing at a damp, fading wallet photo through many nights and days, clinging to hope. A wheelchair-bound Corporal sat alone, ignored by both the airport crew and his fellow soldiers.

Otis approached. "Hooke" declared the man's pocket insignia. One of his legs and one arm were truncated; a cast encased his remaining foot. Thin scruff dappled his face like spilled commas on chocolate. A simple metal cross hung around his neck. Otis set Corporal Hooke's monogrammed duffel beside him, careful to keep his eyes away, afraid he would stare at the wrong things and offend him. Curson pointed at a trail of wadded paper towels across the airport waiting area. "It looks like you're coming apart."

As Otis rushed to retrieve the lost makeshift insulation, he thought of the brainless scarecrow in the Wizard of Oz. He returned to Corporal Hooke who fished for his wallet but dropped it out of reach. Otis stooped for it. "Please take a sawbuck for your trouble," Corporal Hooke said.

Otis was tempted by the five dollars, yet the thought also felt like stealing. He handed back the wallet unopened. Corporal Hooke scowled and said that if it made him feel better, Otis could buy him two hot dogs with onions and mustard and keep the change to buy his own. Otis' mouth watered. He bought several hot dogs, dressed all the same, then ate them with Corporal Hooke. For a man with one working limb, he managed well, Otis thought, as Corporal Hooke deftly daubed mustard from his lips.

"My friends call me Curson."

"Otis," said Otis, forgetting too late that here he was Ulrich.

"You serve?" Curson asked.

"Excuse me?"

"You heard me. Did you serve? Like us." He indicated the waiting area.

The excuse Otis had often repeated (that he'd drawn a high draft number) formed on his lips, but before he could speak, a withering inward taunt dissolved it: *It was never your number.* Here with Curson—a man who'd paid a high price doing what Otis was evading—Otis felt he could neither lie *nor* tell the truth. "Uh, no. I haven't served... yet. It's complicated." He felt like a peach stone had lodged in his throat.

Curson's expression stayed kind. He removed a toothpick from his breast pocket and worked it around his front teeth. "Come here," he said and Otis bent down on one knee, his arms crossed tight. Curson's breath smelled of cinnamon. "I watched you distribute the bags. You work hard, but you're shy about tips. Tell me: why is that?"

Otis wanted to voice his fear and dwindling hope, his homesickness and guilt at fleeing. He wanted to share the sadness that ebbed but always returned. No way could he take money from soldiers who'd actually served. *God, he missed Henry.* But all he had the courage to say was, "I'm not sure."

The silence that followed felt interminable, but Curson smiled in a way that seemed non-judgmental. Otis was about to leave when Curson spoke.

"I hope you might do me a favor."

He needed to urinate, he explained, but he didn't want to bother his sleeping buddies. He would be grateful if Otis could wheel him to the men's room. Otis considered. Had his co-workers set him up for a practical joke? It was certainly the *kind* of ugly prank they might pull. But if Curson were on the level—as he seemed to be—and Otis refused, he would despise himself. The help proved much simpler than Otis feared, and as he washed Curson's hand he recalled how his grandfather would place a stepstool at the sink to help *him* wash up. When they finished, Curson said that his wife disliked beards. Would Otis help him shave? That too proved straightforward, and when they finished Otis felt better than he had in weeks. Later though, he wished he'd asked Curson how he managed to be so serene in such a helpless, compromised condition.

Forty-Six:
Balsam

O n his way home, Otis bought milk, eggs, and Pop-Tarts. At the house, mail littered the foyer. Gathering it, he blanched. Two cards stated that packages needing signatures would be returned to the sender if not picked up. "Fidelity, Bravery, Integrity," declared the colorful logo on a letter addressed to Ulrich. It bore no postage. The FBI had come. Heart racing, he set the grocery bag on the stairs; it flopped down. Ignoring the soggy mess at his feet, he tore open the letter.

"Dear Mr. Sterbender, It has come to our attention that you may be acquainted with, know the whereabouts of, or have had substantive dealings with one Mr. Otis Shurwood Fletcher, late of Dirkden, Massachusetts. Mr. Fletcher is a person of interest in, and potentially the subject of, an important ongoing Bureau investigation. We would kindly request that you make an appointment to speak with us at your earliest convenience regarding what you may know about Mr. Fletcher's activities, associations, and/or whereabouts. We would further ask that you not share your knowledge of this inquiry with Mr. Fletcher." *Too late*, Otis thought. "Thank you for your cooperation with the United States government in this vital matter," the letter concluded.

"Cordially Yours, Agent Jeb Cuttler Russo, Anchorage FBI."

Otis cleaned the stairs, scrambled the unbroken eggs with the wet Pop-Tarts, then guzzled the remaining milk. What did *earliest convenience* mean? Did they have photos? Fatigue hit him like a truck. When he woke it was dark, after the start of his regular shift. He sped to work but could not find his time card to punch in. Roy sidled up, holding it out like a soccer referee's warning. "See me for it at six." Otis wanted to argue. He was only twenty

233

minutes late. It wasn't fair for Roy to make him work for free. Otis slunk out to load planes.

He got home late. Boot tracks laced the walk and puddles wet the inside stairs, but the drive showed no sign of recent tire tracks. Otis turned on all the lights, checked the closets, and pulled back the shower curtain. His paycheck envelope rested on the kitchen table. Who had brought it up? Sid and the landlord had keys and the FBI didn't need them. Could it be the Halloween trio? He opened the cupboards. The packages he had signed for after Sid left had been replaced by un-mailed smaller ones, addressed all over Alaska. Each was the size and weight of a paperback book. Separately, each addressee was plausible—Jack Coe, Jake Doe, John Bow—but together? At the back of the cupboard was a manila envelope with Ulrich's name on it.

Otis undid the clasp, splayed it, and tipped out a hundred dollar bill, several times the value of his first paycheck. He'd never held this denomination. Its crisp texture reminded him of the extra fine sandpaper he'd used on balsawood model rockets. His mouth watered for the thick steak he would order rare and eat very slowly. But what did Sid want? Otis slid out a typewritten page.

"Quick stop to say hello. Sorry I missed you. Not sure how long I'll be gone this trip. The C-note's for postage, outbound. Vary the locations and days. I'm counting on you getting this right. Now burn this note, and check the freezer. You're welcome. P.S., no more pick-up delays!"

Why had Sid bothered to type? Otis tromped to the basement, hoping for moose or elk tenderloin steaks, but both large chest freezers were padlocked. Upstairs again he opened the smaller freezer over the fridge. It was packed with TV dinners. Frost-steam spilled at his feet. He was grateful and yet, like Jack the trucker's ride offer, the gesture felt like it had strings.

On a hunch, he set Sid's note beside a draft he'd left rolled in Ulrich's typewriter, stymied to come up with fresh reasons why Ulrich couldn't call or visit Calia. Each 'a', 'e,' and 'h' evinced worn spots while all the 'g' whorls were distinctively inky. Otis completed a sentence: "...and so, I hope..." The lines were offset! Sid must have removed Otis' letter, typed his directive, then re-rolled Otis' letter back around the typewriter's rubber platen cylinder. For such a meticulous man, it was sloppy.

Otis' face heated up. Sid *wanted* him to know—as blatantly as if he'd pinched Calia's rump, confident that Otis, upon seeing it, would do nothing. And Sid was right. Until Otis had money again, he was beholden to him.

An awful thought came: *Sid had likely also made him.* Otis had hidden his old, real driver's license, but his letters from home were right there in an open box in his room. How stupid! Sid knew he was juggling two identities. And in that discovery, the FBI couldn't be far behind him.

Crumpled in the dark crevasse (dire as that had been) Otis had been sure which way was up and, when morning light came, what he had to do to save himself. This felt instead like what had preceded that fall—lost on the plateau in the storm, *waiting* for a jolt to yank him out of control.

Otis pocketed the hundred. In the sink he burned Sid's note. As he washed the ashes down the drain, he wondered not only how he would extricate himself this time but also from what.

Hungry for a familiar reference point, he thought back to when his intact family of five—he, Henry, Billy, and their parents—would go to the parking lot behind Dirkden Congregational as soon as the Christmas trees arrived, bare bulbs strung on wires, sawdust strewn around for mud. Clumps of trees leaned against sawhorse frames, too many to make a quick choice, unless it was cold. He missed his mother's unfailing traditions: cookies and Handel's Messiah, vanilla, ginger and fresh balsam smells. Until Otis turned nineteen, the holiday seasons were hard to tell apart.

The Christmas of '67—with Henry barely two months in the ground—the remaining four of them had faked their way through each tradition as if he were merely delayed getting home. Only upon unwrapping the 1968 picture calendars did each of them relish secret relief that the painful charades the three *others* needed would be over soon. On New Year's Eve, Otis retreated to his room to listen to the top hits countdown. A short song called "The Letter," *almost* made number one. Otis had tried to vote it so, but the station's lines had been jammed. Why couldn't someone get *him* an airplane ticket? *Anywhere.* Any time or place that the war wasn't and home was as it once had been. But 1968 only multiplied agonies and made Otis' day of reckoning seem certain.

The next Christmas Eve, Apollo Eight circled the moon. When the astronauts slipped behind it in silence—more isolated than anyone had ever been—Otis felt the thick darkness: billions of people concurrently anxious. *Would they re-emerge?* Everyone venerated the iconic photo they took Christmas Day ('Earthrise') but for Otis the image only intensified his loneliness. Severed by night, the blue-white ball hung cut off by vast black dead space—*utterly* alone.

If he got a small tree for Sid's too-big empty apartment, it would seem cheerier, a small island of normalcy. He would call his mom for her recipes; make the best of his situation alone. He had free rent and weeks' worth of food. He was back at work. For all he knew, Sid's parcels could be books: gifts for far-flung friends. What did he have to complain about? Why wasn't he happy? He retreated to his room and opened an Ulrich journal where he'd left a marker.

"Monday, March 2nd, 1970, 5:25AM. Excited about Alaska and Light of Grace Fellowship. Reminds me of Psalm 68:6a: "God maketh the solitary to dwell in families.""

Family? Not exactly, but they might have Christmas music, decorations, and cookies. And if they sold trees, it would save him a trip. He found the address in the phone book then jotted it in the notebook's margin. He could sit in the back, glean some Christmas spirit, and then slip out.

A few days later, Otis woke cold. In the glow of his drugstore watch, his breath steamed. On several occasions, he'd come close to tossing it because it reminded him of Henry's finer timepiece, lost on the glacier. Had the boiler cut out? It was too early to bug the landlord he'd not met. He put a TV dinner in the oven and donned his parka. Around seven, he went downstairs and knocked. After several minutes, the landlord's porch light came on. He emerged, his grey hair mussed by sleep, his face days unshaven. "Who are you?" He yelled. "What do you want?" He looked confused.

Through the security chain, Otis identified himself.

"Rick? You need to speak up; I'm hard of hearing. Are you telling me you sub-let from Sidwell?"

"We take it month by month," Otis yelled.

"He's not supposed to sub-let."

Otis shrugged then described the problem.

"Wait here, Rick." Otis stamped and blew into his hands. The landlord returned with sooty fingers. "The tank's empty. Did Sid pay the bill?"

"Beats me."

The landlord let fly a string of epithets. He would call the oil company then come up to check on things. Meantime, could "Rick" light the oven, leave its door open, and set faucets dripping? Otis agreed. He turned and descended the porch, eager to hide Sid's packages.

"Rick" the landlord called after him. "Did Sidwell give you keys to the basement freezers?"

"No," Otis said, suddenly defensive for Sid, who thought this guy nosy.

Otis trudged upstairs and did as the landlord asked, but the oven barely dented the chill. He packed his clothes, his sleeping bag, Ulrich's typewriter, and the next round of Sid's packages in the car then—happy to be footloose again—he drove to find a warm place to wait.

Forty-Seven:
In Flight

The McDonald's Otis had visited his first day in Anchorage looked naked without balloons to accompany the leftover banners: *First in Alaska! Go for the Goodness! Thousands served!* At the drive-through, he tried to pay with Sid's hundred but the server balked. Counterfeit trouble, her manager explained. Otis offered Ulrich's ID and Sid's address, hopeful they didn't record them. In the front seat, with the heater on, he re-typed and finished the offset letter to Calia, then mailed it from a post office he'd never been to, along with one of Sid's packages. At another post office, he retrieved the most recent packages for Sid that he'd failed to sign for.

The clerk palpated them and raised an eyebrow.

"Money orders are safer," he said.

Why was everyone being so nosy today? He visited his Otis box (empty), his Ulrich box (empty), then a third place to send another of Sid's packages off to a funny name.

He then drove around for a while. He could empathize with Calia for wanting to see Ulrich in person. He was no expert on facial expressions or body language, but they helped avoid miscues. Trying to guess how Ulrich might phrase a reply still felt like playing chess blindfolded. If he went to Nebraska he'd learn things and be less blind. He pondered how. He didn't necessarily have to speak with Calia, just get a sense for her and the place. No, speaking was better. Should he pretend no connection to Ulrich or admit that he'd met him? What might be in Ulrich's safe deposit box?

He ran quick mental math: travel costs and time off. The trip would clean him out, but he could trade shifts and just swing it. He had to be careful though. Calia had mentioned her father in retrospect, but what if he was still around? Then there was Jack. The diner seemed to be one of his regular stops. And if Rhonda was working she would recognize him. He was being too anxious, not being bold. He resolved to *make* it work. He changed into nice clothes, drove to the airport, and parked in the long-term lot.

At the Alaska Airlines ticket counter, he conjured George C. Scott's four-star-general brass from his "Patton" monologue. "One way to Denver," he grunted. "Tonight!" Denver meant a longer drive, but it would give him time to figure out how to approach things.

"I can get you on the redeye through Seattle." Otis mentally doubled the price for the return then agreed. He had just enough. "What name should I put on the ticket?"

Why hadn't he thought this part through? Ulrich was on the airport payroll; Otis was wanted by the FBI. "Reinhold Messner," Otis said in a sloppy Austrian accent.

Incredibly, she bought the act, as wide-eyed as if he'd said "John Lennon." She wrote the ticket with a clunky grip. Surprisingly, she spelled the name right. Wincing, she separated the triplicate purple-red carbons, daubed ink from her fingers, and slid the top copy into a ticket sleeve.

"It's an honor to serve you, sir. I'm sorry about your brother."

"What?" Otis' mind churned. *Brother?* Who *here* knew about Henry?

She held up her hands, shiny with scars. "I lost a friend on McKinley."

Frostbite. Oh. She was a climber. And she meant Günther Messner. In June, the brothers had made a first ascent of Nanga Parbat's Rupal Face— "beautiful" in Sanskrit—a relentless three mile wall of rock and ice in the Pakistan Himalaya. Reinhold crawled back to camp a week later, badly frostbitten. Günther did not. Günther stayed missing. She must assume Reinhold was here to scout an audacious climb.

"I don't know who you think I am," Otis said, jutting indignation even as his accent wavered. Why had he thought he could impersonate a celebrity as casually as a nobody? Serious climbers were rare. Reputation mattered. Word got around. To summit North America's highest peak, he needed to *win* people like her around Anchorage, not embarrass himself.

She winked. "Don't worry, Mr. Messner. My lips are sealed."

In the parking lot, Otis folded his nice clothes around his airline ticket and changed for work. Nadine confirmed that he wasn't on the schedule again until next Tuesday. Otis punched in.

Calia. Soon they would breathe the same air. Not a letter or old photo but the actual woman. Throughout his shift, pre-match type jitters kept him energized as he imagined his redeye flight's one-thirty departure and their face-to-face conversation this time tomorrow

Just before midnight, a big plane nosed in. Roy made second shift stay to help turn it but the more Otis tried to hurry his crew, the more they dawdled for overtime. Finally, around one, Otis lined up to punch out. Roy again sidled up. Did this man have a life?

"Sterbender? I might need you this weekend. Call me tomorrow."

"OK," Otis bluffed. Roy would rather lose a limb than pay more overtime. Otis ran to his car, threw on his nice clothes, then sprinted to his gate. As the plane's door clunked shut just behind him and he caught his breath, Otis suddenly wondered: *What have I done?*

***

Driving east from Denver, dimples of snow dotted the brown land. Behind, a peach sky faded to purple, then grey, then to black. The close call with Jack last June had diverted him from California to extremes of bad and good luck he'd never asked for. If he'd kept his cool and continued west, he might not have a safe draft number, but maybe he'd have been a Yosemite climber, ensconced in a friendly underground network of fellow draft dodgers.

Near the Nebraska border, he slowed to look for where he'd fought Jack, but everything was different: season, time of day, his state of mind. The memory shook him. What would Jack have done to him if he'd passed out? What if Otis had let his rage run and shot Jack beside the road? In such a remote place he would likely have gotten away with it, but knowing now what that felt like, he was glad that he hadn't. Leaving the scene did not mean that the scene left you.

He stopped for food, coffee, and gas. Was this a fool's errand? What should he say to her? He thought about bailing to Mexico City. Its snow-topped volcanoes were worthy walk-ups, almost twenty thousand feet. He could return the rental in El Paso, cross to Juarez, and hitch south, visit the '68 Olympic wrestling venue. On TV, right up until his weight class hero

240

missed bronze for the U.S., the faraway Insurgentes Rink had felt more like home than home. But they had probably put the ice back, and he didn't speak Spanish. Plus, the Mexican mail was notoriously erratic.

~~~

The closer Otis got to the Grand Island diner, the more he felt as if Octopus sat in the seat beside him. *Drop him frozen!* The dread sense persisted. Across the street from the diner lot, Otis paused to scan for Jack's semi-truck rig. *Jack could be anywhere along thousands of miles of highway. You escaped him by wits once; you can do it again if you have to. He has much more to lose than you do in a public confrontation.* After an hour watching trucks come and go, he drove across the street into the lot and parked facing the diner's foggy plate glass.

And there she was.

Time and pregnancy had altered Calia's girlish plump cheeks and the forward curl of her thin shoulders, but it was unmistakably her: Ulrich's photo, alive. Panic seized him again. Typing gave him time to weigh what to say and rework it; a visit would be a lit fuse of half-inept invention.

Tomorrow. He would return fresh and ready tomorrow.

He drove off and found a motel.

That night, he dreamed about Pinnacle Gully.

Ulrich was above, leading *without a rope*. Otis tried to follow in the divots left by Ulrich's tools, but a huge hawk buffeted him with its wings, sucking the air from his lungs. Otis craned his neck to see up but gasped and fell backward. The hawk dove and seized him midair in its razor talons, shredding his parka. Then the dream flipped and *he* was the hawk, Ulrich below, some feathers stuck in his blood and some drifting away.

Forty-Eight:
Precious

‗‗‗‗‗‗‗‗‗‗

Last June, Grand Island had seemed a mercurial planet of creosote, fertilizer, and hot dust but now as Otis drove through what passed for downtown, it seemed a lost dreary moon. Cold vapor billowed; shoes and tires squeaked. Stumpy buildings stood cordially distant from one another, their brick façades announcing forgotten brands in old ghostly commercial whitewash. Scarf-clad forms rushed heads-down through veils of wind-driven snow, immune to the archaic cheer of the outdated ads above them. Otis wondered: Who among them might have known Ulrich?

Back at the diner midmorning, Otis ate slowly, pretending to read the paper. The lunch crowd came and went, as did a second plate of scrambled eggs. He motioned for Susan, his waitress.

"Is Calia working today?"

"Who wants to know?"

Her sallow face and grey roots hinted at decades of multiple jobs.

"I'm a friend of a friend."

"She doesn't need strangers." Susan scowled, then wagged a finger. "Wait. I've seen you. Sunburned, last June, headed west. You left with trucker Jack. Now you're back in a rental?"

Otis shrugged, sheepish. "I came for the food?"

"Bull. Jack got beat up. Lost his cargo. Got fired. You know anything about that?"

"No. Sounds terrible."

She glared. "Who are you? Who is this mutual friend?"

Otis gave his real name. It felt odd. "I met Ulrich last summer. He mentioned this place—and Calia. I was in the area and figured I'd say hello." He could justify each partial truth.

Susan drew back her head, turtle-like, skeptical.

"Where is he? Are you in touch with him?"

"Not really. Not lately." He knew she would hear the truth wrongly.

"I used to think Ulrich was a nice kid but now? If I saw him, I'd smack him. Calia deserves better." Otis wanted to blurt his agreement. Calia deserved the best. But he said nothing. Susan said, "You tell him to come back here pronto. No offense, but an envoy doesn't cut it. Calia's a precious jewel." She turned. "She's on six to ten. I'll tell her you came by."

Otis left a big tip then drove back into town, glad that she'd not pressed him further. Grain elevators dotted the horizon, their concrete barely distinct from the drab sky. How had Ulrich come to love mountains in a place where climbing or standing out defied nature? Otis dropped off two of Sid's packages at the post office, then gathered courage for his next errand.

<hr />

From the first moment Otis discovered the key among Ulrich's things, he wondered what it unlocked. When a bill came for a safety deposit box, he'd recalled the etched number and figured it out. He imagined a sandstone bank façade, ornate brass handles on thick glass doors. Perhaps Ulrich's Uncle Walter and Aunt Greta had kept jewelry in the box, or stocks held for decades—Masco, Xerox, Polaroid, Avon—curlicue-engraved certificates worth millions now. To let such wealth revert to the state would be a waste.

He had practiced Ulrich's signature and rehearsed plausible dialogue. He would stroll across a cavernous lobby, shoes clacking on inlaid marble, eyes disciplined to be un-furtive. Grand Island seemed like a scrupulous place, so he brought the receipt. They would not have a photo. Of that, he was sure. If someone knew Ulrich, Otis was ready to say essentially what he'd said already at the diner: he was a friend of Ulrich's running an errand, helping. It was a calculated risk. Ulrich had lived here only five years before departing for college. If things went badly, he could always hop on the interstate. It would be a shame though, the ground salted, Calia further out of reach.

Inside the front vestibule at the First Agricultural Trust, Otis pulled the wood door through a gritty half-circle of sand-scraped beige carpet the same color as a ceiling so low as to evoke the one time Otis had tried spelunking. A man in a green polyester suit sat at a veneer desk beside a puny vault. Spying Otis, Vice President Sven Bowles adjusted his nameplate. His tie was clean but stiff and melancholy, wholly unlike the perfectly knotted flows of shimmering silk Wilson Ward and Fent Carmichael the third had each sported at their Morrison-James interview lovefest.

"We close in five minutes," Sven said. "No exceptions." Even paces away, his breath smelled tomb-like. Otis had waited until nearly closing time, gambling that as three o'clock neared, the staff's focus would be more on punctuality than on scrutinizing a customer holding a key. *Five minutes*. Otis began silently counting down seconds: *two-ninety-nine, two-ninety-eight*.

Sven offered him an ingratiating smile. "May I help you?"

Otis tapped his throat and brandished the key. "Box," he croaked in mock laryngitis, careful to exhale to make obvious the handful of Extra Strength Vicks he'd gobbled just minutes ago.

Sven rolled his eyes across the room to an older man who gave a go-ahead nod, then escorted Otis a few feet to a visitor's log where Otis signed in as Ulrich.

Sven studied the scrawl. *Two-fifty-two, two-fifty-one, two-fifty. Breathe.* Should he bolt? "Go ahead," Sven said at the four-minute mark. Inside the vault, Otis found the numbered box, slid out an aluminum drawer, and set it on a small, scarred wooden table.

On top was a German Bible, "Walter Schrank" inscribed inside the cover. "Berlin, 1899."

"Three minutes," Sven whined, fidgeting at the vault door.

Tucked into Psalms was a sheaf of papers. Otis skimmed Ulrich's will, formalized June 5th, 1970, then another document, formalized the same day. Three days before Ulrich left town, Aunt Greta had signed over the deed to her house on eighty acres *and* given Ulrich power of attorney.

She'd given Ulrich everything.

In turn, Ulrich's will left everything to Calia.

And Calia didn't know he was dead.

"Two minutes!" Sven flicked the vault lights.

Otis wrote down the property's address and glanced back in the Bible, open to Psalm 127. In strokes blurred by time, someone had penciled an English translation. "Except the LORD build the house, they that build it labor in vain. It is vain for you to rise up early, sit up late, and eat the bread of sorrows, for He gives his beloved sleep."

Vain, late, sorrows, sleep. The only thing between Calia and her rightful inheritance was an impossible secret. How could he face her? Numb, Otis kept reading. "Lo, children are a heritage of the LORD, the fruit of the womb His reward." *Ulrich's child.* Sven cleared his throat as he tugged at a heavy brass grating. If Sven locked him in, Otis could hardly object.

"Mr. Sterbender!" Sven snarled an ingratiating smile. "I am *terribly* sorry, but our time is up."

Under the Bible was more but Otis couldn't return. He thrust notebooks, papers, and bundles of cash into his coat pockets. He placed Ulrich's will, Greta's power of attorney, and the house deed back into the Bible at Psalm 127, laid it in the drawer, and slid the drawer back into its slot. He locked it, took the key, and strode out across the lobby. Sven yelled. A burly guard with a saucer-sized key ring blocked the front door. Otis turned, ready for anything. Sven squinted at him in bureaucratic fury. "You must sign out, Mr. Sterbender! It is bank policy!"

Otis complied, but outside as the guard locked the door behind him, Otis felt his coat transparent, the papers he'd pilfered all in plain view. Walking away, he couldn't stop looking over his shoulder.

Forty-Nine:
No One

A unt Greta wrote to Ulrich in Alaska but never mentioned Calia. Instead, she prattled about her husband Walter as if he'd survived his 1968 stroke, of her Nebraska life as if Pearl Harbor were recent, and of being a young, carefree Jew in Berlin. Otis typed short cheery responses to her that Calia mentioned seeing on weekly visits. He figured he could chance a visit and glean ideas to improve his letters. He was also now curious about the house listed on the deed.

Planted well out from town, the Farmview Rest Home looked forlorn, its parking lot almost empty. Two whitewashed cinderblock stories squatted amidst corn stalk stubs that shadowed the snow in long stripes. On the south sides of low rolling hillocks, patches of soil awaited spring.

The overheated lobby smelled of unwashed hair and moldy bread. In neat blue and white chalk, a blackboard easel announced music appreciation and Parcheesi. Otis approached a desk.

"Name?" The receptionist's hands flitted over her humming typewriter.

He could be anyone here—except Otis or Ulrich.

"Alan Shepard," he said.

"Sign in please." She tilted her chin at a loose-leaf log.

He looked for Calia's name. "I'm a friend of Greta Schrank's nephew."

Her face went gushy; she stopped typing.

"Oh, Ulrich! We miss him. How *is* he?"

"He would have wanted to be here."

"His fiancée comes weekly, but you can tell: Mrs. Schrank misses him."

"When does Calia come by?"

Otis could see in the log it was Fridays, but saying her name would dampen any lingering doubts the staff might harbor about his visit.

"Fridays. You might see her. This time of year she's usually here right around dusk." Otis noted the time. He couldn't dawdle.

A nurse emerged and beckoned. She unlocked another door, ushered him through, then locked it behind them. The nurse's white crepe shoes squeaked on the linoleum. Urine and bleach smells competed. Otis tried not to gag. They passed a room where several women wove colored paper strips, eyeing the one older man. At the end of a long hallway, the nurse stopped, peered through a tiny wire-reinforced pane in a white metal door, then knocked and quickly unlocked it.

Otis had expected frail, but except for droopy complexion, Greta looked like she could have just come inside from digging potatoes. She sat erect, blue eyes vibrant against white hair, her thin, brightly colored cotton dress appropriate for the room's near-desert heat. She set down her knitting and peered over her glasses at Otis.

"Why hello there." Her words were clear, her accent distinctly German.

"Press this buzzer when you're done," the nurse said. "Or if you need help." She caught Otis' eye and glanced at the low sun. "She should be good for a bit." She turned and raised her voice. "Won't you, Mrs. Schrank?" Her polite smile evinced condescension. Greta smiled back in kind.

As the nurse's footsteps faded down the corridor, Greta motioned Otis to a floral-patterned plush chair and resumed her knitting.

"Some of the girls think we are deaf."

Otis leaned forward. "Do you remember me?"

"No. But I am sure they checked you out." She didn't look up. "That is one nice thing about a place like this. One does not mistakenly kiss the paperboy." She said it so offhandedly that Otis choked to imagine the incidents that might have required Ulrich to coax her here—or more likely force her. She looked Otis over. "You are handsome, but you are not my husband. That is him on the dresser, next to his sister Sophie and her husband, Martin."

Even in the small old black and white photo, Otis was struck by how much Ulrich's parents resembled how he remembered him.

"You are not the preacher. He always carries his Bible." She narrowed her eyes. "And if you are from the IRS, you are too late. This place is draining me dry." She winked.

He cleared his throat. "I'm Otis. A friend of yours said to drop by to see how you're doing." Ulrich had said no such thing of course, but the way Otis felt being there—virtuous, visiting an old lady he didn't have to—made the bald-faced lie feel less wrong.

"Otis." She masticated the word then repeated it like a toddler. "Otis. Well, it is high time. You brought your tools, yes?" She stared past him and Otis twisted. The painted cinderblocks remained glossy light yellow. He turned back around to her crying. "Poor Sadie!" she sighed. "Our piano lessons with Mrs. Stein were on the sixth floor. We always raced down. That day it was my turn for the stairs. Sadie shut the lift cage." Aunt Greta paused, pained by the memory. "Young man, I don't mean to offend your employer but ever since that day, I take the stairs."

"I'm sorry about your friend," Otis said. "I prefer the stairs too."

Needle clack sounds and a table clock's ticking mixed with snowmelt drip sounds outside. Irregular clunks and whooshes from a steam radiator augmented the jazz-like mix to create a complex, soothing effect. Minutes of only those sounds hinted that Aunt Greta had forgotten her expectation that Otis would repair the elevator in her piano teacher's Berlin building before World War One began.

"I knew your nephew Ulrich."

Otis kicked himself for using the past tense.

"Ulrich!" Her face brightened. "My goodness. What day is it?"

"Friday. The eleventh." It was true.

"Then we must get ready!" Her voice rose with tender excitement.

"For what?"

"A lovely Saturday! Everyone will be about. Last I come you are so small. But now? I will enjoy to hold your hand on the full trams. You do not need such a thing now. You are a man, but so kind to come with this old woman. What strudel kind shall we get?"

"Umm, chocolate?" The game seemed harmless if it made her happy.

"The big one there?" She pointed a knitting needle at nothing.

Otis nodded eagerly. He loved upscale sweets, but how would a half-starved thirteen-year-old East German boy respond? If he paused to consider how to nuance it, he might break her bizarre retro trance. "Oh yes, that one! That chocolate one there! Thank you so much!"

"Ah Ulrich, your parents raise you well. A full pastry case and yet you wait to be asked. My dear Sophie remembers the bakery before the war, in the American sector. Let us eat. Then we visit your cousins—an adventure!" Her use of the present tense was disorienting.

"What of Mother and Father?" Otis asked. Without a word, she rose, went to the bedroom and returned with a letter which she solemnly held out. Otis could discern only the date, "11/08/61," "New York," and "Liebe, Mutter & Vater." Hoping draw her out, he pretended to silently read the German then put on a sad, inquisitive expression. "Why?"

Puzzled, she pointed at the letter and whispered. "It is as they say. Best for now. You will see. We will take a train then an airplane then you will stay with us in Nebraska. It is love, Ulrich."

"We're in Nebraska now."

Startled, her eyes battled for focus. Hand to mouth, she whispered.

"No Stasi?"

"No Stasi. America."

"Then we may speak freely! Practice more English! Your parents hate keeping it from you. You could say a wrong thing without meaning to. The soldiers are clumsy though: all those cement trucks and coils of barbed wire. We think you suspect. Your father is too frail to travel. Poor Martin: two wars a conscript, fifty-six when his truck is hit at Dresden and he is burned." She paused. "And Klaus. Poor Klaus. He does not want to fight either. Your parents want better for you."

Who was Klaus? Otis wondered. "Do you have a picture of Klaus?"

She fetched a sepia photo: dreamy gaze and smooth cheeks, Wehrmacht cap buttoned in front. Ulrich's *much* older brother, apparently.

"They trust God, but oh dear—to not have a body? Panzers try a Christmas rescue, but he is lost in Leningrad's snow. Your big brother always hopes for a sibling. We only learn later. It is hard on them. Everyone is sad he will never know you here, in this life."

Otis handed her back the photo.

"Tell me more about when I was small."

"What a blessing you are, Ulrich! They think your father is sterile. Years in the mines for the Russian bomb. Forty-seven she is when you arrive.

Impossible! They laugh—call each other Abe and Sarah. It is years to gain a wheelchair. You do not remember him walking do you?"

"No, I'm afraid I don't."

"That is too bad. You remember your vile West Berlin cousins though."

"I'm sorry. I'm a little hazy on the details. Remind me?"

"I overhear the day we leave. Oh, I am angry. God forgive me. They wake you only to taunt you: *The border is sealed and guards are shooting. Your parents are stuck. You cannot go back. Our clothes would fall off such a filthy urchin as you.* Beastly boys! I hate for you to hear them, but you turn the other cheek and make me proud. I never forget what you say on the train."

Otis bobbed his head as if affirming her version of a shared memory.

"You remember Isaiah." In German, the verse seemed to flow like the Rhine. She translated. "*You keep him in perfect peace, whose mind is stayed on you because he trusts in you.* You see the severe mercy in what your parents do!" She looked wistful then her face re-lit. "We have a good laugh though, yes? Such new clothes for you in Manhattan; two suitcases full!"

She praised Ulrich's quick grasp of English, then mentioned his Nebraska friends, Rufus and Devlen, but with her warped sense of time, it wasn't clear if they were still part of Ulrich's life.

The room darkened and her tales slowed. Then it struck him: to make Ulrich think he was merely on an afternoon outing and keep him from slipping up, raising suspicions, his parents must have sent him away with only the clothes on his back. Otis tried to imagine their turmoil at what they had to have reckoned might be a final goodbye and felt his curiosity about a one-time belayer suddenly grotesque, shame overshadowing his fear of being smoked out. Aunt Greta had flown five thousand miles to rescue an East German refugee nephew and raise him as her own son.

Greta's brow furrowed. "You," she said. "You!" she shouted, shaking.

He deserved whatever this was. She pointed past him. Otis willed himself not to turn. If it was a ghost, he knew whose it would be. "Shh. Shh! Aunt Greta. It's only me, Ulrich."

She yelled louder. He wanted to muzzle her but knew he couldn't. Palms forward, he put up his hands, patting the air. He reached for her shoulder but she scrambled away backward. Her knitting clattered to the floor. She picked it up and brandished the needles. "Who are you?!"

Running footsteps echoed in the hall. A man yelled: "He hasn't signed out." A burly male nurse thrust the door open and another like him piled in close behind. "Mr. Shepard?"

"She was fine just a minute ago," Otis protested.

One nurse moved in on Aunt Greta as the other pulled a syringe from his bag. Greta lowered her needles and whimpered, resigned.

"Shepard? Mein schatz Ulrich?"

"You need to step out," the second nurse said. "Tell Calia it will be a few minutes. She's knows about this kind of thing."

Otis peeked into the empty hall then scurried down a staircase, out a fire door, and around the building. Alarms blared as he dashed through snow and mud and hopped in his rental car.

Fifty:
Many Dwelling Places

Otis sped past fallow cornfields, glad that his mirrors stayed empty. There was no sense dwelling on feeling like a miserable lying coward. Aunt Greta would be fine—the nurses had as much as said so— especially with Calia there to comfort her in a few minutes. Besides, he was safe again. Only Aunt Greta had heard his real name and even if she recalled it, nobody was going to take *her* seriously. She and the nurses might as well have encountered no one.

He pictured Aunt Greta's rescue trip to Berlin. Did her muddled memory help her cope with being party to the agonizing decision his parents had made? Someone who'd endured all Greta had would have taken care not to offer Ulrich assurances as to when he might see them again, but neither could she have known that their separation would stretch out to almost a decade—and now to forever.

Otis also imagined Ulrich's parents that first evening without him in the summer of 1961, sopping up cabbage soup with hard bread (as construction noise and soldiers' shouts swirled around them) reassuring each other that sending their last son away to America had been the right thing to do.

Had Greta distracted Ulrich with a window seat on his first plane trip? Explained why the sun hung in the west? Told him to look for Greenland icebergs, tiny as salt grains on the dark ocean? Had Ulrich been startled landing at JFK, the bump and screech of aircraft tires as foreign to him as New York's fast-paced commotion and foreign speech?

Had Ulrich's Jasper postcard reached his mother in East Berlin? And why had he addressed it to her only? Was Martin his crippled father dead? Ulrich's treasure-map arrow to his ice tomb seemed spookier the more Otis thought about it. Waren hier! *We are here.* Would she write him back to ask who else made up the 'we'? Would he be crazy to respond if she did?

Otis slowed and flipped on the dome light. A house on eighty acres should be easy to find. He steadied the wheel with one knee and checked the map and address. Several miles down a gravel road, the well-cared-for Victorian listed in Aunt Greta's will occupied a low rise in open country. Two stately trees flanked a long un-plowed drive. Tight rows of younger trees looked like fish skeletons—planted to slow relentless plains winds, Otis guessed. From the gabled third floor, a small window sparkled, reflecting the still-bright sky. Ulrich had written of bookshelves, a cedar chest, and a brass bed up there. Otis imagined it as he shut off the engine.

Outside the car, crisscrossing pink contrails caught his attention—some jets chasing daylight as others chased darkness, their passengers' minds on the hugs and handshakes ahead (at worst, a talkative cabbie). The thought made him homesick. He scuffed through snow to a wraparound porch. The front door was locked. He peered through the beveled panes and let his eyes adjust. Inside, a staircase swept up from a paneled foyer. In bare-walled adjacent rooms, sheets draped furniture huddles. If Greta's departure had been reluctant, Ulrich had brought order, but also left barren anonymity. Otis wondered if Calia had been involved in the work.

He waded into a back door alcove clogged by snowdrift. Searching for stairs, he kicked steps. Feeling for a rail, thorns pricked his hand, red drops staining the snow. On the porch, he cupped his other hand to a window. Except for a propped-open fridge and vacant mousetraps, the kitchen was bare. He imagined standing at the sink, gazing out at monotony. How did people live here?

He trudged back to the car, brushed snow off his pants, and started the engine, better able now to make sense of Ulrich's first journal entries. He closed his eyes and recalled one. *October 4th, 1961—no letter yet from Mutter and Vater. I miss them, but here I read and pray in quiet.* The car warmed and Otis dozed and the two grand trees seemed to rustle yellow against a cloudless crystal blue sky: cottonwood guardians, planted by settlers. Book bag in hand, a scrawny Ulrich marched between them up from a school bus, then he and Aunt Greta ate fresh-baked pie out on the back lawn where bumblebees droned around late-season roses.

Soothed, Otis drove into town.

Outside the diner, Otis considered what to tell Calia. After she had implored Ulrich to call or visit, the news that he was dead would provoke shock. He would have to take it slowly.

Fifty-One:
Table for One

Inside the diner, rich food aromas engulfed him. Hands in his pockets, Otis waited beside the cash register. At booths, tables, and along the counter, clutches of men in wool shirts tossed opinions as efficiently as the farm equipment brands emblazoned on their polyester caps tilled and sowed their fields each spring. Clasping thick mugs, some tapped at glass ashtrays and sized Otis up.

Calia stepped forward. Her smile matched her Ivory soap smell. She asked if he was there by himself or if others would join him, then plucked a plastic menu and showed him to a table. After she left, feeling exposed, he wished he'd asked for a booth but she'd already poured him coffee and moving to another seat might mean he'd get another waitress.

Sipping, he rehearsed his approach. *I knew your fiancé*, he would begin. He didn't have to say *how*. Like the men who'd come about Henry, he'd give the gist, succinct and distant. She would cry, maybe get angry. He couldn't predict or control that. She would ask questions and he would answer—though no more specifically than he had to. Details could make things harder. *Hang on*, he would say at some point. *Don't shoot the messenger. There's a silver lining here—some good news too.* But was it news? Did she know about Ulrich's safe deposit box? Some of its contents were in his pockets but to let on that *he* knew would invite questions that led nowhere good.

An alternative version clawed for attention. *I know how he died*, he would blurt. *I'm the only eyewitness; it's partly my fault.* Rehearsing confession made him feel better, the secret's poison diluted by the fantasy of sharing it. *I know how awful you must feel. My brother stepped on a landmine in Vietnam. It was probably quick for him too. You can take solace in that. I'm sorry, but glaciers are deep and they shift. His body is gone by now. Here's his safe deposit box key and some of his papers and cash. I'll go fetch the rest from my car.* That version was a dead-end also.

A pen clicked. Calia's stood there. "Would you like a little more time?"

He could use a century. "No, no, I'm good." *No,* came a thought. *You are not good at all.* He knew what he wanted to eat, but he ran his finger down the menu so as not to have to look at her.

"Wait. Are you Otis?" She set down the coffee pot, her smile like dawn.

"Yes. Susan must have told you."

If *Aunt Greta* had told her, she wouldn't still be smiling

"Susan's such a dear. She said you know Ulrich?"

Present tense. He half expected a spark to leap between them, connecting what he knew with what she didn't. Either of the discourses he'd rehearsed would be like shooting Bambi's mother.

"We met last June. He mentioned this place and showed me a picture."

Calia wrinkled her nose. "Of the *diner*?"

"No. Of you; from his wallet. I remembered your face."

Shut up, he thought. She's practically a widow.

"Oh that one." She blushed and flapped her fingers. "There's more of me now—I mean us." She rested a hand on her belly. Her face clouded. "Have you seen him lately?"

"No. We shared a campsite in Canada."

"You don't *sound* Canadian."

"I live in Alaska." This is awful, he thought. She really has no inkling.

Her face brightened again. "He does too! What's it like there?"

"The darkness is rough. This time of year, you start to crave sunshine."

She tipped her head. "Why, he said the same thing." Her eyes lingered on him longer than he expected. "He might come home for Christmas. It's darkest up there around then, he said."

"I hope that works out for you."

She blushed. "Oh, my. Look at me. I'm so sorry. I shouldn't burden you with my problems."

"That's OK," Otis said; his scumbag muteness made him want to bolt. Instead, he ordered the small pancakes and thanked her for refilling his coffee. His unease recalled his family's church forays. His mother would insist he and Billy clip on neckties but Otis' always popped loose right as everyone got serious. Fumbling under a pew to find it and reattach it made him want to crawl away, unseen. Whatever he told Calia tonight would only restyle her hard reckoning.

Calia brought his food. "OK, this may sound funny," she said, "but I have a question for you. Ulrich? My fiancé? He has these special mirrored sunglasses with funny leather side flaps. I can see myself in them, but not his eyes." Her voice trailed off. Her uniform bulged and shifted. She rested a hand on it and murmured with a pinched faraway look.

"Glacier goggles?"

"Yes, that's it. Did he wear them with you?"

"Once or twice, if I recall correctly. Why do you ask?" Otis concentrated on not mentioning his own pair lest it raise the question of them having climbed together.

"Oh, I've just been thinking what colors our babies' eyes might be."

"Colors? Babies? Are you having twins?"

"No. I mean when we're married; siblings to this one, Lord willing."

"Are you hoping for blue?" Meeting her eyes, Otis pictured sapphires.

"Why, yes! He must have taken those silly goggles off to talk to you."

Why had he not seen it before? For months, Ulrich had filled their respective thoughts. Moved by that secret, intimate irony, Otis told Calia how he and Ulrich had met, how Ulrich had cooked him pancakes, how thrilled Ulrich had been to encounter a Berlin family and how—when Otis burned down his own tent—Ulrich gladly took him in. He gushed cataracts of detail, mindlessly hopeful that the clarity and force of his stories might breach the dam of what had happened next and carve a different, less tragic outcome. But instead, the unmelting reality of the glacier drama towered even higher in his mind, casting his conscience in hard jumbled shadow.

"After we parted, I headed north. Since then I haven't seen him."

Calia's face fell. The parts he skipped played in his head. Coaxing, ascending, their quarrels; the storm and their fall; his narrow escape; his quick choice to use Ulrich's ID. Could she sense the sleight-of-hand gaps as he spliced together a sanitized narrative for her?

"Well then," she said. Dignity brightened her face as fast as dejection had shaded it. "It's neat that you two met. If you run into him up there, do tell him that we met, OK?"

"I will," Otis said. How did you express sympathy to someone who hadn't gotten bad news? The question gave Otis the sense he'd had on the serac when Ulrich passed out: how best to help without hurting them both. "Tell me," he said, "how do tips work here? Do you pool them?"

"No. It's each girl for herself. I didn't like it at first, but I've come to see the sense in it."

She left the check and walked away. Contrasted against the diner's dark windows, her bulging uniform reminded him of snow piled at the lip of a crevasse. He wanted to protect her, yet by not telling her what he knew, he was leaving her in trouble. Under the plate's edge, he left a fiver for the meal, plus a tip so fat that leftover syrup pooled to the plate's opposite edge.

From his car, Otis watched Calia return to his booth to clear his dirty dishes. Before she could lift the wad of hundreds and turn to catch him relishing her astonishment, Otis was speeding past the empty spot where Jack had parked last June. He could have left her far more, he thought from the highway. Why had he made such a half-hearted move?

Fifty-Two:
No Place

The further he drove through the night back to Denver the fewer options he saw. The bold move here would be to get Calia into Aunt Greta's farmhouse, but that required triggering Ulrich's will, and *that* called for eyewitness testimony to the accident, or else a body. The body was gone and the lone eyewitness was him. The best he could do would be to dribble her cash by mail from Ulrich's safe deposit box money.

Before dawn, inside the Denver airport, Otis looked through the rest of what he'd scooped from the bank box in haste. Ulrich's birth certificate bore the black-bear crest of a Berlin hospital. Fitting his religious devotion (or had it shaped it?) his middle name was Devot, born at 2:22AM on April 25, 1948. Otis counted the time zones, astounded. They were virtual twins! Otis, born the evening of April 24th, was older; Ulrich was ten minutes younger.

The thought renewed Otis' desire to put all of this behind him.

The Anchorage flight was not until noon, but a *Mexico City* nonstop left at eight, no passport needed. He joined that ticket line but each step forward added to his sense of unease. Ulrich's notebooks were still in Anchorage; he couldn't just abandon them. Calia should get a chance to see them someday. He stepped out of line and, at a different counter, bought a one-way ticket to Anchorage. Monday he would call the FBI. He had to keep Ulrich's name untainted. He couldn't afford to have both Calia *and* the FBI suspicious.

Later that day in fading light, his plane dipped below afternoon clouds. A tidal bore roiled up Turnagain Arm, saltwater mixing with muddy fresh. Otis dreaded to glimpse the DC-8's charred hulk but thankfully it was gone, new snow already hiding the blackened spot where it had lain.

At the house, junk lay strewn along the curb under deepening drifts. Otis waded to the front door. His key refused to turn. He jiggled it, tried it again, then checked that he had the right one. Confused, he knocked, then pounded. The landlord cracked his adjacent door and yelled through the security chain. "If you're looking for your stuff, it's out there." The FBI had come by again, he explained. He couldn't risk losing his home. No, Sid didn't know yet. Otis pleaded. Could he just stay the night? No. He was trespassing; his name was not on the lease. The landlord pumped a shotgun and Otis fled. Only once he reached the curb did the landlord slam the door.

Amidst a pile of furniture, boxes, and bags Otis quickly located Ulrich's notebooks (safely dry) and wedged them behind the driver's seat. He was glad he'd taken everything else before. Ulrich's typewriter might not have fared as well. Sid's packages were harder to find. He would rather have left them, but Sid had made clear that if any went missing, he would hold Otis responsible; changed locks didn't change that. Otis set each in the foot well opposite Ulrich's notebooks, tallying against what he recalled. He wasn't sure how he would return all the inbound packages but—as he had done from Nebraska to keep to Sid's schedule—he figured it was easy enough to mail the remaining outbound ones on time and so keep things square.

Only after he'd driven a while did Otis wonder why he'd located neither the TV dinners Sid had stocked in the upstairs freezer, nor the elk and moose steaks he supposed he must keep in the basement ones. The landlord probably pilfered those for himself, but it wasn't his problem; they could work that out. In fact, the more Otis thought about it, the better he felt being out of there. Unlike before, stuck in a crappy motel, he had a job (the first thing any landlord asked) plus cash (from Ulrich's box) for up-front rent. Once he resettled he would replace every penny.

Saturday night. Even if the motels had vacancies—and that was unlikely—he couldn't face them. Through ice smog, he followed a flickering glow to an all-night drive-in, pleased to find movies he wanted to see. He paid for the "All-Nite All-Shows Special," and read the electrical console beside his window: *Engines off. Don't make a fog! No heater refunds after 15 minutes.* He plunked in coins and set the heater inside the car. In the first movie, Dustin Hoffman played a centenarian witness to the Little Bighorn battle. The rolling Wyoming grasslands made Otis want to drive into the whitewashed plywood screen, back to the H3 ranch. In the second movie, Alan Arkin found clever ways to shirk World War Two combat. In the third movie, Otis grew tired of Jack Nicholson as a rich college grad working in an oil field and treating women shabbily.

Bored, he fished out and studied one of Sid's outbound packages, addressed to a pseudonym down in Homer. Like others he'd handled, it felt like Play-Doh. He picked at the wrapping tape with his pocketknife and had almost released it cleanly when his knife slipped and sliced through the cover into his hand. Powder spewed everywhere. He raised his cut hand to his mouth. A salty blood taste mixed with a weird vinegary smell. He flicked on the dome light. The gash was bad. He ripped a shirt with his teeth, and bound the wound. The bandage quickly soaked through. He set down the punctured package. His hand hurt less, and then hardly at all. Burt Lancaster's on-screen airport antics became hard to follow. Otis slept, woke, and mixed-up the two.

A man rapped on the window. The screen was dark, the lot empty, his car cold. "Show's over. I need your heater." Otis handed it out to the man.

Powder covered his clothes and around his seat. One-handed, he brushed it off. What was it? Until trying marijuana at Deden-Fisher (then deciding not to seek more), the closest he'd come to the drug scene had been startling a clutch of Chandler toughs popping pills and drinking a case of Pabst in the swampy no-man's-land woods on the Dirkden town line.

A sudden thought chilled him. With one drug package breached, what could he tell Sid? *Thanks but no thanks, here are most of them back?* He needed space to think. He drove to Earthquake Park, hopeful it was empty but as his headlights swept the huge clay mounds the '64 quake had extruded, the shadows seemed to leer and dance. He shut off the engine and lights, reassured by silence. Sid couldn't *prove* he had the drugs. Anyone could have pilfered them curbside. He sat for a while.

He needed to wash his hands (and the car) of this mess—blood, drugs, and Sid. He could not let a traffic stop or a curious postal clerk put him away. He gathered Sid's outbound packages and traipsed toward Knik Arm to toss them. A brisk breeze cleared his head but as he crested a rise his heart sank. Tortuously buckled sea ice stretched far out from shore. What now? The ground was frozen too; he couldn't just leave them. His tire and boot prints crisscrossed the snow; his fingerprints were on the tape. Anchorage was small. Nebraska plates stuck out, but driving to the lower forty-eight in winter was impossible, not to mention the border crossings.

He returned to the car with the drugs, curious about Sid's *inbound* packages. He slit one open and fanned two fat stacks of crisp hundreds. The rest all had the same texture. He could now fly away! He envisioned the house he could buy: balcony, views, a hot tub. No. He should re-tape the open packages and place a classified:

"Lost and found white & green things for S.R.; call..."

Call who? Call where? The seat where he'd weighed the two wallets last June was home. He had to clean up, but emergency rooms would ask questions, and it was *Sunday*. Motels would be full. *Sunday*. He and Ulrich had met on a Sunday. The following Sunday—as if a thousand years had elapsed—Otis was taking Ulrich's name. *Sunday*. Didn't churches offer sanctuary to people in desperate straits?

He recalled an Ulrich notebook entry about an Anchorage church and found the citation. He set down the notebook and checked a map. The one Ulrich had planned to attend was close by, at the end of Fourth Avenue. He could scrounge food and coffee, dress his wound properly, and make it through to the afternoon when the motels would empty.

Fifty-Three:
Prepared Place

Otis idled, facing the church. Across its empty lot, light from mullioned windows gilded the snow like honeyed waffles. A block-lettered lawn sign declared the pastor: "Dr. Joseph Massey Lifton." Otis wondered: Was his doctorate from a decent school? He checked his gas gauge and shut off the engine. The service wasn't for hours. The car chilled. He thought about leaving to find a gas station. Instead, he tried the church's front door, surprised to find it unlocked. The foyer smelled of new carpet. He ran his good hand over a Christmas tree's branches, soothed by the spruce smell. He peeked into the sanctuary. Empty. He tiptoed in. Silence gave no clue as to the source of a coffee aroma; once people arrived, he would blend in and follow them to it. He picked a pew spot where he could see every door. To kill time, he opened a pew rack Bible.

"For ye are not come unto the mount that might be touched." He thought of Mount McKinley utterly inaccessible in winter. Summer would make it touchable again. He fanned the Bible's pages and let his eyes drift down another random page. "The lot is cast into the lap." Wait. *That* verse again? He glanced around, half expecting Mike to appear and yell "surprise!"

Instead, a man with a huge red beard entered the sanctuary and strode toward him with two steaming mugs. "Good morning," he boomed. Otis blinked. At first glance, he looked and sounded like Coach. He wasn't, but the positive impression lingered. "You OK there?" The man indicated Otis' hasty, seeping bandage. Otis accepted a mug and gulped greedily.

"Yeah. Stupid pocketknife accident. I'll be fine." Did he look and sound as stoned as he felt?

"I'm Pastor Joe." Closer up, he looked much younger than Coach—perhaps in his late thirties.

"Otis," said Otis, glad when Pastor Joe stepped a body length back before plunking into what Otis already considered his pew.

"Otis like in Homer; Odysseus versus the Cyclops?"

"You're kidding," said Otis. "*No one* gets that."

"My wife tells me I read too much. Are you Greek?" Pastor Joe swiveled his legs toward Otis and stretched his arm along the pew back. A bulge of flesh around his wedding band suggested sedentary indoor pursuits. Otis scanned the room for exit options.

"No, I'm total white bread; not much of anything. It's just that my dad liked to read me the classics."

"Sounds like a great dad."

"He meant well." The coffee's zing made it easier to feel charitable.

"How so?"

"He wanted me confident in my abilities. Odysseus watches the Cyclops eat his companions and knows he's next so when the Cyclops gets drunk and insists on knowing his name, he thinks on his feet and makes a clever escape. Cagey caution my father called it."

"Because to give your name was to cede power. Don't you love Odysseus' response?"

"Of course! He tells the Cyclops his name is 'No One.' In Greek, it's 'Otis.' His flair lets him hide in plain sight. Kids at school had their cliques, but the secret behind my name made me feel above all that garbage—like Doctor Strange in the comics, invincible because he's invisible."

Pastor Joe smiled. "Where are you from, Otis? I hope you're not fleeing a drunken Cyclops!"

"Out east," he said, envisioning Sid.

"What brings you to The Great Land?" Pastor Joe seemed unruffled by Otis' vagueness.

"Initially? The pipeline."

"I see. And how is that going?"

"I got laid off."

"I'm sorry. A number of our people were laid off as well. Did one of them perhaps point you to us?"

"Actually, I was hoping you sold Christmas trees."

"Sorry. We're more into growing than selling."

Pastor Joe's unblinking gaze reminded Otis of infants he'd held, creepy but comforting at the same time.

"Well, so yeah, there was a guy who mentioned this place but I doubt you'd know him." Otis pursed his lips, bracing for Pastor Joe to call his bluff (*try me; I probably do know him*—and he had). But instead, Pastor Joe looked down, silent as if thinking deeply.

"Otis, would you be able to join our family for midday supper in our home after the service?"

Whoa. Where had *that* come from? The question exuded a quality Otis admired in all his top wrestling opponents: patient poised power. Octopus, although a brute, had buckets of it. Shaun emanated it like a lighthouse, brighter the closer one got. Otis found the trait attractive largely because he was not naturally endowed with it. He'd honed his imitation only slowly and he still hadn't mastered it. Pastor Joe's easy manner had led Otis to assume he was a Jesus freak doofus but cloaking his ability long enough to deploy this under-the-radar move was *beyond* impressive.

"Yes," Otis said suddenly. "Yes I'd like that. Supper would be great."

Pastor Joe smiled and abruptly stood. "I'm glad. Now, come with me."

Otis followed as Pastor Joe fetched a First Aid kit, glad he didn't ask why he'd been messing with a knife. He helped Otis to clean and re-bandage his hand then Otis excused himself to fetch fresh clothes from his car for the service. On his way out, he grabbed a handful of Fudge Town cookies from a snack table an old lady was setting up. In the parking lot, he debated. Why stay? He had what he came for: warmth, coffee, medical help, and food, even a tiny taste of Christmas cheer. But if he left, where would he go? What was his rush? Why pass up a hot meal?

He returned inside with clothes to change into. Inside the front foyer, Pastor Joe was hunched on his hands and knees beside a bucket, singing. "Oh God our help in ages past." He flashed Otis a smile, crab-walked a step and sponged the floor. "Our shelter from the stormy blast." Another crab walk, sponge, next verse, repeat. Otis looked closer. A trail of damp spots led from the front door to where Pastor Joe scrubbed. A trail of blood drops led on from there to where they'd sat.

From sporadic visits to churches in Dirkden and neighboring affluent towns, Otis recalled a pastiche of sermon tidbits. A few days before Easter or Christmas, his mother would insist they "go as a family," and propose a church where she knew someone from the League of Women Voters or the PTA. His father would say something like "oh not that place again." Then, if he didn't win the tussle to "just stay home this year," he would mention a church on his commute that rotated clever lawn sign sayings or one they had visited long enough ago that the reasons they'd never returned *there* (e.g., noisy kids; too many blue-hairs; pastor mentioned money) had gotten muddled with reasons for eschewing *other* places. His mother would parry with a church she'd looked up in the Yellow Pages and his father would acquiesce. They'd all go, do their time, stand around awkwardly, then talk about Santa Claus or the Easter Bunny on their ride home.

A few times at school, Lucius had caught Otis without an excuse and guilted him into coming to his church there. The sermons Otis had heard over those two life eras seemed to come in two types. The first type was so picky and overbearing that he imagined the pastor railing at his wife for burning his toast. The second (more common) type was so smarmy and vacuous that eating jelly beans while watching Mister Rogers seemed like an easier way to produce the same fleeting agreeable outlook: that most things were mostly right with most people most of the time, and that as everyone tried harder to be even nicer, they and everything would get even better.

Pastor Joe's sermon felt different: urgent, cogent, warm. Despite a few rhetorical theatrics, it was honest and intellectually rigorous—like a good steak that stuck with you. Though the pews were nearly full, Pastor Joe seemed to be looking right at him every time Otis glanced up.

"We have a huge problem," Pastor Joe said, pausing just long enough for Otis to think, *what problem?* (Precisely the purpose Pastor Joe had designed the pause to serve.) "God is good."

Everyone knows that, Otis thought, pleased with himself through another long pause before Pastor Joe enveloped the microphone and dropped his voice. "And we're not."

Now wait a minute, Otis thought, but before his thoughts coalesced, Pastor Joe released the proverbial brakes, his proverbial foot mashing a proverbial gas pedal to a proverbial floor.

"The moral currency we hold is no good with God. We can't bribe him with what we think of as good deeds but which in fact are filthy rags. And yet He didn't *leave* us in that bind. The God-man came as a baby, lived the life you and I can't, and died to take the full rap we deserve."

Otis was intrigued; the God-man sounded like a comic book superhero.

"If you turn from your sin and trust Jesus, he'll forgive every wrong you've ever done or *will* do across every *category* of wrong." Otis was puzzled. Was the God-man Jesus? "He'll forgive the worst things you're ashamed to admit you even imagined. Things buried so deep that only He knows because you've worked so hard to forget them. The God-man is the sole cure for the fatal disease we all want to ignore. He is *the* Christmas gift. Not boxes or bags but Himself. And on a glorious winter morning like this, I can't help but think of the prophet Isaiah, who assures us that Jesus can and will wash the red stain of our sin white as snow—fresh, bright, and pure."

Pastor Joe looked at Otis, then to the back of the sanctuary. Was his look expectant? Was this a sting? Had he deduced that Otis was bad news and called the cops? Had he aimed his sermon at working Otis up to confess while they searched his car? Otis swiveled but no one looked out of place; outside the window, his car looked untouched. He settled, relieved. If he kept his mouth shut, no one had to know about what had brought him here.

Otis' first impression of the Liftons' home behind the church was of a storybook place: snug, cluttered, but clean. Pastor Joe stoked a fire in the stone hearth. His wife Esther served the midday meal—a cabbage/potato/hamburger/cheese casserole—with her long braid tucked under one of her apron strings. Pastor Joe asked their youngest (six-year-old Benjamin) to bless the meal which was tastier than Otis had feared. All six Lifton kids behaved far better (and their parents seemed much less harried) than families half as large back in Dirkden. Their offer of wine surprised him, but lest he discover the limits of their welcome, he stopped at one glass. After dessert, Esther dismissed the children to watch Mother Moose.

"And nothing else," Pastor Joe clarified with a jovial bellow before cajoling Otis to split the last slice of apple pie with him. The dollop of vanilla ice cream atop it reminded Otis of a snow drift. Esther opened the back door to a cold blast, snapped her fingers, and two husky dogs loped in

267

to clean scraps from plates set on the floor. Each dog eyed Otis briefly but didn't approach or snarl. After Mother Moose ended, the older children grabbed books to read to the younger ones. Without intending to, Otis fell asleep on the couch. He woke well after dark.

"I should go," he said, embarrassed. They offered a cot. "But you just met me," he protested.

"If you've wandered down Fourth Avenue," Esther said, "then you've passed by some of the people we've been blessed to have under our roof. We're glad to have you here too."

"Besides," Pastor Joe added, "the dogs haven't growled at you yet."

Fifty-Four:
Badlands

Enough snow fell overnight that Ulrich's car looked like a marshmallow. Midmorning, as the sky lightened, Otis, Pastor Joe, and his two older sons went out to clear the drive. Pastor Joe leaned on his shovel to catch his breath. Steam rose from his neck. He indicated Otis' license plate. (Otis was glad his first view did not include the bear claw marks still across his trunk lid.)

"Amazing! You're a Husker? I interned at a church in Grand Island."

Otis tried to sound surprised. "Are you serious? Wow. When?"

"The early sixties. Where are you from in Nebraska?"

Otis' mind raced to recall the state's geography. What was his best bet to sidestep the do-you-know-so-and-so game? City or small town? Made-up or real? His last hitchhike to Grand Island had been in the dark. On the way there, his driver had pointed out the University of Nebraska's mothership Lincoln campus. Even far from the highway, its football stadium ruled the night like a bright alien insect. Otis had estimated it would take a quarter century's worth of Deden-Fisher commencements to equal the attendance at one UNL home game. The following harrowing day, all he recalled of the interstate west from Grand Island was Jack's grease-stained map blurring in and out of focus. From chit-chat overheard on his diner visits, Grand Island locals seemed view Omaha (despite the stink of its vast stockyards) as culturally akin to Paris—a bastion of elegance and erudition, glittering and unreachable across a chasm of sophistication. Omaha was also the only Nebraska city big enough and far enough from Grand Island to hide his fib.

"Omaha," Otis said. "That's what I meant yesterday by, 'out East.'"

"Did you go to school in Lincoln?"

"No. Lincoln was west of me. I wanted to wrestle and the Big Ten is too competitive. I chose a small place instead—out East where I'm from."

"Ah, a wrestler! Like Jacob. He wrestled with God."

Otis ignored the baited hook comment. It had been almost two years since he'd thought about the Big Ten athletic conference but now, suddenly, Octopus memories taunted him afresh. It still seemed unfair that a cheater like him had won a full scholarship to the University of Iowa while Otis had battled his father's small-minded threats to consign him to UMass. What if the ref had done his job, called Octopus' illegal choke hold, and Otis had won the state championship as a junior? Would he have gotten a wrestling scholarship and top coaching? Probably. Would he now be training for the 1972 Munich games alongside his old rival? Very possibly.

Pastor Joe broke into Otis' bitter reverie.

"And how did you like the small place you chose out East?"

How did he *like* it? To trot out the DF name unsolicited seemed haughty, yet with only himself to be (DF's prestige halo could not illumine him here) Otis felt as if he were wearing burlap pajamas. In Dirkden or Dedentown, anyone would have begun brazenly sniffing (snarling only if needed) to establish alpha order. *Where out east? Which small place? My uncle was class of '55 there; magna, a hair shy of summa; word is, they still enforce a grade curve; how was that for you?* Pastor Joe's tack was refreshing but also unnerving. Without an elite college pedigree, Otis was left to wonder: who was he?

"I liked it enough to come here."

To his surprise, Pastor Joe waxed reflective.

"Many people we meet here express something similar, Otis. It was exciting for us but hard to leave family and friends. Other than Christmas cards, we've stayed in touch with fewer people than we would have hoped. Fresh starts are thrilling though, don't you think?"

"Thrilling? Yeah, I guess." How had he landed on that? Did he know how truly he'd spoken? Through the maze of half-truths and full-on shams Otis had laid down, Pastor Joe had pinpointed something Otis would never have dreamed that they shared. After years of relative predictability, Otis had become accustomed to 'thrilling' fresh starts by virtue of *needing* them.

"A young man from our church youth group wrote us last spring with news of *his* fresh start. He wrote to say he was taking a job on the pipeline. He said he planned to drop by, but so far we've been sad not to see him."

"He was probably busy. Our crew worked almost nonstop."

"If you knew Ulrich you would understand our concern."

Stop now, Otis chided himself. He was grateful for refuge, and company, but to toy with being found out was reckless. Ignoring his hurt hand, he thrust his shovel into a snowbank and heaved. "Ulrich, you say? The name doesn't ring a bell." He clenched his teeth, glad for pain to keep the lie sharp. He threw another shovelful. "Humble had lots of crews." He lifted more snow, panting with effort; he felt a trickle of blood inside his mitten. "Alaska's a big place." A gust blew sharp snow grains back in his face. He hated doing this to such a nice guy.

Pastor Joe sighed. "Perhaps Ulrich went home to Grand Island."

Otis waved at the leaden sky. "That would make him the smart one."

Pastor Joe chuckled. "Winters in Nebraska can be hard too. Say, I have photos from when we lived there. Ulrich is in a few. You might recognize him. Remind me when we go inside."

"I'd like that. Thanks. You never know."

They shoveled awhile at a more leisurely pace.

"So, tell me, Otis. What have you been doing for work since October?"

Otis told him about his airport job, the plane crash, and being evicted. Were pastors sworn not to report confessions? It seemed a bad time to ask.

Pastor Joe offered that Otis could stay as long as he needed. "Everyone needs a safe place to anchor." The image made Otis recall hundreds of protection placements he'd set on climbs, some solid, some sketchy, some mere charades to keep terror at bay. The best hardware was useless without a good belayer. An anchor could be bomber—a tourist-route bolt, deeply set and years old—but if the guy paying out rope did not pay close *attention*, the best pro was moot. The wrong belayer could make an ugly fall as likely as if the rope were woven from red licorice, the protection anchored in Jell-O.

Offhandedly, Pastor Joe asked Otis again how he'd found the church.

"A guy I met on the road. I couldn't tell you his name." Otis envisioned a casual encounter: two guys at a bar, half watching a game, popping the occasional peanut: *Oh by the way, when you get to Anchorage, there's this place my third cousin went. Give it a look.*

Why did Ulrich fill his thoughts more now than when he'd used his name? Why did he feel worse closer to truth than far from it? Why hadn't he said he'd been driving by and stopped in on impulse for Christmas cheer?

Now that simple lie was closed off, and it brought back the edgy sense he'd had retreating from the Icefield, fighting off deadly sleep and cold.

⁂

Later, Pastor Joe showed Otis the old photos he'd mentioned. Otis spotted Ulrich right away but shrugged and asked Pastor Joe to point him out. Like the four dozen or so boys around him, Ulrich wore khaki shorts bound by a cloth belt with a shiny buckle. His olive shirt matched the others, but was stained with more sweat. Behind the group, hardy scrub pines poked out from cracks in a wall of yellow-brown rock like fancy garnish on a plate. Ulrich's forearms were full and sinewy, not Popeye proportions, but notable beside other boys roughly his age. Otis asked where the photo was taken.

"The buttes. Up near the Badlands."

"Oh, of course. The Nebraska National Forest."

"You've been?"

"No, but someone told me about it. It's supposed to be beautiful."

Pastor Joe's face softened. "Oh, it's gorgeous. I have many fond memories. A Friday or two each fall, the leaders and several of the fathers would caravan up. The boys would set up camp by kerosene lanterns. Ulrich was shy at first, but a spider on anything vertical. He qualified for our Colorado trip his first outing—the youngest boy ever."

Otis thought of how different Ulrich and Shaun were as men, yet as climbing partners much the same: serious and competent. "It sounds like Ulrich was—I mean like he *is*—courageous."

Pastor Joe cocked his head.

"That's very perceptive of you, Otis. Yes, Ulrich is quietly fearless."

"What else did you guys do on those trips?"

It surprised Otis that he was growing curious.

"Well, let me see. We burned bacon, froze toes, and blew bugles."

He chuckled. "After the Sunday services in camp, we would tour the boys through Fort Robinson and have them debate the U.S. government interning Indians there in the 1870s versus it interning German soldiers there during the war. Ulrich had no idea how much his presence shifted those discussions. He'd absorbed good theology from a young age. His parents knew Dietrich Bonhoeffer before the war. Ulrich never mentioned that—most of the kids would not have known or cared—but it made me smile. Once Ulrich learned enough English, those Sunday afternoon scout trip dialogues could be fascinating. One time, he used Augustine's Just War Theory to defend interning German soldiers and to question interning Indians. That took some boys off guard—many leaders and fathers too! So yes, Ulrich is quietly courageous but I also admire him for his *thoughtfulness*."

Impulsively, Otis added, "Yeah, in both senses of that word."

Pastor Joe nodded. "Yes exactly! It's almost as if you..."

Otis lunged for another photo.

"How old was he when *this* one was taken?"

"Oh goodness, that one. October, 1961. I remember it like it was yesterday. Ulrich was thirteen. He'd been in the U.S. only two months."

"Wasn't that the Halloween the Russians tested that H-bomb?"

Pastor Joe closed his eyes as if in pain. "Yes, it was."

Otis pictured one of Ulrich's crossed-out German notebook entries: "Fünfzig Megatonnen! Erbarme dich, Herr!" Or, according to Ulrich's later translation adjacent to it: "50 Megatons! Lord, have mercy!" The photo of Ulrich from that time caused Otis to feel an enfolding sense of *déjà vu*.

"That day still gives me the creeps," he began "My junior high was doing duck-and-cover drills—all of us under our desks like normal except for our Halloween costumes—until all of a sudden these sirens we've never heard before start going off super loud and some kid yells, *it's a real attack!* I've only ever told my brother this, but as soon as he yelled that, these other two guys, Ed Service and Vic Reede—I can't believe I remember their names; they're dressed as ghosts—they suddenly start laughing all crazy and sinister, whispering nasty things to Susi Glendon and Leah Garrott, who are dressed as witches. Things no one should ever say in front of a girl. Man, telling you this, it's like I'm still there between them. So Susi and Leah start sobbing and I tell Ed and Vic to cool it. 'Shut up,' they say but it I swear it sounds like a wolf bark. 'Who made you the police? We're all dead anyway so what does it matter? Who's going to punish us? You?' And they were right. None of the teachers did anything."

Pastor Joe shook his head. "I'm sorry you had to go through that, Otis. It's not fun to dwell on, but people can say and do terrible things. With Elmendorf here, so close to Russia, we're a prime first-strike target. It's a sobering reality, but it's led to some fruitful conversations."

Pastor Joe stopped sorting photos and let his thinly-veiled offer linger, but Otis was still back in eighth grade, troubled by what he'd witnessed. Immediately after the drill—as quickly and as thoroughly as if the teacher had made them scrawl fifty times on the chalkboard, *nothing to see here!*—the class had snapped back to a boring lesson on the Sumerian Empire. Pastor Joe must have sensed Otis' distress because he resumed reviewing photos.

"Ulrich's first Scout trip was that Columbus Day weekend. He hadn't heard from his parents yet, or made any friends, but that began to change with this one boy who'd been on the trips before. Devlen Koss was dirt poor. 'Devil-in' they teased him or 'Redman' for his sunburn. He was a real handful; picked fights with everyone. Ulrich's Uncle Walter had sponsored him for merit badges to try to tame him—Insect Life, Bookbinding, that sort of thing—but Ulrich took another tack. Whenever Devlen went after him, Ulrich would throw Devlen off balance before he could land a punch. Ulrich's always been agile like that. After enough failures, Devlen stopped trying. When Ulrich learned that Devlen's father drank and beat him, he befriended him. Eventually they became pals."

Pastor Joe showed a picture of a grazed meadow dotted with dung mounds, pup tents rimed with frost. Blond cliffs rose like a ruined ziggurat from undulating dunes. Like Cape Cod, Otis thought, only without shore birds or ocean smell. Beside one of the tents stood three boys who looked like they'd just woken up. Ulrich was one. Pastor Joe pointed to a wiry sunburned boy with deep-set eyes. "Devlen was assigned to Ulrich's tent with Rufus Conner. That's him there on Ulrich's other side. Total opposite of Devlen. Ellwood, they called him, Lord knows why. As you can see, he's large and so he played football, but rather poorly I'm afraid—Lord forgive me for saying so. He's gentle as a lamb, shy and scared of heights. Ulrich taught him to belay so he wouldn't have to climb. Let's just say that he made a good anchor. The three of them clicked."

As Pastor Joe spoke, Otis wondered if either man might pose an obstacle to his using Ulrich's name. Might they even be in touch with Calia? Cautiously, he asked, "Did they stay friends?"

"Honestly? I don't know. Which reminds me: I should write Ulrich. Hear how his summer went. See what he's up to."

Fifty-Five:
Paper Thin

Pastor Joe put away the old photos and went next door to his study while at the kitchen table, Esther helped the children with their lessons. Otis flipped through the newspaper. The Alaska Federation of Natives wanted their fair share of the state's newfound oil wealth. Vietnam might or might not enjoy a holiday cease-fire. President Nixon and Elvis Presley were slated to meet at the White House. Yet as enticing (and improbable) as those things were, Otis was on a mission.

He moved to his objective: the classifieds.

"Certify as an EMT! Always in demand! No $$$ down! Call today!"

A year ago, Otis would have abominated such a lowbrow spiel. If his father viewed his plans to teach and coach as a dereliction of a Fletcher man's duty to raise the clan's respectability, then a bloody late-night blue-collar job was beneath mention. *Chandler* guys aspired to be Emergency Medical Technicians only if the refrigerator factory refused to hire them out of high school. If his father knew he had even *glanced* at an EMT ad, he would not dignify the idea by acknowledging it, but would instead swerve the conversation to *Billy's* latest achievements.

Even so, Otis' desperate acceptance of the airport job had validated aspects of his father's wisdom. There had not been a day loading baggage—exhausted, cold, doing his best to get along with people wholly unlike him—that a sense of disgrace and futility had not plagued him. Why had he rebuffed the draft counselor's help? Why had he not applied to grad school? Why had he looked askance at *all* his father's attempts to help? If he'd not been distracted with Louisabeth last fall, he might have called his father's old acquaintance Ed Fishender, and gotten an inside track into Morrison-James *before* his campus interview debacle. (Wilson Ward's draft number was high and safe but the scuttlebutt was that—unlike as was now the case for teachers—big firms like MJ had ways of fixing draft problems for any of their own at risk of induction.)

Otis pictured Wilson Ward and Fent Carmichael III in a plushly appointed Morrison-James office late on a Friday, their custom suit jackets draped across chair backs, sleeves rolled up and neckties loose. In large hands (soft, but athletic) they would stand cradling crystal tumblers of golden liquor and—peering out floor-to-ceiling windows across the darkening Hudson—toast another week of financial conquests. Fent would make an offhand remark.

"You remember that loser classmate of yours?"

And right on cue, Wilson would sneer.

"I know. Seriously. What was a guy like that *thinking*?"

"He wasn't." Fent would quip, then offer Wilson a fat cigar.

Otis seethed to imagine it. Yet even as he did, he realized that the airport job had begun to cauterize the shame he felt at his father's censure. EMT work would be tough but honest and noble. The skills were portable to other cities, useful on climbing trips too. The next six-week class started in January. Otis borrowed one of the children's rulers and tore out the ad.

That night in the break room midway through his shift, Otis picked up the paper's evening edition. "French Connection North!" screamed a banner headline. "One Arrested, One Dead in Local Heroin Ring; Body in Earthquake Park." His mouth turned to cotton; he'd left mazes of boot and tire tracks there. He skimmed the article. Pending further investigation, authorities were withholding names but how could it *not* relate to Sid? Was the body Sid himself or one Sid had dumped? Might Sid be roaming free, wrapping-up loose ends? The cash and the heroin were still in Ulrich's car, in the employee lot—*and Sid knew he worked here*. Were his chainsawed, frozen hunting trophies really moose and elk? Otis had never seen any antlers, heads, or hooves.

Roy sidled up. "Anything important enough to keep us from loading planes?" He pinched the paper dramatically, tilting his wrist so Otis could see the time on his gold watch.

If Sid were in custody, Otis was hardly safe. Sid would scapegoat the man he knew as Ulrich, then the FBI would scurry here to arrest him. Otis tore the paper out of Roy's grip. "I quit," he said. Roy's faced flushed in mute shock. Otis turned, relishing each step he took away.

He found Nadine. "I'll miss you," he said, feeling the depth of his sincerity only as the words left his mouth. His first impression of her—during her world-weary job phone screen—had been premature. She had become a small island of comfort, someone he truly hoped the best for.

She located his paycheck envelope. "Merry Christmas," she said.

There seemed no way to give Sid back his cash (or keep it) and not end up dead. He might not even live out the day. Borrowing Nadine's pen, he signed his paycheck over to her. "And Merry Christmas to *you*." He darted around the desk, kissed her on the cheek, then rushed out before sentimentality could drive him to lie about keeping in touch.

The next day, Otis stuffed the FBI's letter to Ulrich in his pocket, called Agent Russo from a phone booth on Fourth, then hailed a cab. It was only a ten minute drive from the Liftons' to the FBI office, but with Sid's packages in his car, he didn't want to take any chances parking it in the FBI lot. In the FBI lobby, an Agent Corbet introduced himself. His shirt was white, his tie plain. Barely older than Otis, he said he hailed from Kansas but would, "try to give a Husker a fair hearing." He winked so much at his own joke that Otis figured he had something in his eye.

He handed Otis a card: Agent Erl Justus Corbet.

Otis resisted a laugh. "Seriously? Your middle name is *Justus*?"

"Dad's a career bureau man. He *almost* named me Edgar. My friends call me Agent Erl."

"Not Erl?"

"No. *Agent* Erl." He swiveled briskly and motioned Otis to follow, leading him through mazes of corridors at a near trot. Finally, he slowed to let Otis come alongside. "I have to warn you, Ulrich. My boss Russo? He's a by-the-book, cross-the-t's-dot-the-i's kind of guy. He likes wrapping up every penny-ante case. Right now we're working down the Selective Service backlog." He rolled his eyes. "Young guys like us have to go along to get along, if you know what I mean. Follow his lead and we'll be out of here in a jiffy." Agent Erl patted Otis' shoulder, set a fawning smile, and held the door open. "Please. After you."

Good cop, Otis thought, glad he had figured it out early so the bad one wouldn't fluster him. Inside the windowless room, Agent Russo sat behind a small table, his hair swept straight back from his forehead, tight to his skull as if glued. He shut a manila folder, his voice as devoid of emotion as if he were typing up a rote report form. "Do you know Otis Fletcher?"

Otis sat. "Yes, I do." He tingled with excitement. Agent Erl's face slid toward subtly smug.

"When did you last see him?"

"This morning, while I was shaving." Otis laced his fingers behind his head and leaned back. Recently he'd learned that less than one percent of draft violators ended up in jail. He liked those odds better than what would happen if the FBI learned that he'd fled the scene of a fatal accident, stolen a dead man's life, and was hiding a wanted man's trove of drugs and cash.

Agent Russo turned the manila folder ninety degrees toward Agent Erl, then opened it and pointed. Agent Erl nodded.

Like a game of Battleship, Otis thought.

"Then how did you know to call us?" Agent Russo asked. "How did you get my number?"

Obvious move; the first thing Otis had thought of. "Ulrich told me."

Agent Erl's eyes flared for half a second before returning to impassive.

Agent Russo pressed. "*How* did he tell you? *When* did you last see him?"

"Last week," Otis lied. "Funniest thing. I bumped into him downtown." They probably had phone, mail, and bank records for them both, but Otis was confident the FBI hadn't tailed him.

"Does Mr. Sterbender know you're a draft dodger?"

"No. Vietnam never came up. We split after climbing. You knew that, right?" Unconvincingly both agents nodded. All was going according to plan. If he'd dallied on the Cambridge sidewalk last June, they would have led with desertion, an offense that carried much harsher penalties.

They grilled him for an hour. Otis remained unflustered. Other than at Pastor Joe's church, his real name had left few recent footprints. He wove true details through a fictional tapestry. He'd hitchhiked a lot, stayed at the Calgary Y, ridden up the Alcan Highway in some guy's car, slept through the border crossing back into Alaska. (He mused that he practically had.) Since then? Odd cash jobs, crashing at different pads. Details? Hard to recall. The agents failed to hide their growing boredom with Otis' minor variations on a hippie-life story they'd heard all too often.

"Do you have a place now?"

Agent Erl sounded almost sympathetic so Otis told the truth.

Agent Russo's tone started out harder to read.

"The Liftons are good people in a tough part of town that needs them. Anchorage is grateful. But I'm surprised, Otis. A history student like you should know better. The principle of church sanctuary ended with the Middle Ages. You can expect a court summons within thirty days—then you can expect to lose your case and go to jail. You're in Alaska, not Massachusetts. Draft hearings are different up here."

Otis blinked in shock. The newspaper had cited only national statistics, not state-level numbers. "Thanks for letting me know," he said.

Agent Erl escorted him to the lobby and had the receptionist call him a cab. "I must admit Otis, I didn't see that one coming. But what's your end-game? I just don't get it."

Otis held Agent Erl's stare. There was no sense in conceding. He had a month. He shrugged. "I was tired of running, I guess." It was true. He hated to run again, but neither could he stay. He would research a better place, somewhere with big mountains and no extradition—Argentina, or Nepal, or New Zealand. End game? Good question. They stood silent a while. A cab pulled up. Otis pushed open the lobby's glass door. Snowflakes swirled in.

Agent Erl shouted over the whooshing wind. "Oh hey, Otis, one more thing!" Otis stepped back inside and let the door thump closed. The last-minute query was clunky, but it was best to play this out. Agent Erl spoke with rehearsed deliberateness. "Did you see today's paper?"

"Yeah. More snow's on the way."

"You can say *that* again." Agent Erl's eyes seemed aflame. Otis held up a finger to signal the cab—one minute, hang on. "What's the FBI coming to, Otis? I mean, here we are, grilling a guy like you, trying to do the right thing and meanwhile a key of uncut smack is hitting the streets." Somewhere a dog barked, but because an old neighbors' unremitting beagle had inured Otis to yapping, he tuned it out. "Over two *pounds* of high-grade heroin. Half a million dollars' worth. Enough to addict the state!" Otis had tracked the story in both local papers. Neither had cited those details. "Pipeline money will keep us busy with OD stiffs in snowbanks for years."

If only Agent Erl knew why there weren't more ODs already. By unwittingly fetching Sid's heroin out of the snowbank after being locked out of their apartment, Otis had rendered the State of Alaska a public service, but now it was too late to confess and turn it in. They would assume he was working an angle. How naïve he'd been! Sid had played him. Sid effectively owned him. Sid would dispose of him once he'd outlived his usefulness—a point he'd likely passed already. How ironic it would be if, like Ulrich, he met his end in a snowbank.

Otis addressed Agent Erl sharply. "Why are you telling me all this?"

"I'm guessing you get around in circles we don't. Here's my card. If you hear anything, call me, OK? Anything you notice or that occurs to you—any time, day or night. Anything."

And there it was—less than he'd feared—a rookie playing a hunch, clamoring for his first bust. That was easy enough to fix. He would toss the drugs, clean the car, and hide the money. Sounds of scrabbling claws joined the barking he'd been ignoring. *Wait. Dogs? In an office building?* Before church he'd changed his pants and shirt, but not the down coat he'd worn Saturday night. His sole outer garment was a canine narcotic olfactory beacon!

He waved Agent Erl's card. "OK, thanks. See ya!"

He pushed the glass door, lunged too hard and tumbled out. Agent Erl moved to help him but covered with snow, Otis leapt to his feet and sprinted to the cab. Inside it, he locked eyes with Agent Erl.

Otis recognized that look. Agent Erl was betting Otis would lose his nerve and talk himself into giving up. Fat chance of that.

Fifty-Six:
Duck and Weave

That afternoon, alert for tails, Otis visited both his PO boxes. On the way back to the Liftons' he glimpsed a blue sedan he'd seen parked near one of them. He made abrupt turns, indifferent to angry honks. The car seemed to follow—or was it only a similar one? Amidst dusky ice smog, it was hard to tell. He stopped into a dirt-floored, sawdust-strewn pawnshop and dawdled a while. When he emerged, the sedan was gone. To be sure any tail had lost interest, he drove aimlessly for a while then swerved down a narrow alley to park out of sight behind a neon-lit club.

In a dim back booth with a view of the door, he ordered a beer and went through his mail. His mother echoed his father's earlier letter (this Christmas would likely be his grandmother's last) but offered no new details. Instead, she described how unnerving and intrusive the FBI visits had been, then begged him to come home. Did she get that the one made the other unsafe—likely a trap? Did she get that the Feds were conscience-free and well-practiced at exploiting motherly worries to catch men they couldn't? In a terse postscript, his father added to the pressure:

"It would mean a lot to your mother for you to see your grandmother."

Otis re-read the line. It would mean a lot to *her*? What about *him*? Did *he* want to see him? And if so, how did he expect that to happen without Otis ending up in jail—or else like Henry? Otis inferred that his parents were holding things back and that the air at home was even tenser than usual. Billy's P.S. confirmed his hunch.

"I'm only three days into my Christmas break. Help me out here, bro. Please!" Beneath his plea, Billy had drawn a self-caricature on a surfboard, balanced on stylized waves made from block capital letters: TENSION. Otis laughed so loud that the whole bar turned to see.

The first lines of Calia's letter to Ulrich offered further relief from his insoluble drama. "A big tipper named Otis said you two met last summer. He left me a thousand dollars! He's up in Alaska too and seemed nice. I'm surprised you didn't mention him. Were you friends? With the baby (I think it's a girl—she kicks and hiccups!) the money he left *would* be a godsend, but what if Otis made a mistake and miscounted? What if he needs it? Could you look him up in the telephone directory and ask him discreetly? I'll put the money aside until I hear from you—*or see you*. Please come home for Christmas, darling. If Otis intended such a big tip, then it will more than pay for your trip here! I got us a small tree and put it in a stand. I water it every day, but I'll wait to decorate it until you're here. We're almost a family!"

How could he reply? What could he say that would keep her hopes from going as dark as they eventually must? He had kept his fibs small when he could, but the fact was he had ignited a love triangle with a guy he had left to die. How could that not end badly? He wished he could take the pious diligent Ulrich and the big-tipping dynamo Otis and fashion from them a new man, Calia's white knight. They'd elope and live happily ever after. *Lunacy.* All his fake Ulrich letters would stalk and torment them. *Why didn't you tell me?* In Calia's shoes, Otis would want someone like him to be publicly flogged and then hung.

As he pondered Calia's letter, Ulrich's face lodged in his mind. Sure he was using his name, but names were so arbitrary, symbols on paper, sounds and furies signifying—*what?* Shakespeare had made Juliet say that a rose by another name would smell as sweet, and Mark Twain had become a hotshot writer by trading in a five-syllable albatross of a name, Samuel Clemens. Norma Jeane Mortenson started life with six syllables, but slimming down to five hadn't kept Marilyn Monroe from dying young. And what kind of conceit had led so many parents—after the JFK assassination—to name their baby boys John, blind to the homogenizing, ego-deflating confusion each of them would face amidst classes full of them?

In a similar way, Otis was the first to *honor* Ulrich by taking his name. It didn't matter that no one knew. Ulrich's name provided him freedom and that was good, right? Was his ruse unique? Maybe once; hardly now. Every year, more men evaded. Almost no one Otis knew had been inducted against his will. Some had hurt themselves to accomplish that, but their methods mostly ended there. Some girlfriends and wives volunteered to go underground with their man or wait out a prison term, but (like Joan Baez a few months ago) most politely moved on. Otis realized he'd done the ignoble inverse. He'd dragged a stranger into a mess she knew nothing about. He didn't like it, but for now it ensured the least harm to the fewest people, he decided. Over another beer, he weighed his Christmas options. His family and Calia had each made heart-rending cases. Should he risk another trip? If so, to where? And using whose money? Sid's or Calia's?

Pastor Joe and Esther insisted Otis stay with them. "Save, wait, and get your own place when you feel ready." Otis briefly protested—the standard courtesy dance. Inwardly, it was pure guilt. Their house was small. He ate a lot. He had more money stashed in their house than they'd ever see. But he was relieved. Hot meals were wonderful and safety priceless. A church seemed the last place Sid would look for him. (The public library seemed a close second.) Besides, Pastor Joe felt like a wise uncle, Esther like a dear aunt, and the Lifton kids like cousins. Along with thanks, Otis offered money for his share of groceries. The Liftons refused.

Otis debated what to tell the Liftons about his airport job. His first week with them, he spent his days at the library. (With Sid's cash, why work?) He read a Civil War tome he'd not finished at school, then several books on Mount McKinley. On Friday, for a change of pace, he plucked Patricia Highsmith's latest novel, Ripley Underground from the new books rack. Riveted by the intricate identity theft plot, he failed see Esther before she spied him. She brought the kids once a week, she said, but what was *he* doing here on a work day? Her tone was down-to-earth, curious but not judgmental. Otis confided that his job had ended. (He did not say how or why.) Clustered around his carrel, Esther and the kids prayed for him in sympathetic whispers.

That evening over dinner, Pastor Joe mentioned that the church sexton had left. The work was only part time and paid almost nothing, but could Otis think about tiding them over? Otis said he welcomed the chance to pay back their hospitality, but one of the middle Lifton boys interrupted. "Jesus does not do *quid pro quo.*" Both Lifton parents beamed; Otis stared, stunned. He had not learned the phrase *quid pro quo* until he was fifteen.

All through Pastor Joe's Sunday sermon, sashaying snowflakes outside the church windows made Otis think of the Icefield's surface covered and covered again. The road was closed for the winter—fifty miles in each direction—not a soul could hear the ice groan and crack as crevasses sealed shut. Ulrich's body might as well be on the far side of the moon.

Not wanting to stand out, Otis closed his eyes for Pastor Joe's prayer. What if Ulrich were there in the pew when he opened them? *Why did you leave me?* Would Ulrich wag an accusing finger? Like dust to a vacuum, Pastor Joe's booming voice drew back Otis' attention.

"Thou hast trusted in thy wickedness: thou hast said, 'no one sees me.'"

On the congregation's echoed 'Amen,' a simple question fluttered then settled in Otis' mind: *What if God saw?* In the crevasse and in the Yukon, thoughts hard to distinguish from his own had blamed and mocked him, inciting old panic. This notion came gently, an invitation to think.

What if God saw? He was glad no one knew he was mulling the question. Like a candy, he would roll it around a bit, reduce it, and try not to choke.

The service ended in a bustle of chatting and tending to children that distracted Otis from a man sidling along his pew toward him.

Pat, his tent-mate from Humble was grinning.

"Ulrich!" Pat extended his arms wide to embrace him.

Polite but spear-like, Otis thrust out a hand. "Hey there, Pat." He should have known. Pat had often tried to steer conversations to the spiritual. Once, to change the subject, Otis had asked him about his unusual name—Patrizio BT Shipley—a compromise between his doting Italian mother and exacting British librarian father. Pat's further explanation had cemented their friendship: "In a thesaurus, 'BT' stands for 'broader term.' Dad has always had high expectations for me." *That* topic had filled many late nights. Pat dropped his arms without looking any less cheerful.

"It's great to see you, Ulrich. When did you start coming here?"

"I dropped in a few weeks ago. And you?"

Pat explained. Last September, unable to find work, he'd returned to a Manhattan publishing job his father had arranged for him. Recently, he'd quit and returned here. He planned to stay.

Pastor Joe strode up.

"Otis! Marvelous! I'm glad that you're meeting non-Liftons!"

Pat shifted his gaze quizzically between them. Pastor Joe excused himself and, like a winsome salmon wove away down the crowded church aisle. Otis fought fear. Had Pat seen his real IDs? No. He had hidden them in Ulrich's car. He hated to do this. Pat had been a steady ally. "I hope you'll forgive me Pat, but it's a long story. Complicated family stuff. Pray for me?" Otis congratulated himself on how quickly he was mastering church lingo.

Pat studied Otis in a way that, from anyone else would have meant: *that's a ridiculous load of hooey, a total smokescreen; fess up and spill the real deal, man.* But Pat's face, while expectant, stayed harmless. "Of course I'll pray for you... Otis. It's good to meet you—again!"

Pat thrust out his hand and they shook good-naturedly and Otis felt refreshed to realize that Pat didn't care *what* his name was. Last summer Pat had helped without question; it seemed he would do so again. Still, Otis did not want to press his luck. Making excuses, he returned to the Liftons to stoke the fire and feed the dogs.

Fifty-Seven:
No Place and Home

onday morning, Otis began his church upkeep duties as sexton. He enjoyed cleaning and fixing, working at his own pace, but each hour he spent in the building raised his dismay. He was a prodigal fraud, a covert deceiver. The Liftons' geniality depended on their ignorance of his real life. They would be appalled at even a slice of the truth.

Each morning on his cot, he tried to ignore dog licks and children's whispers even as he took delight in them. *Shh! Mr. Fletcher is sleeping! I know. I can see him too. You touched him. Dad said not to. There. Look. He blinked. I think he's squinting. I think he's awake. Shh! No he's not.*

When he fled again he would miss this more than he'd ever missed Dirkden. He hoped to raise kids of his own in a home as loving someday. Could you buy a house with cash? Did realtors deign to talk to people his age? After the EMT course, he would get his own place—and an EMT job—but where? Strict draft enforcement (plus Sid's presence) ruled out Alaska. Returning to Boston would be nice, but there he would have to be Otis, and he could never explain his sudden wealth. What good was money you couldn't use? Agent Russo had said Massachusetts was lenient on the draft, but what if Mr. Metcalfe pushed the Dirkden draft board to make an example of him? What was the use of evasion if you landed in Vietnam after all and your father's boss brick-walled his career because of it?

So then, Massachusetts was out. Should he wait for his draft hearing or leave Alaska sooner? And when should he fess up to Calia? He began a longhand letter to her as Otis, but stumbled on the same things that had plagued him in person. How could he keep from coming within range of her grief and the desire to lay blame that would ensue? How much detail did bad news require? After ripping up his fifth attempt, Otis returned to the drive-in. With the typewriter perched on the seat beside him, he wrote her as Ulrich instead. Was that so cruel? This letter was it though—Ulrich's last. New Year's Day he would stop the fake letters cold turkey.

The next day over breakfast Pastor Joe complicated Otis' already thorny conundrum about where to spend Christmas. (He had no idea he was doing so. He was just being kind.)

"You're welcome to celebrate God's incarnation with us."

"I need to go home," Otis said, not quite sure where that was anymore.

"We haven't been back in years," Esther said, "but we liked it there. Surprise us with something Nebraskan!"

Otis mused inwardly. What might that be? Corn, cattle, dirt?

"I'll try to remember," he said.

The problem of how to dispose of the heroin still stymied him. Leaving it inside the Liftons while he was away was reckless. Their dogs might have a nose for the stuff, and if the kids got into it he would never forgive himself. Flushing it down their only toilet might leave residue or create a clog, and the seldom-used wood outhouse was no good. Leaving it in the car in the long-term airport lot made him nervous, but for now it was the best bad option he could think of.

To avoid the Alaska Airlines counter agent who knew him as Reinhold Messner, he paid cash for a roundtrip to Seattle on Northwest Orient under another name he'd made up and jotted down so he wouldn't trip himself up again. In Seattle, he would purchase his second flight leg in cash on a different airline under yet another name, which he also wrote down.

Christmas Eve morning, Otis slouched off his first flight, thankful he'd been seated beside a sleepy Japanese businessman and not a returning soldier. Families thronged to greet uniformed arrivals. The order was nearly always the same: wife, kid(s), then the soldier's mother. Fathers and brothers held back, waiting their turn with manly-fond steely stares.

Scratchy-eyed, still half asleep, Otis wandered to a big window and watched the baggage handlers work in the rain. He was glad he had not been required to unload, transfer, or deliver caskets but only to check that they were secure in airplane holds.

He sat on the floor with his back to the scene. What was Calia doing? *How* was she doing? He was helpless to halt what must be her growing intuition of trouble, but he could brighten her day. While in Nebraska, he had looked up her number. He retrieved the slip of paper from his pocket and dialed. As the phone rang, he envisioned steep avalanche slopes he'd tested with snowballs then mincing steps after heavy snowstorms. Should he ask if she knew who he was? No—too contrived. The unadorned 'Hey' that married people used was definitely inappropriate. 'Hi, it's me,' wasn't much better—way too cute and familiar.

Calia picked up halfway through the first ring.

"Alright Thea, that's enough! I'm sorry you've had trouble finding another place and that the shelter is loud. I'm sorry you got fired and that you're having more car trouble. But Ethel and I were very clear and patient with you. The drinking and the men staying overnight here had to stop. You may not believe it, but we set that rule because we love you. Now, you need to hang up and call your sponsor—take responsibility for yourself. I'm not going to say it again. If you continue to harass us, we will call the police and take out a restraining order. Is that clear?"

"Calia?"

"Who is this?"

"Otis Fletcher. You probably don't remember me."

"Oh my. Oh my goodness. Hi."

"Merry Christmas."

"Um. Merry Christmas. Sorry to give you that earful but our former roommate has been calling here every hour since two in the morning."

"Sounds heavy."

"We've been frazzled trying to help her. But I'm glad *you* called."

"Phew," Otis said, quickly wishing that he'd said something wittier or more substantive. If his visit to the diner had been half-crazy, this was triple crazy with a dollop of brash and it sounded like she had plenty to deal with already. He should hang up, wash his hands of this mess, and forget her.

"I set your tip money aside. I hope you haven't been inconvenienced. If you give me your address I'm pretty sure the post office is open until noon today. I can get you a money order. I haven't seen many hundred-dollar bills but I suppose that if you were in a rush you could mistake them for the ones. Either way, your tip was very generous. Thank you."

How could she shift from righteous anger to utterly guileless so fast?

"There was no mistake," Otis said, feeling the words shore up his resolve as they left his mouth. "I left it for you to help with the baby."

"Oh my. That's so much. Are you sure?"

"Yes." He touched the wad of bills in his jacket. She was right. It was a lot—and not enough. He should give her more. Later.

"What a blessing. Thank you."

He totally didn't deserve this. Posing as her fiancé, he'd fed her tasteless poison, yet her trust in him as Otis had only grown. He and Louisabeth had never extended each other anything close to such trust. At single-gender schools, each had craved the abstract notion of *I'm-taken* status because it freed them from the heartaches and hassles of casual dating. They'd grown adept at mutual flattery, stupidly sure it was what lovers did. But routine salvos of praise had cauterized trust. Was a compliment real or self-serving? Who knew? And frankly, who cared? Sex kept the arrangement functional (and mostly fun) until it produced a result that threatened to grow up.

"Well, it was a great meal," Otis said to Calia then, hoping to hit the right repartee timing, he added: "OK, I lied. The bacon was a little fatty." Calia laughed, easy and light and Otis hated himself. Even half-confessing he couldn't help blowing smoke, saying nothing—flirting.

"It *is* just a diner," she said.

"So... what are you doing for Christmas tomorrow?"

Like he was asking her out. He couldn't believe he was stumbling like this.

"Sorry. I meant what do you *typically* do?"

But if Calia noticed his nerves, she didn't show it. Her church would hold a candlelight service tonight. She hoped to get an afternoon nap so she could stay awake for it. Tomorrow she would visit Aunt Greta. (He should have asked who that was, but she seemed not to infer his familiarity.) Then she would eat Christmas dinner at the home of the older couple who hosted their weekly Bible study group. Otis asked after her baby.

"I'm getting excited. I think it's a girl. I don't know why I think she's a girl, but it seems right whenever I talk to her. She's kicking and hiccupping, especially when I get upset like that. I've started thinking of names."

Otis had read in her last letter to Ulrich about the in-womb gyrations and her speculation about the baby's gender, but his surprise at her selecting a name—and at the feud with Thea-the-drunken-promiscuous-roommate—was real. Calia had *not* shared those pieces of news with Ulrich. She quickly turned the conversation from herself to ask Otis how *he* was.

Otis mentioned the meal he'd passed up at "a church friend's house." *Her old pastor!* It felt wild to walk so close to the line. He stammered that he would like to call her again, and though he'd thought it over, he did not quite believe he would say it until the words left his lips. She said she would enjoy that, but also that she knew calls were expensive. Otis said he didn't mind—he had money—but she gave him her address just in case. He didn't let on that he already knew it.

Euphoric, he found a departures board. The next Boston flight left in three hours. An Omaha flight left in one. It would take only a couple of hours to drive west from Omaha to Grand Island. He fished a quarter from his pocket and poised it on his thumbnail to flip it but returned it to his pocket. This wasn't Friendly's. This decision was his: one he could make—one he *should* make. As his nonstop flight to Boston climbed over Puget Sound, Otis wondered if Calia had ever seen an ocean, and whether his plane today might pass over her house.

Fifty-Eight:
For the Holidays

The Logan Airport cab driver was playing a Simon & Garfunkel eight-track when Otis gave him directions to Dirkden. They listened in silence. Otis *was* weary—tired of running angry and scared amidst strangers. The cab pulled up at his parents' house. Roast turkey smell helped ease his unease. Several years ago, scuffles about which church to attend on Christmas Eve had given way to a new early Christmas family dinner tradition. Otis was glad to have made it in time and also to see no guest cars. Ringing the doorbell, he felt like a ghost asking to haunt.

Footsteps. The living room curtain moved. His mother's startled yell recalled another surprise on this spot: an unending wail. What if the pair of soldiers had not come? What if the last three years were a bad dream. What if *Henry* answered the door? The outside light blazed on. Through his bright breath steam, Otis squinted and tried to smile as the inner door opened.

"Oh my," his mother mouthed through the glass storm. Otis pulled it open and stepped inside and her arms exploded from slack to umbilical around him. "Oh my," she repeated.

Octopus, he thought, but only for a fraction of a second.

Billy, clean-shaven, held back, shaking his head.

"Never in a million years," he said.

Their father stutter-stepped forward in his signature moccasins, a linen napkin tucked high between his dress shirt buttons. His face flashed a cascade of emotions too fast for Otis to read. The congenial ambiguity reminded him of Sid—if Sid were trying his best to love him instead of to kill him. "There's no fatted calf, but if you've been good, there may be dark meat." His napkin fluttered to the floor. Otis retrieved it and handed it to him. His father waved it dramatically and Otis wondered who might broker the truce it implied. "Ho, ho, ho," his father said to salvage the tangled metaphors, but his comment came off like a jaded department store Santa Claus. "I'll get an extra chair," he said and scurried to the basement. Since Otis could recall, his father had used his workbench there to attempt salvage of virtually anything he could fit down the stairs.

"I'll lay out another setting," his mother said and darted to the kitchen.

"Basement and kitchen," Billy said. "Going to corners."

"Just like old times," Otis said and they both chuckled.

"Almost." Billy corrected and they both nodded, suddenly solemn.

"Happy birthday," Otis added and Billy bear-hugged him.

"They so needed this, bro," Billy whispered. He held Otis longer than he expected. Billy had grown at least an inch and added surprising muscle. "You need to see Grandma too. I'll fill you in later." He pushed Otis back, one hand alongside each shoulder like Henry used to do. "You look like absolute crap," he deadpanned and they both laughed so hard that Otis blew snot on the sofa. Then—cleaning it up while telling their parents it was nothing—they laughed even more.

Otis couldn't remember a time when he hadn't cringed any time Billy opened his mouth. At any opportunity, he would recount his little brother's latest folly to all who would listen—as well as to many who squirmed. What had happened? Who had changed? And would it last?

On Christmas Day the family waited to unwrap presents until Otis shuffled downstairs a little past noon. His mother handed him his stocking. It was stuffed with his favorite vanilla/ginger cookies.

"A homemade wool hat and mittens should be there for you when you get back," his mother said. "At your Anchorage post office box. They're from us both." She glanced at his father.

"If we'd known you were coming," his father began, gruffly, but his mother quickly turned her lighthearted glance into a withering glare and his father left off midsentence.

"Thanks, Mom. Hat and mittens are great." For the first time in a while, he recalled losing his others in the storm on the glacier. "I didn't get anyone anything." Otis considered: should he troll the mall tomorrow for picked-over belated gifts? The idea made him tired. They might smile politely but then return them or give them to Goodwill, a complete waste.

Snow fell gently all afternoon. Billy waxed and tested a pair of cross-country skis, then the two of them built a snowman. Standing beside it, neither spoke. Otis was glad that the dusk hid his tears.

"You want company?" Billy asked the next day. He'd cleaned and gassed the Dauphine for Otis' trip to see their grandmother. An air freshener hung from the mirror. Otis couldn't detect any odors that needed covering.

"Don't you have stuff to do?"

"I've been home two weeks already. You and she are all they talk about, Otis. Besides, they don't exactly advertise these kinds of places. Last week I got lost trying to find it."

Billy drove. Otis was grateful. Light rain filled low spots with fog, the trees brown and bare. Billy's blue denim shirt and the green Mass Pike exit signs reminded Otis of his ride this way last June with the musician. "Billy? I know Grandma likes it in the Berkshires, but once she got sick, why didn't she continue staying with us—I mean Mom and Dad—in Dirkden? They're a whole lot closer to the good hospitals in Boston."

"We're kind of past that now, I'm afraid. But before? That's a good question. They didn't say. I know she has friends at the nursing home, but I think they were also just overwhelmed—that it was too much for them to take after... after, well, you know."

They drove in silence for a while. Near their destination, Billy pulled over for coffee. "So," he began. He poured in sugar and stirred, taking his time as if equally happy to remain there or turn back and head home. "Do you have a girlfriend up there in polar bear land?"

Did he? What was Calia? If Otis counted the work he'd put into the Ulrich letters, he'd spent more time thinking about Calia than he had about any woman before. "No, not really. Between the military and the pipeline, Alaska's a weird place for dating; the ratios are all messed up."

"You only need one."

"Thanks, bro. I know."

Besides an artificial floral smell, the first thing Otis noticed about the special wing where his grandmother lay dying was a deep hush imparted by a thick lavender carpet. Billy greeted her briefly then returned to the lobby to read. Otis sat by her bed. Her face looked like half-cooked biscuits: yellowish, puffy, and pinched. Her hands were warm. Otis didn't expect that.

"Your grandfather," she murmured. "He would be so proud." Her expression melted into a gentle smile and Otis thought *no*, he would not be proud, not anymore. No one in his family would be. They would be shocked and he would be ashamed; none of them would ever speak to him again if they knew what he'd done. Every few minutes his grandmother would gaze adoringly, murmur similarly doting words, then slip back into narcotic sleep.

Finally, a nurse crept in and bent down, her voice low.

"Your brother says it's time to go."

Otis leaned to kiss his grandmother. "Goodbye," he whispered, and though she did not open her eyes he thought she cracked a wan smile. He was glad she would not know the truth.

In the car on the way home, as casually as if he were remarking, *How 'bout them Bruins?* Billy shared that he was thinking of asking his girlfriend Laurinda Westleigh to marry him.

Otis jerked sideways. "Are you kidding? You just turned nineteen."

"She's from South Carolina. It's really different there. Her father's this high-profile General. They're very traditional, into all this high society stuff. Debutantes. Country clubs. Scruples."

Otis' head swum. "Is she pregnant?"

"Hehe. I hope not. The General would shoot me and hide the body."

Otis wanted to help his little brother by sharing hard lessons he'd learned, but instead, he told him about "a couple I met in Nebraska who put off getting married. And it was a good thing they did because, a week later, the guy died in a freak accident."

Fifty-Nine:
Faulty Metaphor

Otis felt bad using Ulrich and Calia that way and so, back home, he thought to call Lucius to cheer himself up. On draft lottery night, Lucius had kept Otis from trouble; and the day of Kent State, facing his own problems, Lucius had stayed shockingly tranquil. Otis figured they would chat only briefly, but Lucius sounded thrilled and insisted they get together. They went for fried clams at a rustic place by a tidal marsh on the North Shore. Lucius said a prayer over their food. (Otis could barely hear his soft voice over the restaurant's bustling din.) Lucius then comforted Otis about his grandmother. Later, he related seminary anecdotes that made the Sound of Music seem ribald. Otis offered a carefully edited saga of his travels, his jobs, and Alaska weather.

Lucius listened with interest and once Otis finished, he asked:

"So Otis, how are you doing?"

Was Lucius really that oblivious? Was he deaf to Otis' apprehension, blind to the subtext of his hollow eyes? Could he not *see* that his old roommate was not doing well, offer him kindly sympathies, and spare him having to illustrate? The last six months had been lonely and strange. Otis hungered for the home he recalled as carefree, but he no longer trusted those memories. And if his recollections of the life he had *actually* lived were suspect, then what hope was there for a happy life so long as he needed— for safety's sake—to fake the past of a man whose life he knew only in broad brushstrokes? To keep their conversation upbeat, Otis considered the closest thing to a happy home he'd experienced lately.

"I've been staying with a pastor up there. He and his family are nice."

Lucius set down a French fry. "That's tremendous! Tell me about it."

"I walked into this church for some Christmas cheer. You know: carols, ho-ho-ho, that kind of thing. Before I know it, the pastor invites me to lunch and I fall asleep on their couch. They pull out a cot and tell me I can stay as long as I need to. I'd been thinking of looking for a new place anyway, so for now it's a great situation." Otis continued in the same buoyant vein, careful to obscure facts that might identify the specific church or connect it to Ulrich, whom he described as, "a friend of the road; a Midwest guy I bumped into and climbed with last June."

Otis was glad Lucius let him duck the most obvious question: Why was he not in Vietnam? Lucius had learned Otis' draft number before he did that awful night but had never pressed him (then or since) about what he would do. In his shoes, Otis would have wearied of such elephant-in-the-room tactics, trading on the easy affability that being roommates had habituated, yet Otis also sensed that, in continuing to tiptoe past the one big thing that had colored every facet of his recent life (and that of *all* their acquaintances) Lucius might be scared of conflict. Yet when the clam place closed and Lucius proposed they continue at an all-night diner Otis wondered if there were more to it. Surely Lucius had better things to do, yet he seemed content, almost joyous, to extend the evening. Why did he care? What did he expect? The more they talked, the more Otis felt his impossible secret move toward the surface. To let Lucius in on it could hardly make his life worse. He shouldn't trust anyone, but there was no one he trusted more. He told Lucius how he and Ulrich had met, chronicling every turning point through his recent phone call with Calia from the Seattle airport. He kept expecting Lucius to scowl, or scold him to clean up his act; but all Lucius did was to nod and say "oh dear," or, "I see," or ask, "what do you mean?"

When at last Otis finished, they sat in silence. Lucius' eyes grew moist until in a steady tone, he said, "I'm so sorry you're in this so deeply, Otis. I've prayed for you every day."

"Too bad it didn't work."

Otis ran his finger around the rim of his chipped coffee mug.

"No, you're being open about what you've done. That's important."

"Did you pray for that?"

"Confession is always good."

"That's not what I asked."

"I've prayed that you'd come to the end of yourself."

"Great," Otis snapped. "Thanks a bunch. I could have gotten *that* in Vietnam." Lucius stayed placid. "I'm sorry," Otis said and they each slumped back against the red Naugahyde booth seats. "I appreciate you trying to help but I can't exactly press rewind and re-record the last year."

"No, you can't. This is serious stuff, Otis. You've hurt people and you're *still* hurting them, and now people want to hurt *you*. It's bad all around. I can see that you appreciate that."

"I'm sorry. I've put you in an awkward position, haven't I?"

"It's hard to see how you don't end up in jail," Lucius said. Otis was glad he didn't say dead.

"If you felt you had to turn me in, I'd understand."

"I'm not saying that, Otis. It might be wise for you to turn *yourself* in, but I'm not a lawyer. I'm not even a pastor yet. I'm just your friend. And I'm human. It's a lot to take in."

Otis had never seen Lucius struggle like this and it unnerved him.

"If you turn me in, will you warn me?"

"Of course, Otis, but first I'm concerned for your safety. It sounds like Sid might harm you."

Lucius was playing it down. Sid would not stop at harm. Sid would kill him. Like Shaun's witness to Otis' ill-fated attempt on Pinnacle Gully last Thanksgiving, Lucius had an ineffectual front seat to potential catastrophe. And like Shaun, Lucius must be ticked off about playing that role. But as Otis thought about it, he realized he had the wrong metaphor. His life since fleeing induction was not comparable to taking a calculated risk, fifty feet up. *He had already fallen.* And while it was true that everywhere else was up from here, and that having made Lucius aware of his plight he had a little more hope, it only mattered if Lucius could offer him practical help.

Lucius went and spoiled even that.

"I'm concerned for your *soul*, Otis. You've been hiding from God."

Otis balked. What did Lucius mean? Couldn't he see that Ulrich's death was accidental? That white lies were sometimes justified? That he had not set out to harm Calia? That he'd given her money and planned to do the right thing? That the situation with Sid made him a victim too?

They jousted about how God could allow evil, then about hell. Around two in the morning, recalling an Ayn Rand novel he'd read in his early teens, Otis went on a ten-minute jag extolling selfishness and ambition as the best foundation for a just society. But it had been years and he'd forgotten details and Ulrich's and Calia's faces kept coming to mind; he lost his train of thought. Finally, he asked for the check, proud to help a poor pastoral student by underwriting *two* meals.

Lucius grasped Otis' forearm.

Softly, he said, "You need to at least come clean with Calia."

"I know, I know." Otis broke free and waved as if dispersing gnats until he recalled how Roy used the same gesture. He folded his hands on the table and spoke more slowly "I've thought of telling her. I've even drafted the letter, but I can't see how sending it doesn't end badly."

Lucius leaned across the table. "Otis? It's *already* ending badly."

"You don't think I see that?"

"I know this is painful Otis, but when Jesus talks about sin, he speaks of it in the most severe terms. If a part of your body causes you or someone else to sin—your eye or your hand or your foot—He says it's better to cut it off and throw it away than to continue down the same road, hoping for the best. It's easy to think of it as a metaphor, and many do, but the shocking thing is, He doesn't qualify it. He doesn't say, 'hey, this is only a parable; hell isn't so bad; don't sweat it.' No. He says it's better to enter the kingdom of heaven lame than to end up in hell. This is life-or-death serious, Otis. You may not have another chance to change. Once you're dead, it's too late."

"I suppose," Otis said. Lucius' monologue was completely outrageous, but something in his earnest departure from mildness made Otis want to think about it some more after a good night's sleep.

"I suppose? C'mon, Otis. You're a tough guy—tougher than most. You've made tough decisions before. You can keep this from getting worse. Will you take responsibility and level with her?"

"I'll try, Lucius. I'll try."

The next day, the Fletchers ate a big late Sunday brunch. Otis pictured the Lifton kids eating pancakes then tromping off to church early for choir rehearsal. He missed them. He missed their Sunday routine. The fact that he missed it so much surprised him. That evening, his father drove him to Logan Airport. On Storrow Drive they hit bumper-to-bumper traffic. Stopped in a stream of red taillights, his father tapped Otis on the shoulder.

"Look at that." He pointed across the Charles. "Pretty reflections."

Otis followed his father's finger to where colored lights along Memorial Drive in Cambridge met the river's rippling surface, sparkling like fairy wood sprites enjoying numbered days until the water froze solid. His father's relaxed manner was so at odds with last June's white-knuckled drop-off at induction that all he could think to say was, "Yeah Dad, nice, pretty."

After a while, they descended into the Callahan Tunnel; Otis zoned out as the wall's dirty tiles flitted by, close on each side.

"It was good to see you, Otis. I'm glad you came."

His father had called him by name!

"It was good to see you too, Dad." Otis almost sang.

"I'm glad you're doing well. Call us if you need help."

Otis was grateful that his father did not demand affirmation by asking, "Alright?" or "OK?" or "Will you promise?" He was also glad he didn't pry into jobs or girlfriends or the draft. But most of all, Otis was glad his father had not noted that Henry's watch was not on his wrist.

In Seattle, fog cancelled Otis' Anchorage flight. Rain pelted the observation windows through which he'd watched men transfer soldiers' caskets a few days before. He lay on the hard airport terminal floor but caught only snippets of sleep. He wondered about Calia's Christmas. He didn't want to wake her or seem too eager by calling again so soon.

Finally, in Anchorage, knee-deep in snow, he walked the airport lot. Where was Ulrich's car? On a second circuit, fresh boot prints startled him. They were his own. The white mounds made him think of Calia's bulging uniform. He brushed snow off several cars before finding Ulrich's.

Sixty:
Whiter Than Snow

T he Lifton kids welcomed Otis back like a long-lost older brother, pleading for piggybacks and foot rides, and inquiring about a Nebraska they'd heard much about but never seen.

"It's still flat," Otis quipped, winking at Pastor Joe.

The misleading cue pained him.

That night, he woke in the wee hours, mind at full throttle. In the airport lot, the passenger seat of Ulrich's car had been dusted with snow. Had it blown through a crack? Fallen in when he opened the door? Or had someone broken in? In sock feet, he tiptoed outside and felt under the seats. The packages were where he'd left them. He brought them all inside and briefly pondered selling the heroin. *But to who? How?* No. It was less than useless to him. He hid the cash in sock balls deep in his duffel bag under his cot. Later that morning he flushed dozens of times to get rid of all the dope. He took a shower, scrubbed down the bathroom, and washed his clothes. Worried that he might have the flu, Esther brought him Ginger Ale and Pepto Bismol. He sipped each and skipped lunch to round out the picture. *I'm a total dirtbag,* he thought. At a car wash, he tipped the attendant to vacuum the car—twice—and kicked himself for not doing all this before.

The first Sunday of the New Year, while it was still dark, Otis went next door to church to set up coffee. A man he didn't recognize ambled past the kitchen. Otis hailed him and he stepped in. Compact and athletic like Shaun, his eyes seemed to crouch, deep and intensely dark, in his weather-creased face. Otis offered his name, then asked the man if he was visiting.

"Pleased to meet you," the man said, pausing as if Otis should *guess* his name. "Visiting? You could say that. I'm Ralph Waterer. I've been around a long time." He said he'd recently returned from "many long years doing missions in Latin America," ascending high peaks and Mayan and Aztec ruins. "But I've always had a heart for Alaska. If the Russian Czars had stayed patient and held onto it, perhaps they would not have come to such an abrupt end. Poor girl, that Anastasia."

Otis shrugged. "$7.2 million was worth a lot more a century ago."

"Indeed it was—the wealth of a great kingdom. But how can you put a price on *The High One*?"

Otis shivered. Ralph had used the insiders' term for Mount McKinley. As casually as if noting what he'd had for lunch, Ralph detailed his three successful ascents by different routes.

"I've climbed a bit too," Otis said, hoping it sounded equally casual. Could Ralph be his new Shaun, the chance he'd hoped for to reach the summit? It was all he could do not to bow at his feet and mumble, *I am not worthy.* Otis gave Ralph a sanitized summary of his best climbing credential—his Icefield adventure. Unblinking, Ralph hung on each word.

"Excellent, Otis," he said. "That is a most impressive story." Still unblinking, he narrowed his already narrow eyes. "Yet I sense you are holding back—that you have done and seen more than this, gambled your life at steep odds and come out on top. It is a rare quality, vital in a climber. We would need to speak further, of course—should you fancy my offer— but let me be direct. My desire is the Wickersham Wall. I have returned to gather a team to ascend it next June. You know it, of course."

"Of course!" Otis blurted, barely able to contain himself. "The first ascent was only seven years ago."

Was this really happening? McKinley's near-vertical Wickersham Wall route was notorious for colossal avalanches that swept its face bare at capricious intervals. More men had circled the moon than had climbed it.

Would Ralph accept him? Could he prepare in time?

"Yes—that first climb took place just months before the first Kennedy was killed. I remember both events rather well. But let us talk about you and me." Ralph glanced at his watch—oddly like Henry's, lost on the Icefield. "In a moment, I must assist with Sunday School," Ralph said, "but from my perspective our meeting here is fortuitous, the start of what could become a mutually beneficial partnership. Shall we plan to speak over lunch today?"

Otis flushed with the same ecstatic hope he'd felt that April afternoon, standing at the mailbox, ripping open his Deden-Fisher acceptance letter.

"Yes!" he said. *Yes, yes, yes,* he thought.

After the service, he went to find Ralph. He searched the building and asked around, but no one at church had ever heard of someone by that name, nor seen anyone who matched Ralph's description.

That afternoon, the Liftons huddled around their tiny black-and-white TV, waiting for it to warm up. Pastor Joe adjusted the rabbit ears to get better reception. Compared to Boston, hardly anyone here talked team sports. *Nothing* was live. Even news tapes were flown up from Seattle to be broadcast hours late, sometimes lagging the papers. A year and a half ago, a satellite feed of the Apollo Eleven moonwalk had marked a proud civic milestone for the state, but since then no other TV had been live. Alaskans' patience with the dearth of professional sports was about to be rewarded. The afternoon's NFC Championship game promised a new era. (Sid had rightly anticipated that live sports would fuel a hunger for illegal betting.)

The Liftons placed no bets—monetary or otherwise. Instead, they laughed and ate popcorn, cheering based on whims without internecine strife for *both* the Forty-Niners *and* the Cowboys. After the game, Pastor Joe set a hand gently atop Otis' shoulder.

"I'd like to hear more about your trip. How 'bout we two grab a bite?"

Seated at a diner where the waitresses all greeted Pastor Joe warmly, Otis scanned a laminate menu then copied Pastor Joe in ordering his "usual": milkshakes, meatloaf, and mashed potatoes. He then related highlights of his trip home, careful to set it in Omaha instead of Boston.

"So, how are you doing?" Pastor Joe asked.

The phrase, the timing, and even the setting echoed his meeting with Lucius to such an extent that Otis wondered if the two men were telepathic. Each face conveyed the message: *nothing you could say would faze me; from me you have nothing to fear; I have your best interests at heart.* Otis was inclined to credit Pastor Joe with the sincerity he intuited largely because Pastor Joe did not claim it. Still, he'd known him barely a month. As Otis considered how to give a cautiously true answer, he slid Agent Erl's card from his pocket.

"Things are good," he said. "I like Alaska. It's been nice of you to take me in." Out of sight under the metal-edged diner table, he folded the card in half, then again, then a third time. Then he unfolded it. He took a leftover boarding pass from his other pocket and folded it with card into what felt like a vaguely tent-like form. Then, still expounding, he brought his creation into view where he absent-mindedly tapped it on the Formica between them. Eventually, he ran out of things to say about Alaska's beauty.

Pastor Joe exuded warmth. "What's troubling you, Otis?"

Their food arrived. The reprieve felt like an open window in spring. Otis set his paper wad next to the salt shaker. Pastor Joe said a quick blessing then dug in, mopping up maximum gravy with every forkful. Otis shaped his mashed potatoes with the back of his fork then set it down.

"I met Ulrich last summer," he said.

"That's wonderful," Pastor Joe said between mouthfuls.

A food gobbet lodged in his beard. Otis couldn't take his eyes off it. He studied Pastor Joe's face for signs he was upset at him for pretending not to know Ulrich when they went through his Nebraska photo album.

"We climbed together," he added.

"Fantastic. Tell me about it."

More meatloaf; more gobbets. Why wasn't Pastor Joe grilling him?

Otis crept through an upbeat, truncated version of their time on the Icefield but the further he went, the more his temples throbbed. When he got to Ulrich's last-morning sermonette about storehouses of snow, Pastor Joe threw back his head in genial laughter.

"I love it! That's Ulrich. Earnest for scripture. What happened then?"

Otis engulfed the paper wad in both hands.

"We hiked then went our separate ways."

"Have you kept in touch?"

"Not really."

Otis sipped at his milkshake. The gravy on his plate had clouded over.

"I wonder where he is," Pastor Joe said. "I'd love to see him again; to see you two together. That would be something!"

"That would be neat," Otis whispered. He excused himself to the restroom, ran the tap, and threw up. Briefly soothed by the old routine, he wiped his mouth then closed his eyes. Winter would re-knit the glacier around Ulrich's body like a fly in amber. He pictured Ulrich as a speck inside the huge solid block—a century or more until he emerged. Otis returned to the table and stared out the window so as not to look at his food—or Pastor Joe. It was up to him not to blow this.

Pastor Joe tapped his forearm. "Otis, could I pray for us?"

"No. Sure. I mean whatever, go ahead."

It was excruciating to consent and yet rude not to.

"Heavenly Father," Pastor Joe began, barely audible. The adjacent booths were empty but Otis' heart raced. It felt like Pastor Joe was shouting. He wanted to slink away. Shoulders cramped to his neck, he held a long breath, his eyes half open in case the waitress came by and needed to talk to someone normal. Pastor Joe continued in a relaxed tone.

"I thank You for who You are, and for sending Jesus, and for the wonderful cross. I thank You for bringing Otis to our home and for giving him rest here. Thank You for Ulrich's testimony to Your glory in glaciers and sunrises. Thank You for arranging for Otis and Ulrich to meet."

Without meaning to, Otis sighed. He had not told Pastor Joe about Henry yet—or thought about him in days. But now for some reason, the brother Otis last saw zipping off in a taxi settled into a pleasant, sun-dappled spot in his mind—the only way he could describe it—*sitting beside Ulrich.* (*That* pairing surprised him.) All the sad seemed filtered out of both situations. The time with the Liftons *had* been restful, Otis reflected. Almost like home; maybe better than home.

Pastor Joe continued. "Father, thank You for letting us get to know Otis. In Your great mercy and love, please open his eyes to his need for You." Otis peeked in case he meant it literally, but Pastor Joe's eyes remained closed. "By Your amazing and sovereign grace, please unburden Otis from his sin and guilt, and from any sense of needing to hide in shame. Grant him the freedom that comes only from knowing You in the deep pervading peace of Christ and His cross. Amen."

Pastor Joe usually took time to open his eyes after prayer so Otis kept his closed too and let the verbal images linger. He pictured the Icefield, broad and white, surrounded by toothy peaks. The mishap had spoiled the expansive promising sense the place had held for him since Shaun first told him about it. He could never return. Ulrich would forever be underfoot.

Otis pictured him pitching headfirst in their conjoined fall, arms stretched over his head like a gymnastic peace sign until he lay still in the dark, his life ebbing away, maybe instantly gone. Then, as if someone were turning Otis' mind upside down, the peace sign flipped and became a man on a cross.

Otis bolted up, startled, eyes wild. Pastor Joe met his gaze, curious. Had he sensed what he'd just imagined? Had he *planted* it by ESP? Otis wished he could ask what it meant, but that would mean admitting—and trying to explain—what had happened, and he was already having second thoughts about having spilled all of that even to Lucius whom he trusted more.

Sixty-One:
Fingers of a Hand

The next day, Otis fought evening Anchorage traffic to take one of the last seats in a junior high classroom. In a tiled closet with a drain in the floor, a janitor sat smoking and reading the paper beside a mop that suffused the air with a damp antiseptic odor.

The three EMT instructors opened the class by relating details of car wrecks, armed domestic disputes, and house fires at thirty below. The barrel-chested senior trainer remarked: "Fifteen years in this job has fueled more nightmares than a month surrounded by Red Chinese troops at the Chosin Reservoir, serving as a Marine Corpsman." Otis sat up, intrigued.

Each story they told topped the last until two students walked out. The sound of indignant demands for refunds drifted in from the hall, along with the scent of hot meat. Otis' stomach rumbled. The class ran six to ten and he'd missed dinner. At a break, he was therefore happy to find card tables laden with snacks: extra crispy pigs-in-a-blanket, egg-shaped Jell-O blobs on toothpicks, and red Kool-Aid. Peculiar selections—but he was starving. He loaded a plate, snarfed it down, then went for seconds.

After the break, the instructors dimmed the lights for a slide show. Pens, pencils, and knitting needles protruded from eyeballs at varying angles and depths. "Stabilize with a paper cup," one advised. "Resist the instinct to pull." There were pictures of mangled fingers. "If you use heavy equipment, it's dumb to wear rings," quipped the veteran. "Wrap gently with gauze," said a third instructor. Other slides depicted cavernous lacerations reminiscent of a supermarket meat display case. An unrelenting series detailed the barely recognizable parts of still-living people, blackened by frostbite, charred in fires, crushed in countless ways—skin of all colors bruised, blistered, or bloated, some sloughing off in great grisly sheets.

Someone gagged, then someone else. Scraping chairs and muttered curses joined a chorus of retching. A dozen pallid soon-to-be-former students filed out. The instructors ignored them. Otis swallowed bile. He would see this course through! He lifted his feet as the janitor mopped and the slide show continued. The janitor confirmed the next EMT cadre's start date with the instructors (six weeks hence), then locked the closet and left.

In a breezy tone, the instructors invited the remnant of students to come forward and take one of the empty (but still warm) seats in the first two rows. The senior instructor took attendance, writing each student's first name on the chalkboard. "Let's go around. Tell us why you're here."

When his turn came, Otis stared at a long deep scratch on the desk's surface and spoke softly. "I'm taking this course because I once failed to save a friend's life."

⁂

Later that week Otis jogged in place, waiting for a phone booth. Feeble midday sun failed to keep the air above negative ten. Inside, a woman in stiletto heels mumbled dejected OKs through pursed gaudy lips. Fishnet stockings poked from beneath her full-length fur. The bars and strip clubs on Fourth had indoor pay phones, but even on weekday mornings, most were in use and Otis didn't want Calia to think he went to such places. The woman hung up and stepped out.

"Sweetheart," she said to Otis, her tone devoid of seduction. "I don't know who *you* answer to, but I hope it's not someone like my pimp." She wobbled off in a cloud of perfume.

Otis stepped in, eager for Calia's voice to dampen his empty reflexive arousal and growing vexation. Careful not to burn his fingers on the sub-zero metal, he inserted a dime. Calia's recent letters to Ulrich had grown distant. Reading a few out of context, one might not think anything wrong, but the decline was clear. She never came close to unkind, but she also no longer shared mundane details like forgetting to water the plants, or what she'd had for dinner, or the human-interest stories from the Grand Island Independent. Concurrent with that waning, these phone calls were warming up. For Otis' part, the oppositely shifting moods of the two relationships made it hard to keep what he wrote as Ulrich separate from what he said (and wanted to say) as himself. If any comingled details had caused Calia to suspect he and Ulrich were linked (beyond the abridged story he'd shared with her), she had not voiced those concerns. And yet how could she? Such a hunch would sound bizarre and paranoid. She had to be exasperated. A fiancé—and especially an expectant father—should show up. Guys Otis had no respect for did more.

He recalled the first Calia letter he'd opened. "Oh that you were like a brother to me." If she *were* his sister, he would strongly press her to dump the Frankenstein's monster "Ulrich" he had stitched together. *No one treats my sister that way,* he would tell the guy, his stare close, cold, and dead, his arms loose and low. *No one. If you <u>ever</u> want to see her again, you <u>will</u> come to me first. You got that?* Violence would be permitted, the suitor scum, the brother her noble protector. Yet he was both men, at war with himself, the monster hard to kill, lurching along as it wreaked havoc. And as if that weren't complicated enough, there was now the baby to consider—as if he had stolen a car and found it asleep in the back. He couldn't just park it somewhere and walk off.

"Otis, are you there?" Calia sounded unperturbed. Otis rewound several minutes of distracted half-hearing about her Christmas dinner with friends.

"I'm sorry. The wind is whipping today. You were talking about ginger cookies." He wanted to be there to smell them, taste them, and see her.

Sweetly, she repeated what she'd said. Otis listened, then said he had to go, not because he had run out of dimes or things to say to her, but because his fingers and toes were going numb.

Sixty-Two:
Shadowing

At a bodega, Otis noted a short feature in the Anchorage Daily News Metro section: a house broken into, the landlord tied up and beaten into a coma. *His old address.* Sid must have returned for his things. Having not found them, he would now come after him. Otis' head spun. This also put him in the FBI's crosshairs. They knew Ulrich had lived with Sid and Otis had *told* them he was in touch with Ulrich. They would find no drug traces anymore, but a trail of hundreds he'd spent would solidify Agent Erl's fly-casting hunch that Otis might work for Sid.

A mix of curiosity and guilt pushed him to the hospital where the landlord had been taken. He found the room and crept in. Tubes dripped and monitors beeped. Otis felt lucky—and sick. The landlord's face was unrecognizable. It could have been him. It could *still* be him.

Sid knew him only as Ulrich but Sid was resourceful—and determined. Neither of them would feel safe with the other free. Rather than fast-track his plans to leave town, Otis stopped shaving and bought clear-lensed glasses and popular coats and hats unlike any he'd ever owned. He traded in Ulrich's car for a nondescript Ford and checked more carefully than ever for tails whenever he went out. The Liftons could handle the FBI, but if *Sid* tracked him there, he would never forgive himself.

Once bearded, Otis browsed gun shops, paralyzed by the variety. No one back home owned one. "For personal protection," he told the salesmen. The shotguns seemed a bit much. One store showed him a used revolver. It felt solid in his hand, about the weight of his ice axe, a lot like ones he'd seen in movies—and far bigger than Jack's. The clerk cut off the string price tag, placed it in a paper bag, and reminded him to buy ammunition. He stashed the handgun and bullets under his car seat and thought how he might use them.

Sid would not broadcast his approach. Waiting for ambush, vaguely hoping to gain advantage represented all Coach had taught him not to do. *Never* let a rival set the tempo. Go into a match thinking five moves ahead then from the opening whistle, show an opponent no mercy.

He didn't like it, but the logic was unavoidable. He had to take the initiative. He had to shoot Sid dead without warning.

A darker thought infiltrated his mind like venomous fog. With a single phone call, Lucius could destroy his life just as easily as Sid could. Why not kill him? More cold logic poured in. Either of the park rangers—the first, who had suggested he share Ulrich's campsite, or the last, who had quizzed him after the accident—could also link him to Ulrich. Neither had a reason to care *yet*, but they would if Ulrich's body emerged prematurely.

The logic burst forth in a raging torrent. Based on his own words, both Calia and Pastor Joe could link Otis to Ulrich and both wanted to know what had happened to him—she especially. Rationally then, in terms of his freedom, Otis would be better off with both of *them* dead as well. The idea so horrified him that for more than a minute he did not breathe. When at last he did, he tried not to cry.

***

Throughout January, Otis studied, cleaned the church, and shadowed EMT crews. When the house got too busy, he would read or sleep in the church sanctuary; it felt safer the more time he spent there. Sometimes he recalled the simple ways the Lifton kids prayed at meals and he would toss up a few silent ones of his own. *Hi, God. If you exist, could you fix the messes I'm in? Soon? Please? Pretty please? Hello?* He figured he was only talking to himself— thinking seemed more like it—but such mental exercises cost nothing and most Christians he'd met said the upside was huge. If a casino provided free chips, why *not* place bets to cover long odds?

Otis had spared the Liftons the burden of knowing about his FBI interview, but—expecting his draft hearing summons to arrive at their house any day—he ran to intercept the mail truck as soon as it came each morning. With the parsonage attached to the church, the Lifton's doorbell also rang often; Otis would leap up to answer it in case it was a process server. Often

310

he faced someone worse off than he was. If the Liftons invited the person in for a meal, Otis would feel bad about occupying a cot he didn't need, but he rationalized it until, gradually, the feeling lost its sting. He worked for the church and he needed protection. After weeks of FBI silence, Otis began to entertain hope. Maybe his file had been lost or their priorities had shifted.

By late January, he was giddy to think he might have dodged the bullet. His buoyancy didn't last long. One day he returned from the sanctuary and all the children looked down and stopped talking. Esther handed him a sheaf of papers. "It seems you've been served." She said no more, nor did Pastor Joe when he got home later. Otis supposed it was because they'd received similar papers for worse people but after days in that liminal state, he wondered if he'd imagined it. He checked the papers. He hadn't. His hearing was real, a month away. The Liftons' wall calendar showed the date in red: Ash Wednesday. The only hint that they knew came one day when little Benjamin gently touched Otis' ear.

"I pray for your hearing," he said.

By agreement, Otis called Calia each week at set times, then twice a week. He couldn't recall if she'd proposed the change, or he had, or if the idea had just emerged. The one time he missed, she forgave him before he asked. She referred to Ulrich as "my fiancé" only once, then as "my boyfriend," then as "the father of my child." Finally, she stopped mentioning Ulrich altogether.

Otis typed one last note to her as Ulrich. "I'm very busy and tired," he wrote. "Not sure when I might write again. Sorry. I hope you're doing OK." He hated himself for being so harsh, trashing a dead man's reputation. What sort of man skipped the birth of his own child? But for both their sakes, it had to end. He enclosed a thousand dollars in cash, "for the baby," hopeful that she'd be angry at Ulrich buying her off and take the hint.

On his way to mail the letter, he found a dumpster. The thunderous sound Ulrich's typewriter made hitting its empty bottom spoke of lasting damage. Regret overwhelmed him. He'd cut her off. Yet the prospect of continuing to call her felt as exhilarating as climbing solo. *Everything* hung on his skill in the moment. Free to be himself, he was actually quite good.

Leaving the post office, Otis opened a letter from Davey. He walked as he read, thankful for *one* low-stakes old contact. Davey's social studies teacher had assigned a paper on recent events. It scared him at first; then he found a topic. He recalled Otis talking about the draft lottery. (Otis thought he had mentioned it only once, but clearly it had made a larger impression.) Aware of his birthday, Davey had looked up Otis' draft number. Why wasn't Otis in Vietnam like his dad had been? Otis must have, "an amazing fantastic story that will knock my teacher's socks off!" His paper was due next week and Davey wanted to feature him. Could he write him back fast or call? "Thanks Big Brother! I know you'll come through!" Davey included his Atlanta phone number.

Otis stopped walking, heart heavy. He pictured Davey brimming with trust in his former mentor. Months ago, Otis would have relished receiving Davey's number so he could call him. Otis' story *was indeed* "amazing fantastic," yet he cared enough for Davey to admit the adverse effects on Davey's moral compass if he shared the truth. Instead, Otis wrote him a warm succinct note. While he was "amazingly glad" to hear from Davey, he wasn't able to share enough to help him. He enclosed a newspaper clipping on Apollo fourteen—a *more* recent event. Alan Shepard planned to hit a golf ball on the moon. Why didn't Davey write his paper about that?

A week later, Otis and the Liftons got up early to watch the golf ball hitting feat. "It's been a long way," Shepard said, voice crackling with time delay across empty space. It made Otis think back across a span of time that seemed just as vast—to the Doors concert and watching Apollo thirteen lift off, drinking too much with friends he had long since lost touch with.

———

"Everything's fine," Calia said on their next call. Her doctor was just being cautious, but he'd advised her to get off her feet and cut back her hours. "He's been kind to discount his bills," she added. Her old pediatrician had assured her that he would do the same next month—also a kind offer because she needed to buy diapers and infant clothes too. She said it offhandedly, but Otis surmised that because she'd been budgeting carefully, his final Ulrich letter had not arrived with the thousand in cash. He asked outright if she needed money. She sounded abashed.

"Oh that's OK. The church is helping out." She hesitated. "I guess I'm just a little upset at him, that's all. I don't know why I'm telling you this, but you've been so kind to me, Otis."

"He sounds like a good man," Otis said, loathing himself. Evasions popped into his head. He held them back. The worst one he quenched was: *I'm sure he'll show up for the baby's birth.*

He stopped at a pharmacy to buy a toothbrush but wandered the aisle for Valentines cards. Most were either gushy or crude. A friendly one stuck out as funny. He pictured Calia laughing. Along with four almond Hershey bars, he bought the card and penned a note.

"A little something for the anticipation. From a 'secret' admirer."

He bundled the chocolate, the card, and two thousand dollars in hundreds and made sure the bills' serial numbers were sequential with those from his final Ulrich letter. Floating the clue to his connection with Ulrich felt reckless but also apt—the kind of thing worthy opponents did for each other out of respect. Did he want her to know? It made no sense, but he had wanted that for a while, optimistic that things would somehow work out once she did.

The post office clerk offered him two kinds of stamps. Otis chose the ones commemorating fifty years of disabled veterans rather than the ones lauding General Douglas MacArthur. After sending the package, he could see no good next move but that didn't mean one would not show itself. True, now that the typewriter was gone, Ulrich would be unresponsive from her vantage, but she'd grown cold to him too. Based on how things were going with her as Otis, more phone contact would likely have her asking him for advice. But while that prospect felt flattering, even titillating, it was also treacherous. As such, he thought it best to take a brief vacation to think and get perspective. He would not check his mail or call her for two weeks.

Sixty-Three:
In Her Possession

In mid-February, homesick for his mother's Valentines, Otis visited his PO boxes again. The seclusion had helped clarify his next steps. He was resolved to surprise Calia in person in early March, slip her more cash, and see the newborn. It seemed like a good thing to do—for her, and for his state of mind. (He was also curious.) But if his draft hearing went as he feared, he might not get that far.

Alone on a church pew, he went through his stacks of accumulated mail. Within minutes, he filled with regret. His grandmother had died— expected, yes, but the memorial service had been last week. If he'd picked up his mail, he *could* have made it. He recalled driving her home, cleaning her gutters, restless as she told stories. Why had he refused her offer to stay for dinner? Why had he been in such a hurry to meet Shaun and impress him, his mind ahead on his climb up Pinnacle Gully?

Low sun peeked from beneath flurrying clouds to fill the sanctuary with amber glow. I *hope* she's in a better place, he thought to himself—or to God. He still wasn't sure which.

The next letter was APO, Saigon. *Shaun. Oh man. They got him.* Shaun distilled all the reasons Otis was glad he was not in Vietnam with him.

"Every patrol reminds me of our Thanksgiving Huntington trip where you got stupid high up without placing pro and I backed away from the fall line. I was sure I'd have to scrape your guts off the deck and call your folks. If you're in-country, you know what I mean. I did finally call them—from Basic—to see where you were. Your mom said you might be Special Ops. Good for you, man. I'm just biding my grunt time. The doctoral programs I applied to turned me down and my draft board killed my exemption. For guys like us boredom's the worst, don't you think? Last week we saw some pretty heavy action. I didn't mind it so much, but then this sniper nailed *the one guy* in my platoon who had half a brain. I "inherited" his books. You'll appreciate this: I'm reading his copy of Moby Dick. Let me know when you snag leave; we can hang out in Saigon or Bangkok—or sneak off to Nepal or Tibet. Now *that* would be something!

Yours in chasing "white whales" (mountains), Shaun."

Otis tried to picture what Shaun depicted—the brutal futility, the loss of control, the resigned matter-of-factness. Unlike on a climb, he couldn't help. He couldn't even respond without piling up self-serving lies. He set Shaun's letter aside.

Among utility bills for the Grand Island house and the expected Valentines from home was a letter addressed in familiar handwriting—with an Anchorage postmark. *Pastor Joe.* He'd said he was going to write Ulrich; the Grand Island address was all he had. His letter had forwarded here *according to Ulrich's instructions.* How had Otis missed that? He could have fixed the forward in Grand Island. But now, if he marked it addressee unknown and tossed it back into the system, it would pick up a second Anchorage postmark. To respond to Pastor Joe as Ulrich was nuts—and yet *not* to respond to him would amplify his alarm. Otis tucked Pastor Joe's unopened letter into his back pocket. There must be a move he could make here. He would think of something.

Calia had written to Otis. *Unusual. Wait. The box was wrong: Ulrich's. How could that be?* He flicked through the other mail. A second letter was addressed to Ulrich—*at Otis' box.*

In both notes, beside doodled checkerboard patterns, Calia asked the same thing: "Who are you and what's going on!?" He held the letters side by side, hoping it wasn't checkmate. It was. His sudden sense of freefall felt freeing. There was nothing more to do: no nuances to maintain, or odds to work—nothing to keep consistent or forget he knew when he called her. Beneath her innocent exterior, Calia wasn't stupid. Somewhere she'd picked up street smarts—resilience and dignity too. He had no idea what came next, but now that this day had finally come, he felt giddy to be an insider— the only one able to admire her so much.

Otis tore open another letter—to Ulrich, in unfamiliar handwriting.

"You have what's mine, 'Rick'. I expect it back. Thursday, 6PM, Earthquake Park. Come alone or else."

Sid. Sunset. Three days. Advance notice was no help. To return most of Sid's cash wouldn't appease him and the drugs were gone. Sid's allusion made it plain he knew Otis had taken his stuff. The landlord had misheard Ulrich as 'Rick'. Sid would not restrain himself to a disfiguring beating. And yet the authorities could offer no help either. They would pull them both in, then search the Liftons' place. The cash in Otis' duffel bag there would damn him and exonerate Sid. Otis was literally left holding the bag.

But if Otis skipped the meeting, Sid would be just as wrathful. He would seek out anyone Ulrich cared for. *The Liftons;* their *kids*. Distinctions between leverage and vengeance wouldn't matter. Sid would be ruthless. Otis imagined the scene; the mere possibility incensed him. They didn't deserve to suffer for his dumb mistakes. He calmed himself down. If Sid had known about the Liftons, he would have come already. All Sid knew was Ulrich's PO box, and Otis was being super-careful going out. Calia should also be fine. Aside from the safe deposit box which Otis had cleaned out, no records he knew of linked her to Ulrich.

A sudden thought chilled him. To keep to Sid's schedule, he'd brought two drug packages with him to Nebraska. Willfully clueless as to their contents, he had not considered the delivery delays from Nebraska to Alaska. Sid's customers would have received their goods late. Baffled (perhaps infuriated) about the unexpected out-of-state postmarks, they would have told Sid.

Otis felt like he was in one of those carnival bumper cars where the steering wheel responded only sluggishly. How hard you gripped it wasn't the issue. Sometimes the car went the way you expected it to. Often it didn't. Eventually you ran into people—and people ran into you. Mailing Sid's packages from Nebraska had put Grand Island on Sid's radar, and in a place that small, Sid could easily learn that Ulrich had lived at Walter and Greta Schrank's farmhouse. The thought of Sid inquiring at the diner—the obvious nexus for gossip—made Otis queasy, but the waitresses there had proven fierce at guarding their own and besides, the house was empty. Calia had no reason to go there.

Queasiness gave way to horror. What if Sid talked to Calia directly? No. The waitresses didn't wear nametags. She might pour him coffee and he'd never know. Aunt Greta was the more likely Grand Island target and she should be safest of all. After Otis spoofed his way into the Farmview to meet her, Calia had written to Ulrich about the facility's tightened security. Other possibilities swirled like a swarm of bees. What if Sid learned that "Ulrich" was Otis and tortured his Dirkden family? Sid wouldn't hesitate to act on such information. The thing Otis had thought would save him—the thing he'd worked hardest to conceal—might be his undoing. Everything traced back to the snap choice he'd made in the Icefield parking lot. Some bold move. If he'd simply given the ranger his Otis ID and hitchhiked back to Calgary, none of this would be happening. He had put at risk all the sources of light in his life. He could take no more half measures.

Protecting them was the only *really* bold move left to him.

He would stuff clothes with pillows, go to Earthquake Park early, and prop the dummy in the front seat. He would leave the car running, stomp tracks in every direction, then select a vantage amidst the clay mounds. He would set up his shot, wait as long as it took, then take Sid out. He would dump the gun, drive to the airport, and vanish. His break with his past had to be total this time. No family, no Calia, no Lucius, no Davey. *No one.* He was disciplined. He would make it work. If the new place had no mountains, so be it. For their sake, the sacrifice would be worth it.

Who was he kidding? He'd only ever shot at fat fixed targets that didn't shoot back—Jack's truck tires, just that one time. Sid would not be as easy, nor would he likely come alone.

Still, though the odds were long, he had to try. He thought of Calia forever in the dark about what had happened to Ulrich, doing her best to raise her child alone. Maybe the clash with Sid was divine retribution catching up with him. He had impersonated Ulrich while passing himself off as his friend. To not-so-subtly woo a dead man's fiancée, he'd used money rightfully hers to cast himself as a sympathetic and generous benefactor. He recalled a sixteenth century tale he'd read in high school French—a true (if bizarre) account. An imitator had won over the wife of a man off at war. When the real man returned, the impostor had been hanged.

Maybe that was how this should end. Send Ulrich's things to Calia; let her know how Ulrich died. With Calia warned and informed, he could die with a clear conscience. But what if, after sending off a box and a detailed letter, he wasn't martyred? What if he got the drop on Sid after all? What if, like Sundance and Butch had—for well, OK, *most* of the movie, until that last bit in Bolivia—he drew first and took Sid out? What if he *survived?* He wouldn't exactly get to hoist a trophy, now would he? After tidying one secret's loose-ends, he would then have a new one to hide: killing Sid.

More things he'd never considered entered his mind.

Upon reading his confessional note, Calia would re-assess everything "Ulrich" had written—and all Otis had ever said too. She already had in her possession a false "Ulrich" letter in which he'd pushed her to abort her child. Whether Otis killed Sid Thursday night or Sid killed him, her opinion of him would change utterly once she knew the truth behind that. Instead of Sid out to get him, *Calia* would be Otis' nemesis, stopping at nothing to bring him to justice.

From his first letter to her, all their relations were tainted. Sid might kill everyone he loved—and Calia too—but he, Otis, had worked to deny her hope in the future *and* trust in the past.

Unembarrassed by hot tears, he half-choked, half-whispered.

"God, I deserve *all* of this, but if you can hear me, oh God please, *please* protect Calia and the baby."

And, for the first time—somehow—Otis *knew* he'd been heard.

Sixty-Four:
Dry Ground

radually, the sanctuary darkened and Otis regained his composure. Two months ago, he'd feared that a pastor's home would be a cage papered with rules, hemmed-in and tense, no better than Ulrich's car or a cheap motel. Now he envisioned the Liftons as a warm, breezy sunflower patch, growing and swaying together. Even when the children got coughs, spilled milk, or woke him, the house seemed joyful. It made him yearn for the home he missed and knew he could not have again—three brothers like plaid flannel puppies, their tussles always with love. He would call Billy tomorrow. If he waited, Billy might think he was asking for help.

Otis approached Pastor Joe's office door, his steps muted by carpet. A plane of light bisected the hall. He paused in the shadows beyond it. Where else could he go? What else could he do? The answer came fast—scary, but clear, the plan he'd just rejected out of cowardice. He could hunt Sid down and shoot him—that's what he could do; what he *had* to do. Sid would never expect it, and he did not need Pastor Joe's permission for it. No one would shed a tear; all his other problems would fade.

Otis thought he heard footsteps. He swiveled, but in the gathering gloom, the light from Pastor Joe's office had spoiled his vision. The sense was uncanny—down to the same sick sharp sweat smell. He could swear that Octopus (a.k.a., Theo Behm, a.k.a. The Bomb) was beside him again like before their state title match six years ago. *The-O! The-O! The-O! The-O!*

Surrounding the two of them in that pregnant moment, a shoulder-to-shoulder mob of ardent Chandler fans had roared their favorite's first name without ceasing, drowning out the handful of cringing polite Dirkden devotees. Before Octopus had slipped in the mouth guard he would soon

319

spit in triumph beside Otis' ear, he'd asked Otis: *How much do you want it?* Barely able to hear over the crowd's stomping chant, Otis had avoided his archrival's gaze. Octopus leaned in and shouted. *Look at me! Answer me!* Otis had stayed mute, stunned to realize that the answer he *wanted* to give—the answer he knew he *should* give—was wholly at odds with his terror.

Chagrined by the memory, Otis felt his feet step forward as if someone were walking for him. He watched his arm extend and push open Pastor Joe's door. It felt as if Coach were beside him, the referee strangely fine with him being there in the fray, helping. In the time it took Pastor Joe to glance up in surprised delight, Otis felt as if Coach had whispered inside of him:

Don't you worry; I've got this; all will be well.

Otis desperately wanted to believe that the sense was real.

"Am I interrupting?"

"No. Not at all. Please. Have a seat. Coffee?"

Otis refused. It wouldn't help. He'd grown used to sagging weight on his eyelids and a sloth-like pause as words tried to form but then fled. Despite being safe at the Liftons, he'd lain awake many nights, recounting last June's events to himself, walking down countless dead-ends. Pastor Joe's black lacquered wing chair sported his seminary's gold colored emblem—a gift he blushed to acknowledge. The first time Otis had sat in the chair, he'd noted how closely it resembled the one in the Deden-Fisher career office. This time it felt different, the association defanged.

"So, you finished your EMT course. You must feel good about that."

"Yeah, I guess." Otis explained. His practicum had gone well—shadowing with ambulance crews all over town, at all times of day. He liked the work: restoring order, helping people start to heal. His instructors said he would make a good EMT. Yet privately he wondered: Why was he so bad at restoring order in his own life? Why did he end up hurting people he did not set out to hurt? How could he tell Pastor Joe of his desperation, much less the reasons for it? His most recent disappointment was only part of it. He should have seen it coming.

Otis could not serve as an EMT. In his enthusiasm to sign-up for the course, he'd not thought ahead to EMT *certification* or the fact that any EMT *job* required a social security number. In the EMT world he was credentialed as Otis, a draft evader facing a fait accompli draft hearing next week.

Getting his Master's degree? Teaching? Coaching? Finding a wife? Settling down? They were all mirages now.

How could he begin what he wanted to say? He recalled the huge serac he'd watched fall the day he and Ulrich met, its thunder delayed—a harbinger he should have heeded. Why would a pastor let a guy like him eat at his table, roughhouse with his kids, ruin his reputation? Once he revealed the truth and gave up Ulrich's name, he would be driven out, a fugitive wanderer again, easy prey for men like Jack or Sid. His other options were jail or war, prey for sure in those realms too.

"You seem troubled, Otis. Do you think it might help to talk about it?"

Otis spread his palm over his brow like a visor and stared at the rug.

"Ah, crap," he choked, eyes welling up.

In his mind as in their match, Octopus pressed him face-first, hard to the mat, his foul breath grunting words Otis feared to refute. *You ready, Fletcher? Because I'm going to flip you and pin you and win.* Otis had grunted, *drop dead,* hopeful the phrase would suffice, but Octopus' fans were screaming, waving their arms, pounding the bleachers. Over the din, inches away and barely breaking a sweat, Octopus had delivered his verdict. *And your people? Your rich, prissy, egghead Dirkden people? They're going to watch me do it. Right. Now!*

Octopus had exploded with precise, overwhelming fury and pinned Otis like a bug. The ref's whistle had come as if through water. Done. Over. Nothing to do. How could a thing so weighty transpire so fast? Far worse than the defeat had been Coach's gawk—statue-like, hands to his temples: *Oh no! No, no, no!* The team which the previous week had elected Otis to lead them the following year looked on in shocked dismay. With their hero fallen, what hope did *they* have?

Pastor Joe came around the desk, closed the door, and pulled a chair alongside. With a soft intent gaze, he leaned in and as he did, Otis felt his old memories shrink back.

"It's alright, Otis. Take all the time you need. I'm not going anywhere."

But instead of calming him, Pastor Joe's comment released a flood like distilled internal trash-talk from all his old foes at once.

Ha! This fat low-paid loser? Help you? Get real. He's out for himself. He keeps his wife pregnant and cooking; he homeschools their kids so they won't think for themselves and refute him. He'll persuade to you spill your guts, then in a New York minute he'll drop a dime and turn you in. He's paying out rope for your noose.

321

Otis coughed, about to blurt: *sorry to bother you; this was a mistake; I'll be fine once I get some sleep*, but Pastor Joe rested a hand on his shoulder. Otis jumped as if it were a live wire. "I'm going to pray," Pastor Joe said—not a question. His voice rumbled with an assurance that reminded Otis of his best climbs, fluid, washed of all fear. He asked God to grant Otis repentance and trust in Christ. "In Jesus' name," Pastor Joe concluded, "please cleanse Otis of his guilt; free him from all his fears."

Otis' mind tumbled back. Ulrich must have sized him up in their first conversation. Yet he'd cheerfully cooked for him, washed up, and given him shelter. Content to snap photos, hum hymns, and read his Bible, he'd never voiced a need to get up on the Icefield. Their odyssey had been entirely Otis' idea. Yet even after Otis pushed him to the point of fainting, he'd continued without complaint, yielded to Otis' ambitions. Why? Fearing he might jeopardize their fragile pact, Otis had not asked him nor, until now, had he reflected this deeply. He'd needed a competent belayer, period. He'd failed to see Ulrich's courage. When the storm struck, Ulrich had *volunteered* to walk point—and not in ignorance either. He'd seen the crevasses. He knew what could happen. With no ice axe to stop a fall, he'd forged ahead through the maelstrom hoping to find the tent and keep them both from freezing. That took *serious* brass ones. On a coin toss, they could have switched roles—Ulrich's light for Otis' axe. Otis knew why *he* hadn't proposed it, but why hadn't Ulrich? Why had he freely risked death for a virtual stranger?

Suddenly, Otis sat up, alert to a strange inner calm. Incessant mental replays of Octopus' taunts and the Icefield's horrors had vanished, burned off like June fog at high noon. It seemed like the most natural thing in the world to pull Pastor Joe's letter from his back pocket and hand it to him.

Quizzically, Pastor Joe took it and examined it.

"Ulrich is dead," Otis said and felt an icy updraft of renewed fear; but as unplanned words burbled out, it quickly gave way to the sense of a clear mossy spring. "The more I try to cover it or make amends, the worse I make things. It was just us two on the glacier. No one else is to blame and now his fiancée Calia and their baby are in danger."

Pastor Joe's eyes widened.

"*Grand Island* Calia? Fiancée? Baby?" His voice stayed calm.

"Yes," Otis mouthed, but no sound came. Seconds crept by and a thought formed to which he gave silent voice. *I'm so sorry, God. Ulrich was*

322

Yours; I led him to his death. There's no reason You should forgive me, but oh Jesus, please, if You're willing. And in response the quiet sense he'd felt before seemed to say, *'I AM,'* and burst like a thousand suns, as much a person as Lucius, Coach, or Pastor Joe, but stronger, better, trustworthy, inside him.

Pastor Joe's eyes softened, sensing or maybe seeing. He reached for his Bible and as if by feel found a verse in Isaiah. He held it out so Otis could see, pointing as he recited aloud from memory. "Though your sins be as scarlet, they'll be white as snow. You remember when I last preached that?"

Otis rubbed the knife scar on his hand, unable to even picture Octopus, or recall why he'd been afraid. "My first week. We'd just met."

"That's right. I didn't know you, but God did—from before time."

For almost an hour, Otis told Pastor Joe all he could think of. His real home and draft status. The family's chill since Henry's death. How he'd misled Calia. The mess with Sid and the FBI and why he'd bought a gun—even what kind and where it was. He was eager not to leave anything out.

"You're in way over your head," Pastor Joe said.

He encouraged Otis to go to the authorities, but he wanted Otis to make his choice freely. His motivations mattered. He walked Otis through the Apostle Paul's letter to Philemon to show him. Otis sensed he was right, but pushed back to be sure. Why risk it all blowing up? Why not tip off the FBI anonymously? Give Pastor Joe Sid's cash to turn in. Tell them to protect Calia. Why risk being sent to Vietnam?

Pastor Joe expressed sympathy. "This world is broken in sin. Its justice is flawed but God's is not. He sent His Son to achieve perfect justice *and* perfect mercy. Jesus lived the life we never could—totally righteous—then took the punishment we deserve for cosmic treason. He credited both those things to anyone who will trust Him. Compared to the riches He gives us in Christ, anything we suffer here is a light, momentary affliction."

"You've said things like that before, but it makes more sense now."

"Good. I suspected it might."

Pastor Joe admitted to wrestling with the war. He credited those who'd planned, fought, and led it with noble motives in sometimes ultimate service to freedom. Yet he'd also comforted, counseled, and grieved with hundreds of people from every walk of life bothered or broken by it. Otis got the sense that—like Henry—Pastor Joe was holding a lot back.

Last week alarming accounts had trickled out from a media forum in Detroit. Dozens of Vietnam veterans had borne witness to things they never imagined they'd see, much less do. Were all their accounts true? Pastor Joe sighed. "All men are liars. Only the unchanging God is totally reliable, all the time right in His words. But if even *some* of what's come out there is valid it makes me very uncomfortable."

Otis' efforts to stay out of combat had a similar quality to them. He'd faced each decision with good intentions. Each door had made sense to step through at the time. Yet whether he acted on instinct or took time to weigh his options, proverbial flies always seemed to buzz in. White lies turned rancid, spreading ruin he never intended. In avoiding harm to himself, he'd heaped it on Ulrich and Calia instead: their baby too—and his own soul.

"Our choices matter," Pastor Joe said. "They have real consequences. Yet *every* tomorrow is in God's control. Once you trust that God in eternity ordained everything with exquisite care from outside the bounds of time— for His glory and for the good of those who love Him—you'll know a peace that surpasses all understanding. I can't convince you of that, but He can."

Pastor Joe prayed again and Otis felt himself being reeled up from a deep dangerous place, the sense entirely contrary to his climb from the crevasse where even the tiniest misstep would have meant certain death. He felt warmth radiate to his fingers and toes, a surge of serenity that made no verbal sense and yet perfect sense. It reminded him of a time-lapse grade school filmstrip of seasons—a green stalk thrusting up through melting snow and soil, its buds swelling-out leaves, then flowers, then fruit. Even the thought of them browning and falling off seemed beautiful.

Later, next door, Otis heaped up thirds of Esther's spaghetti casserole, which seemed more delicious than any food since Ulrich's pancakes. He recalled the rush of meeting him, persuading him, charting their route, dividing gear, then the wee-hours alarm and they'd been off, their fates and bodies tied together, the whole thing serious and thrilling, and yet they'd barely known one another. The last few hours in Pastor Joe's office had likewise felt rapid and weighty, a turning point in his life. What lay beyond the next few days? He could scarcely guess.

Sixty-Five:
All That He'd Carried

The next day, Otis gave Pastor Joe the keys to Ulrich's safe deposit box plus everything he'd taken from it. He gave him the keys to the nondescript Ford and reminded him about the never-loaded gun and box of ammo under the front seat inside it. He gave him Ulrich's journals and all the other things he had carried—relics of his former life, muddled up with the life he'd stolen. It pained him to ponder the hurt he had caused. Pastor Joe said that was a positive sign—evidence that God was disciplining and shaping him to be more like Jesus. God would empower Otis to face and help to heal the wrongs he had done.

Pastor Joe suggested that Otis write Calia a *brief* note. Otis drafted one in careful longhand. "Dear Calia. I have greatly harmed you, Ulrich, and the baby. By the time you read this, an old friend will have called. Words cannot convey my full sorrow. I beg your forgiveness."

He thought to qualify his request (what right did he have to ask her for *anything?*) but Pastor Joe explained how relatives and friends of people whom Saul of Tarsus had tortured and killed reconciled to him after Jesus arrested him on the Damascus road and made him the Apostle Paul. Otis shouldn't think Calia had any less reconciling power available to her. Otis owed her—his new sister in Christ—the chance to seek God's help in *her* struggle. Otis wasn't sure which part of that statement astonished him more: the idea of such total, mind-changing power or the sister label he'd once misread. After thinking a while, he concluded simply. "I would appreciate your prayers, Calia. Sincerely, Otis (your former enemy)."

He wrote to Lucius to thank him for his persistence, recount his conversation with Pastor Joe, and report his baptism that Sunday. He also

325

outlined his plans and asked Lucius to pray. Several times he had to stop, overcome to reflect on how patient and hopeful Lucius had been. In less detail he wrote to his parents, to Davey, and finally to Billy. He concluded each note with a caution: it might be some time before he could write again.

The next day (the first-ever Presidents' Day Monday) he helped Pastor Joe shovel the drive. The sun lingered longer and higher than the first time they'd done this. They talked of the joys of not hiding. Later Otis watched Mother Moose re-runs with the Lifton children, who were unsure why their parents were allowing a sudden glut of TV—but they happily went with it.

Early Tuesday, Otis called Agent Erl, whose unsurprised informal manner briefly made Otis wonder if he was walking into a trap. The thought vanished like a soap bubble. *He was free.*

As if Pastor Joe had read his thoughts, he handed Otis a slip of paper. "You know the Truth now, and He knows you. The name above all names has set you free indeed." *Jesus.* The thought tasted sweet. He would *never* have thought he'd be *one of those people*—but here he was. Pastor Joe prayed in the car outside the FBI office. "You're through the worst," he said.

"I guess," he said, still unsure. He would miss the long fatigue-free Arctic days brimming with bird sounds and the smell of everything green. On the sidewalk, Pastor Joe hugged him. Otis thumped him then stood back, hands in his jeans pockets, arms straight as pillars. Snowflakes tickling at his eyelashes made him recall waking up inside the crevasse.

"I'll hang onto your break-ups," Pastor Joe said, his arms pillar-like also. Far ahead of spring melt, Otis had purchased the pair of uniquely Alaskan tall rubber boots with thick studded treads to get through the wet, icy-mud season. Otis thought of how much the Liftons had done for him. "The boys are almost my size," he noted. What was he saying? It would be years until they grew into them. His chin quaked. *He might never see that day.* He swiveled to hide his emotion.

Pastor Joe kicked at the snow. "Otis?"

"Yeah."

"You'll be OK."

"I know. Thanks for everything." It felt inadequate. They stood awkwardly. Finally, Otis turned and trudged toward the glass FBI office doors. With each snow-muffled footstep, he expected a chasm of doubt to swallow him whole. Silently he prayed for courage. Just as he was about to conclude it was silly to pray for something so vague, Pastor Joe shouted.

"Hey!" Otis spun and caught his softly lobbed snowball. "Remember, nothing is chance."

Otis laughed. "Someone else told me that." Overhand, he threw it back.

Pastor Joe ducked. "Alright, now get out of here. I'll see you later."

"I'm counting on it," Otis replied, giddily sure that he *would*.

Sixty-Six:
On Belay

In the same FBI interview room again, Otis clutched Pastor Joe's slip of paper. He did not need to unfurl it. *You will know THE Truth and THE Truth will set you free.* He did not need a lawyer, he said. He admitted wrong right away, then did his best to relate all he knew.

Agents came and went, as did Anchorage police. Alternating waves of aftershave and body odor provided his only clues to time passing. Cigarette smoke was the only constant. They kept probing, asking him to repeat things: induction, hitchhiking, Jack, crossing the border (Mike and Mark had done nothing wrong, he made clear), Ulrich and their climb, deceiving the park ranger, impersonating Ulrich, taking Ulrich's car, Sid, the drugs, even the Thanksgiving plane crash.

"You're a walking one-man disaster area," quipped one.

Otis was thankful when they brought sandwiches and Cokes and let him stretch his legs. He wondered if it was still light outside or still snowing. One agent referred to Otis' draft dodge as "marvelously slick." What Otis once would have swelled with pride to hear now seemed like a poison ivy T-shirt—flattery he'd rather be rid of. During what he guessed was the second night, the authorities changed tactics.

"You fled induction, beat up a truck driver who tried to help you, then fled the country with a stolen firearm. A Saskatchewan farmer dug it up; we traced the serial number. You were homeless and jobless. When you learned of Ulrich's draft number, you got jealous. An immigrant like him gets a lucky break and you don't? That doesn't seem fair to me; does it to you?"

"I didn't know about his draft number until after the climb," Otis said, as calmly as he could, which wasn't as calmly as he would have liked.

"Oh, c'mon. Weeks after Kent State, two American college kids bump into each other in *Canada* and you're telling us the draft never came up?"

"We never talked about it."

Another agent weighed-in. "Here's how I think it went down. You're in close quarters in the campground. His wallet falls open or maybe you snoop. Doesn't matter. You find his draft card and job offer. His low number fends off a big stick. The job? Big, fat carrot. Most twenty-two-year-olds don't pull down half of *his* salary. Who could resist? Am I on the right track?"

Otis prayed, silent and (he hoped) expressionless.

"You lure him up onto the glacier, bide your time, then cut the rope. Crevasse hides the body. He's frozen solid—a hundred feet down, I'd guess. The place is vast, they tell me. The Canucks could spend a month up there with their best sniffer dogs and never find him." The agent clapped in mock slow-motion. "Well done. Perfect crime."

"No. That's not true." Otis found it hard to steady his voice. "It wasn't like that. That's not what happened."

"You're right," said a third agent, mute until then. "It's much worse. Most common motive for murder there is. You wanted his fiancée. And you wanted her so bad that you wove a web to get her." He gestured toward a stack of file boxes with his name on them. "Those are phone records—interstate and international—and lots of letters. We have witnesses in Grand Island who will testify that you stalked them both in Nebraska a week *before* you said you met him *by chance* in Canada."

Otis didn't know where to begin with the labyrinth of half-truths, back-handed slander, and blatant lies.

"That's premeditation," the first agent noted. "Malice aforethought. Canada and Alaska don't have the death penalty, but Nebraska sure does, and for a scheme this complex, including flight to escape prosecution, we may recommend that U.S. *federal* attorneys apply it."

Otis prayed for help to combat his growing distress. He took a deep breath. Even if they weren't bluffing, he would be OK in the end.

The third agent spread his hands on the table, leaned over them, and spoke softly. "A love triangle like this? I'll lay odds that this Calia woman was in on it all from the start. She told you where to track him. I'll bet it was her idea that you set your tent on fire to gain his trust."

"No!" Otis shouted. How could all things work together for good through a sham twisting of motives and facts? Their fanciful narrative made him seem diabolical, an incorrigible beast that should be put down. Calia too! How could he convey his *actual* selfish motives—and his horror looking back on them—without feeding their bogus scenarios?

His words came in bursts. "I didn't meet Calia until much later. I didn't want to hurt anyone. The fall was an accident. The draft card was unplanned. I wish Ulrich were alive. I wish I could have saved him. I'm sorry about hurting Jack. You have no idea how sorry I am about all of it."

But Otis could not let *himself* off the hook so easily. Could he honestly say he'd not known it might end as it did? He'd had no active plan to hurt anyone, yet his laser fixation had made him cavalier. Why had climbing shone so blindingly bright? How had it become the one vital thing he had to do at all costs—to fingers, toes, even lives? How had it gone from a fun alluring break from wrestling to the undisputed best way to invest every ounce of his attention, vigor, and love? Why had he been sure that the ecstasy he felt with each conquest would last? And why, when it faded each time, did he keep on believing that the next conquest—a larger dose or harder 'drug': a tougher mountain like Columbia, or McKinley, or the Himalayas—would fill the chasm in his soul and not widen and deepen it? Why, in pursuing self-glory projects had he never questioned using people like Shaun, or Ulrich, or Calia to help feed his appetites? Was he better than Jack? For that matter, how could he look down at Sid? He couldn't come up with a clear distinction anymore. He was in the chasm right along with them.

The fact was, the rope in the crevasse was cut. That meant a cutter. Sin was sneaky; he was guilty of something. His inability to recall precisely *how* it happened didn't absolve him of the obvious: no one else had been there. He thought of Mike Running Bear. Nothing was random.

Driving over here, Pastor Joe had talked Otis through Jesus' Sermon on the Mount. "He calls anger murder," he pointed out. "If no one else learns what you think and you deceive yourself, God still knows what's in your heart—far better than you do, in fact."

Up on the glacier, for the pettiest irritations, Otis had been angry enough with Ulrich that, for a cartoon second, he'd fantasized taking his ice axe to him. He would never have actually done it. Or would he? He'd come close with Jack. He'd come close with Sid. He'd rationalized both.

Eventually, the FBI broadsides ceased. Because Ulrich had died in Canada, they admitted a lack of jurisdiction on that portion of the tangled mess. (Alberta provincial authorities couldn't care less. Until a body turned up all was conjecture, covered by *habeas corpus*.)

The agents called a break. Instantly, Otis fell asleep on folded arms. He dreamed of a tar pit. Dinosaurs were all around him. He was struggling and sinking. Tar clogged his mouth and nose. Then suddenly, he was floating, cavorting like the astronauts in happy slow motion.

A rough hand grabbed his shoulder.

"Otis! I asked you if Sid had prostitutes at the house."

The question surprised him. "Not that I ever saw."

Later reports chronicled how heroin was a mere fraction of the criminality Sid had brought to Alaska. His organization's tentacles stretched to Arizona, New York, Florida, and a guy named Frank Lucas who had pioneered the innovative practice of transporting heroin from Vietnam in the caskets of fallen soldiers. One investigator quipped to the Anchorage Daily News that Sid's operation was "a lot like Alaskan king crab: hidden, lucrative, and dangerous to haul up."

Sure enough, the padlocked chest freezers held hacked-up human bodies. The agents showed pictures. Even with EMT training, Otis felt ill. He wished he had paid more attention and shared his suspicions earlier.

Pastor Joe verified that Otis had flushed a lot the day he said he'd gotten rid of the dope. Because Pastor Joe and Esther had plucked countless wretches from Fourth Avenue, the police searched respectfully. They let the Liftons take the kids out for ice cream then came to the empty house in unmarked cars. They found the new owner of Ulrich's car down in Homer and searched that too. Dogs verified traces of drugs in both places.

Misleading U.S. and Canadian officials made for serious charges, as did importing a stolen vehicle, but in the end all agreed that Otis was no drug kingpin or murderer. The Anchorage draft board was unbending though. Otis pondered the irony. If he'd never fled, Massachusetts likely would have been lenient. His five-thousand-mile freedom odyssey had backfired.

On the FBI's recommendation, a judge let Otis plead guilty to evasion instead of desertion. Otis made known his desire to put his EMT skills to use and the Army agreed. The medic role would be risky, but no worse than mountains he'd once vowed to climb. Pending an honorable Army discharge, he would serve a year's probation in Massachusetts. The police accepted Pastor Joe as liaison to Ulrich's estate executor, and typed up an inventory of items in his possession.

Lucius' reply to Otis' last letter was waiting for Otis when he arrived at Basic Training. Lucius tempered excitement with counsel. Otis should, "expect spiritual fire-fights as well as physical ones. But remember, your house is built on The Rock now, not on sinking sands." Otis mused again about the house he could have bought with Sid's money. In his imagination, it had always been empty and pristine—shiny hardwood floors; track lights on smooth white walls—but because of its view it was also perched precariously on a hillside, poised to topple or slide.

Otis and Pastor Joe wrote each other often. In July, in the shade of a moss-draped live oak, Otis waited for a grubby outdoor phone. Specialist Training nearly complete, he would ship out in two weeks. He was hungry for a friendly voice. Before Otis left Alaska, Pastor Joe had quoted C.S. Lewis to him. *I shan't say goodbye. We'll meet again. Christians never say goodbye.* Waiting, Otis swatted at flies—and a gloomy thought. *Where* would they meet again? After they'd talked awhile, Otis said, "I saw a movie last week."

"Oh? Which one?"

"Le Mans. Steve McQueen."

"You're not into cars."

"No, but I can't get it out of my head. McQueen's character is this ultra-competitive race car driver who causes a fatal accident; then it's a year later," Otis' throat tightened, "McQueen and the guy's widow—the widow of the guy he killed—are face to face, just the two of them. She's very composed, and she asks him why he risks his life for something that's not important. They began filming the week I met Ulrich."

Pastor Joe said, "Oh my, yes," and though Otis' phone time was up, he knew that Vietnam was exactly where he needed to be. It didn't matter when he saw Pastor Joe again. Being sure that he would was enough.

Part III

Sixty-Seven:
The Strength to Bring Forth

September, 1971...

A fter the baby came in early March, Calia's funk was blessedly brief. Her doctor assured her they were both doing well, and her church family left her no time or reason to worry. Mere friends did not remove hampers of soiled cloth diapers, sneak them back clean (*ah, that fresh line-dried smell!*), and stack them neatly folded over the changing table. Mere friends did not shop, cook, clean, and change the baby without fanfare to let Calia nap. She looked and smelled like a disaster victim—marinated in spit-up and other emanations, eyes puffy, teeth furry, hair frowzy—but when they spelled her to take a shower, they never showed signs of feeling coerced or inconvenienced.

Grief for Ulrich proved harder to staunch with a shower, fresh air, and covered dish meals. She should expect that, her pastor said. *We all weep with you.* With the news so delayed, and the reason for that delay so distressing—plus with no body to bury—her process might take longer than most, he advised. How long? He couldn't say, but he didn't need to. The church's steadfast support helped the worst parts pass quickly.

In what she now knew were not Ulrich's letters but Otis' fakes, she had sensed something off, but assumed her negative intuition was a side effect of pregnancy. Ulrich had a difficult job, a lot on his mind. She cut him slack. When an August letter alluded to ending their pregnancy though, she was speechless. How could he? He had to know the baby was his—that it could *only* be his. The Ulrich she knew would never evade responsibility or propose to end a life. Some unnamed gloom had befallen him, she concluded, and she'd prayed fervently for it to lift.

But after reacting to that letter, she'd also chastised and prayed for herself. Who was she to insist he be perfect? Had she not entertained similarly selfish thoughts? Her life *would* be easier without the crying, pooping, insistent evidence of one passionate mistake narrowing her options, draining her youth, sapping her freedom, reminding the world of its dubious origin by its very existence. Plumbing her own cold, dark motives, she'd been horrified to find them bottomless.

Last October, when she'd laid all his letters across the kitchen table to compare them, she'd sensed some kind of hard, irrevocable change in him, yet the feeling had remained vague. She'd talked with Vietnam MIA widows-in-waiting and chosen, like them, to hold out hope for him.

Then, one evening last February, Calia's pastor came by unannounced with his wife. Calia's phone rang moments later. They both stood stiffly as she waddled to answer it. For an instant, Pastor Joe's voice delighted her. Then she connected his dutiful tone with the impromptu visit.

"I'd like you to sit, Calia," Pastor Joe said with the same gentle firmness her father exuded when he would nestle her tight for the scariest part of their bedtime fairy tale routine. Her Nebraska pastor brought her a chair.

"Ulrich is dead," Pastor Joe said.

The phone line hummed. Ice filled her veins.

Calia's longstanding hunch had made its confirmation no easier. Like an unopened parachute, she had tempered her fears with hopeful explanations. This news was like hitting concrete. She breathed too quickly and got lightheaded. They got a paper bag and consoled her. Ulrich was with the Lord. She knew it before they reminded her, but her wracking sobs seemed like they would squeeze out the baby. Her pastor's wife stayed. Her doctor made a house call. Finally, Calia slept. Each day, someone from church had come to help, talk, or simply sit with her.

———

Now, despite lethargic late-summer heat, Ulrich's death no longer made waking a ravenous disappointment. Not an hour passed when Calia did not think of Ulrich, but six months had given her a sense of God's work in it, tumbling her like a stone in a stream, smoothing her sorrow's flintiest edges. When the pace felt glacial, she would call to mind God's Bible promise to wipe away *every* tear. Some days it seemed absurd. Her grief was her parasite friend: cranky, but loyal. How could God wipe it away and still preserve the good memories? Yet her inability to imagine *how* He would bring total joy only made her love Him more. His thoughts and His ways were far above hers. He would finish what He had started.

She had much to be grateful for—having known Ulrich; the gift of his child, a girl like she'd guessed. Most Sundays at church the baby slept in Calia's arms. Only if Calia sang especially loudly would she open her blue eyes and melt Calia with adoration—a feeling Calia was sure must be mutual. She was sorry Aunt Greta had not met her. Her death so soon after the news of Ulrich had been a blow, but it also relieved money pressures. She missed their weekly visits.

At nineteen, this was hardly the family she'd hoped for. When her parents separated the fall she entered kindergarten, Calia had found solace in cutting beautiful people from the Sears and Roebuck catalog and pasting them into idyllic domestic scenes. Two years later, Sleeping Beauty had come out in theaters and her father had taken her to see it. After he died, worry and might-have-been musings had burst around her like the evil queen's thorns. Was she letting thorns grow up again? She felt forgotten—neither a bride nor a widow—cast-off like scissored catalog scraps. Was lack of forgiveness for *Otis* the root of that? It made her furious that Otis had duped her for so long. Yet like a fatal diagnosis that made sense of protracted pain, she had felt an odd relief to learn of the ruse when news of Ulrich's death finally came. It was better than naïve wondering.

The extra time—and her experience with bad news—had let her avoid traps she'd seen others plunge into. Whenever she got upset she would pray. *Get back, thorns! Jesus wore them for me. Talk to my big brother! He hasn't thrown me away.* And God always answered, filling the voids in her soul. Those who'd gone through tragedy would sometimes act as if all were well, but draw attention with a subtle pout, their eyes theatrically bright inside hollow orbs. *How are you?* Calia might ask a person like that at church who might then reply, *Oh, fine; by God's grace I'm fine!* But behind a charade that fooled few, the person was usually crumbling to dust.

That was not Calia. *She* had an inexhaustible fountain. When she spoke of Christ that way, people at work, around town (even some at church) would gently suggest she was impractical. They would stare baffled, then say, *I wish I had your faith!* No one who said that *ever* asked her how to get such faith for themselves. Instead—like her former roommate Thea—such a person would mulishly push her to validate *their* unease by being as angry or sad as she *should* be. Did Calia not understand herself to be a victim? Because she was. *All* women were.

Calia reminded herself to forgive more, trust God more, think more often and deeply on how much God had forgiven her. She didn't hate *God* for what happened. Or did she? How could you not, a little? And how could you know? Fervent weedings of sinful thoughts had not erased her anger at the intent bound up in what Otis had done for eight months. Eight months! Did she need to forget? Pretend it hadn't happened? Pretend there was no damage? Or could she consider the harm and the harmer (she could not think his name without anger) like a book to pick up and put down, nothing to resent or be scared of, but to revisit and find forgiveness as God gave it?

Forgive us our sins, as we forgive those who sin against us. What if she couldn't? What if she didn't? Some days it made her head hurt. She asked God to help her trust Him more for all of it.

The number of people who urged her to nurse her anger at Otis shocked her. Co-workers at the diner pitched in to buy her darts and a dartboard. *Put his letters on it! Better: his picture! We'll come by to help.* She'd laughed nervously, tempted. Would her anger work *out* that way, dispersing like smoke? Or was it like grease on a fire? After her father's death, no one had said anything so vile about her scheming mother as they'd said about Otis, yet *her* crimes had been *blatant*, felonious, without a hint of remorse. Calia supposed that not having Ulrich's body (plus their child being illegitimate) emboldened some to shed like snakeskin the somber respect they *would* have offered (albeit insincerely) at a proper funeral.

Some at church did it more subtly. The few times she'd lost control and verbalized how she felt about Otis' betrayal, they'd nodded vigorously. *Oh, that's awful, honey*, one would say as more gathered. *Wow*, several would say, cocking ears, waiting for more. *Incredible,* one would say, then whisper a juicy story. *I've never told anyone this*, she would say, *but I'm sure you will understand.* Then the confidante would pour out a flood of festering gripes about a husband's bad habits and failures. Younger women would unload about a father, brother, friend, or boss. Some tales were genuinely horrific. Calia could sympathize. Yet she often left with a sad sense of the tale-teller in a cesspool, urging onlookers to dive in to help bail for more treasure.

The image helped Calia sidestep that trap with Otis. His testimony was lovely, his conversion clear, backed-up by change Pastor Joe amply vouched for. Plus there was his brief, humble letter from Alaska. No one described themselves as a "former enemy" if they didn't mean it. Who was she to condemn? The same grace that covered her also covered him.

She had more trouble forgiving herself. Part of the difficulty lay in Ulrich having been older, a godsend when he first showed interest, yet she'd let him become far more, not just a godsend but a god, an idol, the perfect man to fill her late father's shoes. That had been unfair of her, and unwise. She'd placed too much hope in his voice and presence making her happy. Unable to talk back and forth, she'd coalesced bright shining lies: Ulrich as white knight, her functional savior. Sure, he'd taught her the Bible and prayed like an angel from heaven, yet the real man was also clay-footed. She had to remember him whole. The real Ulrich had fathered a child with her out of wedlock just weeks after her eighteenth birthday then split town and gotten himself killed.

Sixty-Eight:
Pristine Feet

Calia lay sticky in her loft room in the big house. Moon shadows sliced across her sheet. How odd Ulrich must have felt here at thirteen, far from all he'd known. They'd gone to the same church, but she'd been nine when he came, immersed in girlish things, politely aware of him, but put off by his foreign accent and what often seemed his terminal shyness.

The June before last, she and Ulrich had moved Aunt Greta from here to the Farmview Rest Home. Ulrich had already packed for Alaska when she'd come by to help close up. On her way, knowing they'd be alone, she had pondered the dangers until an armed mob of rationalizations took hold of her and asserted its flawless reasoning. They both went to church. They thought of each other as brother and sister. They both read their Bibles daily. They knew right from wrong. They were going to be married someday. What was the difference? God was forgiving. Ulrich had seemed unlike his usual self. Had he been thinking the same things? One year in Alaska and then they'd marry, he'd said. *Then* her living out here would be proper. Besides, the upkeep was expensive and time-consuming. Calia was best where she was, in town with Ethel.

They'd worked up from the basement together, setting mousetraps, draping furniture, draining pipes. Here on the third floor, dusty and sweaty, they'd sat on the bed's edge a moment, *this* bed. Neither one had planned it. All he'd done was brush her arm, and it was as if they were the only people in all creation, a primordial spark crackling between them. A few minutes right here, groping and quivering. She recalled the shame, praying. It felt *years* ago, another world—two different people. For his good, she had quickly dressed and left. The next morning at the diner, she'd begged him

339

not to go. He would write her soon, he'd said. She'd been mute, but resolved at last. He was the right man, the only—diligent and kindhearted, a keeper of promises. His job was *their* future. She would patiently wait.

Driving home from work the next week, a ribbon of violet had lingered in the west, the moon blue-white on her hood. She'd felt a distinct, sharp anxiety for him, like sudden cool after sultry thunderstorm build-up. Ten days later a postcard came—two smiling stick figures astride a great glacier. "We are here!" She'd laughed, reassured that he'd found a friend. Later, she had chalked up that night's sharp anxious sense to the baby growing inside her before she knew it, preparing her with precision, changing how things smelled and tasted and how she reacted: tired all the time, not always thinking straight. She re-read his old letters and relaxed further. In time he would return for her—for his bride and now, too, for his blood, the baby.

Recently, she'd leafed back through her journal. The morning of his accident, for no reason she could recall, she'd written the verse he'd shared with her the first time she'd noticed him noticing her. "You keep him in perfect peace whose mind is stayed on You because he trusts in You." Her unknowing pen strokes had flowed as Ulrich lay dying! The thought gave her chills, but also comfort. Providence was scrupulous. "All things work together for good to them that love God." Whenever she was tempted to see her life's hard turn as bitter or ludicrous she would repeat it. *All* things: her father's death; her mother's abuse; whatever tough things were next.

She didn't like that Ulrich had died, nor did she understand it, but she was confident she was where God would have her. God would provide and protect and make sense of it all in His time. To catch tiny glimpses of Him doing it gave her more strength than any she could muster on her own. Ulrich's old friend Rufus had helped her resolve Ulrich's and Greta's estates (a tune-up for law school). Then over the summer, a huge team from church had helped her ready the house.

She was still getting used to it. The wind sometimes whined through the eaves. She wasn't sure which windows to open for the best air flow to avoid a draft on the baby. The floorboards squeaked as she crossed the hall to the baby's room, then under the rocker as she guided the eager tiny mouth through the gap in her nightshirt. As she did every night, the baby murmured and glanced up before settling in to the earnest, slightly ticklish business of tugging and slurping. So strange at first, it had plunged them both into frustration and fear until they figured it out and came to delight in it. Calia mourned the routine's predictable end. Pureed carrots, bananas, and peas had already sparked curious surprise, leading her into cascades of giggles which the baby echoed with splatters and spews, launching more giggles, mopping, and laundry. To think that they would be apart from one another someday felt outrageous.

Still, adult company would be nice. Ethel had moved to Los Angeles and joined a church with a new young vibrant pastor. (They joked that his Scottish last name was the same as a great Army general.) Perhaps she would take in a boarder who needed help—another single mom to share sitting and let her take classes. She hardly needed the rent. She could decide later.

"Tomorrow, let's shop for a puppy," she cooed and took the baby's gurgles as agreement. Ulrich would have liked a dog. She would not get a yippy, nervy, unstable one. Robust, friendly, and smart was better: a dog tolerant of a little girl jumping on its back, taking its food, tugging at its ears; one to bark fiercely if the wrong kind of person came around but which would wag its tail then nuzzle and charm everyone else.

"In town, we'll visit Aunt Susan and Aunt Rhonda too." Calia had taken the baby to visit her former work only a few times. Without a wedding band, pregnancy had led some people to cast cruel glances that spoke volumes—*Fornicator! Harlot! Single mom!*—as if a brief loss of control stained her forever in scarlet for stoning. Those same women were always first to ask to hold the baby, dissolving with affection once they felt her warmth.

Calia patted the baby's back until she belched and slipped into sleep. She drew in the scent of her downy hair then set her back in her crib. Calia marveled at her daughter's regular breaths and tiny flawless hands. Her pristine feet would gain strength to crawl, stand, and walk. She needed no cover on such a warm night. On her way out of the room, Calia nudged the felt-clad paving stone doorstop to prop the door wider so she would hear the baby sooner the next time she cried.

Back in bed, Calia prayed, "Thank you, Lord. We are truly blessed."

From downstairs came the sound of breaking glass, then footsteps.

Sixty-Nine:
Raining Dirt

The Central Highlands of Vietnam, at that same moment...

Eight thousand miles from Grand Island, prone in a hasty trench, midday sun hot on his neck, Otis felt the thump of incoming mortars. One landed close. In the sudden cotton-wool deafness, a month's worth of faces filled his mind—guys he'd saved and failed to; a bunch he'd stabilized for Med-Evac and never seen again. With each dash and kneel to help, Otis felt the fierce focus he'd loved about climbing and wrestling, but with a resolute calm. On their last phone call, Pastor Joe had cemented Otis' certainty that God had prepared him to go where he was needed, do what he was meant to, and risk his life for something important.

A familiar voice pierced his muffled hearing. "Medic!"

Otis evoked the face that went with it: black kid, thick glasses, keen reader. He'd memorized the eye chart to get into the Army. By hanging out playing chess, the two of them had broken unwritten rules. How could Otis forget his name? A month of sleep deprivation interspersed with panic had obscured the simplest memories behind an impenetrable mental haze.

The voice came again higher, desperate. "Medic! *Otis!* Oh God, help!"

Then Otis remembered his name: Glenn; Glenn Jefferson from Wheatland, Missouri. He'd lost his big brother too.

Otis peeked up. Beside a clump of elephant grass, both Glenn's thighs glinted white bone. Around him, as if the earth were retaking him, bloody brown skin was hard to distinguish from red-brown mud. Glenn rolled back and forth as if thrashing away a bad dream, eyeglasses gone, one arm draped over his face. Lots of them did that, not wanting to see, then startled when

342

Otis lunged in beside them to work. To avoid wasting precious seconds, he'd learned to warn of his approach.

"Hang on!" he yelled. He had three minutes, if that. He leapt up and sprinted, head down. Bullets sang around him like angry drops on an over-hot pan. He rehearsed the sequence of grabs for compresses and tourniquets while another part of him prayed not to have to pull another dog tag and drape a tarp. With maybe five steps to go to reach Glenn—while he was yelling "It's me!" but before he could think why the trail beneath his descending foot looked unnaturally patterned and smooth—Otis tripped, flew, and landed hard.

He gazed at the sky. A wild boar, confused by the firefight must have dashed out and clipped him on the knee the way he'd done to Jack the trucker. Acrid black smoke wafted past. Glenn's time was ticking down. Tingling all over, Otis lurched to stand, but pitched over sideways into a warm crater. Shreds of knee hung loose. Not a wild boar: Charlie.

Shaking, ears whooshing, heart pounding with shock, Otis cinched a tourniquet around his thigh then wriggled to Glenn. It took all his strength to bind one of Glenn's leg stumps, then rip strips from his uniform for a second tourniquet on the other. He wasn't sure he could hold on one more second—or wanted to. He chastised himself. *Stay with it.* Plug oozing shrapnel holes. Insert an IV line. Stab in a morphine syrette. His own relief could wait; he had to keep a clear head.

More mortars thumped in, raining dirt. Bullets sang, inches above them. Yells broke out (*Stay down! Hang on! We'll get you!*) But no one came. Otis prayed a feeble "Help," and a deep peace steered his thoughts. His brother had gone out like this—the brother who'd become a third-rail topic at home—the brother Otis had been sure he would never live up to. But the landmine with Otis' name on it had been smaller than the Bouncing Betty destined for Henry's midsection. Otis might not make it home alive either, but he was sure he would *be* home soon enough.

He took Glenn's wrist, slippery with blood, and counted the second-hand's crawl around his watch's face. Glenn didn't have long, his pulse thin, thready, and fast. Otis slid his hand up to Glenn's fingers and felt him weakly clasp back. Tongue thick, mouth dry, Otis prayed.

At "forever and ever, Amen," Glenn whispered, "Thank you."

And then he was gone.

Seventy:
Paired Socks

T he two other uniformed soldiers on Otis' cross-country flight walked slowly alongside as he crutched up the jetway. In a letter he'd told his parents what day he thought he would arrive. He wouldn't know which flight until the last minute though. "Don't worry," he wrote. "I'll take a cab. If it's late, I'll use the spare key under the mat and try to be quiet."

He'd heard rumors of returning soldiers being treated poorly. He hadn't believed them. He'd forgotten how different Boston was. A woman spied them coming up the jetway and raised her middle finger. Emboldened, a man beside her yelled "Baby killer!" Inside the terminal, epithets that even combat soldiers hesitated to deploy whizzed around them. Spit splat nearby. "Hippie!" someone shouted and Otis laughed. He'd let his beard grow again.

A greying black redcap raced to their rescue, thrusting an airport wheelchair forward like a Boston driver. Grateful, Otis plopped in. The redcap leaned down. "I see this stuff every day. Don't you pay them no mind." Otis' companions stood awkwardly for a moment. They should all try to get together, one said. Have a beer and hang out, said the other. They were going to find a restroom and change into civilian clothes, he added. Otis said he would wait for them. They said he didn't need to. Really. Go.

"I see that too," the redcap said as the companions strode away. He tilted Otis' chair back, its small front wheels off the ground. "Hang on tight and do *not* make eye contact." As they sliced through the crowds at near running speed, the redcap hummed a jaunty tune, pausing only long enough to shout, "Look sharp! Coming through!"

344

Outside, a chill mist smelled of low tide, wet concrete, and the distinctly Boston scent of oily metal and traffic. *Ah, home. Unchanged.* The redcap rushed him past a line of briefcase-wielding trench-coat-clad men, grumbling about a cab shortage that had triggered burdensome ride-sharing rules. Otis wished he'd not written his parents so hastily not to wait up. Now that he could smell home, he was ready to be there.

At the line's front, the redcap spun the chair so Otis faced the men, then he scooted to stand in the gap between them. Otis quickly saw why he'd moved. Half the men sported primary election campaign buttons. Otis had been off U.S. soil only three months (after six in training in Georgia and Texas) yet in that brief time, a push to end the war by ousting Nixon seemed to have become a pressingly passionate object of fashion. "Come Home and Stop Killing Little Babies" read the man's button closest to him, for McGovern. Other buttons took a different tack: "Trust Muskie," said one, and, "President Muskie (Don't you feel better already?)"

Under the men's glares, Otis wasn't sure what to feel or who to trust.

A black car swerved toward them. The driver shut off the engine.

A man in line yelled, "Hey buddy, cabs only!"

Others joined in with choice words, fueling a raucous tirade.

The commotion diverted Otis' attention such that he failed to recognize the blur bursting at him until his mother was kneeling, sobbing, hand to his face, avoiding a glance toward his safety-pinned pant-leg. His father strode calmly over, shook Otis' hand, then bent and gave him the type of hug reserved for good report cards. His father stood and faced the cab line, his hand on Otis' shoulder. He began in a commanding voice Otis had never heard. "My son here..." The men all shut up and Otis felt his father squeeze his shoulder as if to say: *Here we go; now watch this!* "My son here has served our country in Vietnam. We will be out of your way in just a moment."

Otis was stunned. He supposed his father must use this persona at work because—though his words seemed unrehearsed—Otis could think of nowhere else he might deploy such in-your-face strength. The redcap handed Otis his crutches. At the same instant, Otis and his father held out to him over-generous fivers. The redcap refused both bills.

At home, his parents hovered behind as Otis crutched up the stairs.

"If these are too much, we can get a lift installed," his father said.

Otis reached the landing, glad his parents could not see his face, pinched with the effort of getting this far. Brotherly reveries lent the spot a sense of timeless detachment. "I'll be OK," he said. His stump throbbed. Home seemed dream-like and small, tidier than he recalled, a physical place he'd been unsure he would see again. His mother scurried past him to his room where she rolled back his covers and fluffed his pillow.

His father pulled down his shades.

"If you need anything, don't hesitate to wake us."

"Even a Dixie cup of cold water," his mother said. "Like when you were little." Her smile wobbled toward anguish. She grabbed his father's hand, clenched it, and her expression settled closer to relieved.

"We will get through this together," his father said.

Since the surprise at the airport, his father had remained more composed than Otis recalled him being in years. On the ride home his mother had spoken animatedly about weather forecasts, food he might like, and new birds at her feeder. If his parents had looked less tired, and if his leg were hurting less, Otis might have lingered to inquire into how they were doing, to reassure them how well *he* was doing, and to explain why—in his new hobbled condition—he could say that with certainty. All they knew was that, in Alaska, he had lived with a pastor and gone to church.

His mother brought him the water she'd offered. Otis took a sip—cold, clear, and lovely, the best he'd had in a long time. They each kissed him goodnight, then gently shut his door behind them.

For nine months—since plowing through his stack of mail in the Light of Grace sanctuary—Otis had not been alone. It felt different now, deliciously odd, not a state to crave, but neither one to fear. He hung up his uniform jacket. His closet smelled faintly of his grandmother. In his top dresser drawer, Otis nestled his Purple Heart and Bronze Star among paired sock balls. No more chore of matching. The thought amused him. The dresser had moved a few feet, revealing where the charred plug socket Henry had covered a decade ago was painted, new, as if time had wound back, his brother a teenager off at his fish-frying job.

He plunked down on his bedside. Lace doilies had sprouted. His room seemed like that of a friend he'd known well who'd died and bequeathed it to him. On graduation night, he'd sat here to weigh the choice he'd put off.

His plan—such as it was—now seemed nebulous and hasty, its aftermaths hard as concrete where before countless options had churned. He looked for the faint ice dam stains that had sprouted the winter after Henry died. They were gone too; no moldy smell. Whoever had painted had done the whole room in two coats at least and perfectly matched the color.

Before gulping two prescribed pain tablets, Otis thanked God for a safe return and for his parents coming to meet him against his instructions.

***

Otis woke to snapping shades and bright sun. A full breakfast tray sat at his bedside. Blinking and groggy, he struggled to arrange extra pillows that had appeared overnight and hoist himself into a sitting position. It surprised him that his mother didn't hurry to intervene and help him. "What time is it?"

"Almost noon. Your father said to tell you good morning. He's picking up Dirkden Gardens on his way home—extra cartons of all the old favorites in case you get hungry later."

Otis salivated. *Chinese.* VA hospital fare had been drab at best, sometimes little better than C-rations. Yet what should he think? Dirkden Gardens had been Henry's favorite. After he died, without anyone ever saying so, or saying why, it had stopped being an option for takeout.

"Isn't Dad's big twin-blade launch coming up? Didn't you say they've been working late and every weekend?"

"Yes, he's busy, but he was emphatic. He'll be home no later than six."

His mother sat beside his bed, adjusted a pair of horn-rimmed glasses, and opened the Boston Globe. Glittering cords ran behind her neck. Was he seeing rightly? Was this the carefree mother he dimly recalled? Her eyes seemed perkier, free of the fog of grief and dread that had driven her to sleeping pills and back to smoking. "When did you get those?" Otis asked. He pointed to his own eyes then to hers, meaning her glasses but also hoping she might say more.

"Two months after we last saw you. I don't get headaches anymore."

Did her headaches entail more than eyestrain? Two months after they last saw him would have been February—the month his world flipped. When Henry shipped out, her worry had been vocal and constant. Had she fretted for him any less? Had Otis' attempt to shield her by fleeing *increased* her pain? Before heading to Basic, he'd written to ask their forgiveness. The next thing he saw from them came to him there: one of the easy, light cartoon cards the family had always exchanged. The cursory birthday greeting offered no hint to acknowledge his weighty attempt, but did it need to? Were his parents obliged to seal the transaction with explicit words—*yes, we forgive you,* like a receipt—or did their recent actions say all that was needed? And what about him? Had he released *them*? It was a hard question. He was getting there.

His mother peered over the newspaper.

"Otis? Did you see the big H-bomb test?"

Her abrupt subject change peeved him. The Supreme Court's decision to let the epic nuke test proceed had flooded the news. Was she being her quirky self, sharing what made her *feel* or was she trying to elicit talk of the war? Any half-honest account of his combat experiences would dumbfound her. The insight made him feel closer to Henry who, on his furloughs, had limited his accounts to sunshine, tropical fruits, and exotic birds.

As a medic, Otis had anticipated heinous carnage and to a lesser extent, confusion and chaos. Despite his short time in combat, he felt good about the lives he'd helped save and the efforts he'd made with those he'd lost. Reading the Psalms every day eased the impact of ghastly sights, sounds, and smells. What surprised him most though was incessant banter about death's physical particulars. His fellow soldiers' armchair expert attitude—as if verbal lewdness made them masters over what privately terrified them—recalled how Otis and his housemates used to talk about centerfold models.

The verbal banality in Vietnam had been relentless, almost obsessive, as impossible to avoid as the mud. It had made him homesick in ways his time alone in Alaska had not. Until Vietnam, Otis had regarded his parents' norms (decorum, order, loyalty, family) as drearily universal—obvious and natural. He now saw them like greenhouse orchids. Painstakingly cultivated over generations, the values they'd grounded their lives on (and which he'd taken for granted) Otis now understood to have been rooted in Christendom. Before he *or they* were born, vital stems had been cut from a singular root. Moral blooms had slowly drooped, browned, and dried.

In Pastor Joe's office he'd glimpsed the rippling impacts that one selfish decision to flee had made on others' lives. Vietnam had cinched the lesson. Depravity was not exclusive to people in far-off benighted ages and places, but a deadly contagion in all of them. Qualities like love, joy, peace, patience, kindness, goodness, faithfulness, gentleness, and self-control did not sprout up spontaneously in the educated any more than they did in the unrefined. They were precious Holy Spirit gifts. Until Otis had seen the bottomless darkness inside *himself*, he'd been blind to his need for that light. Until he'd seen it unleashed on and by people more like those in Dirkden than different from them—despite different surroundings and histories—he had not realized how close the darkness had come to taking over completely.

With that lesson ten thousand miles behind him and nowhere to go, Otis could already feel the cozy home bubble reabsorbing him. Sure, phantom leg pain caused his hands to shake, his brow to sweat, and his mood to turn grouchy, but neither soporific ease nor distracting distress could justify answering his mother's H-bomb question with a verbal nuke. The briefest straightforward account of what he'd seen in Vietnam could devastate her. No. He would take a cue from Henry and guard his tongue. Eyes open, Otis silently struggled to pray, his mind like a flooded engine. *Our Father Who art... Our Father... Our Father...* He could not get past it. His bottle of pain pills drew his eyes and kept killing his thoughts. *When I am weak*, he prayed, and at last some words came.

"I didn't see the nuke test, Mom. The Pacific's a really big ocean. The stewardesses put me in an aisle seat."

He reached for the pain pill bottle but came up short.

"Help, please?"

His mother handed him his breakfast tray with the pill bottle on it. He gulped two tablets and mentally counted down, waiting for them to kick in. In a bowl of pastel-tinged milk pink hearts, yellow moons, orange stars, and green clovers floated: Lucky Charms, his favorite. For months he'd been forced to settle for Cap'n Crunch—on the good days. The dark-blue steep-sided bowl was his favorite among an oddball antique-glazed set—now mostly broken and gone—salvaged from Shurwood, the rambling Maine house where, May to October each year, "buds out to leaves down," his grandparents had passed their retirement.

He missed the Julys when the five of them would spend a week there. With his middle name Shurwood and an April birthday, the fact that he'd been conceived there embarrassed him when he figured it out. Later it amused him. And later still, after the house was sold to make way for a golf course, the memory of their time there gave him a sense that the universe had an immovable center. His favorite Shurwood spoon lay on the tray too, enfolded neatly in a linen napkin tucked alongside the bowl. Sterling silver and distinctively bent, the spoon was big for a child, but small for a grown-up. Holding it again, Otis felt the ballast of thousands of meals—ice cream, chicken soup, cereal—during which he'd studied and felt its intricate cursive monogram designs on his tongue, artwork commissioned by ancestors who even his grandparents had never known.

Far beyond the dulling glow of the pills, Otis felt comfort down to his bones as he realized that his mother had choreographed *every* detail of this moment based on a compendium of subtle and not-so-subtle idiosyncrasies she'd observed about her second son since before he was born. Only a mother would bother. Only *his* mother would bother so well.

Seeing him notice, she took off her glasses, not needing credit. The glance was enough. She knew that he knew. "Someday you'll pass that on," she said with a quiet poise that made Otis sure it was true despite not knowing *how*. How could a one-legged felon—reviled for shirking his duty, then reviled for doing it—ever get a date, much less a wife, a job, or a home? He had to trust God. The strange years they'd all just been through would recede. He could feel it starting. He just hoped *his* kids would not give him as much heartache as he'd given his parents.

The sun moved. His tray vanished. His mother cleared her throat. Otis rubbed his eyes. His duffel was empty and folded. Outside the window, dryer steam billowed.

His mother pointed to the newspaper, folded on the bedside table within his reach. "I'd never heard of the Rat Islands. Had you? Apparently, they're part of Alaska. Were you there?"

That again. Why did it fascinate her so much?

"No, Mom. The H-bomb test was in the Aleutians Islands, over near Russia. The pipeline route is far east of there."

"Otis Fletcher. Now how would I know a thing like that?"

He was being short with her. She'd never traveled much. Maps weren't her thing. "I'm sorry, Mom," he said softly. "Please forgive me." He was still getting used to the new instinct, deep in the grain of him, not like the half-truth whitewash he'd once spread to hide flaws.

"Apology accepted," she said, but failed to hide a delighted squeak. "This is fascinating," she said. Otis hoped she might ask how he'd come by his new demeanor, but instead, she picked up the paper again. "Listen to this. The explosion was a mile underground, but the surface leapt up twenty-five feet. Can you imagine? It tossed buildings off their foundations!"

Otis could imagine it only too well.

"Sounds powerful. By the way, I lost Henry's watch."

"I know," she said. "I noticed at Christmas. You don't have to explain."

"Does Dad know?"

"Yes. It's OK. Look at this. It says a lot, don't you think?"

She handed him the paper. He examined the quarter-page picture.

A man encased head-to-toe in a protective white suit held a Geiger counter over a black, foot-wide fissure. The underground explosion had severed a gravel road. Both road and fissure snaked to the horizon. The last time Ulrich's feet had touched earth he and Otis had been side by side on a road like the one in the picture. If Ulrich's caution had not slowed them down, they *both* might be dead on Mount Columbia's flanks.

Otis would once have heaped derision on what the picture implied: foolish people dead-set on foolish ventures. But hadn't his quests been equally so? He'd found courage to flee induction, but so what? Coach had seen through his non-plan before they'd reached Route 128.

On the wrestling mat, then on steep ice, he had lurched from feat to feat, hardening his faith that each triumph made him stronger and that dogged tenacity would bring due rewards in time. He could recall his state of mind as if in a museum case—dried, pinned, and dead, drained of all power. He'd been deaf to goodness, blind to the costs to himself and others. Only in Jesus could he accept that the ostensibly benign act of coaxing Ulrich onto the Icefield had led inexorably to Sid hunting down Calia and the baby in Nebraska. Pastor Joe had relayed the news in a letter Otis read in his VA hospital room in Manila.

Late one night last September—in the wide-open farm country outside Grand Island where the houses are too far apart to see or hear much—an intruder had climbed her front porch and broken in. The police found Sid's body, gun still clutched in his hand, his skull staved-in by a felt-clad paving-stone doorstop Calia had dropped on him from the stair landing a floor above. While EMTs tweezered wood fragments from Calia's hands and face, police detectives carved bullets from the splintered railing where she'd stood her ground. Upstairs, right where Calia had left her when she went down to check on the breaking glass sounds, the baby was crying—startled by the sound of indoor gunfire, but otherwise completely fine.

Otis handed the newspaper back to his mother. "It's an evocative picture," he said. "Thank you for showing it to me."

As with the scientists on the ruined Alaska island, Otis was glad that a white garment now covered *him* head to toe, protecting him (and other people) from the sin inside him. But how could he explain that invisible spiritual reality—that sin was as widespread, insidious, and deadly as bomb radiation? The moment didn't seem right. His mother might listen politely, attribute his fervor to jet lag, combat fatigue, or his medication, and move on. She had already noted a change in him, and he'd renewed his fondness for her. That was sufficient for now—a good start. They would likely have weeks together like this.

Before Thanksgiving, Otis vowed, praying for strength. He would tell his parents plainly who he now served and why they needed Him too. He would tell of the patient Christ—the God-man he'd neither sought nor expected who'd removed his old heart of stone and given him a new one of flesh— the God who always saw all His projects through to completion.

Seventy-One:
The Last Duplicate Key

Lucius took his own advice about steadfastness. He wrote to Otis throughout his training, his truncated combat tour, and his VA hospital stay in Manila. Otis wrote back less often than he would have liked, but he took comfort in reading (and often re-reading) Lucius' letters. Now, on his first day back home, Lucius stopped by the house. Otis' mother made tea, then left to run errands and, "let you boys talk."

Otis rested his crutches against a new kitchen chair and recalled the old ones: gaudy covers stapled around bent steel frames. Whenever family conversations got tense, he used to stare at grime in the seat backs' crimped crevices—dried, ancient, hard-to-clean bits of food no one wanted to mention or name. The new ones had smoother lines and smelled of plastic.

Lucius caught Otis up on mutual Deden-Fisher acquaintances. Typical of top colleges, almost every man determined not to be inducted wasn't. (By 1970, except for a handful of pariahs shackled to ROTC, that represented nearly everyone.) Some never said how they bypassed Vietnam. (Some would maintain that silence for decades, even from family, and *especially* at work.) Grad school was the most common, "respectable" tactic to run out the war's clock. The Peace Corps was also popular. Two classmates they barely recalled (an ostracized, dwindling trickle of volunteers) had been KIA. The men's pregnant brides had retreated to live with parents and memories. The North Vietnamese captured Connor on his second tour. Hopeful and childless, Louisabeth was circulating petitions and rallying other POW wives.

"I suppose you heard about Shaun," Lucius said.

"No." Otis braced the way he used to for incoming rounds.

"Oh man, I'm sorry. I thought you knew. He's MIA."

Lucius looked as hurt as Otis felt.

"When?"

"Around the same time as your thing; right before Nixon announced the halt to offensive operations."

Otis stammered. "We'd snagged R&R orders for the same week in October." He and Shaun had talked of the Himalayas, but with no equipment, no time to acclimate, and Pakistan, Nepal, and Tibet not Army-sanctioned as R&R destinations, they had planned to make sake toasts atop Mount Fuji instead. A year before Henry, the Fletchers' neighbors had been informed that their son was MIA. They'd gone door to door with photos and clipboards as if for a lost pet, desperate for a three letter acronym status change to POW. They'd not raked their leaves, hung Christmas lights, or accepted the Fletchers' offers to help with those things. A downspout stayed askew all winter. An icicle formed in its place down their siding. Only later would the Fletchers appreciate how the definitive world-changing shock of KIA spared a family the grinding torpor each MIA's kin endured. Hope *mixed* with grief prolonged the pain.

MIA, Otis thought. *Good as dead.* He hoped it wasn't true but he strongly sensed that it was. A cascade of things too mundane to warrant retelling slid through his mind: shared camp meals and rambling conversations, mental snapshots with no special significance. Shaun had taught him to climb ice. Without him, Otis would not have known of the Icefield or felt its allure.

Now, if he altered something only he and Shaun had experienced, no one could correct him. *Hang on, you've got it backward; you've left out the best part!* He was familiar with the effect from Henry and his grandparents. He'd heard it was what made the loss of a spouse especially hard. Handed the last duplicate key to a library of memories no other pair on the planet shared, one sensed eccentric inventories gathering dust, disintegrating from disuse. A few spotlights on retold one-sided stories hardly did justice to the fleshed-out sum of qualities that made up the living surprising person.

He wished he could keep his mind clearer and feel Shaun's loss more. He would flush his meds New Year's Day. He knew how to endure pain and hold on one more second.

Seeming to sense his distress, Lucius asked, "Why don't we go for a drive?" It wasn't a question.

Low sun flicked through bare trees like an old silent movie. On the Battle Road between Lexington and Concord, they stopped for ice cream at Buttrick's, about to close for the winter. They sat on a stone wall, hands sticky from triple cones. Minutemen had once crouched here. Otis felt better able to envision the carnage than when on a fourth-grade class field trip here, he and all but a few of the other boys had "shot" at each other with sticks.

"Where to next?" Lucius asked once Otis finished his cone.

"We could go bowling," Otis quipped.

"OK," Lucius said. They got back in the car.

He's humoring me, Otis thought. Pitying me. Would this be his life now—driven around, the world passive through glass? His parents used to take his grandmother out to look at fall leaves or Christmas light displays but Otis never saw the point. Why not stay home and watch TV?

Lucius cleared his throat. The sun was down, the engine off. They faced the candlepin alley where Otis used to help out in exchange for lane time before high school sports made it uncool. How had Lucius found it? How had Lucius remembered his sole mention of this place years ago? Otis sat up and rubbed his eyes. "I was kidding, you know."

"Were you?" Lucius' expression betrayed no sarcasm.

Otis had grown used to the faint fleshy smell of puss leaking from his stump, but after ice cream and dozing off, it made him nauseous. His leg was throbbing again. Bowling? What had he been thinking? His next pill dose was not for a full hour. Fear suddenly choked him. Once, on a family trip to Singing Beach, Henry had been off fetching a Frisbee. A wave had knocked Otis down and dragged him out. Soundless and airless, each second had stretched to an hour.

Lucius spoke up. "Nothing says we have to."

"No, it's just that, I guess I don't trust myself anymore. My body, I mean. What it can do."

"Otis?" Otis looked at him. "How about we try one frame?"

Otis opened the car door and sucked in cool air. Against a darkening sky, water-filled potholes twinkled like orange pearls. Lucius held open the alley's glass door. Otis perched halfway out, halfway in. The cacophony of crashes evoked more recent memories: dropped bedpans in the Da Nang trauma ward, his jet engine's roar taking off from Saigon. At the alley's counter, a dome-headed man in a flashy silk shirt glanced in their direction.

"Bert!" Otis yelled, glad for someone familiar to help him decide. He crutched inside toward him and Bert's cigarette fell from his lip. Too big to stoop to pick it up, he ground it out with his shoe. "You know Bert, two full-price patrons who only need three bowling shoes is a good deal for the lanes." Otis winked. Behind him, Lucius stifled a snicker. Otis introduced them, and they all talked for a while. Bert insisted they bowl for free.

Otis tried several methods. Balance was the main thing. Finally, he rolled a strike to applause from adjacent lanes. Fellow bowlers had paid close attention but tried not to make it too obvious. As the pins in their lane reset, a crew cut boy approached him.

"Go on; he won't bite" the boy's father said, flicking his fingers. The boy looked about eight, the age Otis had been when his father brought him here after the clash about the robins' nest.

The boy stammered. "Hey, mister. Does it hurt?" Otis recalled his first hour in Mike Running Bear's car, his missing arm conspicuous—all Otis had been able to think about.

"Yes, it does," Otis said, and the boy blanched. "But I'll be OK." It helped to assert it aloud. *All things work together for good for those who love God.* Much more hurt than his leg, but Otis wasn't about to tell the boy that. He extended his hand. "My name's Otis, what's yours?"

The boy slowly extended his. "Wally."

Otis engulfed Wally's hand up to his small wrist. His pulse felt eager and strong, not trickling away like Glenn Jefferson's had. It made Otis think of mountain rivulets.

When he was ten, his family had visited the Hoover Dam near Las Vegas. Desert heat made him want to dive through Lake Mead's bright shining surface into its cool—a fusion of dozens of streams—but it wasn't allowed. *The turbines might suck you down,* his father explained. They crossed the road to peer over the rail. Sixty stories below, white water thundered out, angry and hard. The blank concrete face made him dizzy. Otis reeled back and almost fell into the road.

Now he stepped back from the memory. Like the dam, the war had subsumed countless small tributaries into a great homogenizing project, tapping great power, yet erasing entire ecosystems of possibility. What would Glenn have done with another sixty years? Married? Had kids? Been first in his family to go to college? Would his kids have read as voraciously and played chess as adeptly as their father? Might they or he have cured cancer? Written award-winning screenplays? Designed motorcycles? The world would never know. Otis recalled the Deden-Fisher graduation speaker struggling to finish. *Names with no special meaning to you—but faces I will not forget.* And with silent understanding, Otis prayed that Wally not have to face the crushing choices they had.

A few days later Lucius took Otis to his North Shore church. As they sang "Amazing Grace," Otis' mind spun back to a time when a wrestling match had been his biggest concern. The rest of that afternoon, he thought and prayed about his future. He also prayed for Calia and the baby.

Seventy-Two:
Making Lists

‹‹‹———›››

O tis found new home routines. First thing each day, he read his Bible and jotted prayers and things he was learning in a bound notebook. Over breakfast, he would chat with his mom, peruse the paper for jobs, and make phone calls. After that, he would steel himself to get through his physical therapy routines. After dinner most days, he hung out with his Dad in his basement workshop—something they'd not done in years.

One day before sunrise, Otis folded a journal page lengthwise. Down the left side, he copied the Apostle Paul's list of love's attributes, a passage he'd once known only from weddings.

- patient
- kind
- not boastful
- not envious
- not arrogant
- not rude
- not insistent on its own way
- not rejoicing at wrongdoing
- not irritable or resentful
- rejoices with the truth
- bears all things
- believes all things
- hopes all things
- endures all things
- never ends

He'd always thought of it as a grab-bag of pretty platitudes—do this, don't do that advice which every couple broke before the honeymoon ended. Now he knew it was more. God had entered history in flesh to showcase once for all the definition of love. Jesus had been patient with him, infinitely kinder than he deserved. Could he be those things by sheer force of will? Content, hopeful, joyful, good, peaceful, gentle, longsuffering, self-controlled? Hardly. Humble? Not on his own. He'd tried and failed.

Each "serious" Christian Otis knew—Lucius, Ulrich, Pat, the Liftons, Calia—had distinct human flaws, yet they shared an appealing dynamic quality he'd never grasped nor credited until it sprang up in him *and kept springing.* He could see new affinities growing (for the Bible and people he'd kept at arm's length) alongside distastes for things he'd once thought of as no big deal: "white" lies, porn, drinking too much. Achievements he'd worn as badges of honor had flipped to reveal ugly scurrying pride bugs. Things he'd loathed but *said* he respected he now found so exquisitely beautiful that he wanted to do them forever: singing old hymns and Psalms and hanging out after church. Sensing that this pace of change would eventually slow, he thought to take stock of what Jesus had done with and for him so far.

On the same creased page where he'd dissected Paul's love sketch, he wrote atop the right column, "By God's grace, I'm a new man and also...

- draft-dodger; Vietnam Veteran; medal winner
- liar and fraud
- EMT and amputee
- cherished son; truncated father
- grieving (now-oldest) brother
- life-saver *and* life-ender
- unworthy (not lucky!) recipient of only probation
- surprisingly proficient candlepin bowler
- man who was briefly rich in one way; now in another
- novice when it comes to prayer
- tolerable/terrible roommate (depending on who you ask)
- future wrestling coach and teacher of history
- potential addict (*don't forget this*)
- former carrier of way too many things
- profoundly grateful

Seventy-Three:
Leaving Dirkden

⸺⸻⸺

The day before Thanksgiving, Billy drove Otis to his first prosthesis-fitting appointment. Billy had gotten home late from school—a five hour drive swelled to eight by holiday traffic—but his eyes looked hollower than they should have from a few late nights finishing papers.

"How's school?"

"Alright, I guess."

"How's Laurinda?"

"Fine."

"Then why aren't you with her down on Hilton Head again? Did General Westleigh scare you off?"

"No. I got along great with her folks." (At Otis' graduation, Billy had noted how that *retired* General seemed totally unlike Laurinda's active duty father, General Westleigh, who was striving to win in Vietnam.)

"Why then?"

"I asked her to come to Boston for Thanksgiving."

"You told me Mom and Dad met her already."

"They did. I wanted her to meet *you*. But her parents were hosting this huge shindig to celebrate her dad's getting his third General star—lawn tent, oysters, tuxedos; the whole nine yards. I've never been to anything like that. It sounded wild. But when I heard you were coming home, I said we should talk about changing plans. But she said she hates cold weather; a holiday weekend up here would be "too much"—whatever *that* means. I reminded her that you served in the same Army. Her dad would understand, maybe even be proud of her. *That* got her going and we had this long fight. Finally, she said that amputees make her sick. I told her we were done."

"I'm sorry," Otis said, simultaneously touched and stunned.

He'd been sure they would get engaged.

Billy shrugged.

"Thanks. Better to see her priorities now than later, I guess."

"I guess."

The VA hospital waiting room smelled sickly sweet and familiar (of iodine and adhesive) yet far more sterile than what he'd grown used to in Manila—no birds flitting through windows, no whiffs of human waste. Billy took a copy of Moby-Dick from his pocket and hung up their coats.

"Hey Otis, what's with the new kitchen furniture?"

"I don't know. It was there when I got back. They haven't said a thing."

"It must be weird. Being back, I mean."

"It's different. Better in some ways."

"You still in touch with those people you stayed with in Alaska?"

"The Liftons? Yeah sure. Some. We write."

"I still don't get why they would take in a total stranger. I mean *I* know you're harmless, but how would *they* know that? It seems pretty reckless of them, especially with kids."

"Their dogs checked me out." Otis grinned.

"Not drug-sniffing ones, apparently."

"You're right. I should have known better. I'm glad I didn't get them in trouble. I didn't get it at first either—why they would be so generous—but they've taken in all kinds of people. It's the kind of thing Christians do because we're grateful to Jesus for what He did for us."

Otis hoped Billy might ask him a question or argue, but after saying, "I can respect that," then sitting in silence, he turned to his book.

A nurse approached. "Mr. Fletcher?"

Billy shut his paperback. Otis stood and faced him. "Would you come with me, Billy? Take notes? Mom and Dad will have questions, and my head's been kind of fuzzy lately."

Several weeks after Christmas, Billy returned to Penn. Otis was thankful for his help driving to appointments. Some days PT made him want to pass out or puke, especially after quitting the pain meds, but he thought of wrestling and climbing and prayed and kept on. He looked forward to retiring his crutches, freeing his hands, but getting used to his metal leg was proving tough. At first it had felt like dead weight, tripping him up, abrading his stump. Each second he wore it had been excruciating. Heavy and rigid, it imposed a hulking gait, tightening his back. If he walked too far, stood too long, or did too many stairs, his stump throbbed. Inclines were also tricky.

He thought of taking the train to visit Lucius, an hour trip, but logistics and being in public felt daunting and he didn't want to impose on his mother. Finally, during the yearly late January thaw, he made the trip. Lucius picked him up at the train station. Lucius lived next door to the church where he interned. The house's wallpaper was mottled and torn. Wind whistled past strips of old flannel shirts stuffed in gaps around windows not painted in decades. The furniture looked like it had been rescued from a landfill.

Lucius made them tuna fish sandwiches. Otis talked about reading through the book of Job and Lucius showed him how the verses Ulrich had quoted to him fit into Bible themes. They lost track of time and rushed to the station. Lucius said that his roommate was moving out the middle of February to get married. Would Otis like a change of scene? An idea that a year ago would have seemed mundane—moving a few miles away—scared him. Had his horizons shrunk that much? Was he getting agoraphobic? His train rumbled in. "Give me a few days, OK?"

"Of course."

The rent was a steal, the first floor a godsend, *and* he could trust Lucius. Still, home life was going well and his "rent" was free. Each time he laid out the gospel, his parents were respectful, and while neither had jumped to embrace it, the three of them were having deeper conversations than ever. That evening, Otis mentioned his potential move and asked them their thoughts. They exchanged surprised glances. Did he feel ready? He was welcome to stay *and* he should feel free to go. Otis could sense their sincerity—hardly unfeeling yet doing their best to let him choose.

Two Saturdays later, amidst a snowstorm, Lucius' Bible study group turned out in cheerful, mitten-clad force with more donuts, thermoses of coffee, and station wagons than they would have needed to move a mid-sized circus. Within hours, Otis was unpacked at Lucius' place.

A few days later, grateful for flat, plowed, well-salted sidewalks, Otis ventured to a nearby bookstore with a sign in the window: "Well-Read Help

Wanted." He spoke with the owner about his physical limitations and his probation status—and walked out with a job and a thankful heart. Later, at a mom-and-pop, he bought two newspapers and a Want Advertiser. If he stayed frugal, and didn't mind a little rust, he should be able to afford a car with automatic transmission about the time his probation ran out.

In the Globe, a local crime roundup caught his eye: "John (a.k.a., Jack) Redbaum of Malden, 59, a former long-haul driver, was sentenced Friday to ten years at Walpole after his conviction last month for child rape." In the Herald Traveler, Jack's picture was unmistakable. Otis was speechless. Justice seemed to have been served, yet it bugged him that his roadside efforts at vengeance might have contributed to Jack's downfall. After talking with Lucius, Otis wrote to Jack in prison to offer forgiveness, ask for it, and plead with him to take the path he had.

Through all his life changes, Otis couldn't stop thinking of Calia. In March, the baby would turn one. He kept wondering what she was like, but Calia had every reason never to speak to him again.

He asked Lucius for his advice. Lucius said, "love reaches out."

But what did that mean? Reach out how? When? With what words? They prayed for wisdom and waited, and Lucius opined that if Otis was gracious, *and curbed his expectations*, he didn't see how it could *hurt*.

Otis drafted a note in pencil, Lucius reviewed it, and they prayed. After a few more, he re-drafted in pen. Mailing the note, he felt butterflies, but none of the old anxious self-loathing. In fact, he felt more himself than in a long time. To his surprise and delight, Calia's reply came within days. She appreciated Otis asking her how they were, she wrote. They were both doing fine and she was glad *he* was doing well. She had prayed for his healing and planned to continue. It was *far* more than he had a right to.

Seventy-Four:
Refining Fire

Grand Island, Nebraska, May, 1979...

Otis thought of Vietnam much less often and when he did, his reflections lacked the dismay that had tainted the war years—subtle as stale cookies or putrid as wormy meat, not the root of *all* evil, but *a* root of plenty enough. Between Henry's deployment (the week he'd been Octopus-humbled) and Jesus' gracious take-down seven years later, sorrow at the war's toll and a low-level dread of it extorting more had trickled to fill every fissure of daily life, even tiny ones distant from it: picnics, sports, fireworks, Thanksgiving, Christmas, incoming phone calls, walks to the mailbox. Everything. He would still wish Henry alive, himself whole, and Shaun found, but without those potent agonies, he would not be alive, whole, and found in the way nothing else approached.

Except for the few times each wrestling season when he took off his prosthesis to show "his guys" the moves Coach had once taught him (and to forestall any carping about arduous workouts), Otis felt no need to bring Vietnam up. Anywhere that his limp plus his age might lead to conjecture, he was glad others spoke of it less often also. Those who knew him well knew enough; the rest could guess all they liked.

Presidents Ford then Carter had stirred and calmed storms of protest and counter-protest with legal amnesties for most draft resisters. A wave of heart-rending refugee sagas had made the papers for a few years, but now that Vietnam was one nation (under God like the rest, though officially spurning that fact) it seldom made the front page. A dark, low-profile war memorial—evocative art or despicable scar, depending on who one spoke with—was scheduled to nudge its way onto the U.S. national mall beside the Lincoln Memorial to try to cauterize a peace deeper and less exhausting than the one the sixteenth president had glimpsed for only a few days.

Yet new hope for healing went beyond formal, public attempts.

The Trumaines' 1978 Christmas card had shown Louisabeth nestled beside her robust and freed husband, Connor, their three children, and as many dogs on their Idaho onion farm. Otis' old wrestling co-captain Tony Burck—whom he'd pretended not recognize in line for induction on the Cambridge sidewalk—had also sent the Fletchers a card, as had Theo Behm. After a humiliating performance at the Munich Olympics (due to illness) Otis' old nemesis had married his high school sweetheart and settled back on the Chandler street where he'd grown up. He'd recently been promoted to night shift supervisor at the refrigerator factory, he wrote. Otis was happy for all of them. The Fletchers' Christmas card wished each grace and peace in Christ (no Rudolph-Frosty-Santa stuff from them, thank you).

Early one late spring morning that following year—not long after Voyager One passed Jupiter with a hopeful gold record greeting no one would ever see or hear tucked inside—Calia wiggled to rest her head on her husband's shoulder. Rounded and due with their third child any day, she often woke first, before their alarm. Otis was not a morning person, but he'd come to relish this routine pause together before the day's bustle.

"I've been up thinking," she said.

Otis credited his wife's well-baked thoughts to her habit of filling the interstices of her days with Bible reading and prayer. He was grateful for the flood of grace that had brought them together. When no one was looking (and sometimes when they were) that fact could dampen his eyes. She made no show of her happy, heartfelt spiritual diligence which seemed to wash her of worry. She had a gentle way of raising issues calmly—issues he had not fully considered, or not considered *at all*. "I'm listening," he said before clearing his throat and opening his eyes enough to show he was trying to hear her properly and not disrespect her with a reawakening jolt and a mumbled drool-wiping, *'oh, um, yeah, sure honey, what did you say?'*

"I'd like it if we burned the letters." She didn't need to explain.

"OK," Otis said, confident she knew he meant he'd heard her, not that he necessarily agreed. *Yet.* As Cece had grown, asked questions, and poked around the house he'd considered it too, but it wasn't his call. To destroy them unilaterally was the kind of move he would have pulled before: bold in his own eyes but impulsive and selfish in fact, adding to a presumptive deception dung heap Calia had covered with mountains of forgiveness. At least on this issue—*emphatically* so on this issue—she was the deceived and he the reformed and reforming deceiver, the former enemy for whom she had struggled to pray (at least as surprised as Otis had been at how God had chosen to answer those prayers).

Downstairs, Otis brewed coffee, brought Calia a cup, then withdrew to his third floor study to read his Bible. Once Ulrich's room—and where Cece had been conceived—it kept him humble. Bacon smell wafted up; a climbing May sun shrank the shadows across his Bible and notebook. Otis closed them and descended one floor, glad for his new, lighter prosthesis. He paused at his daughter's door. He could hardly believe it. Cece was almost done with second grade!

"Morning Dad. I see your foot shadows."

"Good morning, Cece. How did you know it was me?"

Otis opened her door, entered, and raised her shades.

"We spies are sneaky. We use *all* our senses."

In family devotions, they'd recently gone through the book of Joshua, and Otis supposed it had prompted Cece to select 'Harriet the Spy,' from a school reading list. Her father would have been proud. No, Otis corrected himself. Above all, Ulrich would have been *thankful*.

Otis clomped down one more flight and took over tending the bacon and pancakes. As the strips crackled and browned, he gave thanks too. He had no right to these delicious smells and full plates, to this sturdy house, or to the gorgeous godly woman who'd filled it with comfort and joy, changing and nursing their son Samuel as she carried his brother or sister *and* coached Cece on what (and what not) to wear. The woman whom he'd left a virtual widow and single mother had made them a home from the empty house he had waded through snow to spy out.

Throughout breakfast, Gideon the dog waited for his signal to clean up around Samuel's highchair. Cece brushed her teeth and grabbed a jacket, then Otis walked her down their long gravel drive to wait for the school bus.

The ground was damp from dew, the morning's breeze barely a zephyr. The two cottonwoods flanking the drive quivered as the sun touched them, the May sky above an achingly crisp sapphire blue.

"I hope the *new* baby is a sister," Cece said. "Then the girls will be ahead again."

"Wouldn't Gideon make things even?" Cece squinted at his tongue-in-cheek prod, weighing its implications. Otis was awed by her far-reaching mind: blink intuition joined to confident gravitas. His daughter could sift through thousands of dendritic possibilities in the time it took him to pick an ice cream flavor. He and Calia were teaching her to count the cost of that power. Be quick to hear and slow to speak, then keep your word. Any minute now, she would come up with a sober answer outside conventional lines. School bored her, she said; she felt out of place. Otis and Calia assured her (and themselves) that God had made her to think differently for a good reason. Her special gifts would blossom in time—and bear fruit for God's kingdom, they hoped.

Otis worked not to chuckle at Cece's resolute "thinking hard" expressions which recalled some of his own. Recently his father had sent black-and-white photos, separated by sheets of tissue paper between symmetrical pieces of X-acto-knifed cardboard, taped on all four sides. In high school, Otis had been so focused during his wrestling matches that he'd barely noticed his non-athletic father snapping from the sidelines, respectfully out of Coach's way. Otis had thought that his father understood neither the sport of wrestling nor him, yet in shot after shot his father had captured pivotal moments—eyes bulging, spit flying, sinews like cable. Seeing the pictures, Cece had asked, "Why did you like it so much if it hurt?" Calia and Otis had smiled, reminded by her question of Ulrich's similarly straightforward manner.

The school bus chugged into view.

"The new baby can have my Winnie."

"Even if it's a boy?"

"Even if it's a boy."

"That's very kind of you, Cece; extremely generous. I'm proud of you."

Cece's "Uncle" Davey Green and his family had sent regrets for Otis and Calia's wedding three years ago (a few weeks before Bicentennial Fourth of July festivities). Davey was starting pitcher for his baseball team; they were likely to make the state tournament. And though his full scholarship to Georgia State beginning that fall did not ride on the outcome, he could not let down his teammates. Otis had called to offer his congratulations, say how well he understood, and to invite them all for Thanksgiving (Calia's idea). Davey had purchased the stuffed Winnie-the-Pooh toy with earnings from mowing lawns and brought it as a gift for Cece.

'Winnie' was getting threadbare in places. For Cece to pledge it to an unseen and uncuddled sister *or brother* was like letting go of a crown jewel—a move bolder and more sacrificial than Otis would have dared hope. It made him want to lift her over his head and twirl her, laughing like they'd done often when she was smaller and Otis was courting her mother. But as the school bus approached—recalling what public mortification felt like—he bent down instead and gave her a quick hug.

The bus squeaked to a halt before them and opened its doors.

"We're out of ice cream," Cece said flatly.

"I'll pick some up on my way home."

"Peppermint stick," she declared from the bus stairs. Turning abruptly, she walked to her seat as the bus moved abreast of him waving, but not glancing out. He trudged up the drive, wondering how God might use her once she filled out a frame taller than four foot one.

Out of wrestling season, Otis went in to school late. Each fall and winter he made up for it. Before dawn he would weigh his athletes, referee any trash talk that veered too far from team standards, and let them try to guess the after-school workout he planned. *Wind sprints? Weights? Scrimmages? Drills?* His wily-ambiguous hints kept them speculating throughout the day—focused and bonding. Today, his first history class didn't start until ten.

From metal shelves in the basement, he fetched the letters. When they'd married, he'd combined those he'd received from Calia (addressed to the man she *thought* was her fiancée) with all his to her in Ulrich's name. Whenever he went down for tools or laundry, the box stared vulture-like from the shadows as if it could re-impose guilt. He'd leafed through it a few times, recalling the man who'd connived such a bundle of lies. The letters were his alright and yet the man who'd conceived, typed, and sent them was dead, the memories harmless, sin gelded and bound.

Outside on the back lawn, he opened the box. On top was the blank Icefield postcard he'd never sent. He held it, closed his eyes, and envisioned *their* only son Samuel's face. He no longer feared Ulrich's body emerging. Whenever it was, the timing God's—right and good.

Inside the fire ring they'd built from New Hampshire brook stones, gathered on a trip to his parents, he set the postcard with the other letters. Upstairs, Calia cooed snippets of Psalms which drifted softly into the rural silence. Once Samuel soothed, she wordlessly came out to Otis' side. He lit a match, touched it to the letters, then took her hand.

Together they watched until the pile was ash.

Epilogue

Vancouver, British Columbia, December, 2019...

A week-long rain drip improv patter outside Professor Cece Paine's university office window gave way to her Pandora Miles Davis jazz shuffle inside. Cece failed to notice until a rare patch of blue sky drew her gaze. Since lunch she'd been grading exams, pondering whether to flunk half the class or follow university policy over a cliff of falling standards and grade on a curve. The way snow dusted the foothills reminded her of her morning pastry; she should get back to the gym. For December, the snow line was low. Up high, there would be more. Much more.

She pictured their Whistler A-frame. She could *watch* it snow through its wall-sized double-panes; let fat flakes waft down and not feel plunged into reflexive computations of water content and crystal structure; not freeze her buns off faking the *that's-a-good-question!* hearty demeanor UBC paid her to muster; not have to wear the buoyant mask she would need to survive an anti-vacation in Boston—the opposite of rest. How nice it would be to curl up with a mug of chai tea and one of the novels that fell from her grip most nights before she'd managed a single page.

Cece was exhausted in every way she and her therapist had tried to label it. The frozen man had triggered her, they agreed, yet after four months of talking they had not reconciled Cece's curiosity at how he got there (and who he was) with her recurrent nightmares about the grey face. Her therapist advised her to be kinder to herself. *Relax, indulge. Be herself.*

Cece had sighed right as her fifty minutes expired.

"I'm not sure who that is anymore."

Now her therapist was in the Caribbean; e-mails and texts not allowed. Cece knew one thing though: feigning Christmas cheer would make things

370

worse. She could no longer pretend that the gulf between her and her mother, brothers, sisters, and their spouses could be bridged by a six-hour plane ride or reduced to the fiction that nothing had changed since growing up in Nebraska together. *They* all lived within blocks of each other in Boston. *They* were all active in the same church. *They* all bred nephews and nieces like rabbits: names she no longer kept track of (though Alistair tried, bless his heart). Contemplating such a trip felt like dangling over the abyss with the body again. She wished she had left it alone.

She wished they would leave *her* alone.

Her therapist would ask her why she was accepting such guilt: *You're an adult.* What was to stop the three of them—she, Alistair, and Nate—from ignoring traditions and expectations and driving up to *their* condo at Whistler for the holidays? Her East Coast family (essentially all of her family) would accept any half-plausible excuse with unquestioned sympathy. (The three of them *had* been fighting colds. Nate's Pee Wee hockey team *had* booked extra games.) Alistair could delight himself perfecting his ski turns (already as flawless as calligraphy) while Nate took the snowboard lessons he'd been begging for. When they returned from the slopes, rosy-cheeked and full of stories (she having napped and finished a fluffy romance) they'd make snow angels, catch flakes on their tongues, and laugh over Parcheesi and hot chocolate. Yes, that's what they should do—what they *would* do.

Cece would pick up a bottle of schnapps on her way home. She would wink at Alistair. "You know any place we could put this to use?" And he would wink back. "Yes, I think I do." And so they would keep from getting Nate's hopes up until the two of them had worked out the details.

Cece had planned last August's student trip to the Icefield as a respite from her typical pace. The locale was surprise-free, a day's drive away, almost in her backyard; only a week removed from home's comforts. In the late nineties, with only a tiny empty apartment to miss, she'd spent three summers there amassing data for her dissertation, her face and arms coppered to peeling. Every year since—including the one she was pregnant—she returned to get reacquainted. And like visits with Ellen, her childhood best friend, the Icefield always yielded a timeless intimacy.

Until that last morning last August.

In Europe, she had encountered old bodies on glaciers but most were like trash piles, hard to think of as having once been warm, moving and breathing and talking. Torn old-style clothes wrapped bleached bones; hair clumps clung to leathery skin.

The Icefield body was different.

Strikingly preserved in the translucent ice, the man's face had been angled slightly off center, eyes closed, lips relaxed. He'd seemed to her like a swimmer smoothly slicing a flat morning lake with long strokes, sure of his next breath behind the shimmering bulge his head made as his body slid powerfully forward. Except that the water was vertical—frozen and unyielding—and the man's blue-grey pallor screamed that he'd not drawn a breath in a very long time.

Troubled by the memory, Cece stood from her desk, took a deep breath, and halfheartedly worked a series of yoga poses. Her joints crackled complaint. With both her chiropractor and her acupuncturist, the running joke was that decades of neglect punctuated by brief stints of titanic overuse were funding the doctors' kids' private school tuitions. Sadly, it was true. "Why don't you slow down?" Alistair would sometimes ask, sweetly oblivious to tenure's handcuffs.

Researching exotic locales and publishing at a pace others could not sustain had vaulted Cece past older colleagues to chair the department *and* several university committees. That discipline now held off younger versions of herself—ambitious iconoclasts inured to risk and accustomed hard work. The seldom-voiced pact with her docs (and with Alistair) was to withhold judgment and put her back together again long enough to plumb another glacier's mysteries and so burnish her professional brand. Speaking and consulting gigs (plus several books) sweetened the pot.

Until Nate's surprise arrival the year she turned forty, time in the field had always energized her. But each day far from home since then made her feel as dry as multi-day dust storms on the Tibetan plateau. (The fine grit in her teeth was the worst.) Alone in a tent, she would pine for Facetime with "her boys" (Alistair and Nate). But when she got back to WiFi, the jerky images, audio gaps, and sudden hang-ups left her sadder than if she'd not seen or heard them at all.

Her outdoorsy Vancouver friends were jealous that she "got" to visit places they longed to tag in retirement. They had no idea. She'd once coveted the magical *this way ma'am* luggage tags which signaled ring-the-bell elite frequent flyer status, but not long after achieving a clacking set of them—the year she turned thirty—jet lag had forced her to dye her hair.

She'd made repeat research trips to Iceland, Antarctica, Greenland, and much of Alaska; to places erudite friends looked up covertly, like the Caucasus Mountains; and to places they were certain were iceless or else soon would be: New Guinea, Tanzania, and the Alps. She'd been up and down the spine of the Andes, traipsed most of New Zealand's South Island, and visited every Himalayan glacier you could walk to in less than a week—plus several more remote ones inside Pakistan that necessitated special permits and round-the-clock shifts of Pashtuns toting AK-47s, spitting nawar, and leading mules. Now she fantasized about scrapping all that, shredding all her airline program cards, taking a sabbatical somewhere boring, and letting her hair grow out to see what a grey ponytail felt like. Alistair wouldn't mind and Nate would think it was cool.

She cringed to recall her naïve enthusiasm flying for the first time. Alone en route to Germany for junior year study abroad, she'd been mistakenly relegated to the smoking section. Disgusted as the plane droned east through the short night, she'd paced the aisles, shocked to find she was the only passenger awake. How could they all sleep? Could they not feel the thrill? Miles below was a vast ocean and, under that, archaeological mysteries hidden as ancient glaciers melted.

From Frankfurt, she slept on the train and almost past her stop, blocks past the spray-painted half-standing jackhammered wall. Augmenting two years of German with gestures, she found the address she'd torn from a recent envelope. Her grandmother's face was like dried apple, her hug wondrous and warm, not at all like Cece had thought their first meeting would be. Over tea, she showed Cece photos of her late husband—Cece's grandfather—and their two late sons, frozen in time as soldier and pre-adolescent boy. The brothers' lives had not overlapped. Both had died at twenty-two: the soldier—Cece's uncle—in the Stalingrad snows; the boy—Cece's father—in the Alaskan bush (Cece guessed) though the accident *could* have happened anywhere in thousands of desolate miles he'd driven to get there the summer before she was born.

Cece compared the boy's features with her own. She'd gotten her father's one-sided dimple, his liquid eyes, and his angle-free face. The black and white photo obscured features her parents had mentioned: his blue eyes and light brown hair. She tried to imagine her grandparents giving away their last living son for his good as the Berlin Wall went up. Cece's grandmother showed her the last thing her father sent—a kitschy tourist postcard. *We are here!* Despite the picture's old style, the vista was breathtaking. Cece knew the story's outlines from childhood.

Headed to Alaska to work on the pipeline, her father had paused at the Icefield. Somewhere, briefly, her *fathers* had met. (Because she had only ever known one of them, she had no trouble thinking of them each as 'father.' One had been present, well-meaning, and flawed; the other far-off, unspoiled, and seldom mentioned.) The visible corporeal father never spoke of the accident except to say that he'd "hitchhiked a lot that summer". Cece assumed that his silence meant he felt bad because he'd been driving when the accident happened. Maybe he'd fallen asleep.

Ulrich's grave was remote and unmarked, her parents insisted. Whenever Cece had pried, her parents had offered the same refrain: His *body's* locale is not important. *He* was ushered instantly into the presence of Jesus—and there is nothing better! When Jesus comes back, he will bring his "holy ones" with him, Ulrich among them. Then the rest of the dead will rise and face judgment. Like a bunch of zombies, Cece always thought and so, to avoid cueing-up her parents' resolutely standard religious spiel, she wasted little time musing about what it might have been like for her fathers to be alive together. One had been plenty; she had her own life to live.

Her grandmother had given her the postcard to keep. The Icefield looked stunning, and having flown by herself to Germany, a shorter flight in the other direction no longer seemed a big deal. And so, the next summer, for her senior thesis, Cece visited the Icefield—and fell in love.

In her office, Cece flicked her iPhone to life and let it find her face. A text popped in as if the correspondent had been waiting, omniscient, happy to see her. "Hi, Prof Paine." Three grey dots danced in the lower left of her screen. She waited, wary; the dots vanished. Phish schemes were getting slick. Hackers in lawless places aped Caller IDs then let you to reel *yourself* into a scam. The cruelest ones used roving Internet bots to grab names from obituaries. But this area code was safely Canadian—825, Alberta. Probably a forgotten student, pleading for a recommendation.

"Who's this?" she tapped.

"Dr. Eph Shields, Edmonton Medical Examiner (Emeritus). It looks like you're the go-to expert on the Icefield. I'd like to ask you a few questions about it if that's alright."

"K," Cece thumbed, but before she could send it, Dr. Shields sent a link to her pinned Tweet. Cece smiled with satisfaction. Years ago her 3D animation—assimilating aerial drone photos of the Icefield with half-a-lifetime of her data—had made Cece a media doyenne. Yet it irked her that most who reached out to her—eager for any credentialed authority to confirm a theory on drowning polar bears—ignored the scope of her expertise. She now blocked every reporter or blogger who served up her words in convenient sound bites, cut off from setting and sense.

Unlike media inquiries, the coroners who contacted her to help date bodies melted out from snowbanks or glaciers tended to act more professionally. She inserted her Air Pods and called Dr. Shields. He picked up right away and (thank goodness) got right to the point.

"My colleagues tell me you found a body on the Icefield last August."

Oh. That body. She should have guessed. "I did," she said. In the fall, she had e-mailed the ranger she'd met, as well as others she knew at Parks Canada. No one had gotten back to her.

"They extracted him in October."

Extracted. Cece ran her tongue around the back of her mouth. An agonizingly cracked tooth had helped her lose ten pounds. Her dentist explained the months-long process of "manageable discomfort" and "unlikely complications" if she got an implant. After getting the tooth pulled, she elected to leave the spot empty. (The procedure made her think about photos of her parents' honeymoon dinner at Windows on the World atop lower Manhattan, and her recent visit to the Ground Zero 9-11 memorial there.) Days now passed when she forgot the tooth gap entirely.

"Yes, extracted. They like to tidy up before the big winter storms. Summer surprises tend to go viral and attract the wrong kinds of tourists. They called me last month to consult."

Cece recalled how much trouble she'd had clearing enough ice from the man's face to take decent photos. Freeing him entirely would have been complicated and messy. She pictured the details, felt bile rise, and staunched the thoughts. "So you have him. How can I help?"

"We're trying to place him in time. Correlate with old missing person reports. Home in on a year, if that's possible. Can you estimate where and when he might have started out?"

Dr. Shields' question evoked others Cece had asked herself since August. Where had the man called home? Who had missed him? Who might *still* miss him? Had he been married? Had kids? What were his last thoughts? But to ask those of Dr. Shields would make her sound like a raving loon and so, when he asked her something she had data to answer ("I've heard that every glacier is different? That some move faster than others?"), Cece jumped on it with one of her regular Tweet themes

"Yes. Each glacier has a unique personality."

Her software let her fast-forward or reverse hundreds of glaciers. With a few mouse clicks, she could predict where and when an unrecoverable body might emerge. She could also suck a found body back in time, up a glacier's flow to the likely place and date of a mishap. There was more she could say, but a call like this wasn't urgent to finish tonight. She didn't want to miss reading Nate a bedtime story or have to reheat the gourmet dinner Alistair would be preparing. She pictured her Icefield model spitting out color-coded stick figure icons. She also pictured the grey face and imagined his past. No. Not today. The dead were better off hidden from view.

"I ran multiple simulation scenarios on every fatal accident listed in public reports from 1945 to 2000 and sent a summary to the park ranger." Cece multitasked as she talked, closing dozens of on-screen windows and shutting down her computer. "I can say definitively that that body was in the wrong place to be among them. Are there records I'm not aware of?"

"There might be."

Was it her imagination, or did Dr. Shields' pause sound pregnant?

"My wife grew up in Jasper. Her father Doug was a Parks Canada ranger. After my residency, in the late sixties, we moved back there to set up private practice and start a family. The summer before he retired, my father-in-law chatted with a young fellow just down off the Icefield who said he was from Nebraska."

Nebraska? Her family had moved away from there to Boston when Cece was in junior high. The state's population was tiny. As her hard drive spun down, Cece ran the probabilities in her head. Her monitor offered a sigh of crackling static then darkened. Dr. Shields continued.

"Doug said that the fellow had climbed with a partner, but he was alone when they spoke. He was badly banged-up, clearly in need of help, but he refused it at the scene. And so Doug referred him to see me the next day." There was another long pause.

"And you can't say more because of patient confidentiality?"

"The laws are well-intentioned. Until I know *for certain* that a patient is deceased, I need to abide the rules. As for the fellow you found though—the body—we've recovered pictures and documents. Can I send them to you? It's not your main area of expertise, but since you've spent so much time there you might see something I've missed. The first photo I'll send you is one we developed from film in his camera. The other images are of things we found in his pockets."

Cece envisioned gum wrappers, packing lists, and scenery snapshots.

"Faces aren't really my forte. But sure. Whatever. Send them. If I notice anything I'll be in touch."

Dr. Shields thanked her and hung up.

A photo dinged in, its colors Kodachrome crisp: two young men on a vast field of white, their wool shirtsleeves rolled up, faces slathered in zinc oxide. She pegged the spot: facing west atop the Icefield, early summer by the sun's angle. Mount Columbia dominated the background. One man beamed, his eyes bright and blue, arm draped across the other man's shoulders. The second stood with his arms at his sides, glacier goggles on. Another shot arrived, almost the same as the first except both men wore goggles and held ice axes—somewhere near the top of Snow Dome, she guessed. Cece zoomed in to the faces. The second man's eyes were hidden in both pictures, but his expression shouted bleak toleration. Cece could empathize. When her father set up timer shots for family photos, he always urged her to smile through *and past* the click.

Suddenly, she felt a wave of recognition. She shook her head as if the wave had been real—knocking her down and stealing her breath. *No. It couldn't be.* She would *not* trust the hinky feeling of seeing her friend Ellen that had gotten her into trouble at the foreign conferences.

Another image arrived, this one creased and faded: a bob-haired, freckle-faced teen. More recognition rushed in, but before she could analyze its validity, a third thumbnail pinged in, thankfully devoid of faces. Instead, it looked like alligator skin. Curious, Cece zoomed in.

Against a stainless steel backdrop, half a dozen water-stained hand-sized sheets lay as if torn from a flip-top notebook. The pencil script was barely legible—reminiscent of the large rough letters Nate used when he broke his wrist in Pee Wee hockey and had to write leftie. As Cece read, ice plummeted to her gut, her legs like the end of spin class. Her face prickled with heat.

Words of shocking forgiveness and love wove two rare familiar first names together; a third rare familiar first name identified the author of the multi-page note. What were the chances that the three together did *not* relate to her? She looked up the popularity of each name on a website she and Alistair had used when pregnant with Nate. Then she did the math.

Ten billion to one. Half again more than the world's population.

Better than a DNA match.

The last sheet with the poignant sign-off was dated June 18, 1970, eight and a half months before she was born. But she had to be sure.

She opened the facial recognition app Alistair had urged her to try. ("If you lost a leg like your dad, you would use crutches or get a prosthesis," he'd observed; she had ceded the point.) The app churned her phone's photo archives—nose, lips, forehead, eye sockets, head shape—the data-crunching technology far superior to her hasty impulses. The best correlation with the stoic goggled man was her phone's wallpaper: her father helping her blow out her candles at her sixth birthday party. The grinning, blue-eyed, un-goggled man matched her August shots of the frozen body. Her hands shook so violently that she had to set down her phone.

The freckled teen girl was her mother.

Cece wanted to scream, but it would not refute such a mountain of data: names, faces, the date and the place, her own eyewitness, and the chain of custody to Dr. Shields. Unwittingly, she had faced her frozen father. She would have just been conceived when he died: teensy, no more than a week, even her mom unaware at that point.

Lately, Nate had been on a Dr. Seuss kick, chanting the refrain from "Horton Hears a Who." Being small, the story made him feel good. Cece felt hopelessly teensy. She needed fresh air. She grabbed her laptop satchel and plunged toward the door but before she reached it, her grandmother's framed postcard caught her eye.

Waren hier! <u>We</u> are here, plural. Hiding in plain sight. As if *both* sketched stick figures had made it off the glacier alive. She unhooked the frame from the wall and set it face down on her desk. She knew what she would see, but had to see it again. She fumbled with the hasps. With her ID key card, she pried back the cardboard spacer and stared at the Canadian postmark.

Jasper, Alberta, June 22nd, 1970—four days *after* the note on the body.

Back to the wall, she slid to the carpet. Who else *but* her father could have sent it? *This* was why her parents had avoided specifics. Yet what could they have said? When would have been a good time? She'd not been the easiest kid to raise. How could they have made her understand at age five? At ten, twenty, forty? How had *they* made their peace with it? When she declared the Icefield as her thesis study area they must have been horrified.

Did her mother know?

North across the Lion's Gate Bridge, watery reflections twinkled, each paired with a real light on land. One of those was home. Alistair would be cooking something amazing, Nate 'helping' him in his seven-year-old way. On a cold night like this, their wood stove would be well stoked, their overstuffed leather sofa waiting for her to change into her fleece pajamas, flop down with a goblet of Pinot, and read Nate a book.

She replaced the postcard and frame. What could she tell them? And what good could come if she did? She stood quietly for a moment then opened the Whistler app on her phone and bought a week's worth of lift tickets. When Nate greeted her at the door, she would say she had a special early Christmas surprise and to go get his father so the three of them could celebrate and look forward together.

Acknowledgements

Near the end of one of the mountain adventures once integral to my life and longing—weeks before I would meet the woman who would become (and who remains) my wife—I sat beside a campfire high in the mountains, struggling for words. Our team leader had urged us each to acknowledge how each of the *others* in our intrepid band had helped make our epic trip a success. I had some hard acts to follow: humility from hoarders; gratitude from grouches; soothing simplicity from selfish strivers. I was the oblivious summation of all those faults and more.

And when it came my turn, *I left someone out.*

One does not forget such a faux pas. Here, sadly, it is inevitable.

Writing is a solitary endeavor (a mind tells fingers to press keys) yet bringing a book to the point of you reading these words is anything but. Many people have provided priceless help and encouragement. If I've left you out here, please forgive me. I am nonetheless profoundly grateful.

First, my Lord Jesus. Yeah, there, I said it, and without shame. Thanks don't begin to sum up who You are and what You've done for sinners like me. You alone know how often I've stared at a screen, praying, afraid and how You've graciously ushered me through the next sentence, deletion, or interruption. All errors are mine; any brilliance is to Your glory.

Second, thank you Helen. No man could ask for a wife more cheerfully sensible and stalwartly supportive of well, everything, but especially of a husband's surprise sense of midlife calling: a whack-a-doodle flyer of a decision to scrap the corporate grind to write novels like this one.

Thanks to my other editors besides Helen: Tracy Fuller, whose insights protected the world from my many oversights and leant me the courage to see this as mission; my Aunt Sylvia Bell, who rang the bell on grace and faith through four(!) readings, and a lot of remedial grammar; Anne Scott whose providential entrance at the moment I *thought* I was done rescued me from a dead-end no one would want to read. Thanks also to my coach, Joanna Sanders, whose gems of gospel vision set the standard for galvanizing a first-time author, and to Jason Farley for generous advice about storytelling.

An alarmingly long time ago, fellow authors Juliette Fay and Tracey Palmer provided heartening feedback on raw drafts of early chapters. Their reassurance has never left me; their counsel and example have prodded me to continue. April Eberhardt, the first literary agent I ever met, kept this project alive with a jaw-dropping request to read the finished manuscript long before it was finished. (So much for playing pessimistic chicken.) Her sage and detailed advice in gracious rejection was unstinting.

I am hugely grateful to my beta readers for enduring alpha-level drafts with good humor: Kara Miller and Kris Washburn, Ridghi Mathieu and Cassie Hanudel, daughters Emily Finn and Kate Gilmartin, plus S.I.L. Cal Gilmartin who foresaw the story's ending well before I'd written it properly.

Thanks also to Charlie F. for many adventures together, to Ron D. for a power-editing lunch, to Luc L. for moving my climbing jargon into the 21st century, and to Peter H. for not letting one particularly ambitious mountaineering trip keep me from living to see it.

I'm immensely grateful to Betsy and Cliff Groh, Theresa Philbrick, and B.I.L. Tom Curran for insiders' views into Alaska life, to teachers Don Maass and Tim Weed for help and assurance at crucial points in the writing process, and to Jason Anscomb for a far better cover design than those in my mind's amateur eye. In a different vein, I'm indebted to many siblings in Christ (including Kevin E., an unexpected, timely Barnabas) who refreshed me and prayed for this project far longer than I or any of them expected to.

Last but not least, thanks to my parents, Ben and Margaret Hutchinson for making reading a natural, pleasant priority from infancy and to my late and only sibling Ed who listened to a *very* rough sketch of this story. Muffled by a medical mask years before everyone wore them, his firm exhortation that I "go for it," has remained a precious touchstone of inspiration. I look forward to thanking him in person around an infinitely brighter and better fire than the mountain embers around which I once huddled.

Book Group Questions

1. We meet Otis Fletcher amidst a high-stakes high-school wrestling match. What do you think about the way he handles defeat? What kinds of big win-lose moments have you faced? Have you thought about them differently after time passed? How?

2. How would you describe Otis at college? How does he change? When have you acted on impulse, instinct, or intuition? When have you waited to make a "bold move"?

3. Otis' older brother Henry dies fighting in Vietnam. Have you ever lost someone close to you unexpectedly or at a younger age than is typical? How did different people around that person deal with grief? Are some approaches better than others? How can they clash?

4. What does Ulrich Sterbender value? What excites him? How would you describe his worldview? Why do you think he agreed to go climbing with Otis?

5. How does Otis justify using Ulrich's name? What do you think you would do in similar circumstances? Are some lies OK? What factors might impact your decision?

6. Otis helps his girlfriend Louisabeth procure an abortion then urges Calia to do the same. Have your views on abortion changed since you were their age? What factors influenced that change?

7. At the beginning of the story, how might Otis describe the pillars of his identity? ("I am a/an...") How does his answer change in Alaska? After he experiences combat in Vietnam?

8. Calia experienced a significantly more difficult early life than Otis. How would you describe the pillars of Calia's worldview? What sorts of things excite her? What does she value?

9. How would you describe Pastor Joe's ministry to Otis? What factors does he juggle in trying to help him? What does Pastor Joe do that's most impactful to Otis' life?

10. How would you describe Otis' relationship with Lucius? Why does Otis trust him? Why does Lucius put up with Otis? What role(s) does Shaun play in Otis' life?

11. What do you think of Otis' decision to resist the draft? To go to Vietnam? Have you been to war (or known someone who has)? What thoughts weighed on you during that time?

12. What did you think of Otis' reaction to losing a leg? Have you ever experienced sudden trauma? Did your reactions (then or later) surprise you? How? What did you learn?

13. Did it surprise you that Calia forgave Otis as she did? Why? Have you ever felt beyond forgiveness? Have you ever forgiven (or tried to forgive) the seemingly unforgiveable?

14. What does Cece Paine value? What excites her and makes her life meaningful? What are some of her assumptions about how the world works? Do you agree with those? Why or why not?

15. Cece discovers that her parents held back information she thought they should have shared with her. Have you ever faced a sense of betrayal? How did you handle it? What did you do?

A Note from (& about) the Author

First inspiration for *Covered With Snow* came atop an icy mountain cliff I had no business attempting. The guy I was roped to looked spent, about to faint and (I feared) take us both down. The plunge would have left my wife of four months a widow. Instead, ten months after my safe return, our first child arrived. Off and on as that daughter (and then her sister) grew up, I pondered alternative outcomes to that high-altitude tipping point. ("What ifs" were my regular fare as I made a living writing *corporate fiction*—speculative scenarios to animate executive planning retreats.)

Two decades later, as our girls began to take flight, I started pecking away at this story on a vacation/hobby basis. The first draft felt lopsided. Were luck and skill the only factors in my walking away from my near fatal mishap, or had there been more going on?

As a boy, my father had read me classic stories of mountaineering prowess and polar exploration (e.g., Scott and Amundsen in Antarctica, and Tenzing and Hillary atop Everest). Especially gripping were left-for-dead tales. Rob Taylor's, *The Breach* (1981; on Mount Kilimanjaro) made a huge impression the year I joined the adult world, as did Joe Simpson's more widely known *Touching the Void* (1988; in the Andes)—the same year as my close call. Yet becoming a father (then later a Christian) made the genre I'd once loved feel deficient, cramped, even distasteful.

With the possible exception of the movie *The Deer Hunter*, Russian roulette is not a popular pastime, yet one in ten who attempt Mount Everest die trying: odds not far off from that demonic practice. Why? What do they seek? What cost is tolerable? Who gets to decide? Jon Krakauer vividly posed and illustrated those questions with the non-fiction classic *Into Thin Air*, recounting (among *many* tragic facets) Rob Hall's poignant last call to

384

his then-pregnant wife. But to my mind even that heart-rending vignette did not get to the root of the issue which—two generations earlier—George Mallory had famously punted. Why did he want to climb Everest? "Because it's there." Great. So is lots of mundane stuff; big help. The genre seemed constrained by an undisputed quasi-militaristic frame that made any larger moral exploration of the tapestry of consequences to loved ones difficult.

Upon visiting the Italian village where a pre-Bronze Age body *with proven descendants* lay on display (melted from a glacier) I found new inspiration and re-framed *Covered With Snow* as a redemptive family saga. Given the war metaphors obvious to anyone who has ever navigated a crevasse field or scurried through an avalanche zone, marrying my story to another longstanding fascination and question seemed equally obvious. What accounted for the vast worldview gulf between my mid-eighties college classmates (who rushed to Wall Street in upbeat lemming-like droves) and acquaintances ten to twenty years older than us who—whether they went to Vietnam or stayed home—saw their lives (and the culture) *profoundly* altered by that conflict?

As I began to share the story concept with people born in my characters' era, *everyone* had a tale. Some spoke guardedly, others openly, relieved to release decades of pent-up emotion. *I've never shared this; even my wife doesn't know. It was illegal, but you understand; what could I do?* I was honored—and I remain deeply sobered. Who was I to represent the wildly different, often agonizing choices of a time I'd pranced through as a child?

Music offered a bridge to understanding. Neil Young's "Ohio" is both haunting and on-the-nose and so remains one of the best known specific critiques of a watershed event of that era (the Kent State shootings). But subtler musical treatments abound. The river of time tends to obscure from popular view the deeper meanings of all kinds of artworks. But if one drills into the context in which certain '60s-era songs were written one finds some allusive and poignant artistic gems.

My final spur to write this book came from a high school team I coached for nearly a decade. Many of my athletes knew Vietnam-era *music* amazingly well but beyond rote shallow mantras about social emancipation, few knew anything about the hard, irrevocable choices that, only fifty years earlier, people their age had been forced to make hastily and live with since.

Contact & Feedback

If you've experienced *Covered With Snow* as an immersive yarn, I'm delighted. If it has bridged any chasms, I'm ecstatic. I'd love to hear from you. Please leave a review and/or send me your reflections at art@arthutchinson.com.